Studies in the Arab Theater and Cinema

Studies in the Arab Theater and Cinema

JACOB M. LANDAU

Preface by Professor H. A. R. Gibb

Philadelphia
UNIVERSITY OF PENNSYLVANIA PRESS

LIBRARY OF CONGRESS CATALOGUE CARD NUMBER 56–12588

SECOND PRINTING, 1969

SBN: 8122–7188–2

PRINTED IN THE UNITED STATES OF AMERICA

Contents

III THE ARAB CINEMA

Illustrations

Preface

A study of the Arabic theater is one of those things which everyone who is interested in the Arab world wants to have, but which qualified scholars usually leave for "somebody else" to do. If reason is required, a glance at the pages of notes at the end of this volume should be answer enough. To produce a substantial sheaf, the historian of the Arabic theater must prowl through the highways and byways of Arabic journalism during the past century, gleaning from them the insights which alone can transform a shelf of books into a living art. More especially, as the first Western scholar to attempt a major study in this field, Dr. Landau had to seek out everything for himself, for the first extensive work on the subject in Arabic appeared only when this book was already in the publisher's hands. And to this study of the Arabic stage he has added, for good measure, a study of the older shadow plays of the Near East, and another of the rise and development of the Arabic cinema.

Drama is not a native Arab art. Various sociological explanations have been suggested for this fact, but the simplest reason is perhaps the best: that the dramatic art of Greece, from which the Western theater derives, remained unknown to them. Comedy found its expression in the picaresque tale, embellished for the intellectuals by literary graces and verse; dramatic tragedy in the still more poetic setting of romantic and unhappy love. Representation came in with the shadow play in the later Middle Ages, but the attempt to raise it above the level of popular entertainment was still-born, and even as a continuing popular art it owes more to the Turks than to the Arabs.

It was, then, as a self-confessed imitation of the European theater that the drama was introduced into the Arab world in the nineteenth century. Aspiring actor-managers hitched their wagons to Corneille and Molière. Perspiring translators battled with the Anglo-Saxon idioms of Shakespeare and Shaw. But out of all this there has gradually emerged a mixed art, in which Arab elements have been grafted on to a transplanted and acclimatized stock. From the neo-classical dramas of S̲h̲auqī to the colloquial vaudeville, poetry and song play a major part, and the old romantic and picaresque themes reappear in the new medium, as well as in the still newer medium of the film. It is in the literary drama, the play as a mode of written literature, that the new medium may have achieved its greatest successes down to the present time. Alongside this, however, the living theater has steadily enlarged its range and its resources. The comedy of manners in particular has made remarkable advances in the hands of a few talented authors, even achieving a foothold on the international stage. By this achievement the Arab world has found probably its best means of projecting itself into the consciousness of the outside world. This fact alone should ensure a welcoming interest in Dr. Landau's study of the slow and difficult progress of the Arabic theater to its present maturity.

H. A. R. Gibb

Center for Middle Eastern Studies
Harvard University
Cambridge, Massachusetts

Introduction

The Arab theater and cinema have been among the most neglected subjects in the studies of Oriental literature and research into the history of the theater. The Chinese, Japanese, Indian, and Turkish theater arts have been the subject of exhaustive monographs, sketching their development and analyzing their characteristics. Even more and better-detailed books have been published on these arts, ancient and modern, in European or American countries[1]. Few studies, however, have been written on the Arab theater. True, some scholarly books have been published on the mediaeval Arabic shadow plays, but even these were, as a rule, concerned with narrowly defined topics or consisted of annotated editions of texts. Moreover, no detailed study of the subject seems to have been published recently. In so far as the odd-hundred-years-old Arab theater is concerned, only two theses on its *beginnings* have been presented at the Universities of Rome[2] and Cairo[3]; these works appear to have remained in manuscript form. Even should they be published[3a], they would cover, as their titles imply, only a limited portion of the subject. For the rest, as well as for the development of the Arab cinema, one can turn only to a multitude of press articles (chiefly in Arabic), none of which, naturally enough, can aspire to exhaust the subject in a few pages.

This work, an attempt to stop this gap in our information, does not claim to be exhaustive. It is intended to be a survey of the development of the Arab theater and cinema as cultural

[1] See, e.g., H. Knudsen, *Theaterwissenschaft* (1950).

[2] For G. R. Orvieto's Ph.D. thesis see below, Bibliography.

[3] I have been as yet unable to consult Muḥammad Yūsuf Najm's thesis, *Nash'at al-masraḥ al-'arabī*, mentioned in *RY* (*Rūz al-Yūsuf*), July 19, 1954.

[3a] A sizable part of Najm's Arabic study was published in book form (see below, Bibliography) in the year 1956. I succeeded in getting a copy only after my work had been typeset, so that I could make only limited use of his valuable research on the early Arab theater.

and social phenomena rather than a critical study of their aesthetic values, for which the time has not yet come. Indeed, research into the birth and progress of these arts necessarily sheds light on the penetration of Western civilization into the Near East during the last hundred years. While literature, music, and the plastic arts represent a synthesis of local Arabic tradition and European innovations, the modern theater and cinema in the Arab countries were wholly foreign products transplanted in virgin soil. Even in this case, a synthesis of ideas and practice was necessary; for the new arts found receptive audiences, trained to appreciate them by a long tradition of Passion plays and shadow plays. Furthermore, the vehicle of expression had to be Arabic. The language, both in its standard literary forms and in its varied spoken dialects, left its imprint on the development of the theater and cinema.

Three main components are brought together in the present work. The first part is devoted to a description and analysis of those elements which contributed, before the nineteenth century, towards the awareness of the dramatic among the Arab populations. It treats therefore of mimicry, the Passion play and, in greater detail, the shadow play, the forerunner of theater and cinema alike. The second part describes the beginnings and evolution of the Arab theater in the nineteenth and twentieth centuries, its public, the best actors and actresses, and the main themes of the Arabic drama as well as an analysis of some of its exponents. Stress is laid throughout on the cultural and social impact of the theater on modern Arab literature and society. The third part deals with the theater's younger sister, the Arab cinema, which—by imitating the theater's approach, linked to its own technical potentialities—has now become the public's favorite. As the history of the Arab cinema is so much shorter than that of the Arabic theater, both mediaeval and modern, less space has been allotted to it. In addition to the description of the cinema's history and a brief analysis of its thematic problems and the quality of the stars' acting, attention has also been given to the moral and economic aspects of the Arab cinema. Both the special character of the government's assistance and censorship and the unsound economic basis of the local film production are also dealt with. Most of the conclusions apply up to the early 1950's only, as later source-material is somewhat scarce and often not too reliable.

The three main parts are followed by a list of Arab plays since 1848, viz. since the birth of the modern Arab theater. No exhaustive list has yet been compiled, to my knowledge[3b]. This alphabetical list, divided into original and translated plays, is perforce incomplete. Many manuscript plays are being jealously guarded by various troupes (as elsewhere in the world), while others are broadcast and then forgotten; nor has it been possible to include the many plays or parts thereof published in the daily press. The separate Bibliography incorporates only the main works mentioned in this book; for further literature, the reader is referred to the relevant footnotes. This alphabetical Bibliography is divided into three parts: manuscripts (European, Oriental); printed works in European languages (books, articles); printed works in Oriental languages (books, articles).

The preparation of the present book has been a matter of some years. During this period I have had the good fortune of receiving the kind assistance of many librarians in the Near East as well as in Europe and the United States, who were so good as to allow me to peruse various public collections of manuscripts, books and periodicals. Many people have given me their good advice, time and again. I was particularly fortunate in obtaining very important suggestions, as well as unfailing encouragement, from Professors L. A. Mayer, S. D. Goitein, D. H. Baneth, I. Shamush and H. Peri, of the Hebrew University, Jerusalem; H. A. R. Gibb of Harvard University

[3b] I obtained a copy of Dāgh̲ir's important, but incomplete, list in *al-Mas̲h̲riq* (see below, Bibliography) only after this book had been typeset, so that I was unable to use it in full.

(who was also kind enough to write the Preface to this work); M. Perlmann of Harvard University; Bernard Lewis of the University of London; Fr. Rosenthal of Yale University; G. E. von Grunebaum of the University of California at Los Angeles; N. N. Glatzer of Brandeis University. Prof. G. L. Della Vida of Rome and Mr. M. Hairabèdian of Paris sent me some valuable material in their possession. Dr. and Mrs. J. Weniger, by their generous invitation to stay with them in Rome, enabled me to collect materials in Italian libraries. Mrs. M. Klausner and Messrs. G. Fraenkel and A. Levin of Tel-Aviv; Messrs. G. Weigert and I. Cohen of Jerusalem; and Mr. F. I. Qubain of New Haven, Connecticut, read parts of the manuscript and offered valuable observations regarding contents and style. Mr. Thomas Yoseloff, Director of the University of Pennsylvania Press, encouraged me continually during the stages of publication. My wife patiently assisted me with much of the technical work that was involved in the preparation of this book, in all its phases. To them all and to others who have shown interest in this work go my warmest thanks. I alone, however, assume responsibility for everything said in the following pages.

J.M.L.

PART I

THE BACKGROUND

CHAPTER 1

Mimicry

In order to understand the rise of the Arab theater in the early nineteenth century and its later development, it is necessary to consider the dramatic elements in the Near East prior to that century.

The fact that there was no regular Arab theater until the nineteenth century may be explained by two main reasons: *a.* The peoples with whom the Arabs came into close contact had no well-developed theater; *b.* Women, particularly if unveiled, were strictly forbidden to appear on the stage. Only the combination of these two reasons[4] may account for the fact that while a large part of the Greek cultural heritage, in the various fields of literature, science and thought, was translated into

[4] For other, not very convincing, reasons, see Zakī Ṭulaimāt, *al-Riwāya al-tamthīliyya wa-limādhā lam yu'ālijhā'l-'Arab*, in *K.* (the Egyptian monthly *al-Kitāb*), vol. I, fasc. 1, Nov., 1945, pp. 101–108. Also Ahmed Abdul Wahhab, *A thesis on the drama in Arabic literature* (1922), in which the author sets out to prove the dramatic (but not the theatrical) element in classical Arabic literature.

Arabic at various times, no item of the classical drama found its way into Arabic translations until recent years.

However, the dramatic element, considered the chief artistic factor in the theater, as being responsible for the impression left on the audience, was not entirely absent from the Muslim Near East. Its main exponent was mimicry in various forms, while in some parts, at least, Passion plays and shadow plays were performed not infrequently.

Mimicry, since time immemorial, has been a favorite pastime not only of children but of adults as well. Its scope is admittedly narrower than that of the theater, for its range of subjects is strictly limited to amusing imitation, whether of voice or manner, more often than not through exaggeration. This imitation of the phenomena of life—behavior and manner of speech—was found in Greece as well as in the ancient East. The Babylonians and Parthians are said to have had it in their festivals; it seems probable that mimicry had a part in Jewish festivals as well, mainly on Purim[5], although this has not yet been fully proved.

Adam Mez, the Orientalist, has already pointed out[6] that the existence of greatly varied Arabic dialects might have stimulated mimicry in towns where a conglomerate populace met. One may find in the literature of the Abbassid period a number of instances of mimicry (*Ḥikāya*) not so dissimilar to modern mimicry. Another popular literary form which often contains the elements of mimicry is the Arabic *Maqāma*, in which the theme was frequently presented in the guise of conversation, parts of which imitated various characters. However, in this genre the artistic-literary factor is more important than in the

[5] I. Schipper, *Geschichte fun Yiddischer Teater-Kunst un Drame* (Yiddish, 1928), vol. III, ch. 1. Josef Horovitz, *Spuren griechischer Mimen im Orient* (1905), pp. 16–17. On the mime in Greek and Roman times see Hermann Reich, *Der Mimus* (1903); and Otto Weinrich, *Epigrammstudien I: Epigramm und Pantomimus*, in *Sitzungsber. der Heidelberger Ak. der Wiss., Philos.-hist. Kl.*, 1944–1948, l. Abhandlung. On the mime's artistic values see A. Kutscher, *Grundriss der Theaterwissenschaft*, 2nd ed. (1949), part 1.

[6] Adam Mez, *Abulqasim*, Introduction, esp. pp. XV–XVI; and Horovitz, *op. cit.*, pp. 18–21.

Ḥikāya, and linguistic sophistication is valued more than successful imitation. This approach limits the realism of the *Maqāma*[7].

Mimicry pervaded to a larger extent the art of the story-tellers in the Near East, who distinguished themselves by their great powers of observation and still greater talents for imitation. Of particular importance are the Turkish *meddah* (that is, praise-giver) or *mukallit* (imitator) and the Arabic *ḥakawātī* (story-teller).[8] Both enlivened their impassionate tales for generations—as they still do today—not only with many gestures (sometimes amounting to a short pantomime), but also with anecdotes spiced with amusing imitations of behavior and speech. At times they would use this means as a sort of "comic relief" from the tension their captivating stories would create amongst the listeners. As they seldom found time to dress, they limited themselves to a change of headgear in order to represent various professions, age-groups, and types of different nationalities. They often used a handkerchief and a cudgel to aid their mimicry and accompany by the latter's knockings their imitations of beasts and birds.

In Turkish circles, this fondness for dramatized mimicry persisted at least until the First World War[9], while with the Arabs it seems to have remained here and there until today.

[7] The mimetic element of the *Maqāma* has been observed by Horovitz, ibid., pp. 21–27.

[8] Georg Jacob was among the first to do serious research in the character of the *meddah*. He first published a booklet, *Aus den Vorträgen eines türkischen Meddah* (1900); then he wrote a more detailed work on the subject, *Vorträge türkischer Meddahs* (1904). Cf. Hermann Paulus, *Harschi Vesvese, ein Vortrag des türkischen Meddah's Nayif Efendi* (1905). For bibliographical material cf. *Der Islam*, IV, 1913, pp. 130–131. See also Nicholas N. Martinovitch, *The Turkish theatre* (1933), esp. pp. 21 ss., 79 ss. Ed. Saussey, *Littérature populaire turque* (1936), pp. 73–74. Selim Nüzhet Gerçek, Türk Temşası (1942; Martinovitch, *op. cit.*, p. 125, and Ritter, *Karagös*, II, p. XI, also mentioned a 1930 ed.), pp. 5–44. Thorough research is still to be done into the character of the Arab *ḥakawātī*.

[9] Hartmann's letters to Fleischer, *ZDMG*, vol. XXX, 1876, p. 159; cf. ibid., p. 168. Martinovitch, *op. cit.*, pp. 23–24. For a detailed description of a *meddah*'s performance in 1916, approximately, see Friedrich Schrader, *Konstantinopel. Vergangenheit und Gegenwart* (1917), pp. 127–131.

One reads about *meddahs* still being very popular in Algeria in 1903[10]. As late as the years immediately preceding the First World War, a certain Aḥmad Fahīm al-Fār (The Mouse) was beloved by the Cairene population for his skill in imitating the voices of birds and beasts, and especially in his ability to present scenes of village and harem life. This Aḥmad al-Fār used to perform at the head of a troupe of twelve men, who would also act the roles of women. The mimetic farces performed by this troupe were immensely popular[11]. In our days, these performances are limited to the poorer, not yet Europeanized population, and their number gradually diminishes.

Summing up, mimicry can be considered a highly important dramatic element in mediaeval and modern times, having kept alive popular interest in semitheatrical performances. There did exist, however, certain types of histrionics more akin to the theater as such. The first type which surely merits more than a passing mention is the Passion play.

[10] See I. Eberhardt, *Pages d' Islam* (1920), pp. 58–66.

[11] Reich, *Der Mimus*, vol. I, part 1, p. 667, n. 1. Curt Prüfer, *Drama, Arabic*, in *ERE*, vol. IV (1911), pp. 872–873. Prüfer had lived in Egypt and later became one of the Intelligence chiefs of the Turco-German armies in Syria and Palestine during the First World War—cf. R. Storrs, *Orientations* (Defin. ed., 1945), p. 122.

CHAPTER 2

The Passion Play

THE *Ta'ziya* which literally translated means "Consolation," was—and still is—the Persian version of the Mysteries or Passion play in Christian Europe of the Middle Ages, revived in twentieth-century Europe and America[12]. With the possible exception of the ancient Egyptian Mysteries, this seems to be the first Passion play in the Orient[13]. One should bear in mind, however, that the *Ta'ziya* shows hardly any resemblance to the Catholic theatrical performances, in either spirit or form. It is more likely a remnant of religious practices from Zoroastrian Persia, strangled by victorious Islam[14].

The Persian ritual play, always performed in the first ten days of the Muslim month of Muḥarram, is mainly a commemoration of the slaughter of Ḥasan, Ḥusain and other members of 'Alī's family almost thirteen centuries ago. This extermination of the descendants and relatives of the Prophet of Islam by the new ruling house was one of the important causes which brought about a political and religious cleavage in the Muslim community, traces of which are still noticeable today.

The *Ta'ziya*, while based on ancient practices of saint commemoration, lacks a very important element found in both Eastern and Western Passion plays, i.e., the leading character's resurrection. This is even stranger considering the fact that the sectarians who celebrate this ten-day rite *do* believe in the return of a scion from the Prophet's house to serve as a sort of Messiah.

[12] J. T. Smith, *The Parish theatre* (1917), ch. 5.
[13] Joseph Gregor, *Weltgeschichte des Theaters* (1933), p. 79; cf. ibid., pp. 79–82.
[14] C. Barbier de Meynard & S. Guyard, *Trois comédies* (Paris, 1886), Introd., p. VII.

Although the main purpose of the *Ta'ziya* is to represent the suffering and death of the Prophet's descendants and their followers, culminating on the tenth day in the heart-rending slaughter of Ḥusain, the chief incidents of these events are not always rendered chronologically[15]. The narrative is frequently interwoven with occasionally irrelevant episodes, such as scenes based on the Old[16] and the New Testament or on Oriental folklore, meant to relieve the tension caused by the main performance. Even then, feelings run so high that many actors, grief-stricken, commit suicide; while the spectators but a generation ago were often driven to such a frenzy that they attacked and manhandled foreigners (mainly Christians) in the streets[17]. It was this brutality that apparently caused the Persian government, under the iron rule of Rizā Shāh between the two World Wars, to limit the scope of the *Ta'ziya*. Performances were reportedly renewed, although with somewhat restricted fervor, during Muṣaddiq's premiership. The reading of *Ta'ziya-s*, published both in Persian and in translation[18], gives but a scant idea of the impact of their performance on an excited crowd. A more accurate idea of these plays and the impression they leave may be formed from the fairly substantial accounts of the various travelers who witnessed the *Ta'ziya* in the last two centuries, usually under the protection of a Persian garb[19].

[15] Contrast, however, the apparently chronological sequence of events in Teheran, as reported by the organizer of the *Ta'ziya* to E. Aubin, *Le Chiisme et la nationalité persane* in *RMM*, vol. IV, Mar., 1908, pp. 486–487.

[16] Strangely enough, this interpolation of unrelated Biblical stories is a feature of the Christian Passion Play, too, e.g., see R. T. Fuller, *The world's stage—Oberammergau, 1934. A book about the passion play: its history, its meaning and its people*, esp. pp. 41–44. If there has been any mutual influence, this is by no means evident.

[17] See also my *'Al ha-teiaṭrōn etsel ha-'aravīm*, part 1, in *Bamah*, fasc. 47, Jan., 1946, pp. 48–49.

[18] A. Chodzko, *Théâtre persan* (1878). Lewis Pelly, *The Miracle Play of Hasan and Husain* (1879). An. de Gubernatis, *Storia universale della letteratura*, vol. III (1883), pp. 109–134. P. M. Sykes, *The Glory of the Shiah World* (1910). Ch. Virolleaud, *La passion de l'imam Hosseyn* (1927).

[19] Cf. bibliography by R. Strothmann in the *Encyclopaedia of Islam* (*sub voce Ta'ziya*); and of H. Massé, *Croyances et coutumes persanes* (1938), vol. I, pp. 122–136.

These plays are performed, to the accompaniment of music and with varying degrees of pomp, in the theaters, in the mosques, and in the open air. More often than not the half-realistic and half-symbolical decoration is striking by its wealth; blood is real, yet sand is represented by straw. The stage effects, moreover, are often overdone, e.g., Ḥusain's gory head reciting holy verses, or an armless warrior killing his opponent with a sword which he holds in his teeth[20]. Men perform the parts of women and wild beasts (the horses, however, are real). Although untrained and a trifle too declamatory, the actors with all their unadulterated enthusiasm are said generally to leave a deep impression, not only on the native audience but also on Europeans present at the performances[21]. It is probably the sincerity of the actors, combined with the credulity of the masses, that makes the most unreal and fantastic scenes—such as King Solomon's forecasting history's whole course of events—look and sound convincing to the onlookers.

The larger part of the *Ta'ziya-s* were written and performed in Persian[22], although some are known to have existed and been shown in Arabic[23] and Turkish. The impact of the *Ta'ziya* on the majority of the Arabic-speaking communities in the Near East through the centuries, however, was not considerable, as most of them were Sunnites. Still, it is plausible that the masked

---

See also Ch. Virolleaud, *Le théâtre persan ou le drame de Kerbéla* (1950). Matthew Arnold, *Essays in criticism* (1889), ch. VII. Th. Nöldeke, *Sketches from Eastern history* (1892), p. 82. H. Lammens, *L'islam croyances et institutions*, 2nd ed. (1941), pp. 188, 226. *H.* (i.e. *al-Hilāl*), vol. XIV, Dec. 1, 1905, pp. 142–144; ibid., vol. XVIII, May 1, 1910, pp. 466–468; cf. *al-Muqtabas*, vol. I, No. 1, Muḥarram 1324 (appr. Feb. 1906), pp. 52–53.

[20] Fuller details in Jean Hytier, *La vie et la mort de la tragédie religieuse persane*, in *L'Islam et l'Occident, Cahiers du Sud*, 1947, pp. 264–270, and the sources mentioned in his article.

[21] Cf. the valuable as yet almost unheeded testimony of S. G. W. Benjamin, the first Minister of the U.S.A. at Teheran, in his *Persia and the Persians* (1887), pp. 365–406.

[22] Not only in Persia but in other countries, such as India—cf. G. Geary, *Through Asiatic Turkey*, vol. I (1878), App. C.

[23] Cf. Jurjī Zaidān, *Ta'rīkh ādāb al-lugha al-'arabiyya*, vol. IV, p. 152.

performances prevalent until today among some of these communities in the first ten days of Muḥarram[24] were influenced, even possibly derived, from the *Ta'ziya*. These were, then, the only dramatic performances of a tragic character in mediaeval Arabic literature; they probably remained the only ones until modern times. Others were more akin to the comedy, out of which the more important were the so-called shadow plays, many of which were both written and presented in Arabic.

[24] G. Cerbella & M. Ageli, *Le faste musulmane in Tripoli* (1949), pp. 15 *ss*.

CHAPTER 3

The Shadow Play

a. The Beginnings

A "SHADOW PLAY" is histrionics performed by the casting of shadows on a curtain, visible to the audience. This is a pastime which entertained even the rich, intellectual highbrow, but in the main it was an amusement enjoyed by the humblest in various countries. This form of popular art deserves attention not only because of its widespread popularity[25]; it is also the most important forerunner of the theater in the Near East.

Puppet shows fall naturally into three categories: marionette plays, hand-puppet plays and shadow plays. The first and the second (almost nonexistent in the Near East) are more important, while the element of reality appears at its strongest in the last. The common denominator is the puppet's lack of existence or possibility of action outside the will of the hidden manipulator of the strings. The puppet's unsteady steps between the ceiling and the floor are a powerful reminder of our own precarious existence between heaven and earth. And truly, the puppet theater goes into all the tragic and the comic in our lives. More generally, puppet shows symbolize the ultimate futility of human life, while shadow plays, in particular, stress the phantom-like aspect of our life's course.

Consequently, the puppet can never be a true-to-life portrait of a man or a woman; it can only describe a particular trait of character. By eliminating the casual and the individualistic, the puppet becomes a prototype. This is fantasy based on real life and connected with it. The face remains stereotyped, but

[25] For a survey of its popularity in our times, cf. David ben Shalōm, *Teiaṭrōn Bubbōt* (in Hebrew, 1946), esp. pp. 3 *ss*.

variations in speech, imitation of movements, and differences of color enable the puppet show to be quite realistic.

Just as the puppet has no possible existence outside the theater hall, it can have no separate existence from the particular run of events allotted to it. The event and the puppet are inseparable; hence the scope of individualism is very restricted. It would contradict the puppet's special style, if anybody were to try to make it express complicated, soul-searching thoughts. Its very inertness and primitiveness make it suitable for general ideas only. It follows that the puppet is most suitable for the interpretation of popular sketches, while its inherent anonymity has particularly prepared it to voice criticism against the powerful and the rich. While an audience is almost uninterruptedly aware of a stage actor's conscious portrayal, the very nonsubsistence of the puppet may often lend greater credibility to the words put into its mouth.

Because of the striking contrast between the imaginary vitality of the puppet and its lifelessness, a comic element is engendered, whose characteristics are perforce clownishly primitive. This is a kind of buffoonery—rudeness, naiveté, and directness are its main components. Preferably, the simple ridicule is employed, such as comical situations or puns on ambiguous words. The comic effect is heightened, as has been hinted, by the incongruity of the contrast between the puppet's lifelessness and its vitality of movement, the stereotyped nature of its face and the material which is to be interpreted, its known dependence on the strings and its apparent free will. The whole effect cannot avoid being grotesque, thus adding another important comic element to the shadow theater of all countries. This grotesqueness is fully appreciated by the masses, particularly when it is demonstrated by abnormal phalli appended to the puppet's body[26].

[26] For a further discussion of these points, see Luzia Glanz, *Das Puppenspiel und sein Publikum* (1941). K. Fr. Floegel, *Geschichte des Grotesk Komischen* (5th ed., rev. by Fr. W. Ebeling, 1888; it seems that a later ed. was publ. in 1914).

It is unlikely that the shadow-play theater had its inception in the Arab Near East, for marionettes and hand-puppets are almost nonexistent. Furthermore, the first instances when such shows are mentioned in Arabic are fairly late. One naturally turns to Greece, with its recognized contribution to the development of the theater in general. However, although one is familiar with the puppet shows in the Classical World, there is but little information about their real influence on the Oriental shadow plays. Even though the obscene element may have been acquired from Greek mimicry, perhaps through Byzantium, it still seems that the source of the Near Eastern shadow theater was in east and southeast Asia[27].

The evidence for this hypothesis, although suggestive, is as yet inconclusive. India is the native land of important languages, of a great wealth of folk tales and of the puppet shows[28]. The few, none too clear allusions to a shadow theater are not convincing. The same applies to Ceylon. The ancient Javanese *Wajang*, on the other hand, is an easily recognizable kind of shadow play, imbued with a mystic fear of magic, in which religion, art and poetry are interwoven; the themes treat of gods, kings, and other high-ranking personages[29]. The figures are more delicately designed, although less varied than in the Near East. While the Siamese shadow play shows traces of Javanese and Indian influence[30], there are signs of an independent development in the Chinese shadow theater, whose figures demonstrate a certain similarity in their general characteristics to those known to us from the various Islamic shadow theaters[31].

[27] Reich, *Der Mimus*, vol. I, part 1, pp. 669–675 and *passim*. Charles Magnin, *Histoire des marionettes en Europe* (1862), whose arguments are less conclusive.

[28] Richard Pischel, *Die Heimat des Puppenspiels* (1900), *passim*. UNESCO's *Courier*, fasc. 3–4 for 1955.

[29] Carl Hagemann, *Spiele der Völker. Eindrücke und Studien einer Weltfahrt nach Afrika und Ostasien* (1921), pp. 149–161. Joseph Gregor, *op. cit.*, p. 76.

[30] Gregor, ibid., pp. 77–79. D. Sonakul (Dhani Nivat), *Pageantry of the Siamese stage*, in *National Geogr. Mag.*, vol. XCI, Feb., 1947. Id., *The Nang* (Bangkok, 1954), pp. 4 *ss*.

[31] Hagemann, *op. cit.*, pp. 444–452.

According to tradition, China is the home of the shadow theater. Even the designation of this amusement as *Ombres chinoises* was current in Europe for a long time. More important is the fact that it was from China, probably through the agency of the Mongolians, the neighbors of the Turkish tribes, that shadow plays were introduced into the Muslim Near East in the twelfth or thirteenth century[32]. Anyway, although various communities in the Near East show traces of having had shadow-play shows at one time or another, the bulk of these performances was shown to Turkish- and Arabic-speaking audiences. Similarly, almost all shadow-play manuscripts from the Near East were found to have been written in these languages.

b. The Turkish Contribution

The Turkish shadow theater, although of great ethnographic importance, and artistic as well as linguistic interest, will be described here only summarily, since it is actually outside the scope of this study and fairly thorough research has already been done into it[33].

[32] I have dealt with this matter separately in my *Shadow plays in the Near East*, *'Edōt (Communities) Quarterly*, vol. III, Nos. 1–2, 1948, *passim*, esp. p. XXV. See also J. Scherr, *Allgemeine Geschichte der Literatur* (1861), p. 57. Cf. Georg Jacob, *Geschichte des Schattentheaters* (1907), pp. 18 *ss.*, to his *Das Schattentheater in seiner Wanderung vom Morgenland zum Abendland* (1901), p. 6; reviewed by R. Pischel in the *DLZ*, 1902, p. 403. See also Reich, ibid., 1904, pp. 598 *ss.* Siyavuşgil, *Karagöz* (1951), pp. 4 *ss.*

[33] Georg Jacob has compiled the most important bibliographies for the Oriental shadow theater. The last of his Appendices to Enno Littmann's *Arabische Schattenspiele* (1901) was a *Schattenspiel Bibliographie.* Jacob enlarged it several times. In that same year he published a more detailed *Schattenspiel Bibliographie,* which he reprinted, with important additions, under the name of *Litteratur Uebersicht,* at the end of his *Das Schattentheater in seiner Wanderung vom Morgenland zum Abendland* (1901). He rearranged the results of his studies in a yet enlarged *Bibliographie über das Schattentheater* (2nd enlarged ed., 1902). In 1906 Jacob published an even more detailed bibliography, divided according to the centuries, from the eleventh to the twentieth, called *Erwähnungen des Schattentheaters in der Welt-Litteratur.* In 1912 he published *Addenda* to it, and in 1925 an enlarged edition. In 1931 he published some typewritten additions (cf. Ritter, *Karagös türkische Schattenspiele,* II, Introd., p. IX). Five years later Jacob had ended preparing a typewritten *Nachtrags-Bibliographie mit Excerpten als Annalen*

The Turkish shadow theater was influenced, to a large extent, by the mimetic performances of the *meddah*[34], as well as by popular local representations, named *Orta oyunu*[35], a stereotyped play with improvisations like the *Commedia dell'arte*. There might have been a mutual influence, if one remembers the close commercial ties of Turkey with Venice and Genoa. The manner of improvisation as well as many aspects of the characters who appear in the *Commedia dell'arte*[36] resemble in a striking way those in the Turkish popular show.

The shows, which attracted the public in Turkey by their satirical description of local manners and customs, probably date from the twelfth century; however, their roots, like those of the *meddah*, are undoubtedly much older and might go back to the Greek mime, possibly through Byzantium[37]. It should be remembered that dramatic performances, had reached a fairly high standard in Byzantium and that it is quite possible that the Turkish conquerors retained the services of Byzantine actors[38]. The sources of the Turkish shadow play are not very clear and will be examined later on, along with the Arabic ones[39]. The style of its puppets, whose shadows the audience

---

des Schattentheaters im Morgenland (Kiel, 9 January, 1936), in my possession, thanks to Prof. L. A. Mayer, of the Hebrew University, Jerusalem; I am unaware of its having been printed. See further bibl. material in H. Ritter, *Karagös*, in the *Encyclopaedia of Islam* (*sub voce*); Martinovitch, *op. cit.*, p. 125; Landau, *Shadow plays in the Near East, passim*, esp. pp. 70–72.

[34] See above, chapter 1.

[35] Martinovitch, *op. cit.*, pp. 13–21, 49–77. Selim Nüzhet Gerçek, *op. cit.*, pp. 111–159. I prefer throughout the modern, current Turkish transliteration (such as *Karagöz*).

[36] Many works have been written on the Italian *Commedia dell'arte* and its characters. Among these, mention should be made of the interesting work of Maurice Sand, *Masques et bouffons* (*comédie italienne*) (2 vols., 1862). On the connection between the *orta oyunu* and the *commedia dell'arte* see Kúnos's thesis (which should be further investigated), in his *Das türkische Volksschauspiel-Orta ojnu* (1908), pp. 8–9. See also Reich, *Der Mimus*, vol. I, part 2, pp. 619–620.

[37] H. Reich, ibid., vol. I, part 2, ch. 7. Martinovitch, *The Turkish theatre—the missing link*, in *The Moslem World*, vol. XXXIV, Jan, 1944, pp. 54–55.

[38] J. S. Tunison, *Dramatic traditions of the dark ages* (1907), p. 113.

[39] See below, footnote 66.

sees moving on a brightly illuminated curtain, resembles, on one hand, the Chinese one; on the other, this popular amusement seems to be related, through the *meddah* and the *Orta oyunu*, to the Greek mimetic performances. However, while the *meddah* can only give an imitation of a comic scene, and while the *Orta oyunu* hardly ever dared to criticize the powerful and the rich openly, the Turkish shadow play could both give a fuller performance than the first and air a more biting criticism than the second.

The fairly large number of Turkish shadow plays, found in MS. and printed in Turkish or in translation, or summarized by onlookers[40], together with an examination of the modern counterpart of this show—not so very different in its main peculiarities from the ancient one, conveys an idea of the main characteristics of the Turkish shadow theater.

Even though the plot is somewhat stereotyped, this is so only in its general outline. Otherwise the play may describe, to the accompaniment of music partly based on melodies imported from Persia, the amusing adventures of the two heroes, Hagivad and Karagöz (of these two more will be said farther on), who ply various trades[41]. In so doing, they come across merchants, boatmen, usurers, watchmen, woodcutters, policemen, wrestlers, etc. Pathological or vicious characters as well as freaks take part, too; chiefly the opium addict, the hashish addict, the drunkard, the madman, the lame pauper, the hunchback, the

[40] Ignaz Kúnos, *Három Karagöz-Játék* (1886). Jacob, *Schejtan dolaby* (1899). Id., *Bekri Mustafa. Ein türkisches Hajalspiel aus Brussa*, in *ZDMG*, vol. LII, 1899, pp. 626 *ss.* J. Oestrup, *En Tyrkisk Syggekomedie*, in *Studier fra sprog-og oldtidsforskning udgivne af det philologisk-historiske samfund*, Nr. 51 (1901). H. Ritter, in *Orientalia* (publ. by the German archaeological Inst.), I, 1933, pp. 3–66. Id., *Karagös türkische Schattenspiele* (3 vols.). Reviews of this work were published in *DLZ*, vol. XLV, 1924, pp. 2250–2256; *MSOS*, vol. XXVIII, part 2, 1925, pp. 282–286; *OLZ*, vol. XXVIII, 1924, pp. 423–431; *Die Szene, Blätter für die Bühnenkunst*, vol. XV, fasc. 9, Sept. 1925, pp. 178–182; *Der Islam*, vol. XV, 1926, pp. 153–158. Gerard de Nerval, *The women of Cairo scenes of life in the Orient* (1929), vol. II, pp. 209–225. Martinovitch, *The Turkish theatre*, pp. 101–120. For further material cf. Ritter, *Karagös*, vol. II, Introd., pp. IX *ss.*

[41] See for details Jacob, *Geschichte des Schattentheaters*, esp. pp. 95–96.

dwarf, the spendthrift, the prodigal, the debauchee, the dandy (whose dress might be an important aid towards a history of Turkish costumes), the gentleman thief, etc. Less often one sees (and hears!) the stutterer, the nasal man, porters, and acrobats. Manifestly absent[42], no doubt through precaution, were the Sultan, Viziers and other dignitaries of the Empire, the women and eunuchs of the Sultan's seraglio, the Janissaries and other soldiers, and the teachers in the religious schools. Among the women, the commonest types are dancers, witches, Negresses, whores, and go-between, which often bring the obscene element into pre-eminence in the play.

Various national types appear also, and the audience is entertained by that essential characteristic of all the puppet plays, namely, their peculiar mannerisms and dialectal speech as well as by the misunderstandings arising therefrom. Among them are Arabs, Persians[43], Jews[44], Negroes, Franks (Christians and strangers), who change place with Greeks, Armenians, Albanians, Bosnians, Turkish yokels, uncultured and hard-working[45]. The appearance of almost every one of these types is usually greeted by a special melody, made necessary by the lack of suitable scenery and stage decoration[46].

It is very difficult to obtain a true impression of the exact contents of any play, for the printed texts are generally remote from the original; even copies written at the direct dictation of the shadow-theater master are unreliable, because of the large

[42] As has been pointed out so ably by Siyavuşgil, *Le Karagöz dans la société Ottomane*, in the newspaper *Ankara*, Apr. 6, 1939, being a translation from the same article in the *Varlık*. For other works of Siyavuşgil on this subject cf. Ritter, *Karagös*, II, Introd., pp. XI–XII.

[43] H. Vambéry, *Sittenbilder aus dem Morgenlande* (1876), pp. 34–35. Th. Gautier, *Constantinople* (1894), ch. 14. Siyavuşgil, *Karagöz*, p. 13, has ably succeeded in identifying the Persian prototype with a Turk from Azerbaijan.

[44] Georg Jacob, *Zur Grammatik des Vulgär-Türkischen*, in *ZDMG*, vol. LII, 1898, pp. 695–703. Id., *Türkische Litteraturgeschichte in Einzeldarstellungen, Heft I. Das türkische Schattentheater* (1900). I. Kúnos, Das *türkische Volksschauspiel—Orta ojnu* (1908). E. Littmann, *Das Malerspiel. Ein Schattenspiel aus Aleppo*, in *Sitzungsber. Heidelberger Ak. Wiss., Phil.-hist. Kl., 25.3.1918.* Saussey, *op. cit.*

[45] F. K. Endres, *Die Türkei* (1916), pp. 286–288.

[46] Siyavuşgıl, *Karagöz*, pp. 9 *ss.*

part improvisation played in these shows[47]. One surmises, however, that certain subjects were particularly popular. These were apparently handed down from father to son, and a shadow-theater director probably had no less than twenty-eight plays, to enable him to have a different show for each night in the month of Ramaḍān, when fasting Muslims increased the attendance at performances[48].

The best-liked subjects were the following:

a. Karagöz looks for employment under his companion Hagivad's guidance and demonstrates his lack of ability.

b. Karagöz tries to do forbidden things out of curiosity or lust; he is caught by the police, from whom only Hagivad can save him, on his promise to give an even gayer performance on the following evening.

c. Hagivad teaches Karagöz various games, which the latter misunderstands.

d. Karagöz manages to get himself into trouble and finds himself in an unpleasant situation.

e. Plots, based on Persian love themes, the *Arabian Nights*, and Turkish popular legends[49].

The obscene element, remindful both in gesture and talk of the Phallic Mime in Ancient Greece, had a fairly important part. It generally determined the character of those *Karagöz* shows performed in the poorer, nautical districts of Asiatic Turkey rather than of the plays shown to more select audiences. Notwithstanding its obscenity, the Turkish shadow theater (strangely enough) lashed at immorality, for the obscene element was a means of entertainment rather than an aim in itself; thus immoral people are often shown in an unfavorable light in these plays. Family life is sacred—a wife's infidelity is

[47] Ritter, in the *Encycl. of Islam, sub voce Karagöz*. Martinovitch, *The Turkish theatre*, esp. pp. 44–45.

[48] Siyavuşgil, *Karagöz*, p. 4.

[49] Ritter, *op. cit.* in the *Enc. of Islam*. Martinovitch, *The Turkish theatre*, p. 43. Landau, *Shadow plays in the Near East*, p. XXXVIII.

almost nonexistent; but marriages arranged by go-betweens are ridiculed.

The satire is directed at other sorts of people besides the peculiar prototypes mentioned above. True, Islam has no clergy, but Karagöz misses no occasion to expose and satirize the lazy dervishes who exploit people's superstitions for their own private gains. Social differences were also satirized, as illustrated by the great dissimilarity between the poor boorish Karagöz and his inseparable companion, the pretentious Hagivad. However, this not too innocent irony of contrast was not pointed directly at the authorities; these were subtly satirized as policemen, who most probably represented the army as well.

The shadow theater flourished in the Ottoman Empire mainly during the seventeenth, the eighteenth and the nineteenth centuries and by its poignant satire helped prepare the "Young Turk" Revolution at the beginning of the twentieth. Notwithstanding the competition of the theater in the nineteenth century, shadow plays became increasingly popular but changed in certain ways: the curtain was enlarged and became a screen, lit by gas; a multitude of decorations and a box office were introduced, and the very subjects of the plays changed, by the adaptation of then modern Turkish novels. These imitations amused audiences for a short time, then taste changed, becoming modeled on European patterns, and *Karagöz* shows disappeared almost completely[50]. It is chiefly in the Arab countries that shadow plays survive, and to a limited extent only.

c. Arabic Performances in Mediaeval Egypt

The Arabic shadow theater is perhaps even more interesting than the Turkish, as it not only excelled in adapting the Turkish *Karagöz* to its own special environment but also created a new, independent kind of shadow play, not connected with the

[50] Siyavuşgil, *Karagöz*, pp. 7–8, 16 *ss*. Contrast, however, Ritter, *Karagös*, vol. III, Introd., p. X.

Turkish one, describing the life and manners of Muslim Egypt.

The latter sort of plays date from the sixties and seventies of the thirteenth century[51]. Their author, Muḥammad ibn Daniyāl, an Egyptian physician (approx. A.D. 1248–1311)[52], wrote three shadow plays in poetry and versified prose—the only remnants of the usage of poetry in a play that remains from the Arab cultural heritage of the Middle Ages[53].

All three plays were intended for actual production on the stage, on consecutive evenings, and the MS. undoubtedly served as a guide to the master, director, and owner of the shadow theater. The prologue advises on methods of direction and performance and lists suitable lyrics.

The first play is *Ṭaif al-Khayāl* (*The Spirit of Imagination*, or *of the Shadow*). After what probably constituted the then accepted, even stereotyped, beginning—some songs, thanks to the audience, praise of God and his Prophet, a prayer for the welfare of the ruler, and some other preliminary scenes, the main plot is unfolded. Its theme was fairly common in the popular literature and later in the popular drama of the Muslim East. In this case the old sinner, the soldier Wiṣāl, is its hero. Having been reduced to poverty, Wiṣāl is persuaded by a matchmaker to marry a young lady whose charms the matchmaker cannot

[51] Jacob, *Gesch. d. Schattentheaters*, pp. 34 *ss*. The plays have been analyzed by id., in the Hungarian *Kéleti Szemle*, vol. II, 1901, pp. 76–77; cf. id., ibid., vol. I, 1900, pp. 233–236. Id., *Al-Mutajjam, ein altarabisches Schauspiel fur die Schattenbühne bestimmt von Muhammad Ibn Danijal. Erste Mitteilung über das Werk* (1901). Id., *Ein ägyptischer Jahrmarkt im 13. Jahrhundert*, in *Sitzungsber. Kön. Bay. Ak. d. Wiss., Philos.—philol. u. hist. Kl.*, 10 Abh., 1910. Id., *'Agib ed-Din al-Wa'iz bei Ibn Danijal*, in *Der Islam*, vol. IV, 1913, pp. 67–71. J. Horovitz, *Eine neue Handschrift von Ibn Danijal's Taif al-hajal*, in *ZDMG*, vol. LX, 1906, p. 703. P. Kahle reviewed Jacob's *Ein ägyptischer Jahrmarkt* in *OLZ*, vol. XV, 1912. See also Kahle, *Marktszene aus einem egyptischen Spiel*, in *ZA*, vol. XXVII, 1912, pp. 92–102. Id., *M. Ibn Danijal und sein zweites arabisches Schattenspiel*, in *Miscellanea Academica Berolinensis*, 1950. Landau, *Shadow plays in the Near East*, pp. XXVIII–XXXIV.

[52] Biographical notice, with sources, in Zaidān's *Ta'rīkh ādāb al-lugha al-'arabiyya*, vol. III, p. 121; cf. ibid., vol. IV, p. 152. Another, by Sa'īd al-Dīwahjī, in *K.*, June 1951, pp. 611–617.

[53] Apparently these three plays have been reissued by Muḥammad Taqī'l-Dīn al-Hilālī in Iraq (cf. *K.*, vol. IV, Jan., 1949, p. 162), but I was unable to consult this ed.

praise too highly. After the wedding, Wiṣāl lifts the veil from his bride's face only to discover she is a monster: "Her nose resembles a hill, her lips are like the camel's, and her hair is like that of a beetle crawling in the dirt." Wiṣāl threatens both the matchmaker and her husband with severe punishment, and decides on a pilgrimage to the Muslim holy places in the Hijaz, to atone for his sins[54].

Ibn Daniyāl's second play is called *'Ajīb and G̲harīb*, which may be either the names of two people, or their description ("the amazing and the strange"). A shadow play of this name is still popular in Persia today, while folk tales in Arabic about these two characters have been passed on from generation to generation[55]. In this shadow play there is no pretension at a plot, as it is actually a most edifying parade of realistic figures, remindful of those known to us from the above-mentioned *maqāma-s* and folk tales. The elaborately drawn picture of the market life is an important source of information on Arab civilization in those times. The large variety of types makes it appear improbable that they were all created by their author's imagination; indeed, the existence of some of them at the time is corroborated by other sources. No doubt, then, that Ibn Daniyāl portrayed a good number of his characters, possibly all, from real life.

G̲harīb and 'Ajīb, for all the contrast between them, are both rogues. The first, a shrewd traveler, personifies the class of the "Sons of Sāsān," the restless, none too honest, but nevertheless poor, wanderers[56]. 'Ajīb, on his part, is an amazing sort

[54] While all sorts of plays in the Christian Middle Ages are strongly tinged by a religious element—see, for instance, F. J. Mone, *Schauspiele des Mittelalters* (1846), pp. 2 *ss.*—the above is one of the few instances of religious matters being mentioned at all in the Arabic shadow theater, which is markedly secular in its themes and attitudes.

[55] One such collection has been printed under the title *Qiṣṣat 'Ajīb wa-G̲harīb wa-mā jarā lahumā 'alā' l-tamām wa'l-kamāl.* Cairo, al-Maṭba'a al-Ḥamīdiyya, A.H. 1320; 68 pp.

[56] Jacob, *Ein ägyptischer Jahrmarkt*, p. 5. Id., *Gesch. d. Schattentheaters*, pp. 50–51. Horovitz, *Spuren griechischer Mimen*, pp. 23–27. J. H. Krammers, *Sāsān*, in the *Enc. of Islam, sub voce.*

of preacher, who praises Allah for having created wine and calls on all beggars to ply their trade energetically, striving for ready cash[57].

Others that also appear are various popular types from everyday life, whose behavior and expression are described briefly but succinctly. First in the procession are various professions, whose exponents show their skill and praise their wares: a snake charmer, a quack doctor, a hawker of medicinal herbs, an ophthalmic surgeon, two acrobats, an astrologer, a sorcerer trading in amulets, an epileptic boy and a phlebotomist with all her instruments. These are followed by several animal tamers, who present their animals or let them show their clownish tricks: tamers of lions, elephants, and bears, *Abū'l-Qiṭaṭ*[58] (who tries to reconcile cats and dogs), a dancing teacher for dogs, a Sudanese buffoon, a bayonet swallower, a monkey owner[59], and a rope dancer. This gallery of characters, every one of whom recites or gesticulates in accordance with his role, is ended by an enamored man covered with self-inflicted wounds, a carrier of burning coal and a camel driver. G̱harīb reappears to bring the performance to an end by a short epilogue, unrelated to the above market scenes[60].

The third play, *al-Mutayyam* (the love-stricken), treats of love and prize fights. Before going to his beloved, al-Mutayyam and his rival (in love) assist at fights between their respective cocks, rams, and bulls. These fights are naturally seasoned with speeches and songs. The rest of the play is connected to the previous part only artificially. Various characters come to feast on al-Mutayyam's bull which was slain in the fight and then roasted. These provide worthy companions to the people ap-

[57] The humorous exhortations of 'Ajīb have been translated into German by Jacob in *Der Islam*, vol. IV, 1913, pp. 67–71.

[58] Literally, "the father of the cats."

[59] For some of the forms in which monkey owners appear, see E. Graefe and others, in *Der Islam*, vol. V, 1914, pp. 93–106.

[60] See also the description of the market in Damascus by J. G. Wetzstein, *Der Markt in Damascus*, in *ZDMG*, vol. XI, 1857, pp. 475–525 and the *corrigenda*, p. 744.

pearing in the former play. Most of them are sinners or pathological types: a debauchee, wild with carnal appetites; a fat songster and winebibber; a pale, haggard youth who shuns wine and indoor sleeping; a mediator of other people's quarrels; a sick man; a man inclined to masturbation; another who snatches children from their beds to satisfy his fiendish lust on their tender bodies; an uninvited parasite; and the Angel of Death, who takes al-Mutayyam's soul, after due repentance by the latter, driving the frightened guests away.

These three plays are most interesting as being the only extensive work of a playwright in Arabic before the seventeenth century that has reached us (others are only mentioned in our sources). Their importance, however, lies in the picture they draw of Egyptian society of seven centuries ago. The characters are so much alive that one feels one may meet many of them today in the old parts of Cairo. Ibn Daniyāl was at his best, of course, when describing the various kinds of physicians, his colleagues, but he also excelled in the portrayal of all craftsmen, respectable and otherwise.

The comic element is brought about, as in every shadow theater worth its name, by puns[61] and the stress laid on the obscene element (e.g., Wiṣāl's nickname "lord of the *Dabbūs*"[62] in the first play, or the introduction of masturbation into the third) as well as by the clever choice of the characters' names: most of these names are comprehensible[63], and from the rest

[61] For an example see Landau, *Shadow plays in the Near East*, p. XXX, n. 34.

[62] *Dabbūs* is translated in most dictionaries as rod (or stick, pin). In Tunis, the man who operates the figures in the shadow theater by means of a stick was called until recently *Abū Dabbūs* (see Flögel, *op. cit.*, II, pp. 10–11. Cf. Reich, *Der Mimus*, vol. I, part 2, p. 649, n. 2). In Turkish, *topūz* or *tōpūz* (today: *topuz*, as in Roumanian) has the same meaning (see G. I. Jonnescu-Gion, *Istoria Bucurescilor*, 1899, pp. 397, 555, 746). However, in the Arabic dialect spoken in Egypt this term has the additional meaning of the male sex organ; one can hardly doubt from the context that it was the vulgar meaning that was intended in our play. Moreover, the image of the mime with a protruding sex organ is remindful of the phallic theme in the Greek farce in a highly suggestive way—ch. also Reich, *Der Mimus, passim*, and Horovitz, *Spuren griechischer Mimen*, p. 29.

[63] P. Kahle, in his *Eine Zunftsprache der ägyptischen Schattenspieler*, in *Islamica*, vol. II, 1926, has examined the vocabulary of the shadow-play writers and performers.

one gathers that these names were given either because of their suitability or their ridiculous unfitness. For example, the matchmaker's husband, on one hand, is called ʻAflaq, whose meaning is both "fat and soft" and "sexual cohabitation"[64]; doubtless the man looks both fat and lewd. On the other hand, *Ṭaif al-k̲h̲ayāl* is addressed as "proportionally perfect," while he is a hunchback. A further unexpected contrast is caused by the bride of Wiṣāl, as opposed to her previous description by the matchmaker.

As has been said, no manuscripts of shadow plays of the following four centuries have been unearthed, although performances were most probably put on in many parts of the Arab world. Various references mention the Arabic shadow theater unequivocally[65]. The most interesting of these is that of the Egyptian historian, Ibn Iyās, in his Arabic chronicle of Egypt[66]. In his biographical record of Sultan Selim I, the Turkish conqueror of Egypt in the sixteenth century, the Sultan was so excited about the local shadow plays that he told the Egyptian producer: "When we go to Istanbul, come along with us so that my son, too, may see it (the shadow play)."

This quotation, whose veracity there is no reason to doubt, raises the whole problem of Egyptian (Arabic)-Turkish mutual influence in the shadow theater. Mutual influences in other cultural fields have been clarified by scholars, who have pointed out that sometimes one of the two countries, sometimes the other, was the prime mover. In the case of the shadow theater, this approach is, however, more difficult, if one does not want to assume that the growth of the shadow theater was independent, both in Egypt and in Turkey; a hypothesis which hardly seems to be plausible, considering the manifold, close relations between the two countries. Anyhow, one should remember that

[64] *Lisān al-ʻArab, sub voce.*

[65] Collected and analyzed by Landau, *Shadow plays in the Near East*, pp. XXXIV–XXXVI, and the footnotes.

[66] *Ta'rīk̲h̲ Miṣr*, ed. Būlāq (1312 A.H.), vol. III, p. 125, also mentioned by Jacob, in his Appendices to Littmann's *Arabische Schattenspiele*, p. 78.

before the Turkish conquest of Egypt, in the early sixteenth century, these relations were not as close as afterwards; indeed, before this date, influences were more given to chance.

While the first evidence of the performance of a shadow play before the Mongolian son of Ginghiz Khan dates from the end of the thirteenth century or the beginning of the fourteenth[67], Ibn Daniyāl's plays are somewhat earlier, and no doubt are based on a tradition of previous performances—as is evident from their relatively high artistic and literary standard. Truly enough, there are earlier mentions of this theater in Arabic sources of the eleventh, twelfth, and thirteenth centuries[68]. However, the omission of any mention of the Turkish shadow theater in previous times constitutes in itself no proof that it did not exist. Even were it so, one should first prove real contact between the Egyptian and Turkish theaters before assuming an influence of the former on the latter, prior to the Turkish conquest of Egypt.

Considering, firstly, the total lack of proof of early mutual influence, and, secondly, the striking dissimilarity between Ibn Daniyāl's plays and what is known of the Turkish shadow theater of the time, it is safe to assume that the first important contact between Egypt and Turkey in this field occurred when Selim I took the above troupe of shadow-play performers to Istanbul. Even if they possibly returned to Egypt afterwards, maybe amongst the six hundred Egyptians sent back to their country three years later[69], they would have left their mark on the less developed Turkish shadow theater. Presumably they could not have changed the stereotyped character of the Turkish shadow plays with their own wealth of varying characters; for except the Master of Ceremonies, called *muqaddam*[70], and a type

[67] See above, footnote 32.

[68] Landau, *Shadow Plays in the Near East*, pp. XXVII–XXVIII, and the footnotes.

[69] Jacob, *Gesch. d. Schattentheaters*, pp. 78–79.

[70] The *muqaddam*—in some dialects, *m'addam*—often plays the same role as Hagivad in the Turkish shadow play. It is interesting to note that the heads of certain corporations, or rather fraternities, in North Africa, are also called by the

called Ri<u>kh</u>im[71], there are no permanent characters in the Egyptian shadow play[72]. It seems, however, that the Turks did copy some of the Egyptians' names for their characters at this time, probably even that of *Karagöz* himself. This name, which the Turks have slightly changed to mean "Black eye," apparently is derived from Qarāqū<u>sh</u>, as was called one of the best-known of the warriors and officials of Ṣalāḥ al-Dīn (Saladin), who filled positions of great responsibility in the army and government of Egypt. Hostile essays, saturated with irony, described fictitious judgments allegedly passed by him, which unreasonably make him look and act the perfect fool. In the course of years many folk tales, concerning themselves at first with entirely different persons, have enhanced the humorous attributes of Qarāqū<u>sh</u>[73]. The Qarāqū<u>sh</u>-inspired type in the Turkish

---

same name—see Lammens, *op. cit.*, 2nd ed., pp. 171–172; cf. ibid., p. 182. Lammens speaks of the immense power which these chiefs wield in their confraternities; I think this is comparable, in a way, to the relation of the *muqaddam* to his puppets.

[71] The importance of this *Ri<u>kh</u>im* is, however, only secondary. Cf. *Ri<u>kh</u>im's* figure in the shadow play published by Prüfer, *Ein ägyptisches Schattenspiel* (1906), p. 86, to the way he appears in *Ḥarb al-'Ajam*, which describes a surprise attack of the Christians on Alexandria, as mentioned by Kahle, *Das Krokodilspiel*, in *Nachr. König. Gesellschaft d. Wiss. Gött., Phil.-hist. Klasse*, 1915 and 1920, p. 293. Cf. Kern, *Das egyptische Schattentheater*, being App. to Horovitz, *Spuren griechischer Mimen*, pp. 101, 102. Prüfer—*op. cit.*, p. 86—tried to interpret *Ri<u>kh</u>im*= *Wi<u>kh</u>im*, i.e. "dirty," but it is known that the name appears quite distinctly as *Ri<u>kh</u>im* in various Mss. It seems to me that this name might be interpreted ironically, as it means "delicate" (in appearance) or "tender" (in its sound)—cf. *Lisān al-'Arab, s.v.*; A. Barthélemy, *Dictionnaire arabe-français* (1935), *s.v.*; and other dictionaries. All the prints of *Ri<u>kh</u>im* show him, however, as a particularly grotesque figure, whose belly and backside bulge abnormally, reminding us of the Hellenic mime. Thus his name is ironically contrasted to his unattractive appearance, just as *Ṭaif al-<u>kh</u>ayāl* in Ibn Daniyāl's play was called "proportionally perfect" while being a hunchback.

[72] It is Prüfer's merit to have observed and demonstrated the lack of common types in the Arabic shadow plays in Egypt—see his *Ein ägyptisches Schattenspiel*.

[73] Sobernheim, *Ḳarāḳū<u>sh</u>*, in the *Enc. of Islam, s.v.* C. Brockelmann, *GAL*, Leipzig, 1909, p. 160; more details and bibliography in the enlarged *GAL*, vol. I (1898), p. 335, and the first *Supplementband* (1937), pp. 572–573. Also Horovitz, *Spuren griechischer Mimen*, pp. 12, 29–31. S. Lane-Poole, *Saladin and the fall of the kingdom of Jerusalem* (1926), pp. 108, 110, 152, 153, 244, 295, 297, 363.

shadow plays is in its essence the personification of the real and the popularly added traits of Ṣalāḥ al-Dīn's close retainer: though quite courageous, he is presented as stupid, ignorant, and churlish[74]. It is remarkable that the Turkish *Karagöz* was copied by all the Arabic-speaking countries—although to a lesser extent in Egypt—and was introduced into their own shadow theaters, modeled on the Turkish pattern; just as non-Arab countries were similarly influenced by *Karagöz* while under Turkish domination[75].

d. Further Development in Egypt

In the nineteenth and twentieth centuries, information concerning the Arabic shadow theater becomes more easily available. In the intervening centuries, this popular entertainment continued its existence with varying degrees of success. There are very few shadow plays which are the work of a single playwright; and the diverse manuscripts hardly ever include the full text of a uniform play. The players, knowing their audience well, often introduced additional attractions into the text. In this practice, they followed the example of their teachers. For it was apparently a practice for the novice player to develop his talents as manipulator, reciter, and singer under the supervision of a more experienced teacher. A great part of the shadow play was at the time written in verse, the majority of the reciters using other people's verses, for very few among them had the necessary talent to compose their own. In this manner the novices not only learnt from their teachers how to manipulate the puppets or to recite and sing, but also wrote down the various texts or parts[76].

[74] Jacob, *Schejtan dolaby*, Introduction, pp. VII *ss*.

[75] This influence was notable to a great extent in Greece. See, for a bibl. list of works treating of *Karagöz* in Greece, Ritter, *Karagös*, vol. II, Introd., pp. XII-XIV.

[76] Kahle, *Das islamische Schattentheater in Aegypten*, in *OA*, vol. III, Apr. 1913, pp. 103–104.

This characteristic way in which shadow plays were transmitted from one generation to another is best illustrated in the so-termed Menzela Manuscript, to which we owe, in part, the revival of this art on a larger scale in Egypt. In the nineteenth century Ḥasan al-Qashshāsh, who had studied the shadow theater in the village of Menzela, procured a two-centuries-old manuscript of a play, which he then presented in Cairo, where this art had been well-nigh forgotten. He joined forces with another shadow player, but subsequently they separated, al-Qashshāsh importing for his theater puppets from Syria[77], thus introducing a further novel element in the Arabic shadow theater of Egypt. His main merit was, however, the revival of this art in Cairo by using the above MS.

The Menzela MS. has the following heading: "This is the *Dīwān* of shadow plays, [collected] from the song of Sheikh Sa'ūd and of Sheikh 'Alī'l-Naḥla and from the song of the leader of players, *al-aḥraf*, and the director Dā'ūd the spice seller." It would seem that Dā'ūd al-Manāwī or al-Manātī himself had compiled this collection from songs written by himself and from those of two of his predecessors—possibly his teachers—whom he does not fail to praise in his songs: thus he gave us an interesting instance of how people compiled their collections of shadow plays. It might be remarked that this Dā'ūd became a legendary figure soon after his death, and tales were spun in the streets of Cairo of his delightful shows, entertaining songs, and tragic death[78].

The shadow-play tradition and the manner of its transmission are further clarified by the contents of the above MS. Each song has a prologue which contains a reference to its author's name. Even though the MS. which has come down to us is incomplete and written on loose sheets, we are in a position to ascertain the author of each complete song. It is highly interest-

[77] Prüfer, *Ein ägyptisches Schattenspiel*, Introduction, p. VII. Kahle, *Islamische Schattenspielfiguren aus Egypten*, in *Der Islam*, vol. II, 1911, pp. 185–186, 188–189.
[78] Kahle, ibid., pp. 185–187. Id., *Das Krokodilspiel*, pp. 185–187.

ing to note that in the MS. there are many parallel scenes, composed by different authors—a fact which enabled the player to choose the version most suited to the audience.

A comparison between the versions proves the existence of various traditions, obviously handed down through generations on a teacher-pupil basis. Moreover, this MS., written A.D. 1706–1707, includes earlier songs; it is also significant that a popular character, like Ibn Daniyāl's *Abū'l-Qiṭaṭ*, reappears. Although this does not yet prove direct succession from the thirteenth-century physician and playwright, it is still strongly suggestive of a long, perhaps uninterrupted local tradition. This seems to be true also of historical shadow plays, probably dating from the same period, such as *The Lighthouse or the War against the Foreigners* (*al-Manār au ḥarb al-'Ajam*), an apologetic work describing the fighting valor of the people of Alexandria (the lighthouse) against the Crusaders[79].

Al-Qashshāsh collected various traditions to supplement the Menzela MS., possibly from the repertoire of the shadow theater which seemed active at Menzela[80]. It is rather difficult to assess foreign influences on al-Qashshāsh, as even his own son contradicted himself as to his father's country of origin[81]. Anyhow, al-Qashshāsh included in the performances of his shadow plays new devices, besides taking the models of his puppets—as has been said above[82]—from Syria: it is possible that he thought the symbols which the old figures were meant to express were no longer grasped easily and correctly by a totally changed audience. Though he was not the only person to take part in the revival of the shadow theater in Cairo, his share was considerable, in that his texts and puppets were imitated, and

79 Description of the contents in one of Kahle's works, *Leuchtturm*, and in G. R. Orvieto, *La genesi del teatro arabo in Egitto*, doctoral thesis presented to the Univ. of Rome, 1948 (typewritten), pp. 105–107.

80 Kahle, *Das islamische Schattentheater in Aegypten*, in *OA*, vol. III, Apr., 1913, pp. 104–105. Cf. Horovitz's review of Kahle's *Neuarabische Volksdichtung aus Egypten* (1909) in *OLZ*, vol. XIII, 1910, fasc. 3, p. 130, and fasc. 6, p. 279.

81 Kahle, ibid., in *OA*, vol. III, Apr. 1913, pp. 105–106.

82 See above, footnote 77.

his practices adopted[83]. It seems that the main pattern of the performance in its general lines continues, scarcely changed, in contemporary Egypt.

This pattern, in Egypt, was as follows (differences in other Arabic-speaking countries will be pointed out later):

On a simple stage erected outside a café, or in a private home on special occasions, such as weddings, a piece of white linen was hung up and a strong light cast from behind. The figures were usually made of brightly colored, transparent leather and measured about thirty to seventy centimeters (twelve to twenty-eight inches) in height. The more elaborate figures in Egypt were copied from ancient models, in other countries they were simpler. The *muqaddam* moved the figures with the help of sticks inserted in holes previously made for the purpose in the limbs and chests of the figures. These holes were often more numerous than those required for manipulation, for the following reason: at first the use of these figures aroused opposition, because the use of images, forbidden in Judaism, is frowned upon by Islam. Although laws against the shadow theater were passed, many people took up its cause, arguing that the holes in the chest or stomach ensured the figure's lifelessness.

As the *muqaddam* could seldom manage to move all the figures himself, he hired some assistants, at times his pupils. These were sometimes required to read the parts assigned to the various figures. The *muqaddam* was further assisted by three or four musicians: two with tambourines, the third with an oboe, and the fourth with a drum[84]. In Turkey[85] the orchestra was usually composed of a violinist, a tambourine player, and harpist, while

[83] Kahle, in *OA*, vol. III, Apr. 1913, p. 106. Id., *Islamische Schattenspielfiguren aus Egypten*, in *Der Islam*, vol. I, 1910, pp. 264–299, and vol. II, 1911, pp. 143–181. See particularly vol. II, pp. 182–183.

[84] Id., in *Der Islam*, ibid. Jacob, *Schejtan dolaby*, Introd., p. VI, n.l. Id., *Geschichte des Schattentheaters*, pp. 104–106. Id., *Die Herkunft der Silhouettenkunst* (*ojmadschylyk*) *aus Persien* (1913).

[85] Süssheim, *op. cit.*, in *ZDMG*, vol. LXIII, 1909, p. 740. Cf. Reich, *Der Mimus*, vol. I, part 2, p. 621.

in Europe as well as in Siam[86] it was larger. The play or *li'b* (exactly "game," i.e., the original meaning of "play") was divided into several scenes (*faṣl*, plural *fuṣūl*), which were not always interrelated and were sometimes presented on their own. The text was either sung or recited, always aloud, as the audience never forgot that it was sitting in a café and behaved accordingly; so that the *muqaddam* had to rap his stick for silence quite often. The audience was composed chiefly of children and the uneducated; the higher class sought other entertainments and attended the shadow plays only occasionally, even during Ramaḍān, the month of fasting, when these shows were at their best[87].

It seems that few shadow plays were performed in Egypt in the nineteenth century, and most of them probably were modeled on the Turkish pattern, with a local background. The *Karagöz* type of these plays was observed there by the well-known Orientalist, Edward William Lane, in the second and third decade of that century[88]. However, some of these *Karagöz* shows were performed at that time not in Arabic but in Turkish, that being then the language of the aristocratic and the rich. One may assume that some wealthy people had a hand in financing the shows. While the language of the *Karagöz* play witnessed by Didier in Cairo in 1859 is not certain[89], it is attested to a little later, in the 1860's, by the missionary Haussmann. The latter attended a number of such shows in Cairo,

[86] For Siam, see Sonakul, *op. cit.*, in *National Geogr. Mag.*, vol. XCI, Feb. 1947, pp. 210–211, and picture XX (p. 204).

[87] Prüfer, *Ein ägyptisches Schattenspiel*, Introduction, pp. VIII, XII. Id., *Das Schiffsspiel. Ein Schattenspiel aus Cairo*, in *München. Beitr. z. Kenntnis d. Orients*, Feb., 1906, Introduction. Id., *Drama, Arabic*, in *ERE*, vol. IV, 1911, p. 874. Kern, *op. cit.*, pp. 98 *ss.* H. Brugsch, *Das morgenlaendische Theater*, in *Deutsche Revue* (Breslau), vol. XII, 1887, part 3. Jacob, *Gesch. d. Schattentheaters*, pp. 105–107. Landau, *'Al ha-teiaṭrōn etsel ha-'aravīm*, part 3, in *Bamah Quarterly*, fasc. 49, Sept., 1946, pp. 50, 58, and the bibliography, ibid., fasc. 50, Jan., 1947, p. 115.

[88] E. W. Lane, *An account of the manners and customs of the modern Egyptians* (1846), vol. II, ch. 7, p. 116.

[89] Didier, *Les nuits du Caire* (1860), p. 353; quoted by Prüfer, *ERE*, vol. IV, p. 874, n. 8.

all of them performed in Turkish[90]. With the awakening of the national spirit in Egypt at the end of the nineteenth century[91] and the revival of Arabic as a current literary language, the latter became the language of most shadow plays.

At the beginning of the twentieth century there existed only one shadow theater in Cairo, to which a second was added in 1903. Neither survived for long, and six years later another recently established shadow theater was closed by order of the authorities, possibly as a measure intended to prevent the spreading of infectious diseases during that summer. However, even if no theater existed, the shadow-play performers did not disband—it seems they remained organized in a sort of guild. There were five shadow performers (each of whom had his assistants). One of them gave shows for the "higher society," while the others performed in permanent coffeehouses or in Cairo's fish market[92]. Apart from Cairo, shadow plays were performed regularly only in Alexandria, though occasional shows were given elsewhere. The latter were probably of a coarser nature, seemingly interspersed with obscene remarks and even more obscene hints.

Various shadow plays from the end of the nineteenth and the beginning of the twentieth century having been published, we are able to have a fairly accurate idea of their general trend.

The *Crocodile Play* (*Liʿb al-Timsāḥ*)[93] is indeed typical of the description of life near the Nile, which holds a fascination not unmixed with danger for many of those who are farmers and

[90] W. Max Müller, *Zur Geschichte des arabischen Schattenspiels in Aegypten*, in *OLZ*, vol. XII, Aug., 1909, pp. 341–342. Cf. Kahle, *op. cit.*, in *Der Islam*, vol. II (1911), p. 188.

[91] Jacob M. Landau, *Parliaments and parties in Egypt*, *passim*, esp. part 1, chs. 3–4, and part 2, chs. 1–4. Id., *The Young Egypt Party*, in *BSOS*, vol. XV, part 1, 1953, pp. 161–164.

[92] Prüfer, *Ein ägyptisches Schattenspiel*, Introd., pp. V–VII.

[93] Kahle, *Das Krokodilspiel*. Prüfer knew of a play by this name, probably the same, by hearsay only—cf. his *Ein ägyptisches Schattenspiel*, Introd., p. XII. The sources of this play are older, probably from the seventeenth century—see above, footnote 78; cf. also Fu'ād Ḥasanain 'Alī, *Qiṣaṣunā'l-s̲h̲aʿbiyya* (1937), quoted by G. R. Orvieto, *op. cit.*, p. 100.

still would like to fish. Such a *fallāḥ*, who tried to learn the art of fishing, ended by falling into the water, was nearly drowned and afterwards swallowed by a crocodile. From the gorge of the latter, the *fallāḥ* yelled for help, which he eventually obtained. The play is the fisherman's not too subtle raillery of the *fallāḥ*. It is also interesting to note that among those who appear are *Rikhim* or *Abū'l-Qiṭaṭ*[94] of Ibn Daniyāl fame, as well as various nationalities, like Berbers, who are laughed at, and Moroccans, whose powers of exorcism are extolled. Although even Ibn Daniyāl mentions a Sudanese character in his second play, the presentation of foreign characters in this otherwise truly local play may denote Turkish influence.

For the dwellers of the Valley of the Nile, not a few of whom make a living from either their river or the seas adjoining their country, boat-life has a particular significance. *The Ship Play* (*Li'b al-markib*) opens, aptly enough, with soft beating of drums and tambourines and the playing of flutes. This music introduces the arrival of a ship, with its captain and singing oarsmen[95]. When they reach land, an idler quarrels with the captain but later brings him some passengers, with their peculiar garb and mannerisms of speech: a Turkish soldier, a cloth merchant, the latter's evil-smelling young son, the merchant's wife, a Moroccan and a Sudanese. An act is often added to the above play, consisting of the captain's conversation with the passengers, who tell him of their destination. The Captain then discourses with the Moroccan on the merits of Cairo, whose places of interest are talked of in great detail[96]. If the enumeration of the technological innovations is taken into account, this act is fairly recent, compared to the rest of the play. The characters

[94] See above, footnote 58.

[95] This apparently meaningless song was analyzed by me in my *Shadow plays in the Near East*, p. XLVIII, where I tried to explain it. To the sources in the footnotes I now wish to add, for further corroboration of my hypothesis, John Gadsby, *My wanderings*, stereotype ed. (1860), p. 358.

[96] The play has been analyzed by Kern—who witnessed its performance—in his *op. cit.*, p. 102; and published by Prüfer, *Das Schiffsspiel*, in *München. Beitr. z. Kenntnis d. Orients*, Feb., 1906.

are not too clear-cut with the possible exception of the idler, the captain's conversation partner (who is the classical villain type, obscene of language and greedy, but cool-headed, like most other mimes). *The Ship Play* resembles the Turkish shadow play in the form, although not in the essence, of the dialogue or *muḥāwara*; it also shows a striking similarity to the Turkish *Boat Play* (*Kayık*)[97]. Furthermore, it seems to reflect a longer tradition dramatizing boat-life, possibly dating back to ancient Egypt.

Another Arabic shadow play, popular in Egypt at the time, describes the characters of the Cairo market. The play, which possibly dates from the beginning of the nineteenth century, is not so successfully laid out as that originating from the thirteenth. Nevertheless, it is very instructive, and it is of particular interest to note that *Abū'l-Qiṭaṭ* appears again. Indeed, his conversations and arguments with the street vendors, in a fairly vulgar dialect, are the core of the play, and might have been isolated scenes from a cycle of popular poems. The characters are: two honey vendors, two water sellers, two bean sellers, a sweetmeat vendor, a vendor of cakes, and a hawker selling fruit preserved in vinegar[98].

A last example from Egypt is interesting not only for *Rikhim's* reappearance in the dancing prologue, but in reflecting Muslim-Christian relation in that country. The Christian Copts, represented by a monk, his son and daughter, are pictured as thieves and liars in the *Cloister Play* (*Li'b al-dair*). The young girl succeeded time and again in stealing the Muslim's wares, when he tried to reach her under various disguises—a frequently employed and well-liked theme in popular Oriental folklore. The Muslim trader eventually softened her heart and married her

[97] German transl. by Jacob, *Türkische Litteraturgeschichte in Einzeldarstellungen. Heft I. Das türkische Schattentheater* (1900). Original and other German transl. publ. by Ritter, *Karagös*, vol. II (1941), pp. 224–269.

[98] Kahle, *Marktszene aus einem egyptischen Spiel*, in *ZA*, vol. XXVII, 1912, pp. 92–102. For the play's language, see Brockelmann, in *ZDMG*, vol. LXIV, 1910, p. 264 and n. 2 on that page.

after having converted her to Islam, to her father's, the monk's, great despair.

To this expression of the Muslim victory over the Christian, other acts are sometimes added, protracting the play over all the nights of the month of Ramaḍān. These are the *Act of the Engineer*, where one can see the Muslim husband building a new house for his young wife; and the *Act of the Sea Wonders*, where a group of sea monsters parade behind the curtain[99].

A few words on the language of these plays might be said in conclusion to this brief survey of Egypt, the most prolific country in the field of the Arabic shadow play. A small part of these plays is written in literary Arabic, but the greater part is in the spoken language of Egypt; a few have both elements, but they are then clearly distinct, as in the case of the *Cloister Play*, where the last parts are nearer to literary Arabic, in contradistinction to the rest.

One naturally assumes that plays written in a literary style, or of a somewhat more refined type, such as those composed by Ibn Daniyāl in the thirteenth century, gradually degenerated into plays of a less intricate pattern, saturated in parts or in whole with a crude sort of spoken Arabic, seasoned with obscenities[100]. Works written on an erotic basis and abounding in vulgarity, even though of doubtful literary value, can be counted upon to attract the lower urban classes along with the rural population, particularly when the plays contain popular Arabic songs. The better educated strata turned to other amusements when these were available.

e. Shadow Plays in Syria

Next to Egypt, Syria is the Arabic-speaking country with the greatest number of shadow plays to come down to us. They

[99] Prüfer published this play under the name of *Ein ägyptisches Schattenspiel* (1906). The supplementary act is described by Kern, *op. cit.*, pp. 101–102. Although Prüfer knew of Kern's article, he did not notice that Kern had witnessed parts of the same play, named, somewhat differently, *The House Play* (*Li'b al-bait*).

[100] Kern, *op. cit.*, p. 98. Prüfer, *op. cit.* in the *München. Beitr. z. Kenntnis d. Orients*, Feb., 1906, pp. 156–157.

differ from the Egyptian ones in that the plays performed in Damascus, Beirut, Aleppo, Jaffa, and Jerusalem (all towns in the province of Syria before the First World War) show unmistakable traces of Turkish influence; this is particularly true of the first two of the above-mentioned towns. Although they frequently lacked the prologue of the Turkish *Karagöz* and sometimes its typical dialogue[101], the Syrian shadow plays bear the mark of almost all its other characteristics. To a smaller degree, the influence of the local popular tales may be felt, too, although it is not always self-evident.

The Syrian *Karagöz* seems to have been immensely popular, mainly in the nineteenth century. Although it is known that the Turkish *Karagöz*-type of shadow play was introduced into various Arabic-speaking countries even outside the Ottoman Empire, as well as into Persia (by way of the Turkish dialect of Azerbaijan[102]), the period cannot be precisely determined. It is quite clear, however, that not only Karagöz and 'Aiwāz, *i.e.*, Hagivad, were copied but a host of other characters too, often with their full Turkish names. The subject matter was somewhat changed, however, drawing material from local conditions to suit the untutored audiences, eager to see images and hear things they could easily grasp.

Another common link between the shadow plays in Turkey and Syria is the fondness for beating, displayed in many farces in other countries as well[103]. The beloved Karagöz and 'Aiwāz, both of whom suffer from the temper of their wives, are fast friends. The most common among the other characters are an opium addict, a pathological character who chortles through his

[101] Littmann, *Das Malerspiel*, in *Sitzungsber. Heidelberger Ak. Wiss. Phil.-hist. Kl.*, Mar. 25, 1918.

[102] Jacob, *Schejtan dolaby*, pp. III–XVI, esp. p. V, in which he quotes Chodzko, *Théâtre persan*. Cf. Jacob, *Türkische Litteraturgeschichte in Einzeldarstellungen. Heft I. Das türkische Schattentheater*, p. 8.

[103] Littmann, *Arabic humor*, in *The Princeton University Bulletin*, 1902, for blows as a comic element of the shadow theater both in Arabic and in other languages. The use of blows in the ancient Classical farce has been ably pointed out by Reich, *Der Mimus*, vol. I, part 1, pp. 113–114; part 2, pp. 638–639.

nose, and the Turk whose duty is to preserve order (who is naturally on bad terms with Karagöz and 'Aiwāz); among the characters whose pronunciation mutilates the Arabic language, the most important is the foreign doctor[104], who is often the prototype of the whole European community in Syria.

The contents are frequently similar to the Turkish shadow play, up to a certain degree. This is especially true of a Syrian play in which Karākōz (i.e., Karagöz), 'Aiwāz and the opium addict behave shamefully in the house of a certain lady of doubtful reputation[105]. The same play, although with some variations, was witnessed, I think, in Beirut about the year 1875, and described by Perolari-Malmignati, a diplomat[106]. The motive of the above play may easily be found in two Turkish shadow plays, *The Two Jealous Women*[107] and *The Witches*[108]. In the *orta oyunu*[109], also, it is common for men to be thrown out of of a lady's house in succession[110].

Other Syrian plays whose texts have reached us were performed fairly often at the end of the nineteenth century, although they date from earlier times. The themes of a few of them merit consideration:

1. *The Beggars* (*al-S̲h̲aḥḥādīn*). Hagivad informed Karagöz that the townspeople were displeased with his laziness, and taught him to beg in various languages (ample occasion for derision). The comedy reaches its peak when Hagivad, without noticing it, begged for alms from his own wife, who refused

[104] Littmann, *Arabische Schattenspiele* (1901), pp. 3–11.

[105] Id., *Ein arabisches Karagöz-Spiel*, in *ZDMG*, 1900, pp. 666–680.

[106] Pietro Perolari-Malmignati, *Su e giù per la Siria note e schizzi* (1878), pp. 74–77. It is interesting that the author speaks of a *chorus* which sang some melody at the beginning of the performance.

[107] Original and transl. by Süssheim, *op. cit.*, in *ZDMG*, vol. LXIII, 1909, pp. 744 *ss*. Original and a different transl. by Th. Seif, *Drei türkische Schattenspiele*, in *Le Monde Oriental*, vol. XVII, 1923, esp. pp. 124–148; reviewed by Jacob, in *MSOS*, vol. XXVIII, part 2, 1925, pp. 282–283.

[108] Original and transl. by Ritter, *Karagös*, vol. II, pp. 128–171.

[109] See above, footnotes 34 and 37.

[110] See, e.g., the MS. farce summarized by Saussey, *Littérature populaire turque* (1936), ch. 3, pp. 78–82.

under false pretences[111]. Quarrels between the wives of Hagivad and Karagöz and their husbands are frequent in Turkish plays, too[112].

2. *The Foreign Doctor* (*Afranjī*). When Karagöz was ill, 'Aiwāz advised the former's wife to consult the recently arrived foreign doctor, who took money only from those whom he had cured completely (the type of the Christian doctor appears in the Turkish *Karagöz*, too[113]). The visit of Karagöz and his wife to the doctor brought about a welter of linguistic misunderstandings. Back at home, Karagöz scolds 'Aiwāz for his stupid advice[114]. Special mention should be made of the doctor, who is presented in such a way that all foreigners (*afranj*) are ridiculed.

3. *The Opium Addict* (*Afyūnī*), who was the favorite amongst the many aberrant characters in the Turkish shadow play, also had an important role in the Arabic *Karagöz* in Syria and Tunis[115]. Afyūnī tempted 'Aiwāz to a pipe of opium, and when they fell asleep (exactly as on the Turkish stage[116]), they were beaten by Karagöz, who was himself intoxicated[117].

4. *The Bathhouse* (*Ḥammām*). After due consideration, Karagöz and 'Aiwāz decided to go to an underground bathhouse. The comic element lies chiefly in the requests of the owner, who desired the two friends to bring all the paraphernalia needed for a bath (including water!), as well as their swords and shields, which they needed to rout the robbers lurking in the bathhouse[118].

[111] Littmann, *Arabische Schattenspiele*, pp. 16–23.
[112] Jacob, *Türkische Litteraturgeschichte in Einzeldarstellungen, Heft I etc.*, p. 39.
[113] Id., ibid., p. 34. See also above, footnote 104.
[114] Littmann, *Arabische Schattenspiele*, pp. 24–35.
[115] Examples and bibl. in Jacob, *Türkische Litteraturgeschichte in Einzeldarstellungen. Heft I etc.*, pp. 38–39. See also above, p. 14.
[116] See the plays *The Fountain or Kütahiya* and *The Boat* in Ritter, *Karagös*, vol. II, pp. 88, 254, 256.
[117] Littmann, *Arabische Schattenspiele*, pp. 36–43.
[118] Id., ibid., pp. 44–49.

5. *The Evening Party* (*Sahra*). 'Aiwāz invited Karagöz to join him in a visit and an evening meal. He entered alone, however, and subsequently accused Karagöz of theft, before the host, who ordered that a sound beating be administered to Karagöz[119].

6. *The Firewood* (*Khashabāt*). Ashqū, the symbol of law and order, asked Karagöz and 'Aiwāz to carry a bundle of firewood for him. They sold it, however, and went on extorting money from Ashqū under various pretexts[120]. A similar plot is part of a Jerusalemite Arabic story concerning Karagöz and 'Aiwāz[121].

For its comic effects, the Syrian *Karagöz*, like its Turkish model, employs the rougher sort of the comedy of manners (unsuccessful visits to a brothel, frequent beatings), comedy of character with a great stress on neurosis[122] (undignified behaviour of the opium addict), linguistic misunderstandings (Karagöz consulting the foreign doctor), and—more than everything else—false situations (a husband begging for alms from his wife, who does not recognize him; bathers being required to bring all the paraphernalia to the public bathhouse; Karagöz and 'Aiwāz selling another person's firewood; Karagöz, invited to a meal, being mistaken for a thief). Most of these characteristics, guaranteed to produce quite happy results with the unsophisticated audience, can be observed in the Palestinian shadow play, too.

119 Id., ibid., pp. 50–55.

120 Id., ibid., pp. 56–63. For other Syrian *Karagöz* plots see Saussey, *Une farce de Karagueuz en dialecte arabe de Damas*, in *Bulletin d'Etudes orientales de Damas*, vol. VII–VIII, 1937–1938, pp. 5–37.

121 Littmann, ibid., pp. 64–67. For examples taken from the popular legend about Karagöz in the New Aramaic dialect see E. Prym & A. Socin, *Der neu-aramaeische Dialekt des Tur 'Abdin* (1881), vol. I, pp. 154–156, and vol. II (transl.), pp. 223–226. For the development of certain facts, illustrated by such stories, into legends, see H. Petermann, *Reisen im Orient* (1865), vol. I, pp. 26, 164–165.

122 While physical grotesqueness is popular in Arab shadow plays everywhere, one feels that psychological abnormality is put to more frequent use in Syria. See, on the general effect of the presentation of these abnormalities on the stage, W. Strohmayer, *Über die Darstellung psychisch abnormer und geisteskranker Charaktere auf der Bühne*, publ. as fasc. 122 of *Grenzfragen des Nerven= und Seelenlebens* (1925).

When Palestine was conquered by the British in the First World War, the local Syrian tradition of *Karagöz* continued unchanged during the thirty-odd years of the Mandatory rule; today this entertainment exists no more in the same pattern. *Karākōz* is still a by-name for a small festival in the Palestinian colloquial Arabic and in the Jewish children's Hebrew.

Naturally, the majority of performances were given during the month of Ramaḍān, when local troupes vied with performers who came from the neighboring Arabic-speaking countries. The Arabs of the Old City of Jerusalem, in particular, both young and old, were known to be very fond of *Karagöz*[123] and to enjoy it immensely[124]. In the month of Ramaḍān, 1944, for instance, these shadow plays in Jerusalem were directed by a Syrian. They were performed twice a night, the first show being intended for children and the second for adults; the background was at times historical and at others satirical[125].

f. North African Shadow Plays

Exact details regarding the period of *Karagöz's* introduction into North Africa (barring Egypt) are not yet available. If it is true that the shadow play, moving westwards, reached Italy in the seventeenth century, it seems to me that one of the probable ways in which it traveled was via North Africa to Sicily. Unfortunately, no reliable material on the existence of a shadow theater in North Africa (with the exception of Egypt) remains from that period. Anyhow, one way of explaining the striking similarity of the Italian shadow plays to the Turkish ones is to take into account the close relations of Italy with Muslim North Africa. It should be borne in mind, however, that until further

[123] See above, footnote 121.

[124] Th. F. M. (Meysels), in *The Palestine Post*, Sept. 13, 1943, p. 4, Meysels' tale in his article *Karagoes and King Solomon. Topical court case dramatized,* ibid., Jan. 5, 1944, is pure fantasy.

[125] Gideon Weigert, ibid., Aug. 31, 1944, p. 4.

evidence is forthcoming, it is equally likely that it was the Turkish *Karagöz* that influenced the Italian shadow play. The North African shadow theater offers in itself no indication either way, for it is closely modeled on the Turkish pattern.

The information culled from travelers' records is but scanty. In Morocco, on one hand, we know only that delightful shadow plays were performed—tales from *The Arabian Nights* and animal shows, but our knowledge of these plays is incomplete.

Of Algeria, on the other hand, we know more. Pückler-Muskau has described in detail a *Karagöz* show performed early in the year 1835, which abounded in exchanges of obscenities between Karagöz and the phallic god of fertility (this relation between the mime and the god of fertility dates from ancient Greek mimics[126]). At the end of the play, the giant Karagöz put to flight the French military unit which had come to arrest him, by beating the soldiers with the god of fertility, which served him as a stick[127]. In other Algerian plays, Satan dressed in a French uniform[128]. The French authorities, grasping that the shadow play's ironical rough treatment of their occupation forces was indeed an expression of popular anti-French feeling, forbade all performances in 1843[129]. Thus the shadow theater became extinct in Algeria more than a hundred years ago, even though private performances were still secretly given at rare intervals[130].

In contrast with Algerian *Karagöz*, the same type of play in Tunis hardly ever satirizes leaders[131] and opinions, but contains

126 Reich, *Der Mimus*, vol. I, part 1, pp. 18 *ss*. Flögel, *op. cit.*, vol. I, pp. 26 *ss*.
127 Pückler-Muskau, *Semilasso in Afrika* (1836), vol. I, p. 135.
128 Reich, *Der Mimus*, vol. I, part 2, p. 641.
129 O. Spies, *Tunesisches Schattentheater*, in *Festschrift, public. d'hommage off. au. P. W. Schmidt* (1928), p. 695, based on L. Piese, *Itinéraire de l'Algérie* (1882), p. 38. See also Jacob, *Türkische Litteraturgeschichte in Einzeldarstellungen. Heft I etc.*, p. 9.
130 Bernard, *L'Algérie qui s'en va* (1887), pp. 66–67; cf. R. Basset, in *RTP*, vol. XVI, 1901, p. 597.
131 For an exception, see Robert d'Humières, *Through isle and empire*, transl. by Alexander Teixeira de Mattos (1905), pp. 131–132.

an immensely greater wealth of indecent images and vocabulary[132]. These lewd tendencies, expressed in the shadow play, are an indication that the vast majority of Tunisians had low cultural requirements. The general conditions of the Tunisian shadow play were throughout, and particularly in the last generation, not very encouraging. *Karagöz* plays were usually performed only in the month of Ramaḍān, when the need for amusements was felt after long fasting, while in Turkey and Egypt they were often shown at feasts, weddings, and circumcisions. As in Algeria, the French authorities sometimes forbade the performances even during Ramaḍān, by ordering all places of amusement closed during the whole month[133]. Again, as in Algeria, the Tunisians were ready to give private *Karagöz* shows for a certain payment[134].

From various references in the travel literature, one assumes that performances of shadow plays were quite common in Tunisia during the nineteenth century. They were mostly in Turkish in the 1820's, but chiefly in the colloquial Arabic of Tunisia in the second half of the nineteenth century, when French rule was gradually but assuredly supplanting Turkish influence.

Heinrich von Maltzan writes in 1870 of a *Karagöz* performance he had attended in Tunis a short while previously[135]. According to him, these performances were popular in all the countries of Islam. This entertainment was introduced into Tunisia by the Turkish rulers of the country[136]. Von Maltzan describes Karagöz as a figure of ugly countenance and ungainly bearing, who threw European audiences into wonderment and indignation by his strange behavior; moreover, he

[132] Flögel, *op. cit.*, vol. II, p. 10; Myriam Harry, *Tunis la blanche* (17th ed.), ch. 14, esp. pp. 202–205; and others.

[133] For such an instance, see *The Palestine Post*, Oct. 10, 1944.

[134] Spies, *op. cit.*, p. 694. Cf. Jacob, *Schejtan dolaby*, Introd., pp. V–VII, as to the proper time of shadow-play performances in Turkey.

[135] *Reise in der Regentschaften Tunis und Tripolis*, vol. I.

[136] Jacob, *Scheitan dolaby*, p. V and n. 5 to that page; ibid., p. VII. Id., *Türkische Litteraturgeschichte in Einzeldarstellungen. Heft I etc.*, pp. 14–15.

bore a striking resemblance to the ancient god of gardens (cf. Karagöz in Algeria!). The Muslims of Tunis did not see any immorality in the obscene language of these plays and even allowed their children to attend[137], as was customary also in Algeria (before the French authorities prohibited these shows[138]), Syria[139] and Turkey[140]. Women however were but rarely present at these shows in Tunisia, since they were usually barred from their men-folk's amusements; while in Turkey these plays were eagerly attended by a large number of women and girls[141].

In the majority of Tunisian shadow plays there were six or seven permanent characters. Karagöz and Hagivad were almost always among them: the former was dressed as a Turk and, being a Turkish invention, was generally pictured as a man-about-town who annoyed and deceived others, relieved them of their possessions and beat them, for good measure. While Muslims were hardly ever reviled by Karagöz, Jews often were. The latter tried to get the better of Karagöz who, however, saw through their devices. The Maltese were treated even more execrably in those plays, the spectators probably, in their derision, identifying the Maltese scapegoat with all European Christians in Tunis. The *Madama* or European lady often had a bad time, for her broad crinoline usually excited Karagöz's curiosity; however, he never paid her seduction fees. Other characters who suffered at his hands were the Moroccan and the Arab yokel whom Karagöz defeated not by his wit, but by his unending store of obscenities and by fisticuffing or whip-

137 Von Maltzan, *op. cit.*, I, p. 234. For a later period, see M. Harry, *op. cit.*, pp. 202–205; and Spies, *op. cit.*, p. 695.

138 Bernard, *op. cit.*, p. 87.

139 Littmann, *Ein arabisches Karagöz-Spiel*, in *ZDMG*, 1900, p. 662.

140 Lemercier de Neuville, *Histoire anecdotique des marionettes modernes* (1892), p. 70. Mehmed Tevfik, *Ein Jahr in Konstantinopel. Die Ramazan-Nächte*, transl. by Theodor Menzel (1905), p. 59.

141 Hermann Vámbéry, *Sittenbilder aus dem Morgenlande* (1876), p. 34. Cf. de Neuville, *op. cit.*, p. 70. For women spectators of the shadow theater in Algeria, see Bernard, *op. cit.*, p. 67.

ping. In short, Karagöz had a moral code of his own, which was the punishment by force of all and sundry who tried to deceive or rob him[142].

According to all the evidence, the standards of the shadow play declined between von Maltzan's visit and that of Otto Spies some sixty years later (in 1927)[143]. In most of the plays collected by the latter, there appeared both Karagöz (also Karākōn)[144] and Ḥagivad or Ḥāzīvāz (in Qairawan: Ḥājīvāsh, Ḥāzīvān), both of whom were, as in other Muslim countries, the main link between the disconnected scenes of the shadow play. As the performers hardly ever bothered to look even at the general outline of the play, let alone its details, many versions existed concurrently of one and the same play[145].

The contents were naïve and simple, the chief attraction of the play lying in the merry, amusing scenes. There appeared, besides the above characters, Negroes, tribal dancers, and others[146]. The fact that the performers were butchers and cobblers, who scarcely knew to read, assured the use of the colloquial language on the stage[147].

The number of different Tunisian shadow plays is not great and they treat chiefly of matters of local interest. The following may serve as representative examples:

The Play of the Lemons (*Liʿbat al-laimūn*). Karākōz (Karagöz) knocked at the gate of Ḥājīvāz's lemon grove, being accompanied by his tenant. Karākōz then tried to rob the tenant of

[142] Von Maltzan, *op. cit.*, I, pp. 233–237. J. Gregor, *op. cit.*, p. 77, mentions the armed Berber and the lady dancer as other common types in the Tunisian shadow play.

[143] Spies, *op. cit.*, pp. 694, 695. The lack of evidence on the shadow theater between those two dates, if not conclusive, is at least suggestive.

[144] Acc. to Littmann, *Arabische Schattenspiele*, p. 7, this name was also pronounced in North West Africa "Qaragos" and "Garagos"—the pronunciation of a guttural G instead of a Q being not unusual in colloquial Arabic.

[145] Spies, *op. cit.*, pp. 695–697; with reference to Beirut, see Littmann, *Ein arabisches Karagöz-Spiel*, in *ZDMG*, 1900, p. 664; with reference to Turkey, see Jacob, *Türkische Litteraturgeschichte in Einzeldarstellungen. Heft I etc.*, pp. 44–47.

[146] Jacob, ibid., p. 36. Id., *Schejtan dolaby*, Introd., p. IX. Spies, *op. cit.*, p. 697.

[147] Spies, ibid., ibid.

the rent and got killed in the attempt. In the second act, however, he rose from his bier and drove the mourners off with his stick, forcing them to leave their clothes on the stage[148]. This motive was observed, too, in a shadow play performed in Tunis in the second half of the nineteenth century[149], while the popular belief in the rising of the dead was also mirrored in a later Egyptian shadow play called *The Play of Abū Ja'far* (*Riwāyat Abī Ja'far*)[150].

The Play of the Bathhouse (*Li'bat al-ḥammām*). Ḥājīwāz and Karākōz, on the former's suggestion, opened a bathhouse. Karākōz attempted to enter the house while the women were washing themselves, but was prevented by his partner's wife. However, she let the following characters in: an Arab, an Indian, a Maltese, and finally a Jew, by hanging onto whose coat-tails(!) Karākōz tried again to get inside. Defeated in his attempt, he called the authorities, intimating to them that the house was a brothel; so that the play ended with a free-for-all[151]. In the Turkish shadow play bearing the same name (*Hammam oyunu*), which probably inspired the subject of the Tunisian text, a similar procession of foreign characters is paraded on the screen, with Karagöz trying to enter the bathhouse from its roof and falling through the glass into the midst of the bathers[152].

The Play of the Ship on the Sea (*Li'bat al-markib fī'l-baḥr*) shows Karākōz being prevented from catching fish by the untimely shouts of the Negro, so that Karākōz had to promise his mate a tarboosh and red shoes (a grotesque contrast to his black skin!) in order to placate him[153]. Their efforts to sell the fish and cheat

[148] Id., ibid., pp. 697–698.
[149] Paul Arène (1884), quoted by Reich, *Der Mimus*, vol. I, part 2, p. 666.
[150] Kern, *op. cit.*, pp. 102–103.
[151] Spies, *op. cit.*, pp. 700–701.
[152] Id., ibid., p. 701. This is the first of the shadow plays transl. by Kúnos in his *Három Karagöz-Játék* (1886). Cf. Saussey, *Littérature populaire turque*, pp. 88–89.
[153] This motif appears in a very similar manner in the Turkish shadow play, *Balıkçılar* (*The Fishermen*), publ. by Ritter, *Karagös*, vol. III, pp. 589 *ss.* I am grateful to Dr. A. Tietze, of Istanbul, for having kindly pointed out this similarity to me.

the boat owner, Ḥājīvāz, brought about the expected quarrel and blows[154]. In the somewhat similar *Fishing Play* (*Li'bat ṣaid al-ḥōta*) Ḥājīvāz, Karākōz, and the Negro were involved in the same pursuits and quarrels[155]. It appears that the main elements of these last two plays, concerned with common fishing-life aspects in Tunisia, crystallized[156] in *The Play of the Fish*, seen a short time later in Tunis[157].

The last-mentioned play along with *The Play of the Bathhouse* had become by then the stock-in-trade of the Tunisian shadow theater. The arrangements were primitive, the implements being extremely simple. For the former a boat with a black puppet was needed; the Negro held the rudder in his hand, while his companion (Karākōz) held a fishing rod; a fish dangled from the rod, while a pole connected to the boat and to the fish made it possible to move both. The preparations for the latter play were even less elaborate, as a house with a flat roof, whose right side was covered by an awning, sufficed.

In *The Play of the Fish* (*Li'bat al-ḥōta*) a servant and master were fishing. The black servant moved the boat so that the fish escaped time and again, in order to extort from his master, successively, promises of a red hat, a green tarboosh, and a wife. The servant had a number of questions: Why is not the promised wife in the boat? Why has she no children before the marriage? Will the children come the morning after the wedding night? How do men treat their women? Will the master show him the difference between men and women? Will he, the servant, be the husband of his master's wife, too? At this the master's patience ran out and the fishing was given up for the time being[158].

[154] Spies, *op. cit.*, pp. 699–700.
[155] Id., ibid., pp. 698–699.
[156] Cf., however, Arène, as mentioned by Reich, *Der Mimus*, vol. I, pp. 664–666.
[157] Kurt Levy, *La'bät elhotä. Ein tunesisches Schattenspiel*, in *Festschrift für Kahle* (1935).
[158] The text—prob. incomplete—ibid., pp. 120–122, and transl. pp. 122–124, with drawings.

This shadow play, as so many others in Tunisia and elsewhere, tries to achieve its purpose of amusing the audience by repeating the same humorous *motif*, in this case the fish's escape because of the Negro's stupidity, greed, and curiosity. It also makes attempts at humor by fairly broad hints on the sexual relations between man and woman. Indeed, this lascivious ingredient, in an undisguised, rudely exaggerated manner, is sometimes predominant in the Tunisian shadow play[159]. One finds this element in the equally decadent shadow theater in Tripolitania, which, its lewdness notwithstanding, is still often attended by children during the month of Ramaḍān[160]. This again, is evidence of the low cultural level of the audiences. Further proof of the decadence in the shadow theater in these countries is the fact that the figures were rather primitive and sometimes made only of clay; even when they were of leather, they were usually unicolored and hardly ever translucent[161].

g. Characteristics and Importance of the Shadow Theater

To conclude this brief survey of the shadow theater:

From the scanty material at our disposal, it is as yet difficult to trace the gradual development of this popular art. Although the Arabic shadow theater of Egypt might have influenced, at first, the Turkish productions, the Turkish *Karagöz* succeeded afterwards in leaving its imprint on the Arabic shadow play, particularly on shows performed in Syria, Palestine, Algeria, and Tunisia for the last three generations; in Egypt this influence was felt much less.

The Arabic and Turkish shadow plays based their texts on fictional literature, such as the Persian farce or the popular legend of various peoples, as well as on everyday behavior. Although the artificial, unconvincing links between the acts, on one hand, and a certain similarity in the themes, on the other,

[159] See, for instance, M. Harry's account, in her *op. cit.*, pp. 203–205

[160] G. Cerbella & M. Ageli, *op. cit.*, pp. 61–62, 70.

[161] Spies, *op. cit.*, pp. 694–695. See also footnote 84, above.

might serve as a common basis, largely speaking, the Arabic shadow plays differed greatly from one another in their artistic level and their degree of morality (or rather immorality).

The most evident common denominator in the shadow plays, however, was their essential humor, which even unnecessary repetitions did not dull. Only rarely did this humor assume the form of mild irony, being generally of rougher nature. This humor fully exploited the inherent possibilities of this theater: color and movement, easy changes of form and size, mimicry in various forms, and song as well as music.

A happy blending of the satire of manners and the satire of character produced a sort of farce suited to delight a primitive Arab audience with its own peculiar mentality, its beliefs, and its slant on life. This farce was the only outlet for the Arabic-speaking people's hatred of their rulers and dislike for foreigners—this being a true reflection of day-to-day life and the common man's reaction to the then existing conditions[162].

Apart from the teratological elements (giant, dwarf, protruding limbs), mental deformity, too, was used as a humor stimulant. Misunderstandings in speech, vilification of customs (not only in political matters), irony, and parody—not confined to strangers but illuminating the frailties of human beings and the conflicts of their characters—were employed side by side with rougher material, such as a bedlam of simultaneous shouts, sound beatings, or the consummation of a sexual act between man and woman, man and man, and man and beast. Popular backgrounds like the market, the bathhouse, and the coffeehouse assisted in giving a general atmosphere of hilarity to the shadow play, which was further enlivened by music and song.

The central character in the Arabic shadow play was Karagöz or, in Egypt, a parallel type who showed the same char-

[162] For examples, M. Harry, *op. cit.*, esp. pp. 204–205; d'Humières, *op. cit.*, pp. 131–132; M. J. Marcel, *Histoire et description de tous les peuples—Egypte* (*depuis la conquête des arabes jusqu'à la domination française*), 1872, quoted by Orvieto, *op. cit.*, pp. 37–40.

acteristics of the villain, whose obscenity points at a clear-cut influence emanating from the ancient Greek mime (Wiṣāl and G̱ẖarīb in Ibn Daniyāl's plays, or the idler in the *Ship Play*). In contrast to the jester, who invites laughter, Karagöz knew well that he was a fool, and his jokes were not directed only against others' hebetude, but against his own stupidity as well. With his popular humor and rich irony, Karagöz resembled, in his general traits, the Italian Pulcinella, the French Polichinelle, the British Punch, and the German Kasperl. Like them, he introduced an increasingly large measure of local gossip into the dialogue of the play. While in Turkey and in some Arabic-speaking countries, the cast of the *Karagöz* type of shadow play developed from more or less vague images into permanent characters, the Arabic shadow play in Egypt was less stereotyped, frequently changing its choice of exponents.

The great service of the shadow theater to the Arabic history of civilization is in its having preserved, for the future, precious information about little-recorded ideas and customs of past generations. Artistically it prepared the ground, along with the story-tellers' mimicry and the Passion-players' performances (being more important, in this respect, than either of them), for the arrival and acceptance of the Europeanized amusements—the theater and the cinema. Ironically, the popularity of these new arts—whose successful introduction was due, in part, to the preservation of interest in dramatic performances—almost drove the shadow theater out of existence. In our days the theater and cinema have had a complete victory, so that in both Turkey and the Arab countries (including Egypt), the shadow play is gradually moving towards extinction, the very few shows held during the month of Ramaḍān being rarely visited, even by the poorer class; the educated show no interest whatever in it[163].

[163] Acc. to Siyavuşgil, *Karagöz*, pp. 3, 4, 7, the shadow play has completely disappeared from Turkey, being only revived, at long intervals, by folklorist groups.

PART II

THE ARAB THEATER

CHAPTER 1

The Beginnings

a. Local Influences

It is undoubtedly remarkable that so little influence has been exercised by the Arabic shadow play on the development of the modern Arab theater (except possibly in keeping alive interest in dramatic performances). While in some West-European countries the shadow play and the marionette theater left indelible traces on the modern comedy, this is hardly the case in the Near East. In the nineteenth century theatrical performances in Arabic show some similarity in their contents to the shadow play only prior to the far-reaching impact of the European theatrical influence, approximately at mid-century. Since then, the scope of European influence on the Arab theater has become paramount, although rustic performances of a comical nature still preserve many particular characteristics, remindful of means and devices in the shadow theater.

Such rustic plays, it seems, were not uncommon in Egypt.

Interesting pieces of information are supplied by various travelers, whose memoirs have as yet been examined only in part. One of the first mentions of this kind is that of the Italian traveler, Belzoni. His little-known description of a play—or, rather, two plays—seen at S̲h̲ubrā, in 1815, after a wedding ceremony, merits quoting[164]:

"When the dancing was at an end, a sort of play was performed, the intent of which was to exhibit life and manners, as we do in our theatres. The subject represented an Hadgee, who wants to go to Mecca, and applies to a camel-driver, to procure a camel for him. The driver imposes on him, by not letting him see the seller of the camel, and putting a higher price on it than is really asked, giving so much less to the seller than he received from the purchaser. A camel is produced at last, made up by two men covered with a cloth, as if ready to depart for Mecca. The Hadgee mounts on the camel, but finds it so bad, that he refuses to take it, and demands his money back again. A scuffle takes place, when, by chance, the seller of the camel appears, and finds that the camel in question is not that which he sold to the driver for the Hadgee. Thus it turns out, that the driver was not satisfied with imposing both on the buyer and the seller in the price, but had also kept the camel for himself, and produced a bad one to the Hadgee. In consequence he receives a good drubbing, and runs off.—Simple as this story appears, yet it was so interesting to the audience, that it seemed as if nothing could please them better, as it taught them to be on their guard against dealers in camels, &c.—This was the play; and the afterpiece represented a European traveller, who served as a sort of clown. He is in the dress of a Frank; and on his travels, comes to the house of an Arab, who, though poor, wishes to have the appearance of being rich. Accordingly he gives orders to his wife to kill a sheep immediately. She pretends to obey; but returns in a few minutes, saying that the flock has strayed away, and that it would be the loss of too much time to fetch one. The host then orders four fowls to be killed; but these cannot be caught. A third time, he sends his wife for pigeons; but the pigeons

[164] G. Belzoni, *Narrative of the operations and recent discoveries in Egypt and Nubia*, pp. 19–20. For a somewhat earlier testimony (C. Niebuhr, 1780), see Najm, *al-Masraḥiyya etc.*, pp. 73–74.

are all out of their holes; and at last the traveller is treated only with sour milk and dhourra bread, the only provision in the house. This finishes the play."

Another performance, different in contents, but not in general tone, was attended a few years afterwards by E. W. Lane. This renowned Orientalist lived in Egypt during the twenties and thirties of the nineteenth century and on at least one occasion was present at the performance of a farce[165]. In it, an indebted *fallāḥ* is beaten, to the delight of the audience; his wife liberates him only after bribing: *a.* the Copt clerk (well-hated by the Muslims) with food; *b.* the village chief with money; *c.* the governor of the district with her body. The bitterness of the poor *fallāḥin*, which was vented against the foreigners in the second of the plays mentioned by Belzoni, here finds an expression against their own corrupt, lewd officials. The sexual effect, prepondering in the shadow play, reappeared and excited Lane's disgust[166]:

"The Egyptians are often amused by players of low and ridiculous farces, who are called Mohhabbazeen.[167] These frequently perform at the festivals prior to weddings and circumcisions, at the houses of the great; and sometimes attract rings of auditors and spectators in the public places in Cairo. Their performances are scarcely worthy of description: it is chiefly by vulgar jests and indecent actions, that they amuse, and obtain applause."

These "low and ridiculous farces," as has already been said, were still being performed in the countryside even later in the nineteenth century, when the European-inspired new Arab theater had conquered the cities and towns. As late as the winter of 1874–1875, Warner witnessed a play performed by the Egyptian sailors of a pleasure boat on the Nile[168]. In this

[165] E. W. Lane, *An account of the manners and customs of the modern Egyptians* (1846), vol. II, pp. 113–116.

[166] Id., ibid., pp. 113–114.

[167] For the use of this term see S. Spiro, *Arabic-English dictionary of the modern Arabic of Egypt*, 2nd ed., *s.v. muḥabbaz.*

[168] C. D. Warner, *My Winter on the Nile*, 18th ed., pp. 284–285.

unsophisticated farce, the crew performed imitations of various dignitaries and officials, when giving or receiving *baksẖīsẖ* (tips, bribes).

b. Foreign Influences

However, it was the European theater that was destined to induce the Arabic-speaking peoples to improve upon the kind of plays described above. This was a two-way process: Western troupes played in the East—particularly in Egypt—while various Arabs visited Europe, where they acquired a liking for the Thespian arts.

Although the French were to be mainly responsible for the evolution of the Arab theater, this proved to be the case in Syria only at mid-century[169], while in Egypt this occurred even later in the nineteenth century[170]. It is reported, indeed, that French actors and musicians came to Egypt after the Napoleonic invasion and that General Menon founded a French theater[171]. Even were this true, it is doubtful if this French theater survived the defeat and repatriation of the French army. It is not until 1837 that one hears again of the existence of a French theater in Alexandria, and even then its activities seem to be rather limited in scope[172]. Although this is not generally known, it is the Italian theatrical troupes that may justly claim the chief activity in Egypt during the first half of the nineteenth century.

[169] See below, pages 56 *ss*.
[170] F O, 141/202, No. 257, Consul Burrell's No. 35, to E. H. Egerton, dated Port Said, June 8, 1884. Mrs. William Grey, *Journal of a visit to Egypt, Constantinople, the Crimea, Greece*, &c. (1869), p. 20. P. Ravaisse, *Ismail Pacha khédive d'Egypte (1830–1895) notes historiques* (1896), p. 10. P. Giffard, *Les français en Égypte* (1883), pp. 71–72. A. von Fircks, *Aegypten 1894. Staatrechtliche Verhältnisse, wirtschaftlichen Zustand, Verwaltung*, vol. II (1896), pp. 278–279. *The Egyptian Graphic*, Jan. 1, 1905, p. 6.
[171] Edwār Ḥunain, *Sẖauqī 'alā'l-masraḥ*, in *Ma.* (*al-Masẖriq*), vol. XXXII, 1934, pp. 577–578, reported by U. Rizzitano, *Il teatro arabo in Egitto opere teatrali di Taufīq al-Ḥakīm*, in *OM*, vol. XXIII, No. 6, June 1943, p. 247, n. 4. Zaidān, *Ta'rīkẖ ādāb al-lugẖa al-'arabiyya*, vol. IV, pp. 152–153. See also Muḥammad Amīn Ḥassūna, *al-Masraḥ al-miṣrī*, in *al-Sẖarq al-adnā*, Oct. 7, 1951, p. 16 (For Ḥassūna himself cf. *GAL*, Suppl. III, pp. 240–241).
[172] Pückler-Muskau, *Aus Mehemed Ali's Reich*, vol. I, pp. 124–125. Najm, *op. cit.*, pp. 19–20, mentions an isolated French production—by *amateurs*—in 1829.

The Italian theater and opera are known to have influenced the inception and development of other, less developed theaters, e.g., in Roumania[173] and Slovenia[174], and at Zaghreb[175]. One can hardly wonder at the frequent visits of Italian troupes to Cairo and Alexandria, the two cities in which the bulk of the Italian population in Egypt has lived for the last 150 years[176]. Of these, Alexandria, the important port, had a more European character; thus it was natural for it to be visited by Italian troupes frequently[177].

This assumption gathers force from a suggestive document in the records of the Foreign Office in London. This hitherto unpublished document[178] is a printed notice, written in Italian. It is dated October 16, 1847, signed by Artin Bey[179], and was sent under cover of a circular letter (also in Italian), to Sir Charles A. Murray, the British Consul General in Egypt during the years 1846–1853 and the author of a biography of Muḥammad 'Alī[180]. Even a cursory examination of archival material proves easily that the Egyptian authorities of those days would print their letters or decisions only when they intended to give them wide circulation and publicity. It may be assumed, there-

[173] Claudio Isopescu, *L'Italia a gli inizi del teatro drammatico e musicale romeno*, in *Giornale di politica e di letteratura*, vol. XI, quaderno 12, pp. 1348–1378. After its early beginnings, the Roumanian theater seems to have freed itself from this influence. Cf. I. Massoff, *Istoria teatrului național din București 1877–1937* (1937), esp. pp. 46–47, 99.

[174] Stanko Skerlj, *Représentations italiennes à Ljubljana aux XVIIe et XVIIIe siècles*, in *Mélanges de philologie offerts à Henri Hauvette*, 1934, pp. 339–346.

[175] Mirko Deanovic, *Le théâtre français et le théâtre italien à Zagreb du moyen âge au milieu du XIXe siècle*, ibid., pp. 161–173.

[176] As asserted by A. Sammarco, *In Egitto* (1939), p. 52.

[177] Ḥassūna, *op. cit.*, in *al-Sharq al-adnā*, Oct. 7, 1951, p. 16, for the location of the theater serving the Italian troupes.

[178] Analyzed by me, in my article *Lishè'elat reshītō shel ha-teiatrōn be-Mitsrayīm* (Hebrew: *The problem of the theater's inception in Egypt*) in *HH*, vol. II, No. 4, July, 1951, pp. 389–391.

[179] For this Armenian and his career cf. J. Heyworth-Dunne, *An Introduction to the history of education in modern Egypt* (1938), p. 159.

[180] F O, 141/13, Artin Bey's Circular to Murray, dated Alexandria, Oct. 16, 1847. Najm found the same document in the Russian diplomatic correspondence and translated it in his *op. cit.*, pp. 21–22.

fore, that the document under discussion was then sent to other dignitaries, too; and, very probably, was publicly brought to the attention of Alexandrines, possibly with an Arabic translation.

The circular letter informed all concerned that, as the Italian theater was under the jurisdiction of the municipal authorities, the latter intended to prevent any disturbance of the peace in the said theater. The appended document was entitled "Theater Regulations" (*Regolamenti Teatrali*) and embodied an introduction and six paragraphs. The introduction stated that the theater was under the jurisdiction of the municipal authorities. Paragraph 1 threatened all the employees of the theater with arrest if they showed discourtesy towards the public. Paragraph 2 affirmed that anyone—none excepted—who might try to make noise during the performance, would be driven out the first time that happened, and then debarred from all performances if this happened again. Paragraph 3 threatened all smokers in the theater hall with eviction. Paragraph 4 prohibited whistling, cane knocking, and feet shuffling in the hall. Paragraph 5 promised energetic action on the part of the authorities in other cases of disturbance that might arise. Paragraph 6 announced that a sergeant and eight policemen would hold themselves in readiness near the theater to enforce quiet.

These regulations are interesting indeed. They not only show the standards of the local audiences, but also the lack of manners on the part of some of the employees in the Italian theater, most likely Egyptians from Alexandria who worked as ushers, stage decorators, and the like. The disturbances of the public tranquillity on the part of the audience, as well as the rudeness of the employees in the theater, was probably a long-standing matter, if they aroused the proverbially apathetic municipal authorities of Alexandria to promise such drastic action and to detail a section of its small police force to enforce the warning. Foreign consuls were also asked to warn their respective nationals. Among these nationals were many natives who enjoyed foreign protection; disturbances in the theater were undoubtedly anticipated from them, rather than from the small, educated minority of Europeans residing in Egypt.

All this goes to show that the Italian theater had by then a standing of at least some years and was popular (undesirably so) with the natives. Therefore, it may be presumed that the Italian theater in Alexandria had at least some share in preparing the local population for a truer appreciation of the Western theater. Thus one may understand more easily how the European-modeled Syrian theater was soon to find such favorable reception in Egypt.

CHAPTER 2

The Theater in Syria and Egypt

a. The Birth of the Theater—Syria

Italian and French influences in Egypt during the first half of the nineteenth century undoubtedly helped to make the town population theater-conscious, but were insufficient nonetheless to ensure the inception of a local theater in Arabic. For such developments, a certain cultural *niveau* had to be attained first; and illiteracy in Egypt was then almost general. Even the literates—generally living in or around Muḥammad 'Alī's court—wrote and talked Turkish rather than Arabic, in deference to this Albanian ruler and his family.

Such was not the case in Syria, which in the nineteenth century comprised the Syria, Lebanon, Israel, and Jordan of today. There, since the beginning of the century, Presbyterian missionaries from America had vied with the Catholics (chiefly Jesuits and Lazarists from France) in educating the younger generation. Ibrāhīm Pasha's conquest of Syria, in 1834, had also given a strong impetus to the enlargement of the Muslim scholastic system. Printing presses were soon established by the missionaries, and cadres of teachers instructed. By mid-century there were evident signs of an Arabic literary revival in Syria, which was to reach its peak some years later and start a national movement rolling[181]. One of the symptoms of this literary revival was the inception of the modern Arab theater.

All considered, therefore, one can hardly wonder that the first modern play in Arabic was performed in Beirut, whose port like Alexandria in Egypt was one of the most important gates for European cultural penetration into the Arab world and

[181] For further details see, e.g., G. Antonius, *The Arab awakening* (1945), ch. 3.

which was, besides, the center of missionary activity in Syria.

One need not wonder, either, that it was a Maronite who wrote and directed the performance of this play, for the Christians were much more susceptible to the Western impact than their Muslim neighbors. Mārūn al-Naqqā<u>sh</u> (1817–1855) had spent a few years in Italy, where he had probably attended some theatrical performances. Possessed of a fairly adequate reading knowledge of French and Italian (besides Arabic and Turkish), he adapted Molière's *L'Avare* into Arabic verse, naming it *al-Ba<u>kh</u>īl*. This comedy he presented on an improvised stage[182] at his own house in Beirut, in the year 1848. The select audience consisted of foreign consuls and local dignitaries. Some characteristics in the play and in its performance merit special mention, since they would seem to be criteria of the Arab theater for a long time:

1. Al-Naqqā<u>sh</u> refrained from inserting organic changes in the original plot, but abbreviated or expanded the comedy at will, to suit his taste and the understanding of his audience. For this very purpose, he also Arabicized the names of the dramatis personae and changed the locale of the plays. These methods were soon to become the general practice.

2. He enlivened the play by inserting several airs and tunes, of Oriental character; these were performed by an orchestra and choir and were often, but not always, related to the subject matter of the play. Because of this approach, the play became something midway between a comedy and an operetta (or, as it is sometimes called, a "lyrical opera"). This musical character of the Arab theater has survived, to a great extent, until our own days.

3. No actresses were allowed to appear on the stage (a phenomenon already noticed earlier by Lane in Egypt[183]) and hardly any women were tolerated in the audience: boys and

[182] In modern Arabic *masraḥ*. See article *al-Masraḥ au al-marzaḥ*, in *Mu.*, vol. LXIX, Aug. 1, 1926, pp. 223–224.

[183] Lane, *op. cit.*, vol. II, pp. 113–114.

men played, therefore, the feminine parts[184]. This practice, although reminiscent of the ancient Greek and the Elizabethan theaters, had its own reasons in the Arab East: on one hand, Arab women were more ignorant than their men-folk and were despised by them accordingly; on the other hand, religious opposition—particularly among the Muslims, whose women-folk were guarded jealously in the harems and allowed in the street only if veiled—was always certain to be aroused if women were to act. In Europe, similar religious considerations prevented the participation of women in the Goldfahden-style Yiddish theater.

4. All actors were members of the Naqqāsh family[185]. This, although not always the rule, was still to be a fairly common trait of the Arab theater for some time.

The great success enjoyed by this novel type of entertainment encouraged al-Naqqāsh to build a larger hall, adjoining his house, to be used for theatrical performances. Apparently he also requested, and obtained, an official order (*firmān*) permitting him to present plays in this hall[186]. In these circumstances al-Naqqāsh wrote (1850) a second play, *Abū'l-Ḥasan al-mughaffal*. It has been stated by various authorities that this play was an adaptation from Molière's *L'Etourdi*, but this was not the case. True, Abū'l-Ḥasan, the play's hero, was as naïve and blundering as Molière's Lélie in the above farce and as violently in love; but there all similarity ends. Al-Naqqāsh's comedy employs material from *The Arabian Nights* and is set in their spirit. Its theme is the jolly story of Abū'l-Ḥasan, who

[184] *GAL*, Suppl. II, p. 754. Jurjī Zaidān, *Tarājim mashāhīr al-sharq* etc., 2nd ed., vol. II, pp. 230–231. Id., *Ta'rīkh ādāb etc.*, vol. IV, pp. 153–154; cf. *H*, vol. V, Dec. 1, 1896, p. 260. H. Pérès, *La littérature arabe et l'Islam par les textes les XIXe et XXe siècles* (1938), p. 4; cf. ibid., Avant-propos, p. VII. Landau, '*Al ha-teiaṭrōn etsel ha-'aravīm*, in *Bamah*, fasc. 47, Jan. 1946, p. 49, Id., *The Arab theatre*, in *MEA*, vol. IV, No. 3, Mar., 1953, p. 78. By courtesy of *Middle Eastern Affairs*, I am using some parts of my article.

[185] Orvieto, *op. cit.*, p. 123, and bibliography in the footnotes, ibid.

[186] Id., p. 122, based on Mārūn al-Naqqāsh, *Arzat Lubnān*, p. 11. See also Zaidān, *Tarājim*, 2nd ed., vol. II, p. 231. *H*, vol. XVIII, May 1, 1910, p. 469. Najm, in *al-Adīb*, vol. XXVII, Mar. 1955, pp. 24–25.

became Caliph-for-a-day by Hārūn al-Rashīd's order and then started a series of misadventures when he was unable to readjust himself to his lowly status. This play should be considered as the first original Arabic drama in modern times. The third and last play by al-Naqqāsh was an adaptation of Molière's *Tartuffe*, renamed *al-Ḥasūd*, which in its Arabic version sometimes differed considerably from Molière's masterpiece and rather resembled an opéra bouffe in verse and rhymed prose[187].

The death of this first adapter of French plays, at the early age of thirty-eight, while on a business trip to Tarsus, was a grievous blow to the young Arab theater in Syria. The death of al-Naqqāsh affected the development of the Arab theater in more ways than one. Not only was it deprived of the talents of its first playwright, his enthusiasm, and his material support; but also the hall that he had erected was converted into a church, so that performances of plays became again small, private events. The opposition of the orthodox leaders to the Arab theater, which had never quite subsided, raised its head again and accused the artists of laxity in their religious practices, sometimes even of immorality. In a country where religious feeling ran high, the propaganda of the orthodox circles, coupled with the penury of the artists, forced the Arab theater to look for encouragement and help elsewhere.

Most authorities assume, explicitly or implicitly, that when Salīm al-Naqqāsh (Mārūn's nephew) and his colleagues went to Egypt, Syria was left practically without any theatrical performances until the beginning of the twentieth century, when Egyptian troupes began to visit Syria and thus encouraged local competition[188]. Nothing could be further from the truth. While

[187] Orvieto, ibid., pp. 122-123. *GAL*, Suppl. II, p. 754. Barbour, *The Arabic theatre in Egypt*, in *BSOS*, vol. VIII, 1935–1937, p. 174. Pérès, *op. cit.*, p. 4. P. Perolari-Malmignati, *Su e giù per la Siria*, pp. 160–165.

[188] *GAL*, Suppl. II, p. 759; Suppl. III, pp. 415–416. Muḥammad Taimūr, *al-Tamthīl fī Miṣr*, in *al-Sufūr*, vol. IV, 1918–1919, repr. in his *Mu'allafāt*, vol. II, pp. 22 *ss*. Khalīl Muṭrān, *al-Tamthīl al-'arabī wa-nahḍatuh al-jadīda*, in *H*, vol. XXIX, Feb. 1, 1921; cf. ibid., vol. XLV, Apr. 1, 1937, p. 696.

it is self-evident that the mass immigration of actors to Egypt deprived the Arab theater in Syria of some of its ablest exponents, this theater nevertheless continued to exist in the large Syrian towns. No other explanation but this continuity can be given to the unusually speedy development of play-writing and acting in twentieth-century Syria[189].

Thus it is no mere chance that in the year 1869 Mārūn al-Naqqāsh's three plays were published in Beirut under the suggestive title *Cedar of the Lebanon* (*Arzat Lubnān*). The continuity is still further suggested by the activities of one of the teachers at the St. Joseph Jesuit University at Beirut. Named Najīb Ḥubaiqa, he published in the excellent Catholic bi-monthly, *al-Mashriq*, of 1899 (i.e., before Egyptian troupes came to Syria) a long, detailed study of acting, besides himself adapting some plays of a French Jesuit, named Camille, into Arabic[190]. Between those two dates, further interesting proof is supplied by various chroniclers and some observant travelers (not all of whom, however, knew Arabic).

Various Maronite[191] and Jesuit[192] schools presented, time and again, plays written by their priests. Before the end of the century, at the latest, this practice of play-writing and acting was to penetrate several Muslim[193] and Jewish schools as well[194]. A number of prolific writers devoted a part of their time to the composition of plays. Iskandar al-ʿĀzār (1855–1919), for instance, wrote four, two of which were afterwards enacted with

[189] An idea of which may be formed by perusing the list of published dramas, drawn up by Bustānī in *Ma.*, vol. XXV, 1927, pp. 623 *ss.*, and by Brockelmann, *GAL*, Suppl. III, pp. 416–419.

[190] See below, List of Ar. Plays and Bibliography.

[191] *H.*, vol. XXV, May 1, 1917, p. 689.

[192] *GAL*, Suppl. III, pp. 415–416, who recorded this well-known fact, failed to draw the correct conclusion, thinking that a dearth of dramatic creation was thus indicated. For the wealth of plays performed in the Jesuit College of Saint-Joseph, Beirut, since 1882, see Lūyyis Shaikhū, *al-Ādāb al-ʿarabiyya fī'l-qarn al-tāsiʿ ʿashar*, vol. II (1910), pp. 65–66.

[193] Ign. Kratschkowsky, *Modern Arabic literature*, c., *Drama*, in the *Encycl. of Islam*, Suppl., 1st ed., *s.v. Arabia*, p. 30.

[194] E.g., *The Spendthrift* (*al-Musrif*), by Salīm Zakī Cohen, performed in 1895 at the Jewish school in Beirut—cf. *H*, vol. IV, Oct. 1, 1895, p. 116.

the laudable purpose of donating the receipts to charity[195]. The journalist Adīb Isḥāq (1856–1885)—of whom more anon—adapted Racine's *Andromaque* into Arabic, adding a few melodies of his own. This was performed, at the suggestion of the French consul, by a girls' orphanage in Beirut (prob. in 1875); the funds raised were donated to the poor[196].

It would be wrong, however, to think that theatrical activity in Syria was limited during the second half of the nineteenth century to playwriting and to performances with educational or philanthropic aims. It should be borne in mind that one of Mārūn al-Naqqāsh's admirers, a certain Sa'd Allāh al-Bustānī, formed a new troupe out of young amateurs, and performances continued more or less regularly[197]. Notwithstanding the fact that many actors were drawn to Egypt—both by the liberality of its rulers and the opportunity of taking some part in the artistic festivities with which the guests to the opening of the Suez Canal were honored in 1869—the Arab theater in Syria did not sink into oblivion. It is not strange to note, indeed, that Italians attended theatrical performances soon after and, fortunately, recorded their impressions.

Goretti, who spent some twenty months in Beirut (1874–1876) as a teacher of Italian, visited (besides two French theaters) the Arab theater, where he saw al-Naqqāsh's *Abū'l-Ḥasan al-mughaffal*, with some variations[198]. The same play, with other variations, was attended (in 1875) by the diplomat Perolari-Malmignati[199] The latter also had an occasion to attend another performance, this time of a play named *Pru-*

[195] Jurjī Niqūlā Bāz, *al-Shaikh Iskandar al-'Āzār*, ibid., vol. XXVII, Apr. 1, 1919, pp. 644–645. See also below, List of Arabic Plays.

[196] *H*, vol. II, Aug. 1, 1894, p. 706. Zaidān, *Tarājim*, 2nd ed., vol. II, p. 77. *GAL*, Suppl. II, p. 759. Zakī Ṭulaimāt, *Kaifa dakhal al-tamthīl bilād al-sharq*, in K, vol. I, Feb., 1946, p. 583. Mārūn 'Abbūd, *Adīb Isḥāq*, ibid. vol. III, Feb., 1948, p. 272.

[197] Zaidān, ibid., p. 231. Id., *Ta'rīkh ādāb etc.*, vol. IV, p. 154. Cf. *H*, vol. XIV, Dec. 1, 1905, p. 144; ibid., vol. XVIII, May 1, 1910, p. 469.

[198] L. Goretti, *Venti mesi in Soria*, pp. 76–85.

[199] Perolari-Malmignati, *Su e giù per la Siria*, pp. 160–165.

dence[200], written by a certain Muslim sheikh, Ḥasan al-Qusṭī. In about three hours, the plot unveiled the court intrigues in Persia: the Shah discovered his daughter alone with an unknown youth, whom he wanted to kill, but deferred the execution out of prudence (hence the play's name). It was soon discovered, however, that the youth was none other than the son of the Emperor of China, so the young people married and all ended well[201].

It is interesting that while in this play men still performed women's parts, in *Abū'l-Ḥasan al-mug̱haffal*, according to both our witnesses, women acted in feminine roles. It would seem as if the seventies of the nineteenth century were a transition period for the Arab theater in Syria; during these years, the Arab woman began to take a hand in acting. The participation of women actors might explain the unexpected quickening of interest among the Syrian audiences, which found expression in the country's two main cities. In Beirut, K̲h̲alīl al-Yāzijī's *Virtue and Faithfulness* (*al-Murū'a wa'l-wafā' au al-faraj ba'd al-ḍīq*) was performed in about 1700 lines of Arabic verse. This first play in verse[202] described ably, along with a love sub-plot, the conversion of an Arab king to Christianity[203]. This was in 1878, and five years later, in Damascus, two new theater halls were erected; several Arabic adaptations from Molière were produced there[204]. A short while afterwards, in October, 1899, E. Littmann, the known Orientalist, saw in Beirut the production of a comedy in colloquial Arabic by a traveling Damascene troupe[204a].

[200] The Italian reads *accortezza di mente*, which may also mean cunning, wit, or good sense.

[201] Perolari-Malmignati, *Su e giù per la Siria*, pp. 153–160.

[202] *H*, vol. XIV, Dec. 1, 1905, p. 148.

[203] Barbour, *op. cit.*, in *BSOS*, vol. VIII, 1935–1937. The play was composed in 1876, first performed in 1878, first printed in 1884, then reprinted in Cairo in 1902—acc. to *Mu.*, vol. XXVII, Sep. 1, 1902, pp. 910–911. Cf. Zaidān, *Ta' rīk̲h̲ ādāb etc.*, vol. IV, p. 157; and *GAL*, Suppl. II, p. 767.

[204] H. Brugsch, *op. cit.*, in *Deutsche Revue*, vol. XII, 1887, part 3, pp. 25–26.

[204a] E. Littmann, *Eine neuarabische Posse aus Damascus*, in *ZDMG*, vol. LVI, 1902, pp. 86–97. For further instances, see Najm, *op. cit.*, pp. 51 *ss.*

All this, again, is interesting, because it goes to prove, along with the other arguments, that there was a continual development of the Arab theater in Syria. However, it was in Egypt that this theater markedly strode forward in the second half of the nineteenth century.

b. The Development—Egypt in Ismā'īl's Days

The continuity of the Arab theater in Syria in the second half of the nineteenth century is thus ascertained. It remained, nevertheless, on a low level. It was therefore natural that some of the brighter playwrights and actors—despondent at the hopelessness of the future, the material hardships, and the opposition of the religious circles in their land—decided to try their fortunes elsewhere. It seems that they made up their minds only after playing for a while before Syrian audiences[205]; but they were also attracted, undoubtedly, by conditions in Egypt at the time. The munificence of the Khedive Ismā'īl had by then become almost proverbial, and was probably enhanced by the splendor of the preparations for the opening of the Suez Canal (1869). It was for this occasion that the great Opera House[206] in Cairo had been built and other smaller theater halls erected. So, during the seventies of the nineteenth century, a sizable number of prominent Syrians connected with the stage emigrated to Egypt. A good number of these were Christians, who could not get over their fright and bitterness at the pogroms they had suffered at the Muslims' hands a few years earlier.

The most prominent among those émigrés were two playwrights, Salīm K͟halīl al-Naqqās͟h (Mārūn's nephew) and Adīb Isḥāq, already mentioned for his adaptation of Racine's *Andromaque*[207]. They brought along with them an able Syrian actor,

[205] Zaidān, *Ta'rīk͟h ādāb etc.*, vol. IV, p. 154.
[206] For whose history and description see A. B. de Guerville, *New Egypt* (1905), p. 80. M. Jacobs, *The Cairo opera house*, in *B*, fasc. 33, Mar., 1949, pp. 17–18.
[207] See above, p. 61.

Yūsuf al-Khayyāṭ (1876). The fragmentary records of their progress in Egypt generally imply that they set out immediately to compose plays and produce them. Nothing could be further from the thoughts of these practical men. They soon realized that the Egyptian popular music, that all-important ingredient in the Arabic play, was different from their own. So they devoted three months to studying local music, having found—luckily for them—a free teacher[208]. These studies, however, helped but little the small troupe, which was unable to compete on equal terms with the experienced local companies. The Syrians nonetheless did not give up without a struggle. Salīm Khalīl al-Naqqāsh adapted Ghislanzoni's libretto for *Aïda*[209] and afterwards wrote a five-act drama, in literary Arabic prose and verse. Named *The Tyrant* (*al-Ẓalūm*), it told of romance and intrigue at an Oriental Court, unspecified but resembling Khedive Ismā'īl's. At the same time, approximately, Adīb Isḥāq rewrote for the troupe his adaptation of *Andromaque*; then translated an historical play named *Charlemagne* as well as a lighter one by Comte d'Ache (?), *La Belle Parisienne*, which he named *Gharā'ib al-ittifāq* (viz., *The Wonders of Chance*)[210]. All three were printed later. Anyway, Isḥāq's plays—along with others' adaptations of Racine's *Phèdre*, Corneille's *Horace*, and l'abbé d'Aubignac's *Zénobie*[211]—flopped, so that he and al-Naqqāsh turned to journalism[212]. Both were still to make their mark by their literary activity in the cause of Egyptian nationalism.

Al-Khayyāṭ then continued on his own. He soon grasped

[208] According to the interesting, unheeded evidence of their teacher, Buṭrus Shalfūn, *H*, vol. XV, Nov. 1, 1906, p. 117.

[209] *GAL*, Suppl. II, p. 759; Suppl. III, p. 266, which wrongly attributes to him Isḥāq's adaptation of *Andromaque*.

[210] *GAL*, Suppl. II, p. 759, mentions its name as translated literally, *al-Bārīsiyya al-ḥasnā'*.

[211] Barbour, *op. cit.*, in *BSOS*, vol. VIII, 1935–1937, p. 174.

[212] Cf. *H.*, vol. II, Aug. 1, 1894, p. 706; ibid., vol. V, Dec. 1, 1896, p. 260. Zaidān, *Tarājim*, vol. II, p. 77. Pérès, *op. cit.*, p. 11. *H*, vol. IV, June 1, 1896, p. 741 and July 1, 1896, p. 836, wrongly give play's name as *Charles-Quint*. For a biogr. notice on Isḥāq cf. the Egyptian *K*, Feb., 1948, pp. 271–283.

that he had hardly a chance to make a living without the Khedive's help. When he asked for it, the Khedive gave his support, as usual, whole-heartedly. The doors of the grand Opera House were opened before his troupe and al-K̲h̲ayyāṭ left the Zizinya theater in Alexandria for the Opera in Cairo. Unfortunately the first play was not judiciously chosen, as regards its contents. Probably as a compliment to his friend Salīm K̲h̲alīl al-Naqqās̲h̲'s abilities, the latter's above-mentioned drama, *The Tyrant*, was chosen for the gala opening in the year 1878. The contents of the play were, naturally enough, interpreted by the Khedive as a reflection on his own personal rule. Al-K̲h̲ayyāṭ and his troupe were banished from Egypt and had to return to Syria[213]; there is no available information about their performing there, but this appears likely.

The Khedive's suspicion of the Arab theater and his ire against its exponents had another cause, too. This cause lay in the activities of a young Egyptian Jew, called Ya'qūb ibn Rufā'īl Ṣanū' or—as he often signed his name—James Sanua. Even though Sanua's theatrical output was only partially in Arabic, his was a most important service to the development of the Arab theater in Egypt, particularly to its popularization.

Sanua (1839–1912) had had the benefit of a good Hebrew and Arabic basic education in Egypt and the occasion to contrast it with European education, when he studied in Italy for a period of three years (at the impressionable age of thirteen to sixteen). He put his brilliant knowledge of several Oriental and European languages to good account by earning his livelihood through tutorial work in these languages. His early interest in politics and his connections with the civil and military leaders of the nascent national movement in Egypt[214] drew him into

[213] Zaidān, ibid., p. 155. S̲h̲alfūn, in *H*, vol. XV, Nov. 1, 1906, p. 117; cf. ibid., vol. XVIII, May 1, 1910, p. 470. Al-Rāfi'ī, *'Aṣr Ismā'īl*, vol. II, p. 300. *GAL*, Suppl. III, p. 266. None of these noticed that the play had been written by al-Naqqās̲h̲. For further information on al-K̲h̲ayyāṭ's career, see Najm, *al-Masraḥiyya etc.*, pp. 103–106.

[214] For further details see Landau, *Parliaments and parties in Egypt*, part 2, chs. 1–2.

feverish activity. Not content with being the creator of the satirical press in Egypt, Sanua tried his hand, successfully, at play-writing. He had already written some Italian plays, three of which were produced in Genoa and elsewhere. Now, in the early seventies of the nineteenth century, he pursued his feud with the administration of Khedive Ismā'īl: not abandoning journalism, he found enough time to compose thirty-two Arabic plays and puppet shows, most of which championed the poor man's cause and directed resentment against the Khedive.

Some of these plays were inspired by the Italian dramatists and by Molière (their author was nicknamed "the Egyptian Molière"). However, Sanua ably changed plot and details to suit his purpose. As his plays—produced and often acted in by himself, at his own theater in Cairo—drew large audiences, Sanua simplified his language to suit the colloquial Arabic they would understand[215]. Thus he was not only the creator of the politico-satirical theater in Egypt, but also the innovator of its language. While previously plays had usually been enacted in the traditional, classical Arabic, Sanua performed his comedies in the spoken dialect of Egypt (one of them, treating with the life of actors, in rhymed prose, was later printed in Beirut[216]). In this he was to serve as a model for his successors. However, his plays were regarded as subversive and his two-year-old theater was closed (1872). Sanua did not desist, however, and many of his short, biting plays were still to be printed in his newspapers, both in Egypt and, afterwards, in exile in Paris[217]. As his papers were very widely read, and passed from hand to hand, one may assume that his plays had some effect on the further development of the Arab theater wherever his news-

[215] Ḥassūna, *op. cit.*, in *al-Sharq al-adnā*, Oct. 7, 1951, p. 16.

[216] It was named *Mulyīr Miṣr wa-mā yuqāsīh*—cf. Barbour, *op. cit.*, in *BSOS*, vol. VIII, 1935–1937, p. 174.

[217] For these and further details see Landau, *Abū Naḍḍāra, an Egyptian Jewish nationalist*, in *JJS*, vol. III, No. 1, 1952, pp. 30–44, and the bibliography in the footnotes. To these should be added Ibrāhīm 'Abduh's book *Abū Naḍḍāra* (1953) and Najm, *al-Masraḥiyya etc.*, pp. 77–93.

papers were sold or distributed free of charge in the Near East and in North Africa.

C. The Increase in the Number of Troupes

Although the number of theater halls increased in the Egypt of Ismā'īl's days, as has already been explained, there was no proportionate rise in the number of patrons. Indeed, the performances of the foreign troupes were attended chiefly by the foreign nationals, proportionally rich and numerous in Egypt at the time. In so far as Egyptians patronized these performances, they were chiefly from the ranks of the upper class, to which were added various high officials of the state and the army[218]. The mass of the people had little use for plays which they did not understand and which, anyhow, did not appeal to them. The great success of Sanua's plays, in those two years before his theater closed down, goes to show that the majority of the Egyptians wanted Arabic plays to be amusing and easy to grasp. Therefore, at no time, in the sixties and seventies of the nineteenth century, do we hear of the coexistence of two troupes or more. Even one troupe at a time had to strain its energy to the utmost to make both ends meet.

This phenomenon is easily understandable if one considers the extreme indigence of the Egyptian masses during Ismā'īl's rule. This Khedive needed immense sums of money for his luxurious life and sumptuous entertainment as well as for great construction plans (the Suez Canal, railways, Opera House). Some of these plans were to bear fruit, economically, in future years. In the meantime, however, taxes were extorted most cruelly and little money, if any, remained in the hands of the theatergoers. Thus the actors had to work at odd jobs to make ends meet[219], while the troupe had to rely on the generosity of the Khedive or some other rich person. The above case of the

[218] See Aḥmad Ḥasan al-Zayyāt, *Ta'rīkh al-adab al-'arabī*, 10th ed., pp. 411–412.
[219] Zakī Ṭulaimāt in *al-Muṣawwar*, May 9, 1947.

Syrian Yūsuf al-Khayyāṭ, who had to appeal to the Khedive Ismā'īl for financial help in order to continue his performances in Egypt, is illustrative of the situation.

The British occupation of Egypt, which began in 1882 and lasted forty years, changed matters visibly. Even though in some aspects the British Occupation hindered the natural progress of the Egyptians, it can hardly be seriously disputed that it furthered their material well-being to a considerable extent. Taxation was just and humane; wise irrigation and development projects brought new prosperity to the country, raising the per capita income; the population grew and doubled in number during a few years.

Prosperity increased the number of pleasure-seekers who could afford to pay for a theater-ticket; the advance of education and the great rise in population swelled also the ranks of the theatergoers. It was only natural, all considered, that theatrical troupes sprang up in Egypt under the British Occupation.

The first actor to form a troupe in the days of the Khedive Taufīq, the son and successor of Ismā'īl, was again a Syrian, named Sulaimān al-Qardāḥī (died 1909). He reorganized the remnants of al-Khayyāṭ's band, but before he could make a good start, a military revolt started in 1882, immediately followed by the British Occupation of Egypt and an epidemic of cholera. It took al-Qardāḥī another two years to prepare for performances at the Opera House in Cairo. He was the first, in Egypt, to introduce women on the stage (first his wife[220] and then a gifted Jewess, Lailā[221]). It is more than likely that in so doing he imitated the practice already in vogue with some troupes in his native Syria[222]. So, when one hears that al-Qardāḥī's troupe was not allowed to continue performances at

[220] See *GAL*, Suppl. III, p. 267. Barbour, *op. cit.*, in *BSOS*, vol. VIII, 1935–1937, p. 175. Rizzitano, *op. cit.*, in *OM*, vol. XXIII, June 1943, p. 248.

[221] Shalfūn, in *H*, vol. XV, Nov. 1, 1906, p. 118. Cf. ibid., vol. XVIII, May 1, 1910, p. 470.

[222] See above, p. 62.

the Opera House soon after[223], one may wonder if some religious pressure had not been exercised on the Khedive and his court.

Deprived of Khedivial protection, al-Qardāḥī continued on his own, touring the rural provinces of Egypt. That meant that he could not be content with his repertoire, even though this included, besides previously mentioned plays, adaptations from *Othello* and *Télémaque*. He now had to suit the character of both plot and acting to the tastes of his audiences, instead of trying to mold their artistic appreciation. Hence his stress on musical plays and comedies, both of which types drew the largest crowds; and his hiring and training of some professional singers who were later to become the mainstay of the Egyptian musical theater. It is to be noted, however, that al-Qardāḥī's troupe, on the whole, did so well that by 1895 it was invited to perform at some wedding festivities in the Khedive's palace[224]. This patronage of the Khedive's court did not prevent the Egyptian government from revoking (1900) the concession it had granted the actor to perform at a place he named the "al-Qardāḥī Theater" in Alexandria. Old and disillusioned, al-Qardāḥī petitioned Lord Cromer, the all-powerful British consul general in Egypt, for help[225].

Whatever the outcome of this affair, the sorest troubles of al-Qardāḥī arose from competition with other troupes, which had formed meanwhile in the favorable economic conditions of the country. His first serious competitor was Iskandar Faraḥ. Faraḥ, also a Syrian, had been educated in Damascus at a Jesuit school: it appears that there, at school performances, he first became acquainted with the drama. His first play was performed in a public garden in Damascus, with the encouragement of Midḥat Pasha, the then progressive Turkish governor

[223] Zaidān, *Ta'rīkh ādāb etc.*, vol. IV, p. 155.
[224] See *H*, vol. III, Feb. 1, 1895, p. 436.
[225] F O, 141/357, No. 199 of "From Miscellaneous," al-Qardāḥī's handwritten letter to Cromer, undated (received Nov. 1900). Cromer's reaction is not known. Other details of al-Qardāḥī's career see in Najm, *al-Masraḥiyya etc.*, pp. 107–114.

of Syria. After a trial at Beirut, Faraḥ went over to Egypt, where he took part in a troupe led by another gifted Syrian, K̲h̲alīl al-Qabbānī[225a]. Then Faraḥ formed his own troupe, "The Egyptian Arabic Troupe" (*al-Jauq al-miṣrī'l-'arabī*), which produced a large number of plays over a period of eighteen years[226]. One of the secrets of Faraḥ's success was his presentation of a new play every month or so, lest his audience get bored. His repertoire included adaptations of classical plays, such as Corneille's *Le Cid*, and modern French melodramas, e.g., *The Gamekeeper's Daughter* (*Ibnat ḥāris al-ṣaid*), a mediocre social drama in which a profligate man becomes the rival-in-love of his illegitimate, unrecognized son[227]. As long as al-Qardāḥī performed in Alexandria and Faraḥ in Cairo[228], the latter could earn his livelihood well. However, secessions amongst his actors and the creation of new troupes forced Faraḥ to leave for Syria again[229]. Anyway, the Syrians had already played their part in promoting the Arab theater in Egypt.

The most serious secession from his troupe, from Faraḥ's point of view, was that of Salāma Ḥijāzī, his chief singer. It is a sign of the times that when Faraḥ, through the force of circumstances, formed another Egyptian troupe which presented plays without any singing, the experiment was applauded by the reviewers, but was received very coolly by the audiences[230]. These were much more attracted by Ḥijāzī's new troupe. For

[225a] For whom see Najm, ibid., pp. 61–70, 115–124.

[226] See details, e.g., in *RMM*, vol. I, 1907, p. 423—*Le théâtre arabe*. For al-Qabbānī, see Najm's monograph in *al-Adīb*, Jan., 1955, pp. 19–22 and Feb., 1955, pp. 17–21.

[227] See the N.Y. *al-Jāmi'a*, vol. V, July 1, 1906, pp. 47–48 (Cairo correspondence). For earlier years cf. *H*, vol. V, Jan. 1, 1897, p. 354 and vol. VI, May 1, 1898, p. 669.

[228] *H*, Jan. 15, 1895, p. 396.

[229] Barbour, *op. cit.*, in *BSOS*, vol. VIII, 1935–1937, p. 176. Zaidān, *Ta'rīk̲h̲ ādāb etc.*, vol. IV, pp. 155–156. Landau, *'Al ha-teiaṭrōn etsel ha-'aravīm*, in *Bamah*, No. 49, p. 51. Further details of his career in Najm, *al-Masraḥiyya etc.*, pp. 125–134.

[230] Barbour, ibid., ibid. Zaidān, ibid., p. 156.

Ḥijāzī had an amazingly resonant, mellifluous voice, which impelled his admirers to call him the "Caruso of the East"[231] and is still remembered nostalgically by many old-timers in Egypt and North Africa[232]. Besides his voice Ḥijāzī seems to have possessed a remarkable personality, notwithstanding his limited education, for he left a deep imprint on the character of the Arab theater.

Born into a poor family in Alexandria, Ḥijāzī (1855–1917) received the customary religious training. He soon distinguished himself by his ability in reciting the Koran and his success in singing popular songs at various private festivities. It appears that, as a youth, he attended the performances of various European troupes. His association with the Arab theater in Egypt covers practically all personalities known at the time. He had close contacts with Adīb Isḥāq and Salīm K̲h̲alīl al-Naqqās̲h̲, during their connection with the Arab theater. Later, he joined the troupe of al-Qardāḥī and, after a quarrel regarding the distribution of the chief roles, left him to adhere to the troupe of Iskandar Faraḥ. He was the latter's faithful lieutenant for eighteen years, excelling in musical dramas to the admiration of the public, who knew but little, however, of his inadequate wages and gradually declining health.

In 1905, Ḥijāzī began to perform, with his newly formed troupe, in "The Arab theater" (*Dār al-tamt̲h̲īl al-ʿarabī*) of Cairo, specially renovated according to his taste. Except for some spells of illness, Ḥijāzī continued to act and sing there until his death a dozen years later. He was the first to introduce the practice of touring other Arabic-speaking lands. With his troupe he repeatedly toured Syria and North Africa (particularly Tunis)[233]. The first great Muslim to be associated with the

[231] *RY*, Jan. 11, 1954, p. 34.

[232] Salāma Mūsā, *al-Qāhira fīmā bain 1903 wa-1907*, in *KM* (*al-Kātib al-miṣrī*), fasc. 10, July 1946, p. 300.

[233] Barbour, *op. cit.*, in *BSOS*, vol. VIII, 1935–1937, p. 177. Jūrj Ṭannūs, *al-S̲h̲aik̲h̲ Salāma Ḥijāzī*, in *H*, vol. XXVI, Nov. 1, 1917, pp. 186–189. Muḥammad Taimūr, *op. cit.*, vol. II, pp. 123–130 (repr. from *al-Minbar*, Aug. 26, 1918); cf.

modern Arab theater (another of the reasons for his success with Muslim audiences), Ḥijāzī's greatest impact on the Arab theater lay, however, in his stress of music. If, before his time, music had been only an important ingredient in this theater, Ḥijāzī transplanted the musical element into the center of attention. No actor himself, although possessed of artistic sensitiveness, it is a great tribute to his singing ability that he left such a mark on the Arab theater.

This brings us to the period of the First World War. The picture, however, would be incomplete were we to leave out the popular farce, which developed independently of the Europeanized Arab theater. The vulgar farce, of the same type seen by Lane in rural areas[234], found its way to the cities, too, where it undoubtedly appealed to many uneducated people. It was easier to grasp because of its unsophisticated plot[235] and, as such, was more attractive to the non-linguist tourist who sometimes fell asleep at the verbiage of the melodrama[236]. This type of farce, generally termed *comic act* (*faṣl muḍḥik*), seems to have been fairly popular. An example, witnessed in Cairo early in the twentieth century[237] will suffice:

"The *faṣl muḍḥik* last seen by the present writer in one of these cafés consists of a number of clownish scenes, that always end in the whipping of one of the participators. The chief character of the flimsy plot is the servant Husen, who appears in a pierrot costume. He makes a dupe of his master (an officer) by entering into illicit

---

ibid., pp. 131 *ss.*, 171, 174 *ss.*, 179 *ss.*, 191 *ss.*, 198, 203 *ss.*, 218 *ss.*, 223, 227–228, 234 *ss.*, 243, 263, 269, 270. Contrast the praise of A.L.C., i.e. A. Le Chatelier, in *RMM*, vol. IV, No. 2, Feb. 1908, p. 410, with the criticism in *al-Jāmi'a*, vol. V, July 15, 1906, pp. 78–79. I have not seen his biography, *al-Shaikh Salāma Ḥijāzī*, by Muḥammad Fāḍil, mentioned in *H*, vol. XLII, Nov. 1, 1933, p. 122, and in the Egyptian monthly *Apōllō*, Mar. 1934, pp. 621–623.

[234] See above, p. 51.
[235] R. d'Humières, *op. cit.*, p. 132, for an example.
[236] E.g., D. Sladen, as described in his *Oriental Cairo*, pp. 115–119.
[237] Prüfer, in *ERE*, *sub voce Drama, Arabic*, where further examples are also given. See also d'Humières, *op. cit.*, p. 132.

relations with the latter's wife. The deceived husband notices from time to time, of course, the love-making that is going on behind his back, and the result is a series of roughly ludicrous mistakes and mystifications. For instance, the servant embraces his master, who has seated himself, unnoticed by the servant, in his wife's chair, and receives as a reward a box on the ear. A boastful, silly European—a Greek (dialect type), with a battered tall hat and a bright red British uniform—is beaten continually throughout the play . . ."

This type of comedy is, of course, nearer to the Arab shadow play than the musical Arab theater. It has the same rough sort of humor, using the ancient devices of wanton buffoonery[238] as well as of satire against the moneyed class (the Greek) and the rulers of the country (his British uniform). These, however, are common to all kinds of popular farce. They can be found easily, indeed, in the Italian *Commedia dell'arte*, which in its stereotyped version, presents striking similarities of character to the *faṣl muḍḥik*, described above. The fooled husband is none but Pagliaccio; the sly servant bears a close resemblance to Arlecchino, as does the boastful, stupid Greek to Scarramucia; while the flirtatious wife has too many common characteristics with Colombina to make this only a coincidence.

It seems that the Arab theater, in the period preceding the First World War, shows some characteristics, which may be summed up under the following headings:

1. The birth of the modern Arab theater was in 1848 in Syria. Although it continued to exist in Syria, its main developments were in Egypt, from the seventies onwards. It was there that Syrian actors (as well as writers and journalists) found a wider scope for their talents.

2. Plays were generally adapted from French and the plot and names of characters and places suited to fit local conditions.

[238] Fr. Kern confirms this by further instances in his *Neuere ägyptische Humoristen und Satiriker*, VII, in *MSOS*, 1906, part 2, p. 49.

3. The same plays were often revived or, at least, the same subjects used time and again.

4. Plays were written and performed sometimes in Classical Arabic and at others in the vernacular.

5. Playwrights sprang, in general, from among the actors; they often acted the leading parts in the plays they had written or adapted; they were often the scene directors, too.

6. Actors were still to a large extent amateurs[239], who considered themselves free to break with their troupe and join another (or form their own). Hence the relatively large number of semi-professional or amateurish troupes[239a].

7. The most prized actors were those who could sing: melodramas and musical comedies thus became the public favorites.

8. Actresses for women's parts gradually began to appear on the stage, instead of men. These were, as a rule, Jewesses or Christian girls from Syria, not the more secluded Egyptian Muslim women[240].

9. Most troupe directors put material considerations over and above artistic ones.

10. The number of theater halls grew, a fact which enabled the Arab theater to pass from private homes and cafés to public shows.

11. Large sections of the public, instead of a small élite, thus became the patron of the theater which often had, because of material considerations, to adapt its standards to the tastes of the public.

12. Side by side with the Europeanized, musical theater, there continued to exist—in rural areas and in the cafés of the cities—a lighter sort of comic theater in the grossest vernacular.

[239] In Arabic *Huwāt*.

[239a] For details see Najm, *al-Masraḥiyya etc.*, pp. 168–189.

[240] Cf. *al-Tamṯīl fī Miṣr nahḍatuh al-jadīda*, in *H*, vol. XXXIII, Nov. 1, 1924, p. 186. Sidky, *Le théâtre arabe*, in *RC*, Feb., 1953 (special issue on mod. Egyptian literature), p. 163. Littmann, in *ZDMG*, vol. LVI, 1902, p. 86, n.

CHAPTER 3

The Post-War Years and Their Actors

a. Abyaḍ and the Classical Theater

In the years immediately preceding the First World War, important developments in the Arab theater began to manifest themselves almost imperceptibly. This process was further accentuated by the War. For the first time in modern history, the Arab Near East was flooded by large European armies and their auxiliaries. Large numbers of the local population were brought into direct daily contact with Europeans of various nationalities, speaking different languages. This contact stirred the interest and imagination of the Arabic-speaking peoples; it certainly quickened their interest in the foreigners' ways and habits; and it probably made them more receptive to the theater in general.

The growing interest of the public expressed itself first and foremost numerically. All classes began to be better represented in the audience. The diversity of the spectators' interests and tastes impelled the playwrights to give them a larger choice. Hence the variety of literary output in the realm of the drama and the change in the general attitude to play-writing. Whilst before the First World War actors were responsible for almost the whole repertoire of the Arab theater, after that War this became the task of many others. First, chronologically, came journalists, printers, and booksellers, all of whom could entertain good hopes of their works getting published and sold. These were soon followed by writers and poets who discovered the drama as a new means of expression. It was through such a particular development that the dramatic literature in Arabic progressed considerably, both in quantity and quality.

In so far as the exponents of this art on the stage were concerned, the most significant advance lay in the growing number of actresses. Isolated experiments in letting women appear on the stage have been already cited. The few actresses were, as has been said, Jewesses or Christians. The conquest of the stage by a not inconsiderable number of Muslim women, some of whom belonged to the best families[241], was a symptom of the Western impact on Near-Eastern society. As such it was one aspect of the campaign for the emancipation of the Muslim women, which gathered momentum after the War. Socially and morally, this was almost a revolution. Previously, self-respecting Muslims would hardly visit a cabaret except on the sly, for its singers and dancers were almost universally held to be in the category of women of doubtful morals. After the First World War, however, anyone could have an opportunity of sitting in one of the first rows at the theater and spending his time, so to say, in the company of some of the most beautiful girls in town, without anybody reproving him on this point. Hence the large number of pretty (rather than gifted) girls attracted to the stage in the post-War years. Hence, too, the springing up of many new troupes instead of the single-troupe-per-town customary in the pre-War years.

The continual growth of troupes and the variety of their performances are among the best indications of the quickening pulse of public interest. To a great extent, this is the merit of the troupe directors, who spare no effort to improve both the quality and number of their performances, material considerations seemingly weighing with them less than in the pre-War years. Probably the noblest efforts towards the improvement of quality were made by the renowned Jūrj Abyaḍ.

Abyaḍ, a Syrian Christian by birth, was one of the few Arab actors of the time who had both talent and feeling for the stage. He was lucky enough to be noticed by 'Abbās II, the then-

[241] See Irma Kraft, *Plays players playhouses international drama of today*, ch. 3, esp. pp. 14–15.

ruling Khedive of Egypt, who sent him to study dramatic art in Paris, and covered all his expenses. In Paris, Abyaḍ went to the *Conservatoire* and studied dramatic art with the renowned actor Sylvain, on whose personality and artistic interpretation the Egyptian was to model his acting for many years to come. Returning to Egypt in 1910, young Abyaḍ formed his own troupe and began to present various plays in earnest.

Abyaḍ, feeling himself suited mainly for the interpretation of tragedies and historical dramas, began with these kinds of plays. The first ones his troupe presented, with great care for the proper clothes and decorations, were Sophocles' *King Oedipus* (translated by Faraḥ Anṭūn), Shakespeare's *Othello*, and Casimir Delavigne's *Louis XI*[242] (translated by Ilyās Fayyāḍ). Abyaḍ played the leading role in each performance, probably imitating Sylvain, and became immediately famous throughout Egypt. The reviewers applauded his acting, and the public the richness of the decorations. There was then an excellent opportunity to use this enthusiasm for improving the tastes of the Egyptian public. This opportunity however was partially lost. Abyaḍ, it appears, was rather conceited and his further success in the interpretation of other historical parts (e.g., Napoleon) blinded him to both his shortcomings and the possibility of molding the taste of his audiences instead of adapting himself to it.

It is not unlikely that Abyaḍ let himself be influenced by his partners, for, beginning with Ḥijāzī, he joined hands with most well-known Egyptian actors. Indeed, strange as it may seem, the curious partnership between Abyaḍ and Ḥijāzī flourished so that for a time two performances were given a day, some of the plays running for as long as a month[243]. Most actors, however, were not too anxious to act in historical dramas and still less in polished tragedies, for which they were not artistically trained. It is also possible that the public clamored, as it so often does, for greater variation in the repertoire. Be that as it

[242] Not, as stated by diverse authors, *Louis IX*.

[243] *The modern Egyptian theatre*, in *B*, fasc. 2, July 1, 1946, p. 11.

may, Abyaḍ gave in. Two years after his return to Egypt, he is already reported to present, among other plays, dramas and melodramas in the vernacular, soon followed by 'Uthmān Jalāl's translations and adaptations of Molière's comedies, of which more later. Other performances included plays and operettas on various topics by local writers, such as the versatile, Syrian-born journalist, playwright, and translator, Faraḥ Anṭūn (1874—1922)[244], and others. Soon afterwards, Abyaḍ had to present even more of this genre, bowing to the public's requests, for his troupe was reduced to financial straits because of the outbreak of the First World War and the enforcement of martial law in the country. Worse still, the Khedive 'Abbās II, the protector of Abyaḍ, was in Constantinople just then and returned to Egypt no more.

True, Abyaḍ continued to present classical dramas, such as Shakespeare's *Macbeth*, Pradon's *Tamerlan*, and Germain and Casimir Delavigne's *Charles VI*, with considerable success. However, his troupe—which could have been the beginning of a classical theater, by European standards—split again and again, sometimes over financial differences, but oftener because of the distribution of parts in the nonclassical plays. For Abyaḍ, blinded by success, insisted on being the star of almost every play. This was a great mistake on his part, for he was not really a character actor. He had the mold of a fine tragic actor, but no more. Even though he remained the dean of the Arab theater in Egypt in post-war years and received well-deserved applause in his tours of Syria, Lebanon, Palestine, Tunisia, and Tripolitania[245], his prestige in Egypt is no more what it once was. There are various reasons for this:

[244] For his life and writings see the commemoration vol. *Faraḥ Anṭūn ḥayātuh wa-ta'bīnuh wa-mukhtārātuh* (1923). Mārūn 'Abbūd, *Faraḥ Anṭūn*, in *K*, vol. II, Nov,. 1947, pp. 1736–1747. *Faraḥ Anṭūn*, in *H*, vol. XXXI, Oct. 1, 1922, pp. 65–67. 'Abbās Maḥmūd al-'Aqqād, *Faraḥ Anṭūn*, in *al-Balāgh*, Mar. 5, 1924. See also below, List of Arabic Plays.

[245] He was less successful, however, in Algeria. For his success elsewhere in North Africa cf. Rizzitano, *op. cit.*, in *OM*, vol. XXIII, June 1943, p. 249, n. 4.

1. As has been explained at some length, Abyaḍ often acted in parts unsuited to his character and talents.

2. The bulk of the public preferred, as it still does, light comedies to tragedies. Abyaḍ's troupe often had to perform an act from a comedy of doubtful merit before *King Oedipus*, in order to attract the public to this excellent tragedy. This sort of addition had been common practice a generation before, with al-Qabbānī's troupe, but one is rather surprised at its continuing necessity.

3. Abyaḍ was too tall and rather stout by the criteria the public had set for its actors; he could not sing, either, a serious drawback for any actor in Egypt.

4. The exaggerated polish given by Abyaḍ to his parts, by dint of endless rehearsals, sometimes made his acting appear artificial; this was even more marked when compared to the studied carelessness of many other members of this troupe.

5. The fact that he was a Christian Syrian by birth was not in Abyaḍ's favor either, particularly with Muslim audiences from the twenties of the twentieth century. After independence had been achieved, the temporary union between Muslims and Copts in Egypt was often set aside; religious and racial differences were on various occasions set ablaze again[246].

The service of Abyaḍ to the theater lies mainly in his awakening the consciousness of the Arab theatergoer, in various countries of the Near East, to the existence and possibilities of the classical theater; and in educating collaborators and pupils to new artistic values, such as the need for exact translation of foreign dramas and serious preparation of every play. They were reminded of this whenever he performed in French or

[246] Muḥammad Taimūr, *op, cit.*, vol. II, pp. 131–143, 144 *ss.*, 149 *ss.*, 161–162, 171, 176, 183, 185, 193, 198, 202, 207, 209, 210, 213, 215 *ss.*, 232, 233, 236 *ss.*, 241–258, 263, 272, 276–277, 281, 285–286, 289, 290 *ss.*, 294, 303–304. *Al-Tamthīl fī Miṣr. Jauq Jūrj Abyaḍ*, in *H*, vol. XX, Apr. 1, 1912, pp. 436–438. *Jauq Abyaḍ*, ibid., vol. XXI, Nov. 1, 1912, pp. 125–126. Cf. ibid., vol. XXII, Apr. 1, 1914, p. 559; vol. XXXIII, June 1, 1925, pp. 906, 908–909. Barbour, *op. cit.*, in *BSOS*, vol. VIII, 1935–1937, pp. 178–179. Landau, *'Al ha-teiaṭrōn etsel ha-'aravīm*, in *Bamah*, fasc. 49, Sep. 1946, pp. 52–53.

appeared again in revivals of his great successes in Arabic[247] and even when he took part in Egyptian films.

b. The Progress of the Musical Theater

One of the main causes for the lukewarm reception of Abyaḍ's troupe was the preference of the Arab theatergoer for the musical theater and for the popular comedy. It has been described how even Abyaḍ had to bow after a time to this taste of the public. Some of Abyaḍ's colleagues and pupils, who shared the public's tastes, became its most revered stars.

It would be wrong to assume, however, that the public, as a whole, lacked the power of constructive criticism. Indeed, the local weeklies and monthlies, and—to a lesser extent—dailies, devoted a gradually increasing space to the problems of the theater, whether related to play-writing, directing, or acting. Various journals dealing exclusively, or almost so, with theatrical arts, appeared sporadically and led a brief existence[248]. They served nevertheless as an incentive to young and old. The senior pupils were apparently so attracted towards acting that in February, 1888, a decree of the Minister of Education forbade them this "unseemly profession," threatening the die-hards with expulsion from school[249]! Their elders took no less an interest, however, in the formation of groups and clubs, dedicated to encourage the Arab theater, discuss its problems, translate plays and perform them. Most of these (starting in 1894 and getting more numerous every year particularly in Alexandria[250]) were, indeed, short-lived; but they served their

[247] See, e.g., Barbour, ibid., p. 181. *A.* (the daily *al-Ahrām*), Feb. 16, 1952, p. 3.

[248] E.g. "The Theater," or, exactly, "Acting" (*al-Tamthīl*)—cf. *H*, vol. VIII, Feb. 15, 1900, p. 319; "Art" (*al-Fann*)—cf. *A*, June 9, 1952, p. 5.

[249] A photograph of this decree, still in *ms.*, was publ. in *AS*, June 22, 1949, p. 14.

[250] Barbour, *op. cit.*, in *BSOS*, vol. VIII, 1935–1937, p. 179. *H*, vol. IV, Dec. 1, 1895, pp. 273–274; June 1, 1896, p. 754; July 1, 1896, p. 836. Ibid., vol. V, Nov. 1, 1896, p. 193; Nov. 15, 1896, p. 233; Dec. 1, 1896, p. 274; Jan. 1, 1897, p. 354; Jan. 15, 1897, p. 393; Mar. 1, 1897, p. 513; Mar. 15, 1897, p. 557; June 1, 1897, p. 754. Ibid., vol. VI, Sep. 15, 1897, p. 32; Dec. 15, 1897, p. 306;

purpose, both by arousing the public and governments to support the theater and by infusing new responsibility into the actors (by dint of criticizing them).

A few of the most prominent Egyptian actors, who formed troupes of their own, deserve special mention[251]. It is to be noted that among these there was already an able woman, Fāṭima Rushdī. After a brief experience with other theatrical companies, she formed her own. Differing in her background from Abyaḍ (she had no foreign training and spoke only Arabic), she played for the masses. Her unaffected acting won their sympathy. Aware of her shortcomings, Fāṭima Rushdī appeared mainly in Muslim costume parts (such as a beggar), even though she succeeded in such diverse parts as Cleopatra in Shauqī's *Maṣra' Kliyūpātrā*, Mark Antony in a translation from Shakespeare, and l'Aiglon in Rostand's play bearing that name. Of the troupe's repertoire, however, the most successful have been the plays rendered in colloquial Arabic, on local topics[252].

More renowned in Egypt (and, particularly, in the other Arab lands) are Yūsuf Wahbī and his confederates. Wahbī's career, in itself, is fairly characteristic of the history of both the Arabic theater in Egypt and its exponents. He was born in a well-to-do Egyptian family of Turkish origin. Notwithstanding his talents, he was not overzealous in his studies at school, for he was already attracted to dramatic art. At the end of the school year, young Wahbī used to perform for his schoolmates various "monologues,"[253] as the imitations of various characters

---

Feb. 15, 1898, p. 468. Ibid., vol. XIII, Dec. 1, 1904, p. 191. Ibid., vol. XXII, May 1, 1914, p. 627. *Mu.*, vol. XLVI, Feb. 1, 1915, pp. 162–163. There is even more material for the years following the First World War.

[251] For the names of less successful actors and their activity, see Barbour, ibid., pp. 177 *ss.* Muḥammad Taimūr, *op. cit.*, vol. II, *passim.*

[252] Barbour, ibid., p. 181.

[253] In modern Arabic literature, "monologues" are a genre by itself. Some have been collected, e.g., in *Munulūjāt Ibrāhīm Jaklā*, Cairo, al-Mak. al-mulūkiyya, n.d.; 32 pp.; and in Sulaimān Ḥasan al-Qabbānī, *Bughyat al-mumaththilīn*, *passim*, esp. pp. 38–118, 126–127.

were termed: Wahbī distinguished himself at the time by imitating a cowardly soldier in a most true-to-life manner. After school, during the First World War, he had begun to achieve some notoriety, when he suddenly disappeared: defying his father's wish, who would not hear of his son becoming a "clown," Wahbī departed secretly for Italy. There he was fortunate enough, in his study of the theater, to be one of the pupils of Chiantoni; it was in Italy that he also met the girl who was to be his first wife, the opera singer Louise Lund.

Wahbī returned to Egypt only after his father's death. Out of his large inheritance he financed some of his projects relating to the development of the Arab theater in Egypt. His first company, "Ramses" (founded in 1923), soon became the public's favorite. Its first performance was *The Madman* (*al-Majnūn*), presumably written by Wahbī himself, but actually adapted by him from the plot of an American film; another story has it that Wahbī compiled the plot from two different French plays. Be this as it may, Wahbī undoubtedly excelled in the leading role, that of the madman himself, just as well as he had excelled in his schooldays in imitating the cowardly soldier. It appears that he had a special knack for interpreting characters suffering from some pathological complex or other.

The second play presented by the Ramses troupe, *The Black Devils* (*al-S̲h̲ayāṭīn al-sūd*), was attended by Ministers and other dignitaries, and its success augured well for the future. However, the membership of the troupe changed many times (although changes were now less frequent than in the years preceding the First World War). Fāṭima Rus̲h̲dī left to found her own troupe and took with her some of her former colleagues. As a result, the somewhat crippled Ramses troupe joined hands with Jūrj Abyaḍ (1926). The divergence in outlook between Abyaḍ, the protagonist of the classical theater in Arabic, and Wahbī, the staunch defender of the Arab musical and social theater, was however too great for the partnership to endure for a long time. Indeed, Wahbī and his Ramses troupe did try, then and afterwards, to present various works by the best European playwrights, such as Henri Bataille, Henri Lavedan, Henry Bernstein, Ernest Feydeau, Tristan Bernard, and others. Thus Wahbī undoubtedly tried to vie with Abyaḍ in the creation of a classical theater in Egypt. Box-office receipts, however, determined the troupe's activity in no little measure. The greatest successes were dramas like *La Dame Aux Camélias*, adapted for the Egyptian public, or doubtful melodramas by Egyptian authors, such as Anṭūn Yazbak's *The Victims* (*al-Ḏhabā'iḥ*)[254]. These were welcomed by the public whose tastes were Wahbī's foremost criterion. Bowing to the public's demands, Wahbī composed also some plays of his own, such as the social drama, *The Secrets of the Castles* (*Asrār al-Quṣūr*)[255], and the comedy, *The Days of War* (*Ayyām al-ḥarb*)[256]—performed by him and his troupe, of course. His personal part in the success of these plays can be appreciated, indeed, only if one remembers that he wrote and produced them, generally starring himself.

Wahbī bowed to the wishes of his audiences probably because of his craving for applause and praise, not from a desire for money. For in 1933 he had divorced his wife, the opera singer, and married a rich Egyptian lady, part of whose money he invested in a new theater (after having closed the Ramses), a cinema hall, a café-concert house, and other establishments. When these did not produce the expected returns, Wahbī agreed to head a government-sponsored troupe, first named the "National Troupe" (*al-Firqa al-qaumiyya*) and then the "Egyptian Troupe" (*al-Firqa al-miṣriyya*)[257]. The difference between the repertoires of the new troupe and of Ramses consisted in the government's demand that only a proportion of the Egyptian

[254] For which cf. *H*, vol. XXXV, Mar. 1, 1927, p. 629. G. Kampffmeyer, *Die Anfänge einer Geschichte der neueren arabischen Litteratur*, in *MSOS*, 1928, part 2, p. 174, n. 1.

[255] *AY* (*Akhbār al-yaum*), Dec. 29, 1951, p. 9; cf. *A*, Dec. 29, 1951, p. 3 and Jan. 3, 1952.

[256] *A*, Apr. 28, 1952, p. 5.

[257] For his £E 100 salary and his 25 per cent part from the proceeds of this troupe, see *RY*, Jan. 5, 1954, p. 42.

Troupe's performances be devoted to melodramas. Although the troupe's rendering of Racine's *Andromaque* and Sophocles' *Antigone*—translated by the brilliant Egyptian man of letters Ṭaha Ḥusain—was welcomed with response and apreciation, this was the exception rather than the rule.

Yūsuf Wahbī, who not only knew how to dominate the stage but also how to bring others over to his views, gradually imposed his personality on the activities of the Egyptian Troupe. This performs of late mostly in colloquial Arabic, mainly melodramas and historical plays enlivened by music. Sometimes, but not frequently, it dabbles in vaudeville shows[258]. It seldom tries now to present a literal translation of a foreign play[259]. In this respect, Wahbī has continued Ḥijāzī's life work and improved upon it. True, Wahbī's most important contribution to the theater was his stress on social problems, in the dramas he both wrote and performed; in this respect, his work was to be copied by many people of smaller stature. However he also gave an impetus to the Arab theater (in contrast to Abyaḍ's conception of it) in its decidedly musical aspect. Ironically enough, Abyaḍ himself was appointed director, for a short time, of the Egyptian troupe (Wahbī being too busy in the film industry)[260]; but he was unable to check the musical trend. The musical theater, after all, has been carried forward by Wahbī's enthusiasm in many places besides Cairo and Alexandria, which were formerly its only centers. Wahbī played not only before special audiences such as the Qaraites in 1941[261], or before the Egyptian soldiers, in the Arab-Israel

[258] Ibid., Mar. 29, 1954, pp. 32–33, for the report of such a show.

[259] Barbour, *op. cit.*, in *BSOS*, vol. VIII, 1935–1937, pp. 180–181. Aḥmad Zakī Abū Shādī, *al-Masraḥ al-miṣrī*, repr. in his *Masraḥ al-adab*, pp. 48–49. *AY*, Dec. 25, 1948, p. 10. For some of the performances of Wahbī and the Egyptian Troupe, see *al-Muṣawwar*, July 9, 1948, p. 41; *AY*, Nov. 24, 1951, p. 6; *AS*, Dec. 5, 1951; *A*, Feb. 14, 1952, p. 3; ibid., Apr. 1, 1952, p. 5; ibid., May 9, 1952, p. 5; ibid., May 29, 1952, p. 5.

[260] *Al-Zamān*, Oct. 21, 1952, p. 4.

[261] Jam'iyyat ziwāj al-faqīrāt li'l-Isrā'īliyyīn al-qarā'īyyīn, *Taqrīr al-jam'iyya 'an al-sana al-ūlā al-muntahiya fī 21 mārs sanat 1941*, p. 5.

war in 1948[262], or the crowds in the political struggle against Great Britain in 1951[263], but also in many Egyptian villages, as well as many towns in other Arab lands. His tours took him through most of the Arabic-speaking peoples: his latest was in Algeria, in 1954. Doubting whether his audiences in Algeria would understand the colloquial Arabic of Egypt, Wahbī re-wrote some of the plays in literary Arabic[264] (common to all Arab countries). His talents, however, seem to have appealed so strongly to the local public that even those of his plays that were performed in the colloquial Arabic of Egypt were largely attended and much appreciated in Alger[265]. Earlier tours had taken his troupe even as far as South America.

c. The Success of the Popular Theater

Along with the failure of Abyaḍ's classical theater and the wide acceptance of Wahbī's musical theater, the popular theater developed rapidly. It has been shown above[266] how this light theater in colloquial Arabic based its repertoire in Egypt on vulgar farces and pantomimes in the nineteenth century; and on rough burlesque, influenced to an extent by the *commedia dell'arte*, in the early twentieth. This popular theater was influenced by foreign revues and light comedies, probably shown to the European troops during the war. Thus impressed, the popular theater in Egypt remains to our days a mixture of the tradition of local humor and showmanship with a strong flavor of West-European means of enlivening this local tradition. The result is somewhat suggestive of modern burlesque[267].

Among the three chief creators of the modern popular theater in Egypt, the oldest was 'Azīz 'Aid. A Syrian by birth, his con-

[262] *Al-Muṣawwar*, July 9, 1948, p. 34.
[263] *A.*, Dec. 11, 1951, p. 8. *Ha-Arets* (Hebrew daily), Dec. 20, 1951, p. 2.
[264] *RY*, May 31, 1954, p. 35.
[265] Cf. the weekly *L'Algérie Libre*, June 18, 1954, pp. 1, 4.
[266] See above, ch. 2, section c.
[267] F. H. H. Roberts, Jr., *Egypt and the Suez Canal* (1943), pp. 12–13.

nection with the theater began early in the twentieth century, when he joined Iskandar Faraḥ's troupe, after its singing star, Ḥijāzī, had left it. He was co-founder of the Ramses troupe in 1923, together with Wahbī, and served as the latter's stage director for some years. When his wife Fāṭima Rushdī left Ramses and formed a troupe of her own, 'Aid joined her and co-starred with her in various musical dramas. His main talent was, however, in the lighter vein, in which he was particularly successful when acting together with the late Bishāra Wākīm[268]. If story-tellers are to be believed, his fame is supposed to have been made in a comedy in which he imitated a provincial '*Umda* (head of village) drinking in a bar frequented by European ladies. Since then he has specialized in contrasting humorously native and foreign characters. 'Aid is considered[269], with justice, as the creator of the so-called "Franco-Arab revue," a sort of full-length French vaudeville[270] somewhat modified for his local audience. He also tried his hand at guignol, at least once; it was called *Kiss in the Dark* (*Qubla fī'l-ẓalām*). 'Aid, notwithstanding his fine artistic sensitiveness, failed for two reasons: 1. he insisted too often on playing the lead, even if he did not suit the part; 2. his vaudeville was not Egyptianized enough for his audience to understand and fully appreciate[271], although 'Aid himself tried hard to create an original, Egyptian sort of vaudeville[272].

These faults of 'Aid—particularly the last-mentioned—were apparently understood by 'Aid's ablest follower and competitor, the gifted Najīb al-Rīḥānī (1891–1949). This born come-

[268] *RY*, Jan. 25, 1954, p. 32.

[269] By the newspaper *al-Sha'b*, Aug. 12, 1933, quoted by Barbour, *op. cit.*, in *BSOS*, vol. VIII, 1935–1937, p. 178, n. 2.

[270] On the vaudeville see, among others, E. Renton, *The vaudeville theatre* (N.Y., 1918).

[271] Barbour, *op. cit.*, in *BSOS*, vol. VIII, 1935–1937, pp. 177–181. Muḥammad Taimūr, in his *op. cit.*, vol. II, pp. 159–167; cf. ibid., pp. 117 *ss.*, 139 *ss.*, 156, 168, 171 *ss.*, 174 *ss.*, 199, 202, 206–211, 214, 215, 218 *ss.*, 237, 246, 303–304.

[272] 'Aziz 'Aid's article on *Risālat al-fann al-masraḥī hiya ta'mīm al-thaqāfa al-'ulyā*, in *H*, vol. XLV, Mar. 1, 1937, pp. 561–563.

dian, nicknamed "the Oriental Molière," was attracted to the theater from his youth, but doubted his own ability. So, while an employee in various financial enterprises, he found an outlet for his marked talents: he amused the other employees, surreptitiously playing various airs by making the office doors screech in time. He started his dramatic career in 1914, and soon afterwards joined the troupe of Ḥijāzī and Abyaḍ. A year later one finds him again in the troupe of 'Azīz 'Aid, from whom he certainly learnt much in what relates to the comic and its interpretation[273]. During the war, always eager for new experiments, he began working simultaneously in a cabaret and, as a supernumerary actor (called in Egypt, in the French fashion, *comparse*), in various foreign plays. It was on the latter occasion that he acted together with such distinguished artists as Sarah Bernhardt, Coquelin, and Mounet-Sully, whose acting he thus could study from near by. Later in life, a stay in France brought him even nearer to the French theater. Al-Rīḥānī began, indeed, with Arabic adaptations from Molière and Marcel Pagnol[274]. He soon passed, however, to original creation. It was then that his immortal "Kis̲h̲-Kis̲h̲ Bey" was created.

Kis̲h̲-Kis̲h̲ Bey was the suggestive name given by al-Rīḥānī to a fictitious Egyptian village elder or '*Umda*—always interpreted on the stage by al-Rīḥānī himself—who passed through various misadventures and whose small talk (in the colloquial Arabic of Egypt) reflected the common-sense attitude of the simple man to all matters concerning world developments, state affairs, social conditions and morals. Kis̲h̲-Kis̲h̲ Bey related his adventures and gave free, unasked-for advice to everyone. In this al-Rīḥānī followed in the steps of his master, 'Azīz 'Aid, and drew his materials from the French vaudeville. However, he changed the material almost completely, by dubbing all his

[273] For this period of al-Rīḥānī's life, see his autobiographical notice in the series *Ta'rīk̲h̲ ḥayātihim bi-aqlāmihim* in the Egyptian weekly *Dunyā'l-fann*, Nov. 19, 1946, p. 13.

[274] For these adaptations see N. Tomiche-Dagher, *Représentations parisiennes du "jeune théâtre algérien,"* in *BE*, Aug. 30, 1952.

characters with Egyptian names and adapting most of it to treat satirically of matters and conditions more or less known to his audience. Among the most frequently used subjects one finds everyday incidents, mishaps of the simple-minded, the cheating of naïve villagers coming to the city, tit-for-tat, the behavior of the flirtatious woman, the spending of public funds (by the village head) on women, and the like[275]. The show was further enlivened by airs, many of which became hits overnight. In this way, he was the real creator of the Egyptian vaudeville, in the teeth of the highbrow attitude of the local critics, who (although unable to dislike al-Rīḥānī[276]) scoffed at this sort of entertainment being called art. He was often imitated, hardly ever equaled[277]; and the popularity of this new genre remains secure today even though its creator has been dead for several years.

In his dramatic work, al-Rīḥānī was associated with two bright script writers whom he inspired and directed. The first, Amīn Ṣidqī, wrote one of al-Rīḥānī's greatest hits, *An Ass and Sweets* (*Ḥimār wa-ḥalāwa*), a farce that had an unprecedented run of four months. His second collaborator, Badī' K͟hairī, who was even closer to him, wrote a good many of al-Rīḥānī's scripts[278], including his best-known vaudeville performance (barring the stereotype Kis͟h-Kis͟h Bey), *Ḥasan, Cohen and Morqoṣ*. This had such a success that it was revived quite a few times[279] and filmed afterwards[280], for it was so well-written and finely acted that everybody liked it, no matter what his religion was, Muslim, Jewish, or Coptic. It is thus that an eyewitness

[275] Orvieto, *op. cit.*, pp. 144–145. Ḥasan Fu'ād, *Fann al-Rīḥānī aulā bi'l-takrīm* in *RY*, June 14, 1954, p. 31. Worrell, in *The Muslim World*, vol. X, 1920, pp. 135–137.

[276] Cf. Ṭaha Ḥusain's review of Rīḥānī's *Silāḥ al-yaum*, in *KM*, fasc. 8, May 1946, pp. 704–705.

[277] *RY*, May 24, 1954, p. 34.

[278] Ṭulaimāt, *al-Masraḥ al-miṣrī fī 'ām*, in *K.*, vol. I, fasc. 9, July 1946, pp. 486–487.

[279] See, e.g., *A.*, July 27, 1952, p. 7.

[280] By S͟hirkat Aflām al-S͟harq al-jadīd, starring Muḥammad Kamāl al-Miṣrī and Stephan Rūstī—cf. *RY*, May 31, 1954, p. 37.

described the three characters of the comedy and their dealings:

"Hassan was the handsome, confident, cultured, well dressed Muslim front for the drug concern, but he had no expertness in anything except how to make friends and establish relations with the government. Cohen was the conservative, careful financier who was the treasurer of the company, but he had little front. Murcus was the Coptic member of this drug company, a slightly dowdy chap, a practical operator. His know-how for getting things done in the community was what made the concern a success. When Murcus made a diplomatic engagement for Hassan, Hassan always appeared and did his job well; when Murcus needed funds for some operation he convinced Mr. Cohen and the funds were forthcoming; but neither Mr. Hassan nor Mr. Cohen could quite get along unless they consulted Mr. Murcus."[281]

The above-described comedy, like the greater part of al-Riḥānī's later work[282], was not without its social implications. It ably satirized the various typical characteristics of the different religious and ethnic groups in Egypt. This frank satire, with malice toward none, made al-Riḥānī one of the best-liked comedy actors of his time, both on the stage and on the screen (to which he devoted much time in his later years[283]). His death was the occasion for national mourning[284], a street was named after him immediately[285], and King Fārūq ordered that a theater bear his name, that his plays be collected and printed by a commission, that the same commission supervise the con-

[281] Courtesy of the Middle East Institute, Washington, D.C.—from W. W. Cleland, *Islam's attitude towards minority groups* in D. S. Franck, *Islam in the modern world a series of addresses* (1951), p. 60. For later performances of this play see, e.g., *A*, Apr. 17, 1952, p. 5, and Apr. 29, 1952, p. 5; also *RY*, Jan. 5, 1954, p. 42, and Jan. 25, 1954, p. 33; also *AY*, Jan. 29, 1949, p. 10.

[282] M. Jacobs, *Naguib el-Rihani*, in *B*, fasc. 18, Nov. 1947, pp. 17–18. Cf. id., ibid., fasc. 37, Aug. 1949, p. 13.

[283] Some of the relevant details in Rus̲h̲dī Kāmil, *S̲h̲ahriyyat al-sīnimā*, in *KM*, fasc. 17, Feb. 1947, pp. 162–163.

[284] For some of the obituaries, cf. *BE*, June 10, 1949, p. 4. *Al-Adīb*, Apr. 1954, pp. 14–18.

[285] *BE*, June 30, 1949, p. 3.

tinuity of al-Rīḥānī's troupe, and that the Egyptian Broadcasting Service broadcast one of his plays every month[286]. Three years later it was decided to distribute a yearly L.E.100 "Rīḥānī Prize" to a distinguished student of the Institute of Dramatic Art and to institute a yearly "Rīḥānī Day" in which one of his plays would be performed at the Opera House[287]. Anyway, al-Rīḥānī's troupe is still performing[288] and has taken an active part in the anti-British campaign of the Egyptian theater in 1951–1952[289]. Its activities have been somewhat cramped, however, by the early death of the troupe's founder and director[290].

Al-Rīḥānī's main competitor in the revue was 'Alī'l-Kassār, whose troupe catered, as it still does, to the same popular audiences. His revues were performed in Arabic at the Casino de Paris, where most shows were staged in French. Besides acting in many melodramas[291], he created a new character, so beloved by the Egyptians, that many came to the Casino only to see his performances. Others heard him on the radio[292]. Named the "Barbarin," this character—a Nubian interpreted by al-Kassār—often in jocular mood, imitated various types. Among these were various foreigners talking Arabic, chiefly the Turkish nobleman, the Greek vegetable vendor and café-owner, the Maltese hawker and the English tourist; even the Shaikh al-Azhar and the bishops did not escape the Barbarin's genial ridicule. Many of al-Kassār's scripts were prepared by the above-mentioned Amīn Ṣidqī, the one-time script writer of al-

[286] Ibid., June 22, 1949, p. 3.

[287] Ibid., June 12, 1952, p. 3. *A.*, June 1, 1952, p. 5. Ibid., June 11, 1952, p. 10. Cf. *RY*, June 14, 1954, pp. 34, 35, for further prizes in his memory.

[288] *A.*, May 29, 1952, p. 5. *M* (*al-Miṣrī*), March 27, 1952, p. 4. Ibid., June 1, 1952, p. 5. *A*, July 20, 1952, p. 7. Ibid., July 27, 1952, p. 7.

[289] *AY*, Dec. 22, 1951, p. 8. *M*, Jan. 17, 1952, p. 5.

[290] For al-Rīḥānī's life and achievements, see Muḥammad Taimūr, *op. cit.*, vol. II, pp. 115–122; cf. ibid., pp. 25–26, 165–166, 183, 230, 244, 248, 256, 257–264, 266 *ss.*, 298, 300. *BE*, June 9, 1949, p. 2. Landau, '*Al ha-teiaṭrōn etsel ha-'aravīm*, in *Bamah*, fasc. 49, Sep. 1946, pp. 54, 59.

[291] See, e.g., the Cairene weekly *al-Rādyū'l-miṣrī*, Jan. 9, 1937, pp. 10–11.

[292] Ibid., Feb. 6, 1937, p. 20.

Rīḥānī[293]; others by the prolific Zakariyā Aḥmad, who already has to his credit some sixty musical plays[294].

While 'Azīz 'Aid tried unsuccessfully to create a comedy theater in Egypt, and al-Rīḥānī was the initiator of the revue (of the vaudeville type), al-Kassār may be seen as the real protagonist of the common popular theater. While al-Rīḥānī's shows featured relatively little music and, where introduced, this was Western-timed, al-Kassār's revues had much more music in them, chiefly singing. This was not Oriental either, but a curious adaptation to Egyptian musical taste, an important contributing factor to their remarkable success. Continuing the activity of the farce performers and *faṣl muḍḥik* enactors[295], al-Kassār had no regular theater of his own, but wandered about in various towns and villages, tuning the audiences' ears to the fine, sharp tongue of the Barbarin[296]. His death was a heavy loss to the Egyptian popular theater.

d. The Government and the Public

The Egyptian Government takes some interest in the advancement of the Arab theater. This finds expression in a variety of ways:

1. Distribution of prizes. The above-mentioned instance of the prize instituted by the King on al-Rīḥānī's death[297] is not unusual. Other prizes have often been given for distinguished play-writing. This is generally done on a competitive basis every few years. In the year 1926, for instance, four prizes were

[293] On al-Kassār and his activity, see Barbour, *op. cit.*, in *BSOS*, vol. VIII, 1935–1937, p. 182. For his performances cf., for instance, *al-Muṣawwar*, June 11, 1948, p. 33 and July 9, 1948, p. 36; and Fatma Nimet Rachid, in *BE*, Mar. 23, 1939.

[294] *AJ* (*al-Akhbār al-jadīda*), July 14, 1952, p. 8.

[295] See above, pp. 72–73.

[296] Other actors, who have distinguished themselves more on the screen than on the stage, will be dealt with below, in Part 3, The Arab Cinema.

[297] See the previous section.

distributed for acting and recitation[298]. In 1932, no less than 143 plays in classical Arabic (for the colloquial was banned this time) were submitted[299] for a play-writing competition.

2. Grant of scholarships. Several young men of promise have been sent in the last few years to study dramatic art abroad, chiefly in France and England[300]. Although not all of them have proved to be truly talented (these were given then small parts only), some have become central figures in the local theater. The best-known among the latter is probably Zakī Ṭulaimāt, the veteran stage director and lecturer on dramatic art. He was sent to study at the Odéon in 1924 and since his return four years later his name has been connected with almost every attempt for the improvement of the theater. Another Egyptian student who has lately won high distinction, at the London Academy of Dramatic Art, is 'Alī Fahmī[301]. He seems a possible prospect for continuing the work of the ageing Ṭulaimāt.

3. Support of dramatic schools. The first school of dramatic arts worth the name was founded in 1930, with forty students of both sexes, under the direction of the above Zakī Ṭulaimāt. Among his colleagues was Ṭaha Ḥusain, whose translations of *Andromaque* and *Antigone* have already been mentioned. He lectured on the history of the drama, while other courses included Arabic literature, declamation, general theater technique, decoration, lighting, make-up, dancing, physical culture, and French. Although the school was closed by the government a year afterwards, it was supplanted by free lectures on the dramatic arts and later by a special institute, which

[298] *H*, vol. XXXIV, May 1, 1926, opp. p. 785.

[299] Names of the winners and their plays see in Barbour, *op. cit.*, *BSOS*, vol. VIII, 1935–1937, p. 184. See also *KM*, fasc. 9, June 1946, p. 178.

[300] See, for details, Habib Moutran, *La troupe nationale égyptienne et Khalil Bey Moutran*, in the Cairene *La Semaine Egyptienne*, vol. XXII, Nos. 23–24, 1948, p. 25.

[301] *Student of the drama*, in *B*, fasc. 45, May–June 1950, pp. 27–28.

copied a good part of its programme from the above[302]. These were apparently sponsored by the government.

4. Financing of theater troupes and actors. Sums of money are distributed, almost yearly, to the various troupes and some of their actors, the principle usually (but not always) being need. The funds allocated are not great, and are usually niggardly when compared to those allocated for the encouragement of foreign troupes[303]. This of course gives rise to criticism by the troupes and people connected with the theater. The dramatic critics, who often lash out at the faults of the theater (chiefly at the plot, with less understanding for the subtleties of acting), attribute many of them to the lukewarmness of the government's support.

The public to which the Arab theater appeals is still limited in number, even though Egypt and the Arab lands of the Near East are well populated. The European-educated class, viz. the aristocracy and upper bourgeoisie, scorn the Arab theater, considering it underdeveloped as compared to European standards. The rural population and the lower strata in the towns are more attracted to the popular theater of al-Rīḥānī's or al-Kassār's type than to the musical theater of Wahbī's, although they frequent the latter willingly when it presents plays in colloquial Arabic. The lower bourgeoisie, the government employees, and the educated artisans are the audience which the Arab theater in Egypt may hope to draw. These would probably attend almost equally the popular and musical theater, possibly preferring the latter when it presents historical plays, appealing to

[302] For further recommendations, see *A*, Apr. 11, 1930, summarized by M.N. (Maria Nallino), in *OM*, vol. X, Apr. 1930, p. 184. Cf. also Rizzitano, *op. cit.*, ibid., vol. XXIII, June 1943, pp. 252–254. Habib Moutran, *op. cit.*, in *La Semaine Egyptienne*, vol. XXII, Nos. 23–24, 1948, p. 25.

[303] For some of these sums, Barbour, *op. cit.*, in *BSOS*, vol. VIII, 1935–1937, p. 184. *Al-Muqaṭṭam*, Jan. 22, 1929, summarized by E.R. (Ettore Rossi), in *OM*, vol. IX, Mar. 1929, p. 145. *Al-Balāgh*, July 4, 1935, summarized by E.R., in *OM*, vol. XV, July 1935, pp. 340–341. *BE*, July 27, 1942, summarized by V.V. (Virginia Vacca), in *OM*, vol. XXII, Nov., 1942, p. 479. *Al-Muṣawwar*, Nov. 12, 1948, p. 50.

their nationalistic feelings. However, very few remain to attend the classical theater of the Abyaḍ type (another of the reasons for its failure). One can understand more easily, therefore, why the Egyptian troupes, unable to enlarge their repertoire *ad infinitum* and present a new play every week, regularly tour the Arab countries of the Near East and North Africa; some of these tours have reached the Arab emigrants in South America, too[304]. These tours have assisted, by the interest they stirred, the revival and progress of the theater in the Arab lands outside Egypt.

e. The Arab Theater in Other Lands

The tours of the Egyptian troupes owed their success in other Arabic-speaking lands, in a great measure, to the fact that the local theater had not yet reached the same level. It has been shown above[305] how there was a certain continuity in the Arab theater in Syria throughout the second half of the nineteenth century. Nevertheless, the brightest Syrian actors and some of the playwrights were attracted by the possibilities offered them in Egypt, so that even up to now the Arab theater in Syria has not yet fully recovered from this bloodletting. Amongst other Arabic-speaking peoples, from Iraq to Morocco, there have been signs of the beginnings of an Arab theater (besides the shadow play) at the end of the nineteenth century. This has shown only a modest amount of progress in our times. Foreign influences—British in Iraq and Jordan, French in most other countries—have pervaded this theater as regards play-writing, acting, decoration, costumes, etc. However, in most respects, conditions everywhere followed closely the Egyptian pattern. This applies to the general character of this theater (musical and popular), as well as to its peculiar adaptation of foreign

[304] Barbour, ibid., pp. 184–186. Landau *'Al ha-teiaṭrōn etsel ha-'aravīm,* in *Bamah,* fasc. 47, Jan., 1946, p. 52. See also above, p. 77.

[305] See above, ch. 2, section a.

plays and, even more, to the general attitude of government and public to the theater.

While in Syria and Lebanon there exists a continual and fruitful activity in dramatic literary output[306], only a few plays get performed and even then by amateurs. These have a hard time competing with the French troupes, some of the most distinguished of which tour there regularly[307] (not to mention the frequent visits of the Egyptian troupes[308]). This competition is doubly difficult, since a relatively great proportion of the population is literate in Syria and Lebanon (particularly in the latter, probably some 75 per cent), French-educated or French-influenced. The Jesuit Fathers, who had such a large share in educating the older generation, gave them a keen apreciation of the French theater (a symbolical play, *Monsieur Bob'le*, written in French by the Lebanese Georges S̲h̲ahāda, was favorably received even when performed in Paris[309]). The younger generation, however, is in part attracted to performances of Arabic plays. This usually applies to the less educated, who are the patrons of local troupes such as that of the humorist 'Abd al-Majīd Abū Laban, self-styled "Cecil de Mille of the Near East[310]." The trend is, moreover, encouraged by the local press which makes efforts to encourage the Arab theater. However, this is done sporadically, for example when the novelist K̲h̲aldūn Sāṭi' al-Ḥuṣarī contributed a sum of money to be rewarded by the *al-Maks̲h̲ūf* weekly newspaper to the local author of the best-written one-act play[311].

The Iraqi government appears to assist the Arab theater more than the Syrian and Lebanese authorities (but less than the

[306] See below, List of Arabic Plays.

[307] E.g., for the year 1947, see Georges Duhamel, *Consultation aux pays d'Islam* (1947), pp. 56–57. Cf. the Egyptian daily *PE* (*Le Progrès Egyptien*), Sep. 12, 1947, p. 4.

[308] See, e.g., *RY*, Aug. 23, 1954, p. 35.

[309] *BE*, Dec. 12, 1951, p. 2.

[310] See the Beirut weekly *al-Ṣayyād*, May 27, 1954, p. 29.

[311] *Al-Bilād*, Feb. 6, 1940, reported by L.V.V. (Laura Veccia Vaglieri) in *OM*, vol. XX, March, 1940, p. 153.

Egyptian). It has demonstrated its interest repeatedly: It sent the dean of Iraqi actors, Ḥaqqī'l-S̲h̲iblī, (later head of the Institute of Arts in Baghdad), to study dramatic art in Paris; it exempted some troupes from paying a part of the taxes, helped others with funds, and distributed awards to playwrights[312]. One can therefore hardly wonder that the Iraqi schools are interested in theatrical performances[313] or that various troupes of amateurs are fairly active[314]. Three professional troupes are competing at present for the favors of the Baghdad audiences.

Dramatic literary output, although less prolific than the Egyptian or Syro-Lebanese, is still noteworthy. The most important playwright was, until his recent death, Jamīl Ṣidqī' l-Zahāwī. His best play is *Lailā and Samīr* (*Lailā wa-Samīr*), a six-act drama of romantic love and dark intrigue in early twentieth-century Baghdad, when the Ottoman Empire was crumbling and the younger generation striving for constitutional rights. After al-Zahāwī's death, an increasing number of plays show a clear-cut tendency to treat of social problems; maybe this is why both publication and production of plays is closely supervised by the government. One of the best living playwrights and actors seems to be Yūsuf al-'Ānī, who has recently published in Baghdad a collection of three plays with a marked tendency for social reform[314a].

Many of the plays published or produced in Iraq are translations, mainly from English, which has remained the most important foreign language even in independent Iraq. In the Kingdom of Jordan, though English is commonly known, one hears of hardly any translations from this or any other foreign

[312] *Al-'Irāq*, Feb. 15, 1936 and *al-Balāg̲h̲*, Feb. 21, 1936, both reported by L.V.V., in *OM*, vol. XVI, Mar., 1936, p. 153.

[313] See, e.g., *Liwā' al-istiqlāl*, Mar. 26, 1952, p. 2.

[314] Such as the "Cultural Society for the Theater and Cinema" (*al-Jam'iyya al-t̲h̲aqāfiyya li'l-tamt̲h̲īl wa'l-sīnimā*)—cf. the Iraqi daily *al-Ak̲h̲bār*, Apr. 16, 1952, p. 2.

[314a] Rev. in *al-Adīb*, vol. XXVII, Mar. 1955, pp. 59–62.

language. Indeed, the output of plays is very limited in Jordan: of these only few have been published, such as Muḥammad Mamīsh's *The Prisoner* (*al-Asīr*, prob. 1933)[315] and not many more presented on the stage. There are very few companies, and these all amateurish and short-lived, such as "The Theatrical Renascence Troupe" (*Firqat al-nahḍa al-masraḥiyya*)[316]. This is partly due to the fact that certain promising actors have left the stage for the screen, for instance, Ibrāhīm Hémō, now in Hollywood[316a]. The audiences are partly illiterate and very small, so that the troupes have to limit their activities to the country's little capital, 'Ammān (population 130,000), and even much smaller Rām-Allāh (pop. 25,000). In the last few years, however, it appears that there has been some intensification of interest in the theater, probably brought about by the Arab refugees. Under their pressure, political sketches and plays (bearing names such as *The Tragedy of Palestine*[317]) are being performed off and on, in various Jordanian towns. Other plays, as elsewhere, are broadcast in sketch form[317a].

In Saudi Arabia, Yemen, and the smaller Arab principalities, religious feeling runs so strongly that plays are still performed very infrequently and only by amateurs. When, in the year 1910, a school of crafts at Medina arranged the charity performance of a play (about the horrors of despotism and the benefits of constitutional rule, in the spirit of the times), the attempt[318] caused considerable amazement and appears not to have been repeated. Even when a writer from Saudi Arabia, a certain 'Alī Aḥmad Bākthīr (who was to gain later fame as a prolific playwright), wrote his first play, he had to publish it in Cairo (1934). Named *Chivalrous or in the Capital of the Sands* (*Humām au fī 'āṣimat al-aḥqāf*), it would probably have been

[315] Reported in *H*, vol. XLII, Jan. 1, 1934, p. 378.
[316] The Jordanian daily *Filasṭīn*, May 17, 1952, p. 4; *al-Nidā'*, July 5, 1955.
[316a] *al-Jihād*, Mar. 5, 1956, p. 3.
[317] Cf. M. Asaf, in *HH*, vol. I, No. 3, Apr. 1950, p. 188.
[317a] Various instances are reported by *al-Jihād*, Dec. 25, 1955, p. 3.
[318] *RMM*, vol. XII, 1910, pp. 306–307, based on *al-Mu'ayyad* of May 19, 1910.

deemed dangerous in the author's homeland, not only because of its play-form but also because it called for the general education of the Arab woman, in whose illiteracy the playwright sees the cause for his people's low standards of civilization[319].

Another reason for the nonexistence of the theater in the Arabian Peninsula is the limited scope of the European influence in that region. This probably accounts also for the low status of the Arab theater in Libya (Cyrenaica and Tripolitania), where it is practically nonexistent. In Sudan, after the nationalist playwright Muḥammad Taufīq Wahbī[320] had been exiled by the local British authorities[321], soon after the First World War, there does not seem to have been any significant theatrical activity.

In French North Africa the theater is slightly more developed than in the Arabian Peninsula, although by no means up to the Egyptian standard. There, again, the inhabitants of the countryside, on one hand, are too religious-minded and primitive to care for the theater. On the other hand, the town dwellers are permeated with French culture to such an extent that the educated strata prefer French shows. This state of affairs is remindful of the situation in Syria and Lebanon. In these two, however, the tradition of the Arab theater, dating from the nineteenth century, as well as the revival of Arabic literature, have succeeded in counteracting, to an extent, the overpowering predominance of the French theater. These particular conditions, unfortunately for the progress of the Arab theater, are lacking in French North Africa. Even the French authorities appeared to feel some responsibility for the lowly status of the Arab theater in their areas. Therefore, a short while ago, a project was considered officially for the foundation of a *Conservatoire* in Arabic, whose main aim would be to en-

[319] Reported in *Mu.*, vol. LXXXV, Oct. 1, 1934, p. 256, where I think "Bākīr" should read "Bākṯẖīr."

[320] For whose three plays see below, List of Arabic Plays.

[321] See *al-Muṣawwar*, Mar. 5, 1954, p. 28.

courage the development of the Arab theater in North Africa[322].

There is only scant theatrical activity in Tunisia, even though some translations and adaptations from the European dramatic literature are occasionally being published, for example, Tolstoy's *Rule of Darkness* (*Sulṭān al-ḍalāl*), translated by Muḥammad al-Mus̲h̲īr[323]. Only a few journals devote enough space to the theater's problems[324]; even the Tunis Broadcasting Station, although it invited Egyptians to give performances, did not particularly encourage local troupes of professional actors or amateurs[325]. Therefore, one need hardly wonder that Tunisian troupes cannot often find receptive audiences. Even the consent of the able Zakī Ṭulaimāt, the Egyptian theater critic[326], to organize a Tunisian troupe on the spot[327], does not seem to have altered matters greatly. He found in the town of Tunis eight troupes out of whose members he chose his own troupe, after having enlisted the support of the religious circles. He was then encouraged with funds by the Town Council. Even so, and notwithstanding the signal success of an Arabic rendering of *The Merchant of Venice* in 1954, Ṭulaimāt prophesied cautiously that some five years would be needed to train a truly able troupe in Tunisia[328].

The same discouraging conditions prevail in Morocco too, notwithstanding the development of Moroccan popular literature in other fields[329]. When a local Jew, Samuel, composed a

[322] See the Parisian weekly *Le Monde Arabe*, Sep. 21, 1951, p. 14. Cf. Landau, *The Arab theatre*, in *MEA*, vol. IV, Mar., 1953, p. 85.

[323] *H*, vol. XX, Nov. 1, 1911, p. 128.

[324] Ibid., vol. XXXI, July 1, 1923, p. 1104, mentions a satirical weekly named *The Actor* (*al-Mumat̲h̲t̲h̲il*).

[325] *L'Algérie Libre*, Oct. 23, 1954, p. 2, mentions the invitation extended to Kamāl Barakāt, the Egyptian actor and scene director. On local troupes see L.V., in the *Revue des Études Islamiques*, vol. VI, 1932, pp. 541–544.

[326] See below, the end of the present chapter.

[327] *RY*, Feb. 15, 1954, p. 33.

[328] *Al-Fann fī Tūnis*, ibid., May 24, 1954, p. 42.

[329] For which see H. Duquaire, *Anthologie de la littérature marocaine arabe et berbère* (Paris, Plon, 1943).

drama on the religious persecution of one of the community's most remarkable women, Sol (Zulaik̲h̲a), he chose to write it in Spanish[330]. Even the fact that some youths with artistic inclinations have, in recent years, translated and presented Molière's *L'Avare*[331] does not change the basic situation. Only in Algeria, which, until recently, was less troubled by internal political strife than her eastern and western neighbors, has the Arab theater developed somewhat more visibly.

The Algerian theater, before the First World War, had two forms only, the *Karagöz* and the farce, those components of the Egyptian theater before Khedive Ismāʿīl's times. After the War, Algerian audiences—who had had some occasion to see the dramatic performances of good French troupes at the local Opera House—showed signs of being bored with the local rudimentary theater, even though women and children still seemed to like it. Jūrj Abyaḍ, bringing his own troupe from Egypt, presented two historical plays by Najīb al-Ḥaddād (of whom more will bę said soon). Then a local troupe tried its luck, by giving performances of three social dramas by Ṭāhir ʿAlī S̲h̲arīf and others. When both experiments failed because the audiences could not grasp classical Arabic well enough, some attempts were made to revive the farce in the colloquial Arabic of Algeria. However, since the farce's humor was too much in the raw, the innovators turned to the comedy. Two names should be mentioned in this connection, Ksenṭīnī and Muḥī'l-Dīn.

Born in Alger in the year 1887, Ras̲h̲īd Ksenṭīnī fled from the Koranic studies imposed upon him, to become one of the most colorful Algerian figures of our times. He sailed to America and the Far East, worked in the armament industry in France, and returned to Alger, where he earned his livelihood by woodcarving. Dissatisfied with what he considered a dreary life,

---

[330] A. Hōrs̲h̲ī, *Sōl ha-qedōs̲h̲a mi-Marōqō* in the Tel-Aviv Hebrew daily *Davar*, June 9, 1950, p. 3.
[331] D. Valdaran, *La nouvelle élite musulmane en Afrique du Nord*, in *L'Islam et l'Occident*, Cahiers du Sud, 1947, p. 207.

Ksenṭīnī formed a troupe in 1926 with which he started performing various farces. These, as has been said previously, were no longer popular in the towns; so he toured the countryside, reaping acclamation everywhere. His ambition, however, made him yearn for the admiration of the urban crowds. For their sake, in the main, he composed (until his death in 1944) various delightful comedies of character, such as *My Cousin from Istanbul*. It was then that the audiences discovered that under his clownish exterior, Ksenṭīnī hid an artistic temperament, both creative and interpretative[332].

Ksenṭīnī's life work was exploited to good purpose by a singer, Bāsh̲ṭarzī Muḥī'l-Dīn, who turned actor and playwright in 1930. If Ksenṭīnī may be called the creator of the modern popular theater in Algeria, Muḥī'l-Dīn deserves to be termed its main promoter and the creator of the Algerian musical theater, at one and the same time. He first presented plays as a singer, with a simple plot filled with climactic adventures and embellished by songs. This was according to the Egyptian fashion, but Muḥī'l-Dīn employed, naturally enough, Algerian tunes. While most of the early plays composed and performed by Muḥī'l-Dīn were thus only a sequence of scenes connected by melodies, his later work developed the Algerian comedy of manners (as compared to Ksenṭīnī's proficiency in the comedy of character). His plays, such as *A Marriage by Telephone*, were illustrations of family or street life. Other comedies tried to point out some moral, while still others depicted the main dangers to clean family life in the Algerian society: the too rapid Europeanization, riches dishonestly come by, social inequality, ignorance of the masses, etc. Muḥī'l-Dīn tried his hand also at adapting some of Molière's comedies. He abbreviated *L'Avare* to three acts and made the character a parsimonious Muslim bourgeois, who was persecuted by his family and servants until he revealed to them the hiding-place of his money. *Le Malade Imaginaire* was

[332] For further details R. Bencheneb, *Rachid Ksentini*, in *Documents Algériens, Série Culturelle*, No. 16, Apr. 15, 1947.

rendered more faithfully to the original, although cut down to only two acts[333]. In the season of 1952–1953, the Algerian theater, under the direction of Muḥī'l-Dīn, was to produce at the Opera House of Alger no less than sixteen different plays, of which two were to be by the director himself. Others had been written by Egyptian or local playwrights; the adapted translations included Sophocles' *Antigone*, Shakespeare's *Hamlet*, Jules Romain's *Knock*, and Rostand's *Cyrano de Bergerac*[334].

With such a growing repertoire, no wonder that the Algerian theater progressed, particularly after Muḥī'l-Dīn had become head of the Arab theater performing in the Opera House at Alger. With the co-operation of some younger playwrights and actors, such as Muṣṭafā Badī', he composed and presented an ever-growing number of dramas and comedies for the stage and the radio. A tour in France in 1951, under the direction of Badī', had already attracted some attention[335]. Another troupe of Algerian amateurs had been welcomed too, shortly after they presented a social comedy in Arabic, *Whose Fault Is It?*[336] So one understands why even Yūsuf Wahbī, visiting Alger with his troupe in 1954, expressed his satisfaction at the progress of the Arab theater there[337]. Further hope for the development of this theater may be found in the financial support (inadequate though it is) granted to it by the municipality of Alger[338].

One of the interesting features of the Arab theater is its existence in non-Arab countries, which have a sizable Arab minority. The State of Israel and the Americas are, perhaps, the best example. The Palestinian Arabs, under the rule of the British mandate, had their own theater, modeled to a great extent after the Arab theater in Egypt. Even though a certain number

[333] For further details see id., *Aspects du théâtre arabe en Algérie*, in *Cahiers du Sud*, 1947, pp. 271–276.
[334] *BE*, Nov. 1, 1952, p. 3.
[335] Ibid., ibid. Also *Un conservatoire de langue arabe*, in *Le Monde Arabe*, Sep. 21, 1951, p. 14. *Le théâtre nord-africain à Paris*, ibid., Dec. 17, 1951, p. 10.
[336] N. Tomiche-Dagher, *op. cit.*, in *BE*, Aug. 30, 1952.
[337] The Algerian weekly, *L'Algérie Libre*, June 18, 1954, pp. 1, 4.
[338] Ibid., Oct. 8, 1954, p. 2.

of plays had been composed by local playwrights[339]—of which only a few have been printed, mainly those of Naṣrī'l-Jauzī and Jamīl Baḥrī[340]—they were not performed as a rule by the local troupes. The latter, great in number[341] and amateurish in technique, generally preferred translations and adaptations of English and French plays. Very seldom was any play performed more than once. The Arab-Israel war in 1947–1948 interrupted the progress of this theater, as many of its exponents left the country, to give an impetus (as has been explained previously) to the development of the theater in Jordan. Lately, however, there have been signs of a revival of this theater, chiefly in Nazareth. This is proceeding at a fairly slow pace, despite the hearty co-operation of some newly immigrated Egyptian Jews. These, led by Matthew I͟shma''elī, have had some real theatrical experience in Egypt. To judge by their first production, *Talisman from India* (a play in Arabic about the life of Oriental immigrants in the State of Israel), they are bringing a contribution that augurs well for the development of an Arabic theater in this state[342]. Some Iraqi Jews, with acting experience, have also been trying their hand at producing Arabic plays there recently. Their first experiment, the production of S͟hauqī's *Majnūn Lailā* (October, 1956), proved successful.

339 Further details see in Landau, *'Al ha-teiaṭrōn etsel ha-'aravīm*, in *Bamah*, fasc. 50, Jan. 1947, pp. 107–111. Id., *ha-Teiaṭrōn ha-'aravī be-Erets-Israel ba-s͟hana-ha-aḥarōna*, ibid., fasc. 52, Dec. 1947, p. 43.

340 On al-Baḥrī's plays see *H*, vol. XXVIII, Oct. 1–Nov. 1, 1911, p. 174 and May 1, 1920, p. 752; ibid., vol. XXXII, Dec. 1, 1923, p. 325 and June 1, 1924, p. 997; *Mu.*, vol. LXIV, Mar. 1, 1924, p. 348. For other plays of Palestinian Arabs see, besides Landau, *op. cit.*, in the previous footnote, *H*, vol. XXXI, Apr. 1, 1923, p. 779; ibid., vol. XL, Aug. 1, 1932, p. 1482. *Mu.*, vol. LXIII, July 1, 1923, p. 92; ibid., vol. LXXXI, Oct. 1, 1932, p. 371. Cf. below, List of Arabic Plays.

341 Naṣrī'l-Jauzī, in his *Kaifa nanhaḍ bi'l-masraḥ al-Filasṭīnī?* in *al-Hadaf*, Apr. 21, 1946, p. 11, spoke of more than thirty troupes in Jerusalem alone. They bore such proud names as *al-Nahḍa*, *al-Raqy*, *al-Taqaddum*, *Iḥyā' al-funūn*.

342 R. Bas͟han, in the Tel-Aviv Hebrew evening newspaper, *Yĕdī'ōt Aḥarōnōt*, Jan. 2, 1952, p. 3. Contrast, however, with the Nazareth monthly, *al-Mujtama'*, vol. II, Mar. 1955, p. 14. See also G. Weigert, *Actor-playwright from Cairo*, in *JP*, Dec. 21, 1955, p. 4.

In the Americas, the Arab theater found expression mainly in the writing of plays. There appears to be no regular theatrical activity amongst the large communities of Arab immigrants in South and North America. Performances are given only at great intervals, even though touring Egyptian companies are given impressive ovations. One of the reasons for this welcome to foreign companies, performing local plays, is the sentimental ties of these communities with their homeland; another is the activity of their men-of-letters, many of whom continue to devote their days to Arabic literature. Among their output, Arab dramas have a part, chiefly in the Argentine[343], Brazil[344] and the United States[345]. Many of these are translations of André Gide, Alphonse Daudet or François Coppée; it is amazing how little of the dramatic literature of the peoples among whom they live has been translated. Most of the original plays are historical, often describing the Arabs' struggle against Turkish oppression in the last generation before the First World War[346]. One can understand the importance of this subject for these playwrights, for, after all, they (or their parents) had emigrated mainly because of this oppression.

The Arab theater, whose development has been sketched in this chapter in terms of theater troupes and their actors, has seen the emergence of some main characteristics since the years immediately following the First World War until today. These may be taken stock of as follows:

1. The Arab theater has made progress particularly in Egypt, while everywhere else it has reached, at the utmost, the level of the Egyptian theater before the First World War, after passing through much of the same stages of development.

[343] For names of authors and their plays, see, e.g., *Mu.*, vol. LXXXV, Oct. 1, 1924, p. 256 (two plays). *H*, vol. XLI, Jan. 1, 1933, p. 412. See also below, footnote 346.

[344] *H.*, vol. XXIX, May 1, 1921, p. 815.

[345] *Mu.*, vol. XL, May 1, 1912, p. 509.

[346] E.g., K̲h̲alīl Ibrāhīm al-Nabbūṭ's *Wat̲h̲bat al-ʿArab*, reviewed in *H*, Jan. 1, 1937, p. 354 and *Mu.*, vol. XCI, Oct. 1, 1937, p. 375. See also below, List of Arabic Plays.

2. It falls into three main categories—classical, musical and popular—of which only the last two are appreciated and attended by the masses.

3. The troupe directors have raised—mainly because of competition[347]—the standard of their performances. Commercial considerations have become less all-important than hitherto and management of theater finances[348] has improved.

4. Actors and actresses (the latter of whom had at last insured their proper place on the stage[349]) are not only amateurs. Although these still try their luck, there is a steadfastly growing number of professional actors and actresses. They are usually bound to their troupes by contracts, which take after the European form. After years of experience they retire on a regular pension[350].

5. Singing and dancing continue to be important attributions of the actor. However, he is nowadays expected to act well, too. Unfortunately for the effect, the music does not accompany the acting, nor is it employed to shape the mood of the audience according to the play[351]. It is still often used to enliven the play and bridge over various scenes.

6. Since the actor must sing, dance, and act well, he cannot be proficient, at one and the same time, at stage direction and production. Studies in Europe and to a lesser extent in the United States have brought forward specialists in these various fields[352], so that it is not one person alone who covers them all (even though he may have more than one part in a play). The High Institute of Dramatic Art, under the able direction of

[347] For various competing troupes see above, ch. 2, c. Also *A*, July, 27, 1952, p. 7; *al-Zamān*, Aug. 30, 1952, p. 2.

[348] On which see, e.g., M. Epstein, *Das Theater als Geschäft*, esp. chs. 2–9.

[349] See the arts section in *al-Ṣayyād*, May 27, 1954, p. 28.

[350] Cf. *al-Nidā'*, July 22, 1952, p. 8 for the pensioned retirement of Zainab Ṣidqī, 'Abd al-Majīd Shukrī and Munsī Fahmī (with short biographical notes). See also *AJ*, July 14, 1952, p. 8.

[351] See 'Uthmān al- 'Antablī, *al-Masraḥ al-miṣrī yamūt*, in *M*, Dec. 8, 1952.

[352] None the less, these remain the weak points of the Arab theater. For some of the problems involved, see C. B. Purdom, *Producing plays a handbook for producers and players* (1930) and H. Nelms, *Play production* (1950).

Zakī Ṭulaimāt, instructed actors who cannot study abroad. Various projects exist for its development[353].

7. Egyptian troupes with growing frequency visit neighboring Arab lands, influencing the local theaters and inadvertently forging another link between the various Arabic-speaking peoples, otherwise of divergent political and economic interests.

8. As a rule, the behavior of the public has improved considerably, even among the audiences of the popular theater. Proper bearing during the performances is becoming fairly customary, even if this is not always up to European or American standards[353a]. The education of the public in this respect has been begun, and rightly so, with the school children. The above Ṭulaimāt is responsible for this to an extent, too. After the revolution of 1952, a stricter censorship on school plays was imposed by the Ministry of Education[354]. Of course the standards of these amateurish troupes, even at the Universities, is still rather low[355], as not enough has yet been done to raise their artistic level[356].

9. Dramatic criticism has progressed somewhat in quality and even more in quantity: journals and dailies[357] regularly devote space to serious reviews of the Arab theater and to lengthy, bold discussions of its problems[358].

10. Play-writing has spread, from amateurish actors and troupe directors to the poets, writers, and other men of letters.

[353] See *al-Akhbār al-jadīda*, Oct. 29, 1952, p. 8. The Institute is named *al-Ma'had al-'ālī li'l-tamthīl*. Ṭulaimāt was also the head of a public Higher Committee for the Theater (*al-Lajna al-'ulyā li'l-masraḥ*)—cf. *al-Nidā'*, Apr. 8, 1952, p. 6.

[353a] F. J. Bonjean, *Une renaissance égyptienne*, in the monthly *Europe* (Paris), vol. I, fasc. 5, June 15, 1923, pp. 83 *ss.*

[354] *AL*, Sep. 3, 1952, p. 3. The supervision of play performances in schools was already extant at the time of the revolution—cf. *al-Nidā'*, July 22, 1952, p. 8.

[355] See Muḥammad Aḥmad 'Īsā's severe criticism in *al-Zamān*, Sep. 6, 1952, p. 4.

[356] For what can be done to encourage theater shows in school, see, e.g., K. A. Ommanncy, *The stage and the school* (1932). For some ways to improve amateur performances, see H. Ferris, *Producing amateur entertainments* (1921).

[357] An incomplete list of organs of the press particularly interested in the theater is given by Rizzitano, *op. cit.*, in *OM*, vol. XXIII, June, 1943, p. 254.

[358] For an example see 'Antablī, *op. cit.*, in *M*, Dec. 8, 1952.

Only seldom are plays "adapted" nowadays; a pedantic translation is generally demanded. The number and scope of original plays, too, have grown. This aspect, however, due to its momentous part in the development of the theater, deserves to be treated in greater detail.

CHAPTER 4

The Plays and Their Themes

a. TRANSLATIONS

1. *General Characteristics* As in other literatures, dramatic output in Arabic falls naturally into two main categories—translations and original plays.

It has already been mentioned that in the early days of the Arab theater, approximately from its beginnings up to the First World War, most translated plays were "adapted" for the benefit of the audiences. Transposition of the plot to surroundings known to the theater's patrons was not uncommon in the early days of other theaters, such as the Roumanian[359]. This, however, necessitated also the changing of place names and the names of the *dramatis personae*, sometimes quite ingeniously (Othello appeared as 'Aṭā' Allāh). These somewhat startling ways of adaptation are indicative of the low cultural standard of those who attended Arabic performances of the Egyptian stage. This practice, however, has been gradually dying out in the last generation, not only in Egypt, but among most other Arabic-speaking peoples as well.

2. *Jalāl's Adaptations* One of the most prolific of the adapters was Muḥammad 'U<u>th</u>mān Jalāl (called by his Egyptian compatriots Galāl). The son of a minor official of Turkish ancestry who had married an Egyptian woman, Jalāl (1829–1898), had such good knowledge of French and Turkish that he entered at the early age of sixteen to work in the Egyptian Government's Translation Bureau (*Qalam al-tarjama*). He put his knowledge of

[359] The Roumanians aptly termed this transposition *localizare*—cf. Massoff, *op. cit.*, pp. 46, 130 *ss.*, for examples.

French and his translation abilities to even better use, when he devoted his whole life to the adaptation[360] of French plays into Arabic. To get an idea of his remarkable industry, a list of his drama adaptations—not all printed as yet[361]—is given below. The first five are Molière's, the next three Racine's, while the last two are Corneille's: *Tartuffe*[362], *Les Femmes Savantes*, *L'Ecole des Maris*, *L'Ecole des Femmes*, *Les Fâcheux*, *Esther*, *Iphigénie*, *Alexandre le Grand*, *Le Cid*, *Les Trois Horaces et les Trois Curiaces*[363].

Jalāl translated the tragedies (just as he had done with La Fontaine's *Fables* and St. Pierre's *Paul et Virginie*) into modern literary Arabic, allowing himself but few changes. He took greater liberty with the contents of comedies, however, when adapting them into the colloquial Arabic of Egypt. He often employed the *Rajaz* meter in his verses. His Arabic version of *Tartuffe*, for instance, brought this respectable character to Cairo, dubbing him and his colleagues with Arabic names. Several additions and omissions occur in this and the other plays, as well as anachronisms and errors caused by wrong interpretation of the French text. Jalāl's intention, in adapting these plays, respectively, into modern literary and colloquial Arabic, was probably to improve the tastes of his audience. He failed because the patrons of the theater still often failed to grasp the ideas he tried to convey. This applied particularly to his tragedies, but was not exceptional even in his comedies: an Oriental audience could not easily understand how Tartuffe, for instance, would consult his women-folk in matters pertaining to marriage. Another cause for the failure of Jalāl's plays,

[360] In Arabic: *iqtibās*. For other Arabic technical terms of the theatre cf. Najīb Ḥubaiqa, *Fann al-tamthīl*, in *Ma.*, vol. II, 1899 (see below, Bibliography, for dates and pages) and Barbour, in his *op. cit.*

[361] See below, List of Arabic Plays.

[362] Reprinted in Latin characters, with introduction and notes, by K. Vollers, *Der neuarabische Tartuffe*, in *ZDMG*, vol. XLV, 1891, pp. 36–96. This was produced in Egypt in 1912 with great success—cf. Zaidān, *Ta'rīkh ādāb etc.*, vol. IV, p. 245.

[363] Fr. Kern, in his critical edition and translation of *Femmes Savantes* (see below, Bibliography), Introd., pp. 6–7. *GAL*, II (2nd ed.), pp. 627–628; Suppl. II, p. 725—both locations giving full bibl.

when performed, was due to the almost complete lack of gifted actresses at the time[364].

3. *Al-Ḥaddād's Translations* Not less famous than Jalāl was another Egyptian playwright, named Najīb al-Ḥaddād (1867–1899). Born in Beirut to the Yāzijī family, famous for its contributions to literature—including the composition of plays[365]—al-Ḥaddād produced in Egypt the whole literary output of his short career. Najīb al-Ḥaddād was as industrious as Jalāl, possibly surpassing him. He edited several newspapers (along with his brother Amīn al-Ḥaddād, himself the translator of *Hamlet*[366]), contributed articles to others, composed a great number of poems, and wrote novels or translated some others from the French (chiefly Dumas, Rostand)[367]. His greatest contribution to Arabic literature is, however, his dramatic output: this is his best memorial, for many of his plays are still presented nowadays, particularly by the musical theater.

While Jalāl may have been his model early in his dramatic efforts, Najīb al-Ḥaddād soon devised a system of his own. His translation[368] was no adaptation, but was more or less faithful to the original; but, since he was actively connected with the Egyptian theater and knew well his compatriots' love for music, he interpolated various melodies in suitable spots (e.g., Romeo

364 Kern, ibid., Introd. M. Sobernheim, *Zur Metrik einiger in's Arabische übersetzter Dramen Molière's*, in *MSOS*, 1898, part 2, pp. 185–187. Muḥammad Taimūr, *op. cit.*, vol. II, pp. 134, 219–220, 229, 237. Article on *Dhikrā Mulyīr wariwāyātih fī'l-lugha al-'arabiyya*, in *H.*, vol. XXX, Mar. 1, 1922, p. 557. Brockelmann, *Geschichte der islamischen Völker und Staaten* (1939), pp. 355–356.

365 See above, p. 62.

366 *H*, vol. XVI, May 1, 1908, p. 504. *Al-Muqtabas*, vol. III, June 1908, pp. 355–356. Zaidān, *Ta'rīkh*, vol. IV, p. 252. Further bibl. in *GAL*, Suppl. II, pp. 762–763, III, p. 268.

367 Zaidān, *Tarājim*, 2nd ed., vol. II, pp. 325–327. *H*, vol. VII, Feb. 15, 1899, pp. 290–291, 315; Mar. 1, 1899, p. 349; Mar. 15, 1899, p. 381; July 1, 1899, p. 607. Ibid., vol. VIII, Aug. 15, 1900, p. 703. Ibid., vol. XI, Nov. 1, 1902, p. 94; June 15, 1903, p. 551. Ibid., vol. XII, Oct. 1, 1903, p. 31; Apr. 15, 1904, p. 446; July 1, 1904, pp. 573, 574, 582. Ibid., vol. XIII, Nov. 1, 1904, p. 126; Aug. 1, 1905, p. 567. *Mu.*, vol. XXVIII, Feb. 1, 1903, p. 179; July 1, 1903, pp. 611–612.

368 In Arabic: *tarjama.*

sings about his love to Juliet). Otherwise, not many changes were introduced in the text[369]. The plays' titles were often Arabicized, so that they might attract larger audiences and sometimes the names of the *dramatis personae* were also changed: in al-Ḥaddād's translation of *Hernani*, for instance, Don Carlos becomes 'Abd al-Raḥmān, Hernani—Ḥamdān, and Dona Sol—S̲h̲ams (i.e., "Sun"). To draw his patrons even nearer to the theater, al-Ḥaddād himself wrote a few plays inspired by world literature (which he perused in French). Other plays of his are on Arabic subjects. A list of his main plays[370] gives an idea of the range of his subjects:

i. *Oedipe* (*Ūdīb*, or *al-Sirr al-hā'il*, literally "The frightful secret," transl. from Voltaire, in prose and verse. Probably al-Ḥaddād's first).

ii. *Zaïre* (*Zāyyīr*, transl. from Voltaire's tragedy).

iii. *Phèdre* (transl. from Racine's tragedy).

iv. *Bérénice* (*Bīrīnīs*, transl. from Racine's historical drama)[371].

v. *Saladin* (*Ṣalāḥ al-Dīn al-Ayyūbī*, inspired by Sir Walter Scott's *Talisman*)[372].

vi. *Le Cid* (*Riwāyat al-Sīd*, or *G̲h̲arām wa-intiqām*, viz. "Love and Revenge," transl. from Corneille)[373]. A few additions, e.g., in Act III.

vii. *The Mahdi* (*Riwāyat al-Mahdī*, an original play on the Sudanese Mahdi who drove the Egyptians out of the Sudan in the 1880's).

369 Still, he sometimes slightly abbreviated the text or tried to "improve" it by additions. E.g., in his translation of Corneille's *Le Cid* he added quite a few verses in Act III, Scene 1 (p. 51 in the Arabic transl.) and at the end of the same Act (p. 74 in the Arabic transl.).

370 Zaidān, *Tarājim*, 2nd ed., vol. II, pp. 326–327. Id., *Ta'rīk̲h̲*, vol. IV, pp. 247–248. *H*, vol. VII, Feb. 15, 1899, p. 291. Pérès, *op. cit.*, pp. 44–45, 93–94. *Mu.*, vol. XXIII, Mar. 1, 1899, p. 239. Further bibl. in *GAL*, Suppl. III, pp. 268–269.

371 List on the back cover of al-Ḥaddād's transl. of *Oedipe*, 1905 ed.

372 Reviewed in *H*, vol. X, May 15, 1902, p. 516. Presented in Alger by Abyaḍ—cf. *L'islam et l'occident Cahiers du Sud*, 1947, pp. 271–276.

373 Reviewed in *H*, vol. IX, Jan. 1, 1901, p. 224.

viii. *Hernani* (*Riwāyat Ḥamdān,* a transl. of Victor Hugo's drama)[374].

ix. *Romeo and Juliet* (*S̲h̲uhadā' al-g̲h̲arām,* literally "The Martyrs of Love")[375].

x. *Hope after Despair* (*al-Rajā' ba'd al-ya's*)[376]. An original (?) play.

xi. *The Miser* (*Riwāyat al-bak̲h̲īl,* probably a translation of Molière's comedy).

xii. *The Feuds of the Arabs* (*T̲h̲a'rāt al-'arab*). An adapted play.

xiii. *Cinna* (*Ḥilm al-mulūk,* literally: "Clemency of the Kings," translated from Corneille's tragedy)[377].

xiv. *Le Medecin Malgré Lui* (*al-Ṭabīb al-mag̲h̲ṣūb,* transl. from Molière).

xv. *'Amr the Son of 'Adī* (*'Amr ibn 'Adī,* apparently an original play)[378].

4. *The Literal Translations* The modified translation soon took the place of adaptation, so popular from the days of Mārūn al-Naqqās̲h̲ to those of Muḥammad 'Ut̲h̲mān Jalāl. The example of Najīb al-Ḥaddād pointed the way to a new trend. Budding authors and playwrights set out to improve the world's masterpieces of literature, while rendering them into Arabic. As an example, Ṭānyūs 'Abduh, who was Najīb al-Ḥaddād's younger contemporary, and a prolific man of letters—he was said, exaggeratedly, to have translated some 700 plays[379]—translated *Hamlet* (approx. 1902) from the French[380]. This was done with certain omissions (such as Act I, Scene I), the abbreviation of the longer monologues and even an addition: at the end of the

[374] Reviewed ibid., ibid., June 1, 1901, p. 503.

[375] Reviewed ibid., vol. X, Jan. 1, 1902, p. 227. Performed many times—cf. ibid., vol. XXXVI, Dec. 1, 1927, p. 202, Taufīq Ḥabīb's article.

[376] Reviewed ibid., vol. XI, Oct. 15, 1902, p. 63.

[377] Reviewed ibid., vol. X, Feb. 15, 1901, p. 322.

[378] Reviewed in *Mu.*, vol. XXVIII, Feb. 1, 1903, p. 179.

[379] *GAL*, Suppl. III, p. 269.

[380] *Mu.*, vol. XXVII, Mar. 1, 1902, pp. 293–294.

tragedy, the ghost reappears, to order Hamlet to mount the throne![381] He further translated Schiller's *Kabale und Liebe*, sometimes suiting the dialogue to Oriental understanding[382].

The cause for the disappearance of the Jalāl-type of play adaptation and of the Ḥaddād-type of modified translation may be due, not only to the rising intellectual level of the audiences, but, concurrently, to the fact that the Arab theater has fallen, naturally enough, into its divisions of classical, musical, and popular theater.

On one hand, the classical theater, inspired by Jūrj Abyaḍ, insisted throughout on pedantic (almost verbatim) translations from the world dramatic literature. The musical and popular theater, on the other hand, preferred different material: this may have been sometimes inspired by European or American literature, but more often than not plays composed by local writers are performed. Hence it follows that play translation either serves the classical theater or remains a literary pastime. In both cases, exactitude and fidelity to the original are expected from the translator. Nowadays, it seems accepted that foreign verse may be rendered into Arabic prose, as in the case of K̲h̲alīl Muṭrān's translation of Shakespeare's *Merchant of Venice*, which is almost throughout literal, even in trying to find suitable ways for expressing in Arabic the idioms of the Elizabethan Bard. A large number of other translations of plays by Shakespeare[383], Molière[384], Racine, Corneille, Victor Hugo, Edmond Rostand, Ibsen, Strindberg, and other more modern playwrights (including the Russians) have been published[385]. Many others, no doubt, still exist in manuscript form. It is to be remarked that, unfortunately, plays are not always translated

381 See below, List of Ar. Plays, Translations.

382 *GAL*, Suppl. III, p. 269, n. 1.

383 Taufīq Ḥabīb, *S̲h̲iksbīr fī Miṣr ṣafḥa min ta'rīk̲h̲ al-adab wa'l-tamt̲h̲īl*, in *H*, vol. XXXVI, Dec. 1, 1927, pp. 201–204.

384 *D̲h̲ikrā Mulyīr wa-riwāyātih fī'l-lug̲h̲a al-'arabiyya*, ibid., vol. XXX, March 1, 1922, pp. 555–558.

385 See below, List of Arabic Plays, Translations. Cf. Barbour, at the end of his *op. cit.* in *BSOS.*, vol. VIII, 1935–1937.

from the original, but oftener from their French or English version. Anyway, nowadays the translations cannot vie in number with plays written originally in Arabic.

b. Original Plays

The original plays fall naturally into eight distinct categories: farces and burlesques, historical plays, melodramas, dramas, tragedies, comedies, political and symbolical plays[386].

1. *Farces* Farces and burlesques, as has already been said[387], were the first to appear in the early nineteenth century. These universally popular performances, without becoming more refined, showed an amount of European influence as early as the beginning of the twentieth century[388] and are nowadays the basis of the popular theater's revue. The hilarious performances of the troupes of al-Rīḥānī and al-Kassār—practically always in the vernacular—still often employ somewhat crude devices to obtain the effect of the *comica*: funny imitations, unexpected blows, and rude jokes. However, there is a growing measure of able use of comic situations and well-pointed satire. This may be noticed when listening to various broadcasts from Arab stations, as well as from the Arabic department of the British Broadcasting Corporation[389].

2. *Historical Plays* The above comical performances, whether presented as farces in play or as burlesques in revue form, could never fulfill the cravings and expectations of the whole theater-

[386] Landau, *The Arab theatre*, in *MEA*, vol. IV, Mar. 1953, pp. 81–83. Id., *'Al ha-teiaṭrōn etsel ha-'aravīm*, in *Bamah*, fasc. 47, Jan. 1946, pp. 50–51; fasc. 48, June 1946, pp. 67–75; fasc. 50, Jan. 1947, pp. 107–113. Only a few examples of the contents of these plays will be given in this chapter; for others see the following chapter.

[387] See above, Part 2, ch. 1, a; and ch. 2, b.

[388] See above, pp. 72–73.

[389] Mr. H. F. Duckworth, of the B.B.C., has kindly sent me a number of mimeographed samples of broadcast sketches and plays.

going public. The last three generations have been an era of much suffering for many Arabs and of intense national desire for independence. In such periods of deep despondence and surging hope, all men search the past of their people or their religion for inspiration. Thus most historical plays, written in Arabic, glorified periods of splendor in Arab or Islamic history; sometimes they treated of non-Arab and non-Muslim events, but these, too, frequently had some connection or other with Eastern history. In Egypt, some of these plays tried to revive the great periods of Pharaonic Egyptian life. Only few plays deal with recent history, because this is a period that has not yet brought special distinction to the Arabs; the few plays dealing with modern events bear, in general, a marked political character.

Fairly typical of historical plays is *Lailā, al-Nuʿmān's Daughter, and the Chosroes* (*Lailā ibnat al-Nuʿmān wa'l-aqāṣira*) published by a certain Syrian Christian, Yūsuf al-Ḥā'ik, in 1932. In his interesting introduction, the author informs us of the *raison d'être* of plays: "To polish memory, to stir sentiment, to impress emotions on our soul, to distinguish between truth and unreality." While one may doubt the application of the last-mentioned purpose to the historical play, the others are certainly its part-and-parcel. For al-Ḥā'ik defines the people interested in the theater as "those with a natural penchant towards acting, those yearning for the memories of their forefathers, those moved by their fathers' sentiment, those hoping to revive their ancestors' heroism and those desiring to feel the truth of the events."

The five-act play itself is devoted, as so many others, to events in pre-Islamic Arabia. The somewhat intricate plot describes the Persian campaigns against the tiny Arabian kingdom of al-Ḥīra. The Persian punitive expeditions were sent to retaliate against Lailā, the proud, vindictive daughter of the late king of al-Ḥīra. She refused to marry the heir to the Persian throne, since his father had killed hers, and encouraged the various Arab chieftains to unite against the Persians. She even managed to enter the Persian camp, under false pretenses, and murder their general. The play ends with the complete victory of the Arabs and the recognition between Lailā and a captive general of the enemy, who turns out to be none other than her long-lost brother.

This plot characterizes the style of Arabic historical plays. Arab honor and courage are extolled, to the detriment of all non-Arabs: "The pure Arab spirit refuses to bear molestation patiently and prefers death for the sake of honor and faithfulness"[390] is a characteristic phrase for the historical play. Lailā's call for Arab unity is remindful of Pan-Arab aspirations in our generation, while her pluck in killing the Persian general may well remind us of the Apocryphal story of Judith and Holofernes. While in the historical tragedies of Corneille and Racine —following in the steps of the great Greek Masters—there is a perpetual inner struggle between duty and love, al-Ḥā'ik's Lailā does not hesitate in the same manner. Her blood-feud with the Persian reigning house is a clear-cut duty, a loyalty from which there can be no swerving. Nonetheless, one wonders if the author has really forced himself free from the influence of the French playwrights. In the words of Lailā's captive brother, "Courage is in the hearts not in the years,"[391] one cannot help hearing the echo of Le Cid's boast,[392] "Mais aux âmes bien nées—la valeur n'attend point le nombre des années!"[393]

3. *Melodrama* In the last few years, even more than previously, the majority of the Arab theatergoers have come to prefer

[390] Page 18: "Al-rūḥ al-'arabiyya al-ṣamīma ta'bā'l-ighḏā' 'alā'l-qaḏḥā wa-tastaṭīb al-maut fī sabīl al-s̲haraf wa' l-wafā'."

[391] Pages 85–86: "Fa'l-s̲hajā'a fī'l-qulūb lā fī'l-a'mār."

[392] Corneille, *Le Cid*, Act II, Scene 2.

[393] For exhaustive reviews of another historical play, 'Azīz Abāẓa's *al-'Abbāsa*, cf. Zakī Ṭulaimāt, *Masrahiyyat al-'Abbāsa*, in *K*, vol. I, Dec. 1945, pp. 223–230; and Sayyid Quṭb in *KM*, fasc. 4, Jan., 1946, pp. 588–594. This describes the downfall of the powerful Viziers, the Barmakids. For other plays by Abāẓa, who promises to be an outstanding playwright, see below, App., List of Arabic Plays.

melodramas. The more complicated the plot and packed with sensation, the sweeter and more touching the melodies—the heartier the applause. The prevalence of the melodrama may be taken as yet another indication of the standard of the audiences. It is interesting to note that the plots of many melodramas have been inspired by French or Italian compositions of the same kind. In general, they treat of passionate love affairs, often culminating in illegitimate offspring, coupled with rape, murder, theft, smuggling, and drug addiction. The use of the colloquial Arabic in melodramas is widespread, so that the patrons may more easily grasp the plot in detail.

The Children of the Poor (*Aulād al-fuqarā'*) is the adequate name of a characteristic Arab melodrama, written by the famed Egyptian actor, Yūsuf Wahbī. Its extremely intricate main plot (not to mention a few sub-plots) traces the story of a girl, Bamba, born out of wedlock to a poor woman who had been seduced by a wealthy cousin. Bamba's uncle, to avenge his sister's honor, shoots at the seducer, wounding him. Out of prison, he becomes a drug addict, finally kills the now syphilitic Bamba, and loses his reason[394]. This harrowing story, well calculated to move an audience, has hardly any literary value. Its only merit is to draw a half-accurate picture of some aspects of contemporary life, in a juicy colloquial Arabic. Nonetheless, interpreted by the restrained but intense acting of Amīna Rizq (as Bamba)[395], the play attracted large audiences; up until the year 1952 it had had a record-breaking number of 683 performances, according to its author's evidence[396].

4. *Dramas* Good dramas[397] in Arabic are not many and those which are worthy of the name are generally restricted to the

[394] For further details see Barbour, *op. cit.*, in *BSOS*, vol. VIII, 1935–1937, p. 996. Landau, '*Al ha-teiaṭrōn etsel ha-'aravīm*, part 2, in *Bamah*, fasc. 48, June, 1946, p. 71. For another characteristic melodrama, see Aḥmad Ṣādiq's *Fruit of Seduction* (*Ṯhamarat al-ghawāya*), reported in *H*, vol. IX, Feb. 1, 1901, p. 288.

[395] M. Jacobs, *Egyptian stage actresses*, in *B*, fasc. 22, Mar. 1948, p. 16.

[396] In *M.*, May 10, 1952, p. 10.

[397] In Arabic: *Fāji'a.*

description of family life. An example is provided by Mīkhā'īl Nu'aima's *Fathers and Sons* (*al-Ābā' wa'l-banūn*). To a student of the twentieth-century social history of the Arabs, the drama has great informative value. One can feel, when reading or seeing it, the powerful impact of the West on manners and morals, bringing to the fore differences between parents and their sons or daughters as regards courtship, marriage, divorce, education, and social behavior. Much may be learned, also, from what is left unsaid. Many dramas are written and performed in literary Arabic, others in the colloquial.

Out of several examples[398], a fair idea of the running trend of the drama may be formed by reading *Seduction* (*al-Ighwā' drāmā 'aṣriyya 'anīfa*) by Anīs Dayya, who has also produced other work in the dramatic field[399]. The three-act drama turns around the relations of Maurice, the young nobleman, and Julia, who has borne him an illegitimate child. Various benevolent elements conspire to force the seducer to marry Julia, which he finally does, to everybody's (undoubtedly including the audience's) satisfaction. Even though the action is tense and the effect heightened by some shooting and the appearance of a person disguised as a ghost, it does not detract from the play's merits. The awkward tension of melodrama is avoided both by the "comic relief" provided by the servants and by the indirect social criticism. For this drama has set out to show how spoiled is that part of the young generation (in Lebanon, presumably) which is totally under French influence: according to Dayya, these youths—who bear French names and talk French (introducing French words even into their Arabic conversation)—are naturally sinful. The old doctor, the family friend, and the avowed champion of Arabic culture and language, even if he is sometimes pathetically comic, still has our author's full sympathy.

398 For further examples see Landau, *Drama ḥevratīt-ḥinnūkhīt be-'aravīt*, in *Bamah*, fasc. 51, May 1947, pp. 33–34.

399 Such as *Ma'sāt al-ṣanaubar* (prob. 1932)—cf. *H*, vol. XLI, Dec. 1, 1932, p. 270.

5. *Tragedies* There are hardly any outstanding tragedies in the Arab repertoire worthy of the name, since only a tiny part of the audience could really understand and enjoy a good tragedy. Another cause for the unpopularity of the tragedy is the frequent use of literary Arabic. Because of this very reason most tragedies, whether translated or original, tend to become either melodramas with a sad end or dramas finishing in a few deaths.

6. *Comedies* Along with melodramas, comedies are the stock in trade of every troupe in the Arab Near East as well as in North Africa. The comedy has already replaced the farce in many places, particularly among the more refined city dwellers. While earlier the comedy of character was preponderant, it now seems that the comedy of manners, gaining importance in the regard of the Arab playwrights, will soon predominate. Most comedies are performed in colloquial Arabic, including the many which are regularly broadcast; but a goodly minority are published or produced in literary Arabic.

Not less than the drama, the comedy is a mine of information on Arab character and social life. Many comedies ridicule, more or less subtly, the undiscerning imitation of Western practices by the Europeanized section of the population; this generally includes the larger landowners and the upper bourgeoisie as well as a sizable part of the urban younger generation. This ridicule has been well exploited by Maḥmūd Taimūr[400]. In one of his best comedies, *A Tea Party* (*Ḥaflat s̲h̲āi*)[401], Taimūr directed his ridicule towards a young Egyptian couple. These persons as well as their friends most snobbishly and superficially affect foreign airs in the interior decoration of their homes, table manners, dress, and speech. However, their careless forgetfulness of vital matters leads through a comedy of errors to the failure of their tea party. Even though Taimūr shows in this

[400] See below, the next chapter.

[401] Summarized and analyzed in Landau, '*Al ha-teiaṭrōn etc.*, in *Bamah*, fasc. 48, June, 1946, pp. 73–74.

comedy the influence of Molière's *Les Précieuses Ridicules* (particularly in the pedantry of speech), he still succeeds in laying his finger on one of the basic sores of contemporary Arab society. He has pointed out the danger of superficiality to the new Arab generation, which has lost much of its backbone of tradition, acquiring instead only a thin veneer of European civilization.

7. *Political Plays* It is rather strange that the political play was so late in coming to the Arabic stage. The obvious explanation is probably the severity of the censorship imposed by the non-Arab authorities and continued, after a fashion, by the Arab governments. Still, this probably affected only the printed works, so that one may assume that a number of political plays were written to vent the people's many grievances. These, whether performed on the stage or not, were probably hidden away or lost. We know that in the 1880's the ardent national journalist 'Abd Allāh Nadīm[402]—one of the first who understood the theater's importance as a vehicle of communication[403]—wrote two political plays, *The Fatherland* (*al-Waṭan*) and *The Arabs* (*al-'Arab*). These he produced together with some of his pupils, apparently for a philanthropic purpose[404]. However, since Khedive Taufīq, Ismā'īl's son and successor and the friend of the British, contributed to and attended these plays[405], one cannot suppose that they were very virulent.

Another political play was written and published in Cairo by the journalist Ḥasan al-Mar'ī (1907). Named *The Denshawai Incident* (*Ḥādiṯhat Dāniṣhwāi*), it attacked the British bitterly for shooting and cruelly punishing some Egyptians after a fray between British hunters and local peasants at the above-mentioned place. Because of its virulence, the production of this

[402] For whom see *GAL*, Suppl. III, p. 1313 (additions to Suppl. II, p. 869).

[403] See his words, as reported by Pérès, *op. cit.*, pp. 40–41.

[404] Zaidān, *Tarājim etc.*, 2nd ed., vol. II, p. 108; cf. ibid., p. 112; also *H*, vol. V, Feb. 1, 1897, pp. 404, 408. K. E. Galal, *op. cit.*, p. 110. Rizzitano, *op. cit.*, in *OM*, vol. XXIII, June, 1943, p. 248 and footnotes.

[405] Zaidān, ibid., ibid. Id., *Ta'rīkh*, vol. IV, p. 244.

play was prohibited by the British authorities[406]. The writing and publication of this political play was, however, an almost isolated instance in the history of the Arabic dramatic literature in Egypt, if one overlooks the strong political character of some of the historical plays and comedies written by Faraḥ Anṭūn[407] in the years immediately following the First World War. A similar experiment in Lebanon hardly received the attention it deserved. This was Muḥī'l-Dīn al-Khayyāṭ's translation of *Vatan ve Silistra*[408], the famous Turkish patriotic play of Namik Kemal, published in Arabic soon after the revolution in Turkey. It is only after the two World Wars, however, with the spread of public interest in political affairs, that more political plays have been written and produced. Some of them are directed against Zionism (of this more will be said soon), but by far the larger number are directed against what is considered foreign interference in Arab internal affairs. It is particularly during the Egyptian struggle to evict the British forces from the Suez Canal by political and economic pressure that the political play was fully used: The *Incident of Denshawai* was revived on the stage[409], while various troupes vied with one another for the performance of bitter political plays and sketches[410].

Amongst the plays performed during this anti-British campaign was a comedy concerning the popular character Juḥā[411], entitled *Juḥā's Nail* (*Mismār Juḥā*). It is interesting that the public saw in it anti-British propaganda and flocked to its performances, as interpreted by the then newly formed Troupe of the New Egyptian Stage (*Firqat al-masraḥ al-miṣrī'l-ḥadīth*) led

[406] *RMM*, vol. III, pp. 504–509; cf. *GAL*, Suppl. III, p. 34, n. 1.
[407] See above, p. 78.
[408] *H*, vol. XVII, Mar. 1, 1909, p. 383. See also below, List of Arabic Plays.
[409] *AS*, Dec. 12, 1951, p. 8. *Ha-Aretz*, Dec. 20, 1951, p. 2.
[410] *Ha- Aretz*, ibid. *AL*, Nov. 30, 1951, p. 6. *A*, Dec. 11, 1951, p. 8; ibid., Jan. 19, 1952, p. 3; ibid., Jan. 22, 1952, p. 5. *AY*, Dec. 22, 1951, p. 8. *M*, Jan. 17, 1952, p. 5.
[411] For whose jokes and mishaps see, e.g., the fasc. *Qiṣṣat Juḥā*, Beirut, Amīn al-Khūrī, n.d.; 24 pp. In the title of Bākthīr's play, *mismār* has the same connotation as *clou* in French.

by Zakī Ṭulaimāt[412]. The author of *Juḥā's Nail*, Bāk<u>th</u>īr, has already been mentioned for his first play[413]. During the years he wrote quite a number of historical plays[414]. His fame, however, had been secured by a political play, entitled *The New Shylock* (*<u>Sh</u>ailūk al-jadīd*)[415], published shortly after the end of the Second World War. This play—anti-Zionist and anti-Jewish at one and the same time—sold in thousands of copies. Here was a sure proof that political consciousness was widespread at last and that unscrupulous virulence paid good dividends. Hence the clever, extensive use of the political play in the Anglo-Egyptian conflict over the Suez a few years afterwards. Soon the Revolution found an echo in the political play, in a rather curious fashion: when Najīb was expected to visit the Egyptian prison at Līmān Ṭarra, its inmates prepared a play on his *coup d'état* for him (1953). Named *Right Has Come* (*Jā'a al-ḥaqq*), it was written and directed by a prison inmate, 'Azīz Sulaimān, and presented by fellow prisoners[416]. Nowadays politics have an important role not only in the activity of the Egyptian theater, but also in its inactivity: thus, for instance, the financially hard-pressed Egyptian troupe[417] changed its mind about participation in the Paris Festival of Drama (1954) —where it was to have presented Molière's *Tartuffe* and Taufīq al-Ḥakīm's *<u>Sh</u>ahrāzād*—when it heard that Israel's oldest troupe, "Habimah," was to take part[418].

8. *Symbolical plays* Contrary to the other kinds of plays, which after all, stand a fair chance of being performed on the stage,

[412] Full details, with pictures, in *al-Muṣawwar*, Nov. 14, 1951. Cf. 'Abd al-Raḥmān Ṣidqī, in *K*, vol. VII, Jan., 1952, pp. 94–95, and *M*, June 5, 1952, p. 5. It seems that the plot of this comedy served as scenario for an Arab film, bearing the same name, released to the public a few days later—cf. *A*, Jan. 15, 1952, p. 3; *M*, June 18, 1952, p. 7, and June 30, 1952, p. 10.

[413] See above, pp. 97–98.

[414] See below, List of Arabic Plays.

[415] Summarized and analyzed by Landau, *'Al ha-teiaṭrōn etc.*, in *Bamah*, fasc. 50, Jan., 1947, pp. 111–112.

[416] *Al-Muṣawwar*, Apr. 24, 1953, pp. 50–51.

[417] *RY*, June 7, 1954, p. 34.

[418] Reported in *Zemannīm* (Jerusalem), June 21, 1954, p. 3.

symbolical plays in Arabic are nowadays mainly an intellectual *tour de force*. On very rare occasions, one or another may be modestly produced before a small, select audience. In general, however, these plays are primarily intended for reading (at least for some time yet) and their authors recognize this fact. The French-influenced Bis̱ẖr Fāris, an Egyptian, is the best-known playwright who has written any symbolical plays in Arabic that show a real streak of originality, with the Lebanese Aḥmad Makkī a close second.

Born in 1906 in Egypt and educated there, Fāris pursued his university studies in Paris and stayed for a long while in Germany (he is one of the few Arab men of letters who know perfect German). He has written many literary pieces of criticism[419], stories of an impressionistic genre (psychological rather than descriptive)[420], euphonious poems[421], and reviews of musical and theatrical compositions and events[422]. His most important work, however, is his symbolical play *The Parting of the Ways* (*Mafriq al-ṭarīq*), first published in 1937[423] and reprinted in book form a year later and again in 1952; the first edition was translated by the author and published in a French periodical[424]. Influenced by the symbolism of Paul Verlaine and Charles Baudelaire, this play had some success in translation on French (1950) and German (1951) stages[425], although it was not tried on an Arab one. The whole play consists of a long dialogue be-

[419] For an example of his dramatic criticism see the Cairene weekly *al-Ṯhaqāfa*, Mar. 7, 1939, pp. 44–45.

[420] Pérès, *op. cit.*, pp. 140–141. J.-M. Abd-al-Jalil, *Brève histoire de la littérature arabe*, 3rd ed., p. 248. *GAL*, Suppl. III, pp. 168–169, 280.

[421] See *GAL*, ibid., and the Egyptian monthly *KM*, fasc. 27, Dec., 1947, pp. 392–393, for examples.

[422] Such reviews see in *Mu.*, vol. LXXX, Apr. 1, 1932, pp. 392–398. *KM*, fasc. 22, July, 1947, pp. 301–306; and fasc. 32, May 1948, pp. 628–638. *A*, July 30, 1952, p. 5.

[423] In *Mu.*, Mar., 1937.

[424] By Maṭba'at Miṣr—cf. *M*, June 6, 1952, p. 5. Bint al-S̱ẖāṭi', in her review of the play (*A.*, July 13, 1952, pp. 5, 11), maintains that it was also translated (but probably not published?) into German. It was also reviewed in *Mu.*, vol. XCII, Apr. 1, 1938, pp. 477–478; in *H*, vol. XLVI, July 1, 1938, p. 1077.

[425] *M*, ibid. *A*, ibid. See also Landau, *op. cit.*, in *MEA*, vol. IV, Mar., 1953, p. 83.

tween Samīra, a twenty-seven-year-old girl, symbolizing the ever-searching soul, still tied, however, to the material world; and "he," an elegant thirty-year-old man, the product of society, simple in speech, and incapable of grasping abstractions. The conflict is not only between the abstract and the material, but also between light (the mind) and darkness (the sentiment), both of which want a hold on the soul.

Summing up, one finds that most Arabic plays are of the melodrama, historical play, and comedy genres, with the political play, farce, and drama coming next; the tragedy and symbolical play are as yet few in number. A great many plays are still more suitable for good reading than good acting. Then, the language problem has not yet been solved satisfactorily. Literary Arabic is understood by few patrons of theater[426] and may even cause unintended laughter in an untutored audience by its overpunctiliousness[427], while colloquial Arabic will probably not be readily understood by the crowds in many places outside the author's and actors' country of origin. Notwithstanding the baffling language situation[428], many plays—whether describing the past or treating of present conditions—are on a fairly high level. This is mainly due to the talents of a restricted number of playwrights, who, after experimenting with the various kinds of plays, chose the one suited best to their temperament and stuck to it.

[426] Cf. Rizzitano's evidence, in his *op. cit.*, *OM*, vol. XXIII, June 1943, p. 250, n. 6; see ibid., p. 251.

[427] See the view of Germanus, reported in Orvieto, *op. cit.*, p. 147.

[428] On which see also I. S̱ẖamūs̱ẖ, *Be'ayat ha-safa ba-sippūr ha-'aravī ha-mōdernī*, in *Tarbīts* (Jerusalem), vol. XXIII, 1952, pp. 231–235; J. Harosen, *S̱ẖamranūt ve-hit'ōrĕrut bĕ-sifrūt ha-mizraḥ ha-tīḵḥōn*, in *ha-Aretz*, Lit. Suppl., Oct. 16, 1953, p. 1.

CHAPTER 5

Some Arab Playwrights

THE ACTIVITY of various Arab playwrights has already been mentioned. Most of them were writers, journalists, teachers, or booksellers. While among the adapters Jalāl, and among the translators Najīb al-Ḥaddād[429], are prominent, there are three authors of original plays who deserve mention at greater length. These are Aḥmad S̲h̲auqī, Taufīq al-Ḥakīm, and Maḥmūd Taimūr. All three are Egyptians; the first is dead, the other two are still very active. Their impact on the historical play, the social drama, and the modern comedy has been considerable, so that their life work merits a more detailed appreciation.

a. S̲h̲auqī[430]

1. *S̲h̲auqī's life* Aḥmad S̲h̲auqī was born in 1868, the son of a Cairene family in whose veins flowed Turkish and Kurdish, as well as Greek and Arab blood. At seventeen he began the study of law and was granted a scholarship in France two years afterwards. During the two years which he spent at Montpellier and Paris, he not only studied law, but acquired much information about French literature and met some of the leaders of French letters of the time. After returning home, he was appointed to a post in the French department of the government, and was sent as Egyptian delegate to Orientalist Congresses at Berlin and Geneva.

When ʿAbbās II became Khedive (1892), S̲h̲auqī retired for

[429] See the previous chapter, section a.

[430] I have drawn large parts of this article from my article on *S̲h̲auqī* in *Bamōt*, vol. I, Mar., 1953, pp. 305–309. Cf. also Landau, *S̲h̲auqī ve-yĕtsīratō bĕ-aspaqlaryah ʿaravīt*, in *HH*, vol. III, Autumn, 1951, p. 101, reviewing ʿUmar Farrūk̲h̲'s *Kalima fī Aḥmad S̲h̲auqī*. See also the following footnotes.

a time from his official work, but soon his eulogies attracted the Khedive's attention; 'Abbās II, who was gradually growing more and more interested in Arabic culture, favored the young poet. During the First World War, S̲h̲auqī was exiled from Egypt and went to Spain, probably because of his famous anti-British poems. In his exile, he had ample time to study the history of Muslim Spain and the ruins of its civilization[431]. When he returned to Egypt after the Armistice, he was appointed court poet, and in this position enjoyed honor and fame until his death in 1932[432]. In April, 1927, S̲h̲auqī was crowned with much pomp the "Prince of the Poets" (*Amīr al-s̲h̲u'arā'*), and acknowledged by delegates from diverse Arabic-speaking countries. This honor was not flattery alone, for though S̲h̲auqī had begun his literary life with three long novels, two of them on ancient Egypt[433] and one on ancient Persia, his power of expression lay in poetry rather than in prose. His political verses and love songs were well known; his popular songs were often sung by Egyptian actors and spread throughout the Arab world. S̲h̲auqī's popularity was not to be impugned even by much adverse criticism, his enemies nicknaming him the "Poet of the Princes" (*S̲h̲ā'ir al-umarā'*). However, it is probable that S̲h̲auqī did not write all his eulogies for merely personal motives; he may have been imitating the traditional style of a great part of ancient Arabic poetry.

2. *S̲h̲auqī's plays*[434] Besides his important lyric poetry, S̲h̲auqī made a valuable contribution to the development of the lyric

431 Cf. his letter from Barcelona, printed in *H*, vol. XXVIII, Oct. 1, 1919, pp. 83–88.

432 Cf. ibid., vol. XXXII, July 1, 1924, pp. 1068–1078, for a life story and appreciation by Salāma Mūsā. Further material in the memorial issue of *K*, Oct., 1947.

433 His first long work that was published was named *Riwāyat al-Hind au tamaddun al-Farā'ina*, Alexandria, Maṭba'at al-Ahrām, 1897; 150 pp.

434 Little has been written about S̲h̲auqī's plays. Cf.: S̲h̲aukat, *al-Masraḥiyya fī s̲h̲i'r S̲h̲auqī* (1947). Edwār Ḥunain, *S̲h̲auqī 'alā'l-masraḥ*, in *Ma*, XXXIII, 1935, pp. 68–92, 273–288, 394–427. As'ad al-Ḥakīm, *S̲h̲auqī wa'l-masraḥ al-'arabī*, in: Aḥmad 'Ubaid, *D̲h̲ikrā'l-s̲h̲ā'irain* (1933), pp. 339–344. Drīnī

historical drama in Arabic. In the course of his literary life, beginning with his student days in France, he published six historical dramas (of which five are in verse) and one comparatively unimportant comedy. The comedy, *al-Sitt Hudā*, tells the story of a lady who is married time and again to men who desire her only for her wealth; but, once she is aware of their cupidity, she succeeds in getting rid of them[435].

It should be pointed out that Shauqī has not succeeded—perhaps he has not even seriously tried—in freeing himself from the ancient laws of meter and rhyme; but there is quite a noteworthy innovation in that he often changes one meter for another and alters the rhyme as well when the roles change.

i. *'Alī Bey*

At the end of the last century, Shauqī, while in France, wrote his first tragedy, *'Alī Bey the Great* (*'Alī Bek al-kabīr*). He sent the drama to the Khedive, who liked it, and the play had a fast sale. Nevertheless, it is not very well known among Arabic-reading people, and Shauqī himself did not think much of it, though he mentions it in the first edition of

---

Khashaba, *Fauq jibāl al-Ulimb*, in *K*, vol. IV, Oct., 1947, pp. 1630–1641. Buṭrus al-Bustānī, *Udabā' al-'Arab fī'l-Andalus wa-'aṣr al-inbi'āth*. Fu'ād Ifrām al-Bustānī, *Shakhṣiyyat Aḥmad Shauqī*, in *Ma.*, vol. XXXIV, 1936, pp. 67–75. Zakī Fahmī, *Ṣafwat al-'aṣr*, pp. 636–639. Muḥammad Ḥusain Haikal, in his Introd. to vol. I of the *Shauqiyyāt*. Muḥammad Is'āf al-Nashshāshībī, *al-Baṭal al-khālid Ṣalāḥ al-Dīn wa'l-shā'ir al-khālid Aḥmad Shauqī* (1932); id., *al-'Arabiyya wa-shā'iruhā'l-akbar Aḥmad Shauqī*. Ṭaha Ḥusain, *Ḥāfiẓ wa-Shauqī*. *GAL*, Suppl. III, pp. 43–48, 275. A. J. Arberry, *Ḥāfiẓ Ibrāhīm and Shauqī*, in *JRAS*, vol. XXXV, 1937, pp. 41–58. H. Pérès, *Aḥmad Šawqî*, in *AIEOA*, vol. II, 1936, pp. 313–340. G. Kampffmeyer, *Arabische Dichter der Gegenwart*. X, in *MSOS*, 1926, part 2, pp. 198–206. M. Guidi, *Le onoranze al poeta Egiziano Shawqī*, in *OM*, vol. VII, 1927, pp. 346–353. A. Dablan, *Neuarabische Literatur* (Haifa, mimeographed), pp. 8–9.

435 Cf. Khashaba, *op. cit.*, p. 1641. A small part was published in *H*, vol. XLV, Dec. 1, 1936, pp. 157–164. See also *AJ*, June 6, 1952, p. 8; and *al-Nidā'*, June 23, 1952, p. 8. Shauqī has left at least another unprinted play, called *al-Bakhīla*, cf. Buṭrus al-Bustānī, *op. cit.*, p. 213; *GAL*, Suppl. III, p. 47.

his *Dīwān*. Only when the Oriental Music Congress met in Cairo in March, 1932, did S̲h̲auqī agree to print the drama anew, after Fāṭima Rus̲h̲dī had successfully starred in it at the Congress.

The scene is laid in Mamlūk Egypt of the early eighteenth century and unfolds, though not exclusively, around the person of 'Alī Bey, the ruler of Egypt. 'Alī takes a slave girl named Āmāl to his palace. Amidst wars and troubles, Āmāl is torn between her feelings of duty towards 'Alī and her love for 'Alī's adopted son, Murād. However, at the end of the drama, while 'Alī is dying of his wounds, Āmāl finds out that Murād is really her long-lost brother.

In *'Alī Bey*, besides describing the known historical events of the revolts against 'Alī, S̲h̲auqī has presented his interpretation of the social conditions in those days, together with his criticism of them. The play is not only a tale of Murād's love for his sister or the struggle between the sentiments of love and duty in Āmāl's spirit (an important problem in Greek tragedy; probably S̲h̲auqī chose the subject from Corneille or Racine), but also an analysis of relations between the Mamlūk rulers and their subjects and of the conditions of life in the palaces. One can find at least one faithful reproduction of Mamlūk life—the Mamlūk ruling a great part of Egypt buys youths in the slave market and rears them at his home, so that they may help him in times of trouble. The very need of adopting children testifies to the weakness of Mamlūk rule; and, indeed, 'Alī's adopted children betray him in gross ingratitude.

'Alī Bey himself was bought in the slave market and understands what Āmāl feels about parents cruelly selling their children as if they were animals. Āmāl is very conscious of her personal merits and because of that her inner struggle is the more bitter. These struggles of passion add tenseness to the play. 'Alī's is the personality that emerges most clearly—a very energetic man both in his foreign policy and in the administration of his country: he hopes to free Egypt from the Turkish yoke, but refuses Russian help in order to strengthen his own rule in Egypt; he cares for the poor and distributes money to the hungry, takes some interest in education and is proud to state that his palace has been built by Egyptian artisans only.

ii. *Majnūn Lailā*

A play of this title had been written before S̲h̲auqī's tragedy by Muḥammad Munjī K̲h̲air Allāh and presented in Alexandria[436]. S̲h̲auqī's tragedy, written in highly polished verse, is dedicated to Fārūq, who was at the time heir presumptive to the throne of Egypt. Fifteen years later the tragedy was published in a second edition and performed with some success in Cairo. In 1933 it was translated by Professor Arberry into English verse of charming felicity[437].

The main subject is the unhappy love of Qais and Lailā, against the background of the simple Bedouin life of the desert. The first three scenes show Qais' luckless wooing of Lailā, the Bedouin rules of honor seeming to prevent Lailā from marrying one who is considered crazy and who had sung of his love for her before suing for her hand. Then Lailā marries another and dies soon after, still a virgin and still loving Qais, who follows her into the grave.

The popular legend about Qais, who went mad because of his disappointed love for Lailā, and therefore was known as Majnūn Lailā (the madman of Lailā), has been a subject for many romances, not only amongst the Arabs, but in the classic and folk literature of the Indians, Persians, and Turks. It is rather doubtful whether Majnūn Lailā was an historical personality, and so his epoch cannot be fixed with any certainty. S̲h̲auqī suggests that he lived in the days of the first Umayyad Caliphs,

[436] See below, List of Arabic Plays.

[437] *Majnūn laylā a Poetical Drama in Five Acts translated into English verse from the Arabic of the late Ahmed Shawki, "Prince of the Poets" of Egypt, with the Author's permission, by Arthur John Arberry.*

when Islam was beginning to feel the division into Sunnites and Shiites, in a religious and political contest the traces of which are clearly imprinted on the play. The main addition of S̲h̲auqī to the material drawn from the traditional legends is to be found in the last two acts, which deal with the events after Lailā's marriage.

S̲h̲auqī draws exceedingly well the life of the Arabs in the first generation of Islam, when the Bedouins still longed for the customs of the *Jāhiliyya*. According to what is said in *Majnūn Lailā*, the Bedouins separate the two lovers, if they announce their love publicly (which was what Qais did). The chief of the family lets his daughter choose her own husband, certain that she will know how to preserve the family's honor intact—a suggestion, here, of the privileges of women in Pre-Islamic society. The tragedy reflects the belief of those times when a poet composed his verses under the influence of a "Jinnī" (spirit); and with a sure and poetic touch, S̲h̲auqī describes the Bedouin's pride in his noble descent, his sense of tribal honor, his hospitality, and the ardor of desert love[438].

iii. *The Fall of Cleopatra*

The Fall of Cleopatra (*Maṣra' Kliyūpātrā*) is perhaps the best of S̲h̲auqī's plays, notwithstanding its many defects. It is written against the background of the Roman conquest of Egypt by Octavian, and shows some influence from Shakespeare's *Antony and Cleopatra*[439].

[438] See some information about the production of *Majnūn Lailā* in 1934, in the Jerusalem daily *al-Waḥda*, May 4, 1947, p. 3, col. 2. On the language of the play see 'Alī Muḥammad al-Baḥrāwī in *Apōllō*, vol. I, fasc. 4, p. 398; Muṣṭafā Ṣādiq al-Rāfi'ī, ibid., vol. I, fasc. 5, pp. 534–535; al-Baḥrāwī's reply, ibid., vol. I, fasc. 6, pp. 621–623. The character of the play in general has been aptly described by N. Barbour as "a pageant of Arab life, rather than a play" (*op. cit.*, in *BSOS*, vol. VIII, 1937, p. 1006).

[439] This play has been analyzed by al-Maqdisī, *Naẓra 'āmma fī Maṣra' Kliyūpātra* in *Mu.*, vol. LXXV, Oct. 1, 1929, pp. 285–292. Cf. the review in *H*, vol. XXXVII, Aug. 1, 1929, p. 1265.

The tragedy describes Cleopatra feasting Antonius and encouraging him to victory. Then Antonius, defeated in battle, commits suicide, but not before Cleopatra has taken leave of him to die afterwards of serpent's venom. The play ends with the Egyptian priest predicting destruction for the Roman conquerors.

Cleopatra is the prominent figure in the play: she is not only a beautiful queen, but also cultured, intelligent and nature-loving. She strives to make her country flourish internally and simultaneously to strengthen its external power. She is devoted to her family and kind to her servants. She always greets the priests with respect, though she is too much attached to the pleasures of life to be a bigot, practicing her forefathers' religion; and yet she resorts to it at times of danger. S̲h̲auqī reveals to us her feminine temper in the scene when Cleopatra decides to let the poisonous snakes bite her, only after the priest has assured her that the bite will not mar the perfection of her body.

iv. *Cambyses*

Though *Cambyses* (*Qambīz*) was first played by the Ramses theater in 1931, S̲h̲auqī had written it some time before. The plot tells how Natītās, of royal blood, sacrifices herself for her country, Egypt: she agrees to marry Cambyses, so that she may avert his projected attack on her country. Nevertheless Cambyses discovers that Natītās has only been posing as Pharaoh's daughter, and invades Egypt, in his madness perpetrating horrible cruelties.

Most probably it was not a coincidence that S̲h̲auqī chose a subject illustrating Egypt's resistance to the invaders; it suffices to remember the trend of his nationalistic poems. He contrasts the atrocities of Persian rule with the spirit of sacrifice inherent in the Egyptians, and especially in Natītās' soul. All the *dramatis personae* are quite well drawn, and it may be worth while to point out S̲h̲auqī's attitude towards Cambyses. In an earlier work, a long poem entitled *Miṣr*, which describes the story of the Nile Valley from ancient times to his days, S̲h̲auqī considers Cambyses as the source of all evils which have come on Egypt. According to him, the Egyptians have been accustomed to live under foreign domination since the time of Cambyses' conquest[440]. This opinion of S̲h̲auqī's is reflected in the play, in which Cambyses is represented as possessed of a beastly character.

Cambyses does not have the dramatic vividness of the *Fall of Cleopatra*. Besides, S̲h̲auqī allows himself, in *Cambyses*, to pass the boundaries of poetic license when he does not follow a uniform spelling of proper names; it seems that he does not always resort to this orthographic license merely because of the demands of prosody, but out of negligence as well. It is also rather curious to note that S̲h̲auqī, who emphasized the splendor of ancient Egypt, should name his heroes in the Greek rather than the Egyptian style. He also might have made better use of the legends about Cambyses' time and might have avoided some anachronisms[441].

v. *The Princess of Andalusia*

Amīrat al-Andalus is not only S̲h̲auqī's one historical drama in prose, but is also his longest[442]. It deals with Seville in the

[440] It was a long poem, named *Miṣr qaṣīda ta'rīk̲h̲iyya tataḍamman kibār ḥawādit̲h̲ wādī'l-Nīl min yaum qām ilā hād̲h̲ih al-ayyām*, and presented by S̲h̲auqī to the Orientalist Congress at Geneva, Sept. 1894; then printed in *Revue d'Egypte*, vol. I, 1895, pp. 556–545 (sic). It was translated into French by the name of *Poème historique sur les évenements importants de la vallée du Nil depuis son origine jusqu' à nos jours*, in the same *Revue*, pp. 471–488. About Cambyses see ibid., pp. 553–552 (sic!), and in the French translation pp. 476–478.

[441] I have dealt with this play more fully in my paper in *Bamah*, fasc. 48, June, 1946, esp. p. 70. See also al-'Aqqād, *Riwāyat Qambīz fī'l-mīzān*; and Abū Sa'dī, *Dars taḥlīlī 'alā riwāyat Qambīz*.

[442] This play has been performed even in Trans-Jordan, where the theater in Arabic is still in its infancy: according to *al-Waḥda*, Apr. 13, 1947, it was produced by Wahīb al-Afūynī and presented by a number of youths on al-Baṭrā' Stage in Irbid.

days of al-Mu'tamid, whose daughter Buthaina has manly courage blended with great interest in literature. Her love for a brave and educated Muslim, a love aided by the noble generosity of the writer Ibn Ḥayyūn, is the main feature of the play, which contains, besides, many declamations about the virtues of courage, honor, and the welcoming of guests.

The plot is very interesting, though perhaps somewhat too involved, and resembles an historical novel more than a drama, both by the great amount of material that has been put into it and by its presentation. The historical background is partly true and partly legendary. The poet prince al-Mu'tamid is the last of the 'Abbād dynasty in Spain. Ibn Tāshfīn is a historic figure as well: it was he who was responsible, in great part, for the foundation of the Almoravid dynasty in Spain at the end of the eleventh century. The central personality in the play is Buthaina, who seems to have all the virtues of womanhood: intelligence and cleverness, respect of parents and modesty, steadfastness and courage. The other figures are also drawn well, in particular al-Mu'tamid, of whom the playwright gives a true and tragic characterization. Shauqī finds special interest in delineating the character of the skillful and faithful court jester.

vi. '*Antara*

The folk songs and popular tales about the Pre-Islamic poet 'Antara (or 'Antar) b. Shaddād have crystallized into the long *Sīrat 'Antar*, told and retold by professional story-tellers. From these poems and legends Shukrī Ghānim drew his material for an historical drama in French, '*Antar*, which was performed at the Odéon in Paris, on February 12, 1910[443], long before

[443] Chekri Ganem, *Antar*, Paris, L'Illustration théâtrale, Apr. 16, 1910, No. 146; 1+24+1 pp. Another edition: *Antar, drame en cinq actes, en vers*, Paris, Librairie théâtrale, 1910; 2+108 pp.

S̲h̲auqī's play was published. G̲h̲ānim was a naturalized French citizen and became the leader of the "Ottoman League," a society of Syrians professing loyalty to Turkey and demanding at the same time equality with all Arabs in the Ottoman Empire. He was one of the promoters of the "Syrian Central Committee," which spread a vast amount of propaganda among Frenchmen for the solution of Syria's political problems. G̲h̲ānim's play met with success and was translated into Arabic by Ilyās Abū S̲h̲abaka, a Lebanese poet who distinguished himself by his translations from French into Arabic[444].

S̲h̲auqī drew on legendary material as well as on G̲h̲ānim's drama for his four-act 'Antara, which was published only a few days after Amīrat al-Andalus. In S̲h̲auqī's drama we see the black hero 'Antara doing noble feats of valor against the enemies of his tribe; and at the same time loving 'Abla passionately. 'Abla seems to have the same virtues as 'Antara, and in the end, surmounting all difficulties, they succeed in marrying. While G̲h̲ānim makes 'Antara die at the end of the drama, S̲h̲auqī lets his hero remain alive.

Here, more than in previous plays, S̲h̲auqī employs an abundance of dramatic effects. 'Antara is divided, rather unusually, into acts, scenes and sub-scenes of varying number and length. The whole drama is set against the background of the life of the early Arabs, their battles and raids, their loves and their songs—reminding us of the background of Majnūn Lailā. One may notice, in the characters of 'Antara and 'Abla, unmitigated idealization; they have only virtues. This, again, is typical of S̲h̲auqī, whose dramatis personae are often either wholly good or utterly wicked.

---

[444] See GAL, Suppl. III, pp. 47, 94, 367; R. Hartmann, Arabische politische Gesellschaften bis 1914, in Beiträge zur Arabistik, Semitistik und Islamwissenschaft (Leipzig, 1944), pp. 449, 459, 460, 467; George Samné, La Syrie (1920), Introd., written by G̲h̲ānim, and passim, e.g., 62 ss., 509 ss., 514 ss., 558 ss.; E. Jung, La révolte Arabe (1925), vol. I, pp. 67 ss., 137; vol. II, pp. 20, 82 ss., 95 ss., 152, 164; OM, vol. I, 1921–1922, pp. 196 s.; Ma., vol. XXIV, 1926, p. 795; A. Dablan, op. cit., pp. 6–7. Mu., vol. LXIX, Nov. 1, 1926, p. 338.

3. *S̲h̲auqī the Playwright* S̲h̲auqī's approach to the ancient world in his plays, as in his poems, is sentimental. He enlivens some aspects of ancient Egypt before our eyes, thus showing a romantic tendency to glorify the past when the present is rather gloomy. The history of modern Egypt proves that such an encouragement from a glorious past was needed, and this may account partly for his success.

However, S̲h̲auqī owed his great popularity mainly to the great elegance and melodiousness of his style, which is very pleasing to hear or read in his verse dramas: parts of his plays as well as some of his poems were often sung by Umm Kult̲h̲ūm, Abū 'Ayūn, and Muḥammad 'Abd al-Wahhāb. Yet his work is based on a fundamental contradiction, which even his great talent has never been able to resolve: the attempt, so often and unsuccessfully made, to express new ideas in the old poetic forms.

This is not the only contradiction in S̲h̲auqī's personality and work, for he was born and lived in Egypt, which was one of the main centres of powerful political commotions in the Near East in the last quarter of the nineteenth century. These surroundings undoubtedly left a mark on the young poet, and European culture failed to obviate the influence.

S̲h̲auqī received his primary education in a way too disordered not to have a detrimental influence on his intellectual development. On one hand, the influence of Turkish culture, with which he seems to have been well acquainted, is not very obvious in his literary output. French education and society, on the other hand, left a deep mark on his thought[445], so divergent from the concepts of his childhood that it seems as if two men compose his dramas and poems: one sees the source of life in wisdom, while the other desires only to taste the pleasures of life; one copies faithfully the classical Arabic model with its rigid laws and forms, while the other introduces new

[445] K̲h̲as̲h̲aba, *op. cit.*, pp. 1632-1635, rather exaggerates in his appreciation of the influence of French dramatic art and theater life on S̲h̲auqī's plays.

words and expressions and at times attempts interesting innovations.

S͟hauqī's interpretation of the historical sources is personal. He presents the Majnūn Lailā of the legends, but emphasizes his love and suffering in delicate lines: Majnūn is ready to love more, though that means to suffer more. S͟hauqī rather hesitated to make up his mind whether Qais really was mad, and gave a double answer: a jinnī entered into Qais the poet, and love attacked the spirit of Qais the man. In his *'Antara*, S͟hauqī describes 'Antara and 'Abla calling upon all the Arabs to unite; this is not only unsubstantiated by the facts, but hardly suits the conditions of 'Antara the black in those days. This call fits better, indeed, the gathering power of Pan-Arab propaganda. So S͟hauqī not only didn't follow the historical sources (which is permissible to a brilliant playwright), but strayed away from the spirit of historical truth.

Because of this attitude, one can observe in S͟hauqī's dramas two parallel plots: the historical and the love plot, of which the second is more often fictitious than not. The two are seldom well integrated and because of that some of these dramas impress us as interesting stories rather than plays written according to a certain literary standard and conforming to the demands of the theater. Besides, his historical approach has rather lessened the dramatic tension, as some of his plays evolve only according to the oversimplified principle of stating cause, development, and effect. In *Majnūn Lailā* the love of Qais to Lailā is described with too great an exactitude, systematically covering its development and results—madness; the madness itself is analyzed in the same manner as to its causes and evolution. It seems that S͟hauqī should have paid more attention, instead, to that artistic element which might have given us better insight into the sentimental problems of his heroes, i.e., the complications of love and the inner struggles which they cause.

The unity of action is not very good either. In *The Fall of*

Cleopatra one finds, in addition to the passion of Antonius for Cleopatra, the love of Ḥābī and Helena, which prevents the interest from being focused on the main subject of the play. It is still worse when the play is woven around two centers of interest, equivalent in their importance and attraction: in *'Alī Bey*, 'Alī fights until the end to reconquer his lost provinces; and side by side, there unfolds Murād's love for Āmāl (which reaches its climax irrelevant of the concerns of 'Alī, when they find out that they are brother and sister). Similarly, in the *Princess of Andalusia*, the King fights for his throne, is vanquished and imprisoned; in the meanwhile Bu<u>th</u>aina is in love and the play ends with her preparations for marriage. This parallelism, which lessens the tension of the play, is caused, as suggested above, by <u>Sh</u>auqī's predilection for studding his historical narrative with love adventures. This practice was very common in the European drama of the eighteenth and nineteenth centuries.

<u>Sh</u>auqī's dramas contain a profusion of details. Details in themselves may not diminish a play's intrinsic value, but their numerousness lessens the interest in the main topic. Indeed, quite a number of details brought forward by him are not essential, and seem to have been introduced only to heighten the effect. The multitude of details leads to a plurality of personalities, every one of them just as important as the others. As one cannot really find a center of interest in most of <u>Sh</u>auqī's dramas, it is rather difficult to point out a preponderant figure to imprint its personality on the whole play. Perhaps the most unwieldy part of <u>Sh</u>auqī's dramas is, however, their ending. In *'Alī Bey*, *Majnūn Lailā*, *The Fall of Cleopatra*, and *Cambyses* almost all the *dramatis personae* die or are killed. This tendency to kill off the characters at the end is so strong that *The Princess of Andalusia* and *'Antara*, which finish in marriages, appear artificial in their endings.

<u>Sh</u>auqī's verses flow easily, without any apparent effort on the playwright's part. Before his time, all verse plays were

written in an almost fixed meter; he seems to be the first to allow himself a frequent change of the rhyme, and, in consequence, of the meter of his plays. He chooses a meter fitting the type of the person speaking and the character of the subject dealt with. Even the prose of *The Princess of Andalusia* is sweet and often has the nature of rhymed prose. It is highly probable that these very qualities of style and language have prevented S̲h̲auqī's dramas from frequent presentation in Egyptian theaters, where the public on the whole prefers colloquial melodramas.

It must be recognized, that S̲h̲auqī succeeded in his poetry better than in his plays. Possibly his education and culture, though great, did not really enable him to deepen his outlook in the field of drama. It is true that S̲h̲auqī had some interest in music in his youth, but we do not have any reliable information about his concern in the theater. His style is rather old-fashioned but, dramatically, the ideas expressed and the life described in his plays are new. It is in this last respect that S̲h̲auqī has influenced the poets and playwrights of modern Egypt, even those who strive to find newer models of expression.

b. Al-Ḥakīm

A not less far-reaching influence on young dramatists was exercised by Taufīq al-Ḥakīm. Since his output, as well as that of Taimūr, is so much larger than S̲h̲auqī's, their plays cannot all be analyzed in detail; hence, only some characteristic ones will be dealt with.

1. *Al-Ḥakīm's Life*[446] Although born in Alexandria in the year 1898 (according to his own testimony), al-Ḥakīm grew up in

[446] Useful material may be found in Ismā'īl Edham's *Taufīq al-Ḥakīm*, for a review of which see the Beirut monthly *al-Adīb*, vol. IV, June, 1945, p. 52. *GAL*, Suppl. III, pp. 242–250. Rizzitano, *op. cit.*, in *OM*, vol. XXIII, June, 1943, pp. 254–266. Id., *Il simbolismo nelle opere di Taufīq al-Ḥakīm*, ibid., vol. XXVI, 1946, pp. 116–123. Orvieto, *op. cit.*, pp. 133–143.

the Egyptian countryside, getting to know it well. Continuous quarrels with his proud mother increased the natural inclination to solitude in the child's spirit and probably assisted him to reach intellectual maturity sooner. In 1915 he went to live with some relatives in Cairo, where he was to study in a secondary school. There, almost free from restraint, he had ample opportunities to come to know life in the Egyptian capital. Like so many other youths, al-Ḥakīm took an active part in the anti-British movement led by Sa'd Zaghlūl; and, after the latter's exile in 1919, was arrested along with many others. The time spent in prison served to confirm the youth's retiring disposition; confined to himself, he no doubt nourished his artistic soul with manifold dreams.

After release from jail, al-Ḥakīm studied law for a few years. It was during his later years at the University that he came into close contact with the Arab theater, which in this post-War period developed considerably. Al-Ḥakīm then began by writing a few short plays on Oriental subjects, which (although not printed) were presented at the time, as they still are, by second-rate or amateurish companies[447]. His interest in the theater was sharpened when, after being granted a licence as a lawyer, he went to France to prepare a doctorate thesis in law. Instead, he spent his time there by attending theatrical and musical performances. It was at this time, in 1926, that, possibly enamored of the young ticket seller at the Odéon, he composed, in French, his charming *Devant son guichet* (afterwards translated into literary Arabic by Aḥmad al-Ṣāwī Muḥammad[448]. Registering the compliments of a youth to the girl who sells tickets at the Odéon—for the purpose of obtaining a date—this short one-act play reveals, its charm notwithstanding, the author's inexperience. Returning to Egypt he spent four years in its villages as

[447] Of these Rizzitano mentions four, in *OM*, vol. XXIII, June 1943, pp. 255–256: *The New Woman* (*al-Mar'a al-jadīda*), *The Bridegroom* (*al-'Arīs*), *Solomon's Signet-Ring* (*Khātim Sulaimān*) and *'Alī Bābā*.

[448] Who named it *Amām shubbāk al-tadhākir*.

Prosecutor[449], then worked in the Ministries of Justice and Social Affairs. Thus he came into contact with many people in various circumstances, all of which served him in writing his many plays. His unmercenary attitude has been evidenced on the various occasions when he reaffirmed his appreciation of the Arab theater's artistic mission as compared to the cinema, expressing his readiness to forego the author's fee if in that way the theater would be served[450].

2. *Al-Ḥakīm's Plays* Besides many short stories, articles, and the above-mentioned short plays, al-Ḥakīm published—in the 1930's and 1940's—at least seven larger plays printed separately[451]; eight shorter ones incorporated in the first two volumes of his *Plays*[452]; and then another twenty-one plays (ranging from two scenes to four acts) collected under the title of *The Theater of Society*[453]. A few of these plays, more or less characteristic of his various *genres* of writing, will be selected from his forty-odd plays and analyzed.

i. *After Death*

After Death (*Ba'd al-maut*)[454], a four-act drama in literary Arabic, is one of al-Ḥakīm's best. Its hero is an aging physician, Dr. Maḥmūd, beloved by his women patients. The secret of his success with the fair sex appears to be the rumor that a young

[449] From this period he drew the material for his *Diary of a Prosecutor in the Countryside* (*Yaumiyyāt nā'ib fī'l-aryāf*), Cairo, 1937; transl. into French by G. Wiet, into Hebrew (1945) by M. Kapelyūk, and into English by A. S. Eban.

[450] Cf. his interview to *AS*, Oct. 21, 1953.

[451] See below, List of Arabic Plays.

[452] *Masraḥiyyāt Taufīq al-Ḥakīm*, Cairo, 1937.

[453] *Masraḥ al-mujtama'*, Cairo, 1950. Some of these plays were transl., along with others by al-Ḥakīm, in *Tewfik El Hakim théâtre arabe traduit de l'arabe par A. Khédry & N. Costandi* (Paris, 1950); Reviewed by Landau, *Dramōt 'araviyyōt bĕ-tirgūm Tsarfatī*, in *HH*, vol. III, Autumn 1951, p. 101. Another collection of transl. plays of al-Ḥakīm (again by Khédry) has appeared in 1954 and is named *Théâtre multicolore*.

[454] Renamed *The secret of the suicide* (*Sirr al-muntaḥira*) by the National Troupe, when it produced the play.

lady who had tried to make love to him and failed, jumped from his clinic's window to a sure death. The physician encourages this rumor by hanging the suicide's photograph in his consultation room, to the growing jealousy of his wife. When she convinces him that the suicide actually was in love with another Maḥmūd, her own car driver, he desists from his flirtations.

This drama, although one of al-Ḥakīm's earliest, excels both in its simple but interesting plot and in the brilliance of its dialogue. The characters, indeed (with the exception of the physician and his wife) are blurred, but characterization never seems to have been al-Ḥakīm's chief interest. He mainly intended, in all his plays, to present some of the problems that troubled his ever-active spirit. In *After Death* he drew attention to the problem of the fading of youth and its influence on charming the opposite sex; and then gave vent to his renowned woman-hatred. An embittered misogynist himself, al-Ḥakīm never missed an occasion to use the sting of irony or hurl invective at women. No wonder, therefore, that the physician accuses all women of corruption and hypocrisy, and that his wife pleads guilty to this accusation[455].

ii. *Our Gentle Sex*

In the same line of attack, al-Ḥakīm ridicules women in one of his best comedies, *Our Gentle Sex* (*Jinsunā'l-laṭīf*). The apparently incongruous point is the dedication of the comedy by this woman-hater to the late Mrs. Hudā S̲h̲a'rāwī, leader of the

[455] Al-Ḥakīm attacks the easy morals and lack of scruples of both women and men in another drama of his, *The Box of the World* (*Ṣundūq al-dunyā*), which is divided into 4 acts—*Work, Capital, Principles, Faithfulness* (*Ṣundūq al-a'māl, Ṣundūq al-māl, Ṣundūq al-mabādi', Ṣundūq al-wafā'*). This was produced at the end of the year 1952—cf. *A*, Dec. 1, 1952; *AJ*, Dec. 5, 1952, p. 8 and Dec. 8, 1952, p. 8. Another creation of his, *The Wedding-Night* (*Lailat al-zifāf*) had been filmed—cf. *AY*, July 5, 1952, p. 8.

Feminist Movement in Egypt, "to be performed in the Feminist Union House in the year 1935." However, this is not odd if one discerns the subtle irony which al-Ḥakīm has succeeded in secretly infusing into the play. This one-act comedy, written in colloquial Arabic, is set in urban surroundings. Three ladies—an aviatrix, a lawyer, and a journalist—try, and succeed, in convincing the aviatrix' husband to fly to Iraq against his will. Here the playwright attacks indirectly the extremist demands of the Egyptian woman emancipators and what he considers their over-all conquest of public life[456].

iii. *The Flutist*

Al-Ḥakīm was even more successful in the comedies set in the country than in those describing city life. Of particular interest is *The Flutist* (*al-Zammār*), a one-act comedy in colloquial Arabic[457]. Its hero is Sālim, a medical orderly, who neglects his work and his patients because of his melomania. He leaves his work completely, to go to Cairo in the wake of Sūma (who is none but the beloved singer Umm Kulthūm). The plot in itself is simple, even naïve, but the play abounds in local color suitable to the scope of interest of the Egyptian spectator or reader, and most instructive to the student of Egyptian life in the countryside: the dirty clinic, the neglected patients, the nightly card-playing of the villages' dignitaries, briefly, the frightful emptiness of the villagers' life. The merited popularity of this play emboldened al-Ḥakīm to write a sequel on the same subject, with many of the same characters[458].

[456] In another comedy of town manners, *A Bullet in the Heart* (*Raṣāṣa fī'l-qalb*), al-Ḥakīm scolds the fickleness of the heroine, Fifi, who changes her sweetheart. In a fine, semi-symbolical drama, *The Exit from Paradise* (*al-Khurūj min al-janna*), he hints broadly that the best way for woman to inspire the creative poet is to leave him alone.

[457] Translated into Hebrew by Kapelyūk (1945), into French by Costandi, *op. cit.*, (1950).

[458] *Broken Life* (*Ḥayāt taḥaṭṭamat*) 4 acts in Colloquial Arabic. It is a melodrama, less ably written than *The Flutist*. Still another, more akin to a political satire,

iv. *Muḥammad*

Al-Ḥakīm's talent is at its peak, however, neither in the drama nor in the comedy, but in the imaginative historical play. *Muḥammad* (1936) is al-Ḥakīm's longest play[459], possibly the longest extant in Arabic. Even though other Arabic plays have dealt with the epoch of Muḥammad or his friends, this appears to be the first play treating exclusively of the life and mission of the Prophet of Islam. It is a sign of the weakening of the religious hold on the people that a play on Muhammad could appear at all and its author go unmolested; one wonders if the same would have been the case, were the play to be produced. Because of its length, however, it is doubtful if it was intended to be presented on the stage. It is closely based on the sources, naturally written in literary Arabic and includes many quotations concerning the whole of the Prophet's life. The beauty of it is that al-Ḥakīm could choose the truly important events in Muḥammad's life and endow them, almost throughout, with powerful suspense. Indeed, the reader's interest, assuming that he is conversant with the facts alluded to, hardly flags for a moment, despite the book's length. It is difficult to say whether this would hold true were the play to be presented, even in part, on the stage.

v. *The People of the Cave*

Probably al-Ḥakīm's most famous historical play is his *People of the Cave* (*Ahl al-kahf*)[460]. This historical fantasy had a

---

is called *The Tree of Government* (*S̲h̲ajarat al-ḥukm*); this shorter comedy was fully translated into Italian, with footnotes, by Rizzitano, *L'Albero del potere*, in *OM*, vol. XXIII, Oct. 1943, pp. 440–447.

[459] It has 485 pp. in large 8°.

[460] Summarized and analyzed in *H*, vol. XLI, May 1, 1933, p. 988. *GAL*, Suppl. III, pp. 243–244. Barbour, *op. cit.*, in *BSOS*, vol. VIII, 1937. Rizzitano, *op. cit.*, in *OM*, vol. XXIII, June 1943, pp. 257–259. Landau, '*Al ha-teiaṭrōn etc.*, in *Bamah*, fasc. 48, June, 1946, pp. 68–69.

most unusual success. It went through two editions in its year of publication (1933) and two more since, besides being translated into French, English and Italian[461]. The plot is based on an ancient legend, mentioned in the Koran, amplified and adapted to the requirements of the stage. The four-act play tells, in literary Arabic, the beautiful story of three Christians and their dog, refugees from religious persecution, who awake after a 300 years' sleep. Brought before the then-ruling King, they cannot adjust themselves to the new conditions and prefer to return to their cave to die. A delicate undertone is added when the king's daughter, loved by one of them and the image of his sweetheart of 300 years before, decides to die together with them.

The legend, fragments of which may be found also in the folklore of other peoples, is exploited to its fullest dramatic effect by al-Ḥakīm. Intending to get glimpses—according to his own evidence[462]—of man's fight with time, the play gives place to philosophical and metaphysical discussions, tempered by a light sort of humor. It has an unearthly quality which is still not unbelievable, something akin, perhaps, to Maeterlinck's manner of expression[463] (although al-Ḥakīm's symbolism does not come obviously to the fore in this play). In a way, al-Ḥakīm's brilliance in *The People of the Cave* has not been surpassed in his other historical plays, not even in his fanciful *Pygmalion*, in which he gave his own exquisite version of what happened to the hapless Greek sculptor[464].

[461] By Khédry, in the monthly *RC*, Dec., 1939–Mar., 1940; reprinted in Khédry's *op. cit.*—in French. Of the English translation, by P. J. Vatikiotis, the first act has already been publ. in the *Islamic Literature* (Lahore), Mar. 1955. For the Italian transl., see below, List of Arabic Plays.

[462] In his *Taḥta s̲h̲ams al-fikr*, quoted by Rizzitano, *op. cit.*, in *OM*, vol. XXIII, June, 1943, p. 259.

[463] For different hypotheses of influences on this play cf. Rizzitano, ibid., ibid. and Edham, *op. cit.*, pp. 115, 131, 154 *ss.* and *passim.*

[464] Reviewed by al-Ṣirafī in *Mu.*, vol. CII, Jan. 1, 1943, pp. 87–92. Analyzed by Rizzitano, *Il simbolismo nelle opere di Taufīq al-Ḥakīm*, in *OM*, vol. XXVI, July–Dec. 1946, pp. 121–123. Transl. into French by Khédry, *op. cit.*

vi. *The River of Madness*

Al-Ḥakīm's symbolism is much more marked in his short, literary Arabic one-act play, *The River of Madness* (*Nahr al-junūn*)[465]. In it he retells an old legend about a king, all whose subjects drank from a river which—according to the king's dream—was a source of madness to all the imbibers of its waters. Only he and his vizier abstained, until their subjects thought that these two, being different, were the mad ones; so they had to drink, too. Al-Ḥakīm purposely strips his play of any indications of time and place. One can thus better feel his short but acute protest against the compulsion exercised by society on the individual, forcing him to uniformity.

3. *Al-Ḥakīm the Playwright* Anyone trying to sum up the value of al-Ḥakīm's dramatic output is perforce astonished at its variety. While S̲h̲auqī concentrated his great talents in play-writing on historical dramas and tragedies, al-Ḥakīm tried his hand, with no little success, at composing comedies, social dramas, historical plays, and symbolistic essays in dramatic form. To understand this expansion—not forgetting al-Ḥakīm's writing of stories and articles—one need remember his back-ground and schooling. While S̲h̲auqī came from an old, aristo-cratic ancestry and moved in court or government circles most of his life, al-Ḥakīm's experience, both in his youth and middle age, was socially speaking much more varied. A strong French influence, both during his stay in Paris and through his reading afterwards, shaped his work differently from that of S̲h̲auqī, inspired as he was by Turkish and Arabic classical literature and thought. This foreign influence on al-Ḥakīm's writing may be particularly felt in his symbolical plays.

However, since he was of a retiring disposition, al-Ḥakīm still had something of the dreamer's quality that was such an

[465] Transl. into French by Khédry, *op. cit.*

asset to S̲h̲auqī in his poetical work. The fantastic setting and development of some of al-Ḥakīm's plays, such as *The People of the Cave*, is most appealing. What is so strange about him is that this unreal sequence of events is nevertheless convincing: due to its author's unusual vitality it becomes almost real. One may see or read his plays time and again, enjoying, e.g., his gentle implication of solitude, reflected in a dog's feeling of strangeness among the other dogs of the town, which easily sense that there is something wrong and uncanny about their revived brother (*The People of the Cave*). This matter of the dog is only one instance of al-Ḥakīm's extreme attention to detail, which makes even his imaginary plots and fantastic characters seem true. Another example may be that of Venus (in *Pygmalion*), who is most curious to know exactly what is going on in Pygmalion's house. Thus Venus received another supposedly womanish trait from the pen of this woman-hater.

The attention to detail is only one aspect of al-Ḥakīm's sustained effort in achieving a highly polished style. Although highly literary, it is almost never pedantic and makes easy reading—easier, in fact, than S̲h̲auqī's. Although no poet himself and an almost inveterate prose writer, al-Ḥakīm's style is often no less pleasant than S̲h̲auqī's both in its rhythmical quality and in its musical undertone, sometimes remindful of d'Annunzio's euphonious prose. It was this melodiousness of expression, coupled with the interesting contents of his plays and his dynamism that ensured his popularity. In his dramatic style, al-Ḥakīm generally succeeded in avoiding the tiresome monologue, all-important to his predecessors: his dialogue is often sparkling and most of his plots evolve at a relatively rapid pace. This improvement in dramatic style is partly achieved by al-Ḥakīm's most important contribution to the language of the drama. Himself a member of the Academy of the Arabic Language in Cairo[466], he has sensed that strict

[466] *A*, May 18, 1954, cit. in *OM*, XXXIV, May 1954, p. 239. *RY*, May 31, 1954, p. 42.

1. The Cairo Opera House

ḥmad Sh̲auqī, noted Egyptian poet
nd playwright

3. Taufīq al-Ḥakīm, prolific and subtle
Egyptian playwright

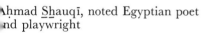

4. Maḥmūd Taimūr, prominent Egyptian playwright

5. Yūsuf Wahbī, famed theater and film star

literary Arabic was often stilted and unnatural for the stage, while colloquial Arabic was often unsuitable. Al-Ḥakīm lets each of his characters, in the plays set in our time, speak in its own peculiar style[467]. Though not the first to fit speech to character among the Arab playwrights, al-Ḥakīm is greatly responsible for diffusing this conception and popularizing it.

The greatest drawback of al-Ḥakīm is the weak, unsatisfactory portrayal of his characters. With the exception of the heroes of his plays (sometimes not even these), most characters are poorly defined and indistinctly drawn. Although the general idea that each character sets out to represent is fairly clear—here al-Ḥakīm's symbolism has the upper hand—one actually knows hardly anything about them as they are, or should be, in real life[468]. The drawing of the characters is far better carried out in the plays of Maḥmūd Taimūr.

c. Maḥmūd Taimūr

Maḥmūd Taimūr had, besides his talents, the singular luck of being born into a family famous for its men of letters. His father, Aḥmad Taimūr (1871–1930)[469], was himself a writer, who gained wide renown as a *Maecenas* and collector of books and manuscripts. His library was to serve as the nucleus of the valuable Taimūriyya Library in Cairo, afterwards incorporated into the vast National Library. Just as well known was Maḥmūd's elder brother, Muḥammad Taimūr (1892–1921)[470], in whose early death the Arab theater in Egypt lost one of its most discerning critics and of its ablest playwrights. He not only tried his hand at acting, but published some of the best dramatic

[467] *Taufīq al-Ḥakīm yataḥaddath*, in the Egyptian weekly *al-Ṯhaqāfa*, Jan. 5, 1953, pp. 7, 16. Ch. Pellat, *Langue at littérature arabes* (1952), p. 210. Cf. Saad El-Din, *Middle East playwrights*, in *B*, fasc. 24, May 1948, p. 42.

[468] With the exception of *The Flutist*.

[469] *GAL*, Suppls. I, p. 283; II, pp. 15, 217; III, p. 217, and Bibl. ibid.

[470] Ibid., Suppl. III, pp. 217–218, 271–273. Orvieto, *op. cit.*, pp. 131–133.

reviews ever written in Egypt[471] (an invaluable source for the early history of the Arabic theater). Moreover. he composed three comedies about everyday life, which were realistic and full of charm[472]. Their vigorous realism represented a break from the then prevalent literary-dramatic tradition. Two of these were ably written in colloquial Arabic. Muḥammad Taimūr thus demonstrated for the first time that fine plays need not necessarily be written in literary Arabic.

1. *Maḥmūd Taimūr's Life* The life work of Muḥammad Taimūr was continued in a way by his even more renowned younger brother, Maḥmūd. Born in 1894, Maḥmūd Taimūr had, early in his life[473], the benefit of literary contacts, in particular his elder brother whom he has always considered his teacher. He first took an interest in economics, but due to his illness interrupted these courses and devoted his life to studying literature and, afterwards, to writing. His industry brought about (1950) his election to the stately Academy of the Arabic Language in Cairo, to replace the late Orientalist, August Fischer[474]. On that occasion, Maḥmūd Taimūr lectured on his credo in linguistic matters. He maintained then that the linguists should never force new words and idioms on the population; they should, on the contrary, listen to the people's expressions and attempt to introduce them into literary Arabic. This lecture clearly aired his opinions on his own literary work. In the last thirty years, Maḥmūd Taimūr has written and published an ever-increasing number of novels and plays[475], which have ranged him among the most prominent novelists and playwrights not only of Egypt but of all countries where Arabic is read.

[471] Collected in the second vol. of his *Mu'allafāt*. See below, Bibl. The excellent Introd. of Zakī Ṭulaimāt to this vol. is of much help in knowing Muḥammad Taimūr's life and in understanding his work. See also *Mu.*, vol. LXIII, Nov. 1, 1923, pp. 303–304.

[472] Collected in the third vol. of his *Mu'allafāt*.

[473] *GAL*, Suppl. III, pp. 218 *ss*.

[474] *Davar*, Feb. 10, 1950, p. 6.

[475] See below, List of Arabic Plays.

2. *Taimūr's Plays* Maḥmūd Taimūr's literary output is so large and varied[476] that a summary and appreciation of only a few plays are possible within the scope of the present work. His plays fall into two main categories: social drama and comedy, the latter being in the majority. One has been described above[477] and a few others are analyzed below, so that an idea may be formed of Taimūr's service to the Arabic theater.

i. *Wine Today*

Maḥmūd Taimūr has tried his hand four times at writing historical plays, but none of his experiments was a signal success. He is so firmly rooted in real life—more than al-Ḥakīm, and much more so than S̲h̲auqī—that he lacks the far-reaching imagination and feeling for the past needed for composing historical plays. *Wine Today* (*al-Yaum k̲h̲amr*)[478] is the romance of the pre-Islamic Arab poet Imru' al-Qais, who vows to renounce wine and women in order to be able to avenge his father's murder. To carry out his revenge, Imru' al-Qais goes to ask the Byzantine emperor's help, gets entangled in court intrigues and at the end gives up the court's luxury to return to the desert. The whole play is an unconvincing song of praise to the desert. Although towards its end, the unintentional meeting of the poet's various *amours* is well exploited to create dramatic tension, the play as a whole is much more suitable for reading than acting. The same may be said about Taimūr's other historical plays: *Suhād*[479], a story of love and intrigue in Islam's

[476] *GAL*, Suppl. III, pp. 217–226, 255–256. M. Saad El-Din, *Mahmoud Taimur*, in *B*, fasc. 21, Feb., 1948, pp. 9–10.
[477] See above, p. 119, for *A Tea Party*.
[478] Cairo, Dār al-ma'ārif, 1949; 271 pp.: 5 acts in literary Arabic. Reviewed in *RC*, Feb., 1953, pp. 190–195.
[479] *Suhād au al-laḥn al-tā'ih*, (Cairo), 'Īsā'l-Bābī'l-Ḥalabī, 1942; 116, IV, pp., 3 Acts in literary Arabic. Reviewed by Muḥammad 'Abd al-G̲h̲anī Ḥasan in *Mu.*, vol. CII, Jan. 1, 1943, pp. 105–106.

days of splendor, or *Ibn Jalā*[480], the life story of al-Ḥajjāj, the great Muslim fighter and administrator[481]; the last of these has however been produced in Cairo.

ii. *Shelter No. 13*

Taimūr has a much truer feeling for the requirements of the stage in his dramas and comedies. This is evident, for instance, when he revels in unfolding the Arab woman's desire to have her will respected by men, e.g., in his *'Awālī*[482]. A still better drama is his *Shelter No. 13* (*al-Makhba' raqm 13*)[483], written twice, both in literary and in colloquial Arabic[484]. The first was probably intended for the reading public and the second for the stage. In this play, a heterogeneous group of people find refuge in an air-raid shelter (its number, thirteen, is undoubtedly intentional, as an evil omen). They are composed of all classes and inclinations who usually keep social distance punctiliously. The true weaknesses of character are revealed when the various peoples face the fear of death, after the entrance of the shelter has been blocked by a near-by bombed building: it is then that the cake vendor gains in importance (for he has food with him). Human nature is further revealed while the rescue party is approaching closer, imperceptibly making social differences distinct again. This social drama reminds one, in many respects, of a comedy of character: the

[480] *Ibn Jalā*, Cairo, 1951; 270 pp. Literary Arabic. This play has been reviewed by Prof. Fr. Gabrieli in *OM*, vol. XXXI, July-Sep., 1951, p. 156; and by Bint al-Shāṭi' in *A*, May 6, 1952, p. 3.

[481] Another historical play, treating of ancient Egypt, is *The Bride of the Nile*: *'Arūs al-Nīl*, Cairo, al-Ḥawādith, 1942; 76 pp., 3 Acts in Literary Arabic, accompanied by music. Reviewed in *Mu.*, vol. C, Mar. 1, 1942, pp. 302–303.

[482] Publ. in 1942, rev. by al-Ṣirafī in *Mu.*, vol. CI, Nov. 1, 1942, pp. 441–443.

[483] *Makhba' raqm 13*, Cairo, al-Ḥawādith, 1941; 141 pp., 3 Acts. Reviewed ibid., Jan. 1, 1942, pp. 106–108 by al-Ṣirafī; and Mar. 1, 1942, pp. 300—301, by B. F. (Bishr Fāris?).

[484] Thus in Taimūr's *al-Yaum khamr*, p. 271.

different persons, often having amusingly unsuitable names (the cabaret singer is named ʿAfāf, i.e. Chastity), are ably shown, in contrast to one another, as subservient to circumstances.

iii. *Bombs*

Taimūr brings the comic element in human nature to the fore both in his historical plays—thus making them readable, despite their tediousness—and in his social dramas, which are fairly akin in character to comedies. However, it is in his comedies that his talents stand truly revealed, apparently since he feels himself more in his element. A comedy of his, *A Tea Party*, has already been described[485]. Another one, *Bombs* (*Qanābil*)[486], merits mention, too. It is termed a comedy[487] by its author, and so it is, despite its bitterness.

Since Taimūr, an already well-known novelist, started writing plays at the beginning of the Second World War, when Egypt was in greater danger, the pulsation of the war is felt here again, as earlier in *Shelter No. 13*. His irony is directed against some town people who, appalled by bombardments, leave for the countryside "to improve the lot of the peasants." Since trouble reaches them there, too, they return to town, "to take part in the hard times through which the nation is passing." Taimūr delights both in revealing the hollowness of most people's pretexts, as well as in pointing out the gulf that exists in Egyptian society between town and country[488]. For descriptions such as these, Taimūr may be considered an important

[485] See above, p. 119.

[486] *Qanābil*, Cairo, Lajnat al-nashr li' l-jāmiʿ iyyīn, 1943; 189 pp., 3 Acts in Literary Arabic. Reviewed by al-Ṣirafī in *Mu.*, vol. CIV, Feb. 1, 1944, pp. 196–197.

[487] Taimūr formerly used the foreign word *Kūmidiya*, afterwards changed it to the Arabic *Maslāt*, the opposite of *Ma'sāt* (tragedy). Today the term *Mahzala* or *Hazliyya* is used, sometimes, for comedy.

[488] For reviews of Maḥmud Taimūr's other comedies, see *Mu.*, vol. XCIX, Nov. 1, 1941, pp. 417–418; ibid., vol. CIII, June 1, 1943, pp. 102–103; ibid., vol. CIV, Mar. 1, 1944, p. 300. *A*, Apr. 4, 1952, p. 5. *Al-Nidā'*, Apr. 8, 1952, p. 6.

reformer, following, perhaps unconsciously, the precept of *ridendo castigat mores*.

3. *Taimūr the Playwright* Rightly considered as one of the leading Arabic story-tellers of our times, Maḥmūd Taimūr has made himself a name among the playwrights in a remarkably short period considering that he has been publishing plays only since 1940. Like Taufīq al-Ḥakīm, Taimūr takes his subjects and characters out of all the strata of Egyptian life, from both village and town. Although the ideas for some of his plots were inspired by that excellent French publication of plays in periodical form, *La Petite Illustration*, the results were purely Egyptian. Then, again, even though the example of Maupassant may be felt in his treatment of various characters, these are none the less real. Indeed, one of the great causes of Taimūr's popularity is the lifelike nature of his types, many of whom seem copied *in toto* from everyday society in Egypt. S̲h̲auqī portrayed his characters as either very good or very bad; al-Ḥakīm often gives them fantastic attributes; Taimūr, keen observer of men and human nature, draws them just as they appear to him.

To a great extent, Taimūr succeeded so well because he concentrated on comedy-writing: his historical plays are rather artificial, while his dramas are good only when they verge on comedy (e.g. *Shelter No. 13*). By concentrating on the kind of dramatic composition most suitable to his temper and talents, he improved upon it. The satire, in his comedy of manners and his comedy of character—at both of which he is a master—is less veiled than al-Ḥakīm's. His readers or his audiences can thus understand him more readily, subtlety being the prerogative of the enlightened few. In this way his satire, when bent on some social reform or other, can carry further with the masses.

The presentation of the material is also more related to the tastes and powers of comprehension of his audiences. While S̲h̲auqī excelled in monologues and al-Ḥakīm in dialogues,

Taimūr's *dramatis personae* carry on a very lively conversation, better suited to the modern conception of the stage. Hence Taimūr's style, taken directly from life, has less finish, albeit it is more natural than S͟hauqī's or al-Ḥakīm's. If S͟hauqī's Arabic is of a highly polished, literary quality and al-Ḥakīm's suited to the various characters, Taimūr's literary Arabic is often mixed with idioms borrowed from the colloquial, while his colloquial Arabic often employs expressions of a purely literary character. This, at least, is a new and original approach to the language problem, so baffling to all Arab playwrights. A mixture of the literary and colloquial Arabic may be a solution of this difficulty.

Aḥmad S͟hauqī, Taufīq al-Ḥakīm and Maḥmūd Taimūr have not only helped to arouse interest in the Arab theater among the educated classes in the Near East and North Africa by offering them plays of high dramatic and human standard, but have also indirectly influenced a host of minor talents by setting them high standards to emulate. The first of the three exercised this influence in the writing of the historical play, the second in drama, and the third in comedy. This influence is to be felt in other Arab countries besides Egypt[489].

[489] In the season of 1952–1953, for instance, the Arab theater in Algeria presented, amongst other works, plays by Taufīq al-Ḥakīm and Yūsuf Wahbī—cf. *BE*, Nov. 1, 1952, p. 3.

PART III

THE ARAB CINEMA

CHAPTER 1

Beginnings and Development

a. The Start

Although a younger art than the theater, the cinema has had no less forceful an impact on the Arab masses in the Near East and North Africa. To a certain extent, one can gauge the reaction of the local public to the cinema from the impression made in mid-nineteenth-century Egypt by the magic lantern, the cinema's forerunner. Two tourists have described its effects: one, a Frenchman, tells us how enchanted the audience was[490]; his words are amplified by a British tourist, who writes as follows[491]:

"When in Egypt in 1853, I had with me a magic lantern. The Arabs were highly delighted with it, never before having seen anything of the kind. One evening I had quite an aristocratic audience

[490] Didier, *Les nuits du Caire* (1860), p. 353, quoted by Prüfer, in *ERE, s.v. Drama, Arabic* (vol. IV, 1911, p. 874, n. 8).

[491] J. Gadsby, *My wanderings. Being travels in the East* (stereotype ed., London, 1860), p. 351.

in the house of Mustapha Agha, our consular agent at Luxor; the nazir[492] of the district, two or three sheikhs and schoolmasters, and several others being present. Mustapha so fell in love with it that he would make me leave it, and gave me in exchange for it a large sepulchral case, containing four wooden cases."

The contacts of the various Arab peoples with Western Europe and—to a lesser extent—America grew much closer at the turn of the century. These contacts aroused great interest in Western technical achievements, which were regarded by the Arab intellectual as the chief reasons for the success of the West in conquering and ruling Oriental countries. From 1903[493], if not earlier, inquisitive readers of the large Egyptian monthlies of those days assailed them with an ever-increasing number of questions concerning the technicalities of cinematic photography, the origins of the cinema and the conditions of its development in various lands, the possibilities of synchronization, etc.; the editors usually obliged. It is interesting to note that an Arabic novel on the Queen of Sheba was, a little later, to be inspired by a film seen on this subject in New York[494]. The interest in the cinema grew even more rapidly in the years immediately preceding the First World War as well as during the war years, as attested to by the press of the time[495] which carried, in Egypt and Syria, not only short notices on the cinema, but full-length articles written locally or translated from the world press.

Such notices and articles, however, reached only a very small

[492] I.e., Local Governor.

[493] *Mu.*, vol. XXVIII, July 1, 1903, p. 615.

[494] Emīl Zaidān, *Malikat Sabā*, N.Y., Maktabat al-ak͟hlāq—reviewed in *H*, vol. XXXI, Apr. 1, 1923, p. 778.

[495] Ibid., vol. XVII, Dec. 1, 1908, pp. 190–191; vol. XIX, Oct. 1, 1910, p. 59; Feb. 1, 1911, p. 317; Mar. 1, 1911, pp. 374–375; vol. XX, Dec. 1, 1911, p. 191; vol. XXII, Oct. 1, 1913, p. 69; Nov. 1913, pp. 132–136; Apr. 1, 1914, p. 557; June 1, 1914, pp. 697–698; vol. XXVI, Feb. 1, 1918, pp. 446–447. *Al-Muqtabas*, vol. VI, fasc. 9, 1911, p. 605. *Mu.*, vol. XXIX, Jan. 1, 1904, p. 97; vol. XXXI, Dec. 1, 1906, p. 1028; vol. XLVI, Feb. 1, 1915, p. 190; vol. XLVII, Oct. 1, 1915, pp. 401–402; vol. XLVIII, Apr. 1, 1916, pp. 411, 415; vol. L, May 1, 1917, p. 517.

part of the population. Even if it sufficed that one person would read aloud such an article and explain it to a large group of illiterate villagers, this did not necessarily imply that they had understood it. In any case, curiosity was whetted sharply enough for the population to abandon shadow plays almost completely and flock to see the silent and, afterwards, the sound film, when they were brought to Egypt. Thus the activities of Pathe, which introduced a great many silent films into Egypt, in the years 1904–1911, attracted considerable notice[496]. It appears that, beginning with the year 1908, short-film shows were given at least twice weekly in Alexandria and Cairo[497]; and, some time afterwards, at Port Said, Ismailia, and Suez[498]. However, by far more important was the influence of the many films brought to entertain the Allied troops stationed in the Near East[499]. These forces were centered in Egypt and a good number of cinema halls was erected for their recreation. The influx of foreign films and the erection of cinema halls were amongst the various reasons (along with the country's relatively high proportion of intellectuals and its favorable climate) which were to make Egypt the center of the Arab film industry.

b. The Post-War Years

Probably through a desire for emulation, Egyptians were the first among Arabic-speaking peoples to start their own film production. This happened in 1917, at the very height of the war. After a few shorts, all silent, were produced and presented in Alexandria, a bolder experiment made available a full-

[496] See Ateek, *Development of the cinema in Egypt*, in *B*, fasc. 51, Jan., 1951, p. 5. Landau, *The Arab cinema*, in *MEA*, vol. IV, Nov., 1953, p. 349. By courtesy of *MEA*, I am using parts of my article.

[497] Zakī Ṭulaimāt, *K̲haiṭ min al-fann al-sīnimā'ī fī Miṣr*, in *K*, vol. I, fasc. 3, Jan., 1946, pp. 416–417.

[498] Note on *Market for films in Port Said district*, in *The Near East and India*, vol. XXXIX, May 14, 1931, p. 560.

[499] For a different view see Ṭulaimāt, *op. cit.*, in *K*, vol. I, fasc. 3, Jan., 1946, pp. 417–418.

length silent film, named *Why Does the Sea Laugh*[500]. This was a comedy acted by some of the Egyptian theater stars of the time. The well-known comedian, 'Alī'l-Kassār, was cast in the lead[501]. Despite its beginner's mediocrity, the film was an immense success. These early experiments stirred dormant emotions, giving way to an enthusiasm no less outspoken than its expression in other lands, upon the introduction of the cinema. Cinema clubs sprang up in quick succession: their members eagerly discussed the mastering of cinema acting technique. Some of these clubs attempted, time and again, to publish periodicals treating of film problems, both in their general as well as local aspects. Most of these—bearing such names as *Cinema Stories*[502] or *Orient-Actualités*[503]—were, indeed, short-lived. Their crudeness notwithstanding, they were sincere, earnest indications of the growing interest in films, and served as models for later publications of similar type, devoted to the cinema wholly or in a great part: *The Future*, *The Art World*, *The Cinema*, *The Novel and Cinema*[504], etc.

It was not until 1925, however, that serious, well-planned attempts at film production were made in Egypt, under the guidance of some foreign, notably American, specialists. After approximately two years, these preparations (led by the aristocratic Widād 'Urfī[505]) resulted in four films, the first and best of which was named *Lailā*, starring the late stage actress 'Azīza Amīr[506]. Its costs amounted to the modest figure of £E1,000

[500] Named, in colloquial Arabic, *Il-baḥr byiḍḥak leih?*—cf. *al-Jumhūr al-miṣrī*, Sep. 24, 1951, p. 9.

[501] See above, pp. 90–91.

[502] *Riwāyāt al-sīnimā*, publ. in Cairo (1922 or 1923)—cf. *H*, vol. XXXI, Feb. 1, 1923, p. 554. This periodical translated into Arabic the plots of famous foreign films.

[503] Edited as a monthly, in French and Arabic, by Victor Stoloff, the film director.

[504] *Al-Mustaqbal*, *Dunyā'l-fann*, *al-Sīnimā*, *Majallat al-qiṣṣa wa'l-sīnimā*, all published in Egypt in the 1940's.

[505] On whom see M. Amīn in *AS*, Dec. 29, 1954, pp. 16–17.

[506] Ṭulaimāt, in *K*, vol. I, fasc. 3, Jan., 1946, p. 419. *Al-Jumhūr al-miṣrī*, Sep. 24, 1951, p. 9. J. Swanson, *Muḏhakkarāt mu'assis ṣinā'at al-sīnimā fī Miṣr*, a series of articles in *Dunyā' l-Kawākib*, 1953–1954.

(£E1 = $5.00 at that time; today it equals $2.87). This primitive production, most of whose scenes had been shot in the streets of Cairo, was a photographed play (even divided into acts) rather than a real film. These shortcomings did not prevent the film from having a six-week run[507]. However, it was symptomatic of the rising interest in the screen[508] that in that very same year (1927) the Lāma Brothers[509] produced, in Alexandria, their first film, *A Kiss in the Desert* (*Qubla fī'l-ṣaḥrā'*). The scenarios of these films drew their materials—probably following the example of the Arab theater—from Egyptian or Arab history as well as from everyday life. The warm reception of these silent films by the public emboldened Yūsuf Wahbī, the famous stage actor[510], to experiment with a sound film. He accordingly took an Arab film, *The Children of the Upper Class* (*Aulād al-d̲h̲awāt*), in which he starred himself, to Paris for synchronization. Thereafter the success of the Arabic-speaking film was assured in all the Arab lands, particularly as American and West European innovations in studio equipment were introduced and the favorable local climate exploited.

In the last generation the young Arab cinema has achieved considerable quantitative progress. In 1934 the largest Arab film company was founded in the vicinity of Cairo and named "Egypt Studio" (*Studio Miṣr*). This was soon followed by other competitors, not only in Egypt but also in other Arab countries. Cinema halls were erected in large numbers in the cities and towns and in smaller numbers in the major villages[511]: In the year 1929, an American Consular report spoke of only fifty

[507] S. Zohny, *The development of the film industry*, in *B*, fasc. 35, May–June, 1949, pp. 55–56. Ateek, *op. cit.*, ibid., fasc. 51, Jan., 1951, p. 5. E. Sidawi, *Le cinéma égyptien*, in the Parisian fortnightly *Le monde arabe*, fasc. 25, June 15, 1952.

[508] In Arabic: *s̲h̲ās̲h̲a*.

[509] Of whom the best-known, Badr Lāma, died in 1947—cf. *The Palestine Post*, Apr. 15, 1947.

[510] See above, Second Part, ch. 3, b.

[511] For some examples, in Egypt and elsewhere, see *AY*, July 24, 1948, pp. 4, 7–10. Ibid., Aug. 7, 1948, p. 10. *Le Journal d'Egypte*, Sep. 15, 1951, p. 4. *Filasṭīn*, May 17, 1952, p. 4. *M*, June 9, 1952, p. 3.

cinema halls throughout Egypt, of which only six had a seating capacity of 1,000 or over[512]; in 1949 there were already 194, with a seating capacity of 190,000[513]; in 1950 there were some 230, of which eighty were in Cairo and thirty in Alexandria[514]; while in 1952 the number had risen to 315, of which seventy-six were in the open air (Cairo and its suburbs alone had 101). Annual attendance, too, had grown from twelve million in 1938 to forty-two million in 1946 to ninety-two million in 1951[515]. This considerable rise, particularly in the towns, was due no doubt to the appeal of the average Arab film to the temperament and tastes of the easily entertained, music-loving Egyptian town dweller. Indeed, both the government and the public combined to give the Arab cinema the chance of its life.

c. The Government and the Public

In Egypt, the government is doubly interested in the film industry: it is one of the state's main sources of hard currency, supplements the government's indirect taxation (through the taxes paid on the medium and higher-priced tickets), and serves the government's propaganda machine. The first point is obviously more important in the present circumstances, for few propaganda films have as yet been produced (even so it is understandable that the government should like to reserve this prerogative for itself).

A semi-official Chamber for Film Industry (*G̲h̲urfat ṣinā'at al-sīnimā*) is affiliated nowadays with the Ministry of National Guidance. It is composed of representatives of the film studios, of the producers (companies as well as private enterprises) and

512 Note on *The cinematograph in Egypt*, in the London weekly *The Near East and India*, vol. XXXVI, Oct. 10, 1929, p. 409.

513 *Statesman's Yearbook*, 1951, p. 947. For slightly higher figures, cf. UNESCO, *Press, film, radio*, vol. III, 1949, p. 162.

514 Ateek, *op. cit.*, in *B*, fasc. 51, Jan. 1951, p. 5.

515 UNESCO, *op. cit.*, vol. III, 1949, p. 162. E. Sidawi, *Le cinéma égyptien*, in *Le Monde Arabe*, fasc. 25, June 15, 1952, p. 21. Landau, *The Arab cinema*, in *MEA*, vol. IV, Nov. 1953, p. 350.

of the owners of the larger theater halls. Its efforts are mainly directed towards the co-ordination of the various branches in the film industry and its development. Some of the problems it has concerned itself with are: the export of Egyptian films, transfer of sums of money from abroad, dubbing foreign films with an Arabic-speaking reel, etc.[516].

The main effort of the Chamber for Film Industry is directed, however, towards contacting similar institutions abroad for the purpose of film distribution. Many Egyptian films are shown in Iraq, Syria, Lebanon, Jordan, North Africa, and even in Persia[517], the State of Israel[518] and Cyprus[519], as well as being circulated among the Arab (chiefly Syrian) communities in France, the United States, Brazil and other South American States. Four years after the presiding council of the Biennale Internazionale d'Arte recognized the cinema as an art (1932), Egypt participated in the Venice Festival with a film, *The Story of Wedad* (1936), and with a documentary the following year[520]. Egypt thus was the only Arabic country to take part in this Festival before the Second World War[521]. The Egyptian government, naturally enough, has encouraged participation in international

[516] Ḥasan Ramzī, *Ghurfat al-sīnimā tas'ā li-yakūn al-fīlm al-miṣrī 'ālamiyyan*, in *RY* May 24, 1954, p. 34. *Annuaire de la fédération égyptienne de l'industrie 1952–1953*, pp. 159–160.

[517] In 1951, there was a curious diplomatic incident, when the Egyptian Ambassador in Teheran was instructed to protest to the Persian Ministry for Foreign Affairs against the apparent practice of the Persian Film Censorship to relegate Egyptian films to second-rate cinema halls—cf. *RY*, Aug. 28, 1951, p. 17.

[518] Where the Arabic film industry had failed even under the British mandate—cf. the Palestinian *al-Muntadā*, vol. III, Sep. 1945, p. 27, and Oct., 1945, p. 22. Nowadays, Arabic newsreels are produced regularly.

[519] In the year 1954, some excitement arose among the Egyptian film producers and distributors when they found out that Turkish agents were allegedly smuggling Egyptian films into Cyprus, to the detriment of the financial interests of the Egyptian film distributors—cf. *RY*, July 19, 1954, p. 33.

[520] The documentary was announced, in French translation, as *Le pélérinage musulman à la Mecque* (Soc. Misr.)—see F. Paulon, *2000 film a Venezia 1932–1950* (1951).

[521] It has remained the only Arabic country to participate even after the war (during the war it could not send any films, of course), excluding Morocco and Algeria—see ibid.

film festivals, for reasons of foreign commerce and national prestige. Several times at Cannes[522], Venice[523], Berlin[524], and New Delhi[525], Egyptian films have been presented and praised.

The latest international success of the Egyptian film industry has been at Cannes, where two melodramatic films were presented. *Struggle in the Valley* (*Ṣirā' fī'l-wādī*, called in French *Ciel d'Enfer*) and *The Beast* (*al-Waḥsh*, called in French *Le Monstre*) both treat of social subjects—the peasants' strife against their vicious landlords—and have been applauded, notwithstanding the patent "Wild West" touch in their ending. Indeed, part of the sound track of the first one was broadcast on Moscow's Arabic program[526]. As a matter of fact, there has been for some time unofficial talk about arranging a film festival in Egypt also[527].

The Egyptian government has aided young directors and actors (of which more later[528]) and organized film competitions. For instance, the Egyptian parliament approved in 1950 a clause in the Budget of the Ministry of Social Affairs for 1951,

[522] At the Cannes Festival at the end of 1946, Egypt presented six films—see their names in *KM*, fac. 13, Oct., 1946, p. 175. For later contributions, see E. Sidawi, *Le cinéma égyptien*, in *Le Monde Arabe*, fasc. 25, June 15, 1952, p. 21; and Ilyās Maqdisī Ilyās, *Nawāḥī'l-naqṣ fī'l-fīlm al-miṣrī*, in *Dunyā'l-kawākib*, Sep. 15, 1952, p. 25.

[523] The greatest Egyptian success at Venice was in Sep. 1951, with *Son of the Nile* (*Ibn al-Nīl*), written, directed and led by Yaḥyā Shāhīn. This was an adaptation of the American novel *Nature Boy*, telling the story of a young peasant married against his will, who has to taste first the disappointment of city life in Cairo before finding peace in the country. Cf. *JE*, Sep. 6, 1951, p. 6; *BE*, Sep. 28, 1951, p. 2. For Egypt's participation in the Venice Film Festival cf. Georges Sadoul in the Parisian *Les Lettres Françaises*, March, 1954.

[524] Where Egypt presented, in June 1952, *Zainab*, a revival of one of the earliest Egyptian films, based on Muḥammad Ḥusain Haikal's renowned novel of country life; it starred Rāqiya Ibrāhīm and Yaḥyā Shāhīn. Cf. *BE*, Feb. 5, 1952, p. 5; ibid., July 1, 1952, p. 5. *Le Progrès Egyptien*, June 28, 1952, p. 2. *A*, June 30, 1952, p. 5; ibid., July 2, 1952, p. 10.

[525] In Jan., 1953—cf. Landau, *The Arab cinema*, in *MEA*, vol. IV, Nov., 1953, p. 350.

[526] Sadoul, *Le septième Festival international du film de Cannes*, in *Les Lettres Françaises*, Apr. 8–15, 1954, p. 6. *The Boston Daily Globe*, Mar. 28, 1956, p. 28.

[527] *A*, Dec. 4, 1951, p. 6.

[528] See the next chapter.

6. Umm Kulthūm, operatic singer and film star

7. Najīb al-Rīḥānī, popular star of stage and screen, in a character scene

8. Nūr al-Hudā, Egyptian film sta

9. Rural Love Scene from Arabic F

10. Ensemble from Egyptian Film

providing for £E9,000 to be awarded to the three best films of the year[529]. Nonetheless, it has had to reduce its £E10,000 (originally £E6,000) subvention to the Egyptian cinema to £E4,000[530]. This was probably caused by the need for financing Egypt's part in the armament race in the world in general and in the Near East in particular. It has apparently been found impossible to accede to the cinema's requests for credit and for tax reductions in favor of the film industry[531]. The Egyptian authorities attempted, indeed, to safeguard the financial interests of the local film industry in another way: they half-heartedly forced the cinema owners to accept a minimum percentage of Egyptian films[532] (one every month in 1949) but this proved to be no great help.

All in all, the Egyptian government's financial support of the cinema was lukewarm; which fact, however, has not prevented it, as other Arab governments, from supervising the film industry closely. This supervision is in itself a most interesting indication of undercurrents in the everyday life of the modern Arab States. The government's supervision is not only political and social—i.e., intended to stop what it regards as insidious, dangerous propaganda (e.g., Communist[533])—but sometimes religious as well.

The influence of the Muslim religious circles is still very large in all Arab lands, and they have never quite given up their strongly worded propaganda against the Arab cinema and its damaging effect (according to their opinion) on the morals of the masses. To give but a few instances: In 1926–1927, religious dignitaries of al-Azhar opposed the inception of the Arab cinema in Egypt, out of fear of the irreverence entailed by

529 Landau, *The Arab cinema*, in *MEA*, vol. IV, Nov., 1953, p. 351.

530 *M*, July 14, 1952, p. 10.

531 *A*., Sep. 15, 1952, p. 5, for requests formulated by ʿAbd al-Salām al-Nabulsī.

532 See, e.g., Rushdī Kāmil, *Inṭibāʿāt min al-sīnimā'l-miṣriyya*, in *KM*, fasc. 12, Sep., 1946, p. 736. *Facts about the film industry in Egypt*, in *B*, fasc. 9, Feb., 1947, p. 7.

533 For the Egyptian Government impounding some Communist films (prob. of foreign make), see *AY*, Dec. 15, 1951, p. 5.

the showing of Muḥammad on the screen[534]. In 1930 the Society of Muslim Youths (*Jam'iyyat al-s̲h̲ubbān al-muslimīn*) protested to the Egyptian Prime Minister and to the press against a foreign film society's wish to film in Egypt a story of the life of Muḥammad and the Four Caliphs[535] (the protest was repeated on a similar occasion in 1954[536]). A few years afterwards, the Islamic associations in Egypt demanded in congress that the government exercise a stricter censorship on love films[537].

The same demands were put forward by organizations of a similar character in Palestine[538], while in Syria manifestors warned away Muslim women in Lād̲h̲iqiyya from attending film shows and sent menacing letters to others[539]. Preaching in the mosques against women's attendance of film shows was decided upon[540], while in Damascus a self-styled Society of Friends of Virtue (*Jam'iyyat anṣār al-faḍīla*) asked the Minister of the Interior to prohibit the entrance of women into the cinema halls and to exercise a stricter moral censorship of films[541].

Other demands called attention to the need for censoring pictures starring scantily clad girls or showing Muslims imbibing spirituous liquors. The French authorities in Syria cleverly exploited these demands and the spirit backing them to tighten their own hold over the cinema[542]. Still the religious propaganda against the cinema went on unabated. The Pan-

[534] J. Swanson, *op. cit.*, in *Dunyā'l-kawākib*, Jan. 12, 1954, pp. 26–27. Also *A*, Dec. 4, 1951, p. 6; and *AS*, Dec., 29, 1954, p. 16.

[535] Full text in *Majallat al-s̲h̲ubbān al-muslimīn*, Ramaḍān 1348 (Feb. 1930), pp. 356–357.

[536] *JP*, Jan. 7, 1955, p. 6.

[537] *Al-Balāg̲h̲*, July 18, 1936, summarized by L.V.V. in *OM*, vol. XVI, Sep. 1936, p. 531.

[538] L.V.V., ibid., vol. XVI, Mar., 1936, p. 143, based on the Arabic press.

[539] *Al-Ayyām*, Feb. 26, 1935, summarized by V.V., ibid., vol. XV, Mar., 1935, p. 123.

[540] Ibid., ibid.

[541] Ibid., Mar. 20, 1939, summarized by id., ibid., vol. XIX, Apr. 1939, p. 215.

[542] Decree of the High Commissioner for Syria No. 165 L/R, publ. in *al-Bas̲h̲īr*, Sep. 7, 1934, summarized ibid., vol. XIV, Oct. 1934, p. 474.

Islamic Congress, which met in Karachi in May, 1952, seriously passed a measure demanding that all governments of Muslim countries close all cinema halls[543]! Not less energetic is the recent demand of the Muslim Ulema Council in the Old City of Jerusalem, urging the Jordanian government to draft a bill prohibiting adolescents from attending certain films and to censor the rest more severely from the Muslim ethical point of view[544]. The last demand was sensible, but most of the other requests for religious censorship or denunciations against the evils of the cinema were distinguished mainly for vociferousness. Few people took the campaign of the religious circles against the cinema seriously: this is one case where religious traditions have crumbled before the expanding tide of Western ideas and of desire for entertainment.

The Egyptian government has been careful, nonetheless, to censor the cinema for years, so as not to give grounds for complaints to the extremist religious organization, the Muslim Brotherhood (whom successive governments have rightly suspected of political ambitions). For instance, a sketch named *The Neighbor's Daughter* (*Bint al-jīrān*) was not permitted to be broadcast, as the setting was the girl's bedroom[545] and its wording was somewhat lewd. Then an Egyptian documentary on the Sudan was withdrawn from Cairo cinemas after a week's showing because of scenes of naked tribesmen[546]. Censorship has also been necessary, sometimes, to see that no offense be given to foreign states[547], or to prevent shooting films prejudicial to Egypt's interests[548]. An extreme case was the reported ban on all films starring Danny Kaye and Mickey Rooney throughout

[543] *Al-Nidā'*, May 22, 1952, p. 9.
[544] Reported in *JP*, Feb. 22, 1954, p. 4.
[545] *AJ*, July 14, 1952, p. 8, See *M*, same date, p. 10, for changes (prob. new restrictions) in the film censorship.
[546] Reported by Reuter in *JP*, Mar. 22, 1954.
[547] In the case of Turkish complaints, see *A*, Aug. 22, 1940, summarized in *OM*, vol. XX, Oct., 1940, p. 508. A case of preventing a misunderstanding with Iraq is mentioned in *RY*, Apr. 12, 1954, p. 42.
[548] *M*, July 19, 1952, p. 9; ibid., July 21, 1952, p. 8.

Egypt, the charge against them being that they had donated to Zionist funds during the hostilities in Palestine[549]. However, film censorship more often served the private aims of the king and his ministers. Thus, during Fārūq's reign, the film *Mismār Juḥā*[550] was not passed by the censors for many months[551], since it satirized the ruling class. To give another instance, Jūrj Abyaḍ was not allowed, in 1952, to play or broadcast his interpretation of *Louis XI*, for it described a despotic king. The same ban was applied to all shows and films about tyrannical potentates[552].

The new regime in Egypt, inaugurated by the armed forces' *coup d'état* on July 23, 1952, did not relax film censorship in any way. If the religious censorship was loosened after the Muslim Brotherhood had fallen into disfavor, there have been no evident signs of it. Even the news that Ṭaha Ḥusain was working on a script treating of early Muslim history[553] is no proof, for the blind man of letters has always pursued his literary convictions fearlessly, regardless of others' political precepts. The government tightened the Ministry of Education's hold on play performances in schools[554] and entrusted all film censorship to the Ministry of National Guidance[555]. While it passed some films previously vetoed by the king's censors[556], it prohibited the showing of others in which Fārūq's picture could be seen hung on the wall in a court of law[557] or which dealt too closely with his life[558]. They not only reimposed the existing censorship on military matters[559], but directed their attention chiefly to the

[549] Reported by A.P. in *The Palestine Post*, June 20, 1948. For later instances, cf. A. Ḥashavya, in *Yĕdī'ōt aḥarōnōt*, Jan. 6, 1956, p. 13.
[550] See above, footnote 412.
[551] *M*, June 18, 1952, p. 7.
[552] *Progrès Dimanche*, Aug. 17, 1952, p. 5, based on *AS*.
[553] *RY*, Feb. 15, 1954, p. 42.
[554] *AL*, Sep. 3, 1952, p. 3.
[555] *AJ*, Dec. 1, 1952, p. 8.
[556] Ibid., Aug. 25, 1952, p. 8.
[557] Ibid., ibid. *Yĕdī'ōt aḥarōnōt* (Tel-Aviv), May 6, 1955, p. 1.
[558] *AJ*, Dec. 1, 1952, p. 8.
[559] Ibid., July 21, 1952, p. 8.

satirical film[560], that great danger to any military dictatorship, revoking all permits given by the king's censors[561] and reaffirming their intention to continue film censorship[562]. While the censorship on films in Lebanon is mainly intended to protect the public morals and to prevent dissemination of ideas prejudicial to the state[563], in Syria it was avowedly exercised on political grounds, as long as the S̲h̲īs̲h̲aklī dictatorship lasted[564]. As one instance of the activities of political censorship in Syria, one may mention the ban imposed by the authorities on two foreign-made "pro-Jewish" films—*Portrait from Life* and *Samson and Delilah*; and, later, on all films showing Danny Kaye, as a reprisal for his interest in the state of Israel[565].

The matter of film censorship imposed by the monarchy and continued by the republic in Egypt has been dealt with at some length, because it is one of the most ardently debated subjects of the cinema critics[566]. No less than the theater, the Arab cinema has its own press reviewers. There is hardly any daily, weekly, or monthly in Egypt, Lebanon, Syria, or Iraq, which can afford to ignore the cinema completely; this is true even of the religious press, which attacks what it considers to be the evil influence of the cinema on public morals. Some journals write exclusively about the cinema[567], but these have few subscribers and must be careful not to antagonize potential advertisers, i.e. the film societies. Most of the press reviews treating of the cinema—Egypt leads the field here, too—do not write

560 *Al-Ẓamān*, Sep. 5, 1952, p. 8.
561 *BE*, Sep. 15, 1952, p. 3.
562 *AJ*, Nov. 24, 1952, p. 8.
563 UNESCO, *Press, film, radio*, vol. III, 1949, p. 176.
564 *Al-Ṣayyād*, May 27, 1954, pp. 28–29.
565 Reported by A.N.A. in *JP*, Oct. 30, 1952; and by I.N.A., ibid., Aug. 1, 1956, p. 3.
566 See, e.g., 'Ut̲h̲mān al-'Antablī, *al-Sīnimā'l-miṣriyya fī'l-'ahd al-jadīd*, in *M*, Aug. 18, 1952, against Government supervision of the film industry; and Ilyās Maqdisī Ilyās, *Nawāḥī'l-naqṣ fī'l-fīlm al-miṣrī*, in *Dunyā'l-kawākib*, Sep. 15, 1952, p. 25, for it.
567 Examples see in Landau, *The Arab cinema*, in *MEA*, vol. IV, Nov. 1953, p. 352. To them *Dunyā'l-kawākib* should be added.

only of government subsidies[568] or censorship, but also of the qualities of various films and, to a lesser degree, of cinematic problems in general. While a very few have acknowledged the necessity of government censorship[569], most demand either its abolition or that it be based on constructive artistic (instead of religious and socio-political) criteria.

The cinema reviewers themselves are, as elsewhere, far from agreeing with one another, except in their tendency to lash the films mercilessly[570]; this tendency seems to have increased under the republic[571]. While some critics desire the Arab cinema to be true to life only[572], others ridicule the tendency to portray only the most up-to-date events[573]. The fact remains that while the theater critics in Arab countries strove hard to make the public theater conscious, this has not been necessary in the case of the cinema, possessed as it is with great powers of attraction. The critics, therefore, have devoted a large amount of time to apostrophizing the producer, director, and minor actors of every film, accusing them of incompetence[574], without, however, offering much constructive advice for the future. This attitude is usually caused by the fact that only a few of these critics have true artistic understanding for the cinema; most reviews are, indeed, veiled propaganda for or against vested interests. Anyhow, the main subject of the critic—just like his brother, the theater critic (he sometimes covers both fields himself)—is the plot. This is usually described at length and analyzed, but more from the literary than the dramatic aspect; it is sometimes ridiculed, particularly because of its routine, unimaginative ending[575]. All this considered, one can better understand the dis-

[568] E.g., Maḥmūd Dh̲ū' l-Faqār, in *al-Zamān*, Oct. 21, 1952, p. 4.

[569] E.g., Muḥammad al-S̲h̲arīf, in *AS*, Oct. 30, 1946, p. 17.

[570] See the plea for moderation, presented by Farīd al-Aṭras̲h̲, the renowned singer and actor, in *A*, Nov. 25, 1953, p. 5.

[571] E.g., *AJ*, Aug. 4, 1952, p. 8.

[572] *Al-Miṣrī*'s film critic, Bairam al-Tūnisī, in *M*, Aug. 4, 1952, p. 8.

[573] Cartoon in *AY*, repr. in *BE*, Dec. 29, 1952, p. 4.

[574] E.g., Fatḥī G̲h̲ānim in *AS*, Dec. 12, 1954, pp. 46–47.

[575] See, e.g., cartoon in *RY*, May 10, 1954, p. 32, describing Yūsuf Wahbī's efforts to suggest a new ending for a certain plot.

appointment in cinema criticism, as expressed a while ago by one of its exponents, Muḥammad Muṣṭafā. In the Egyptian weekly, *al-Ṣabāḥ*, he suggested the following criteria for writing a film review[576]. Even if the order of importance of the points raised may be questioned, one can agree to the justification of most of them:

1. What is the theme of the film?
2. What is its moral?
3. What benefit will the public derive from it?
4. What entertainment value does it have?
5. Why is there a dearth of new melodies?
6. What is the plot?
7. Where are the songs?

The Arab cinema public, however, is interested only in the last two points raised by M. Muṣṭafā, i.e., the plot and the music[577]. This is true both of the rural and the urban population (although the former attends film shows less frequently, due to the necessity of travel[578]). The rural audiences in the Arab countries are often almost illiterate, or at best have only a smattering of reading and writing, just that half-knowledge which enables them to enjoy cheaper Arabic films, but not enough to make them absorb the literary Arabic theater or foreign films. Often the masses still give their emotions free play by commenting aloud on the plot and the acting, and show their appreciation or displeasure by acclamation or catcalling[579].

Strangely enough, because one expects them to be more literate and possessed of better taste, this is also true of town audiences. There is, of course, a small number of Europeanized

[576] *Al-Ṣabāḥ*, first issue of 1952, summarized by Landau, in *MEA*, vol. IV, Nov. 1953, p. 352.

[577] For the part of music in the Arab film see below, chs. 2 and 3.

[578] See above, the end of section b, for the distribution of the cinema halls among the rural and urban population.

[579] Landau, in *MEA*, vol. IV, Nov. 1953, p. 351.

town dwellers, who hardly ever attend Arabic films or Arabic plays, as a matter of either taste or snobbery. The others, whether professionals, white-collar workers, or daily workers, include many who occasionally see American[580], British, French[581], Italian[582], German[583] and, lately, Indian[584] films.

The number of films may be decreasing, for while in 1948, 518 films were imported and shown, this number dropped to 350 in the year 1950 (245 American, fifty Italian, thirty British, ten French and fifteen from other countries)[585]. This can probably be explained by the fact that many audiences do not like or do not understand foreign films. In Jordan, for instance, Charlie Chaplin's *Limelight*[586] had only a three-day run. The great mass of the town dwellers who on the average, go to the pictures at least once a week, still prefer (even if less so than the rural population) Arabic films. This means Egyptian films, which predominate among all Arabic-speaking populations of the Near East, even those that have their own film industry.

In summing up the development of the Arab cinema, the following characteristics are evident:

1. Although it started much later than the Arab theater, the Arab cinema has already made considerable progress, particularly in Egypt.

580 For their influence, probably the strongest, see Mosharrafa, *op. cit.*, vol. II, pp. 59–60.

581 Cf., e.g., *PE*, Oct. 11, 1951, p. 3.

582 E.g., *The Egyptian Gazette*, Aug. 9, 1951, p. 5; *JE*, Sep. 6, 1951, p. 6.

583 For the German films and their small impact on Egyptian society—probably for language reasons (for people prefer to study English or French)—see Centre d'études de politique étrangère, *La politique islamique de l'Allemagne* (1939), pp. 78–79, partly based on *Illustrierte Zeitung*, Nov. 27, 1937. Contrast, on the Neo-Nazi film penetration, the Hebrew evening paper *ha-Dōr* (Tel-Aviv), Nov. 5, 1952, p. 3, and *Davar*, Mar. 16, 1950, p. 2; cf. *al-Ithnain*, May 24, 1954, p. 3, and *RY*, June 21, 1954, p. 33.

584 During the first half of the year 1954 alone, Egypt imported at least 54 Indian films—see *RY*, July 5, 1954, p. 34. For the general character of Indian films and film industry, cf. A. Shaw, *India and the film*, in *The Asiatic Review* (London), vol. XXXVIII, July, 1942, pp. 271–279.

585 Ateek, *op. cit.*, in *B*, fasc. 51, Jan., 1951, p. 5.

586 Reported in *JP*, July 8, 1954, p. 4.

2. The development of the Arab cinema has been better marked in its quantitative than in its qualitative values; this is due both to lack of initiative and to glorification of the box office.

3. The government supports the cinema insufficiently with funds, but imposes a strict censorship—military, political, and moral. This censorship is, in part at least, the outcome of social and religious pressure.

4. Criticism treats chiefly of the plot and less of the artistic and technical problems involved. Generally sharp, it tends to educate the public, but succeeds in reaching only the educated class, not the masses that need the critics' guidance most.

5. The public is greatly attracted towards the Arab cinema (with the exception of a small, Europeanized upper class). The rural masses have fewer occasions of attending films than the urban. Both strata, however, are fond of tear-jerking social films of a musical character. It is to this public that most of the producers and distributors unhesitatingly cater.

d. Arab Cinema in Other Lands

An indication of the success of the Arabic-speaking film produced in Egypt is that it has adapted itself to the mentality of the public in other Near Eastern lands, despite the fact that the colloquial Arabic of Egypt differs from that of other countries. Indeed, the Egyptian film easily reigns supreme among Arab populations, being the despair of would-be emulators. Egyptian films have the most vogue in Syria[587] and Lebanon[588]. Several attempts to found a film industry there—such as the "Umayya Film" at Damascus, in 1935[589]—were foredoomed to failure.

[587] J. W. Crowfoot, *Greater Syria and the four freedoms*, in *JRCAS*, vol. XXXI, Apr. 1944, p. 156.

[588] For the success in Beirut of the Egyptian film *Night of Love* (*Lailat gharām*)—starring Yūsuf Wahbī, Lailā Murād and Anwar Wajdī—see *Bairūt*, Nov. 29, 1951, p. 2.

[589] *Al-Ayyām*, Oct. 22, 1935, summarized in *OM*, vol. XV, Nov., 1935, p. 576.

A later attempt to build film studios in Beirut[590] has apparently not yet borne fruit. This by no means implies that the people in these two countries do not appreciate the cinema and the Arabic-speaking film. In Lebanon there were in 1949 some forty-eight cinema halls, with a seating capacity of 24,000. The seventeen halls in Beirut alone had 12,900 seats, Tripoli being next with ten halls containing 4,200 seats. Total attendance in Lebanon during 1948 was six million, i.e., an average of five times a year per capita. About half of the cinema-goers flock to the Egyptian films[591], which is remarkable when foreign (especially United States) competition is taken into account.

Egyptian films have repeatedly been shot in the wonderful panoramas of the Lebanon, e.g., *An Egyptian in the Lebanon* (*Miṣrī fī Lubnān*)[592]. When filming this picture[593], as well as on many other occasions, local talents were given minor roles to interpret. Local artists usually go for screen tests to Cairo to determine their aptitude for the cinema[594]; others work in the Egyptian film industry and return home afterwards to write their own scenarios or produce local films[595]. In their attempts at writing, acting, or producing, these young men and women are considerably influenced by the impact of the steady flow of foreign films.

In Syria, too, the screen is a great attraction. The silent film and, later, French talking films stirred the interest of the crowds throughout the country. Cinema halls sprang up in quick succession, and in 1950 there were about fifty 35-mm. cinemas in the whole of Syria with a seating capacity of approximately 27,000; since then the number seems to have increased. About half of the cinema halls and two-thirds of the total seating capacity are in Damascus and Aleppo combined. The rest are

590 Reported by A.N.A., in *The Palestine Post*, June 5, 1944.
591 UNESCO, *Press, Film, Radio*, vol. III, 1949, pp. 176–177.
592 Starring Lōlā Ṣidqī and Kamāl al-Sh̲ināwī—cf. the Jordanian daily *al-Difā'*, Apr. 17, 1952, p. 3 and Apr. 29, 1952, p. 1.
593 Ibid., ibid.
594 *Al-Ḥayāt* (Lebanon), Feb. 22, 1953, p. 6.
595 Ibid., ibid. Also *RY*, June 21, 1954, p. 33, and *al-Ṣayyād*, July 15, 1954, p. 29.

in other towns or large rural centers. The total yearly attendance was unofficially estimated at 5,000,000, i.e., once a year per capita, approximately[596].

The predominance of the Egyptian film is marked in Syria no less than in Lebanon. Arabic-speaking films are imported almost solely from Egypt. Until recently, this was done through some distributors in Beirut, but since the termination of the customs union between Syria and Lebanon, agents have been appointed in Damascus, and direct importation from Egypt is likely to follow. All films, before they are shown, must obtain the approval of a censorship board connected with the Security Department and composed of three members representing the Security Department, the director of press and propaganda, and the Ministry of Education. One of the duties of this censorship board is to see that every film without an Arabic sound track should have Arabic subtitles—an interesting manifestation of nationalism.

It appears that no less than half the cinema-goers prefer Egyptian films, which is no mean achievement when the competition of the American and European industry is taken into account (including showings by the United States Information Service, the British Council, and the French Legation). It is usually the villagers and the lower urban classes that prefer the Arabic-speaking films, produced in Egypt. These appeal to them by both their easy-to-understand subject matter and their language, even though this is the colloquial Arabic of Egypt; most audiences can understand it by not too great an effort. The more educated prefer foreign films, chiefly American and French. This need not be taken to mean that any innovation fails to attract the lovers of the Arabic film: in the Damascus Fair of September, 1954, for instance, the Americans showed Cinerama and drew huge audiences composed of all classes[596a].

[596] UNESCO, *Press, film, radio*, vol. IV, 1950, pp. 365–366.

[596a] *Time, The Weekly Newsmagazine* (N.Y.), Sep. 13, 1954, p. 23; ibid., Nov. 1, 1954, p. 9.

It is rather strange that under these circumstances no successful, permanent experiment has been made at founding a large Syrian film industry, after the stillbirth of the "Umayya Film." Since the end of World War II, one studio has been built in Damascus. It has a stage, a recording room, and a little laboratory. Until 1950 (later activities unknown), it produced only one full-length feature film, other productions being documentaries and newsreels. The latter have been financed by the state, and even then exclusively for the parts which the government was directly interested in seeing included. Probably the reason for the all too small development of the Syrian motion picture lies in the lack of capital and of both economic and moral support on the part of the Syrian government.

Compared to the theater, the cinema has developed considerably in Jordan. Although no local motion-picture industry was in existence, there were in 1950 some sixteen 35-mm. cinemas and one 16-mm., all of them together seating some 8,000. Of these cinema halls, five (including the 16-mm. one) were in 'Ammān, as was an open-air one, operated in summertime only. The Arab part of Jerusalem had five, and two new 35-mm. cinemas were then under construction in 'Ammān. The total yearly attendance was unofficially estimated at over one million, i.e., a little more than one time a year per capita.

About 700 different feature films are shown in Jordan every year, divided approximately as follows:

American films	45 per cent
Egyptian films	30 per cent
British films	15 per cent
French, Italian and Turkish films	10 per cent
	100 per cent

The exhibitors order the films directly from Beirut or Cairo, where the subtitling is usually done. All films have to receive the approval of a censorship board, appointed by the Jordanian Prime Minister. Its chairman is the Undersecretary of State, while the two other members represent the Minister of the Interior and the Police. Sometimes the board asks the advice of a representative of a certain Muslim organization if there is any apprehension as to whether a given film may tend to hurt the religious feelings of the population[597].

In Iraq, patrons favor the cinema consistently. In 1950, there were in the whole country seventy-one 35-mm. cinemas, of which thirty-two were open air ones. About twenty-seven cinema halls were in Baghdad, with Basra and Mosul following suit with seven each. Total seating capacity was about 65,000, and, according to UNESCO computations[597a], had an annual attendance of some 25 million which means five visits a year per capita. Egyptian films led the way with more than half the attendance, followed by American and British films. In 1950, the Baghdad Studios, owned by a cinema proprietor, had a small stage, a recording room, and a modernly equipped laboratory. It produced two films and then closed down. Government efforts[597b] to renew film production, in 1952, had no success, probably due to inability to compete with the Egyptian motion-picture industry.

One hears of few public shows in Bahrain. In Saudi Arabia or Kuwait films are, as a rule, shown privately in the houses of the rich. The cause is that the "Government of Saudi Arabia does not permit the public showing of films on the grounds that this is prejudicial to ethical and religious ideals"[597c] (sic!).

The Arab cinema has had no better luck in North Africa, where many Egyptian films are shown regularly. In 1951, Lybia had twelve 35-mm. cinemas, with a total seating capacity of 8,400; of these, eight cinemas were in Tripoli[597d]. At the same

[597] UNESCO, *Press, film, radio*, vol. IV, 1950, pp. 356–357. *JP*, July 15, 1955, p. 5.
[597a] UNESCO, ibid., pp. 357–359.
[597b] *Al-Ahālī* (Baghdad), Oct. 22, 1952, p. 2.
[597c] UNESCO, *Press, film, radio*, vol. IV, 1950, p. 365.
[597d] Ibid., vol. V, 1951, p. 265.

time, the Anglo-Egyptian Sudan had eighteen permanent 35-mm. cinemas[597e]. No attempts at local production are known from either Lybia or the Sudan.

The population of French North Africa has been showing so much interest in the cinema that some modest attempts have been made at local production. During the Second World War, when the Vichy authorities wanted to tighten their hold over their subjects in North Africa, three propaganda documentaries were dubbed with an Arabic commentary[598]. From there it was a short step towards local production.

Tunisia boasted of sixty halls in 1949, visited annually by approximately 8,500,000 cinema-goers, who certainly appreciated the Arabic-speaking films imported from Egypt. Local production was begun in 1945 in the single African Studio, and consisted mainly of documentaries—which the French authorities subsidized—and short musical films[599].

Algeria, which in the same year had some 230 cinema halls, with a seating capacity of 130,000, was even more attracted by the Arabic film[600]. Production, however, was limited to non-native societies, particularly French and American. Special mention should be made here of the good work done by the World Health Organization, which is typical of the penetration of cinema into the farthest limits of Arab countries. Let the WHO itself sum it up[601]:

"On the third of August [1950] at the Palais des Nations, members of the staff of WHO and other UN personnel had an opportunity to see films and hear discussions of the visual education programme which the Government of Algeria is carrying out to

[597e] Ibid., pp. 269–272.

[598] *La Dépêche Tunisienne*, Dec. 19, 1941, summarized in *OM*, vol XXII, May., 1942, p. 218.

[599] UNESCO, *Press, film, radio*, vol. III, 1949, pp. 174–176. See also *al-Kawākib*, Feb. 22, 1955, pp. 16–17.

[600] UNESCO, ibid., pp. 158–162.

[601] *WHO Newsletter*, Nos. 8–9, Aug-Sep., 1950, p. 4. See also the Hebrew educational weekly *Hed ha-ḥinnūḵẖ* (Tel-Aviv), Sep. 16, 1951, p. 8.

promote health and elementary hygiene. M. Joseph Meyer, chief of the cinema service of the Government of Algeria, presented an interesting programme of health-propaganda and entertainment films and reported that since 1947 Algeria has made about 40 documentaries on various aspects of life in Algeria, the most important of which are those on public health.

"The films are made in sound and silent, 16 and 35 mm. versions and are shown to the population through a variety of distribution services, including mobile cinema vans equipped with 35 mm. projection facilities and their own electrical generating systems, 16 mm. projectors in schools and other institutions, and the ordinary entertainment cinema houses. The films are made in French and Classic Arabic but since a large proportion of the populace does not understand either of these languages every team includes an interpreter-translator-commentator who replaces the sound track on the film and gives an explanation and commentary in the dialect of the particular section. The work of these commentators is one of the most interesting aspects of the Algerian film programme. Candidates are chosen primarily for their public-spirited interest in the welfare and health of their people, since the desire to improve conditions is fundamental to a successful approach to this work. They are recruited from among members of the teaching and medical profession, nurses, social workers, religious groups, etc. They are given a thorough training at the Regional Centre of Health Education before they are sent out on their missions.

"In 1949, according to M. Meyer, more than 600,000 spectators saw the educational films presented through mobile cinemas. They travel primarily to villages of the Bled which are cut off from ordinary communications, have no electricity and have rarely seen a film. It is remarkable, he commented, that the Moslem women in these villages, who, as a rule, never venture into public places, come in great numbers to these programmes. After the showings the crowd swarms around the projection team and besieges them with questions. When health films are shown the audience invariably tries to convert the question period into a medical consultation. This is always met with the same counsel: 'Have confidence in your local health officers and in the welfare workers, go to the clinic nearest you, follow the advice of the doctors and abandon charlatans who will bring you only trouble.' The results are most encouraging and many hundreds of villages are now demanding increased modern medical services. The cities are already convinced."

Possibly inspired by the shows, Algerian actors and actresses began to organize. One of them, Ashwāq, was chosen to act in an Egyptian film (*Wahība malikat al-ghajar*)[602], while another, Karīma, got an important though silent role in Carol Reed's *Outcast of the Islands*[603]. Later, Karīma appears to try her luck in the film industry in Italy[604].

Similar work, preparing Arab actors and speakers for their work in a future local film industry, was also undertaken in Morocco. This, having equal success, was continued under the patronage of the French residency, which has also supplied funds for the local production of films serving simultaneously the purposes of instruction and propaganda[605]. These various films, despite their local success, have not succeeded in changing an iota the loyalty of the population to the Egyptian Arabic-speaking film. Many natives still remember proudly the first Moroccan film, *The Seventh Door* (*al-Bāb al-sābi'*), produced during the very brief period of thirteen weeks in the year 1946. This was originally filmed in French, with French actors; but, at the same time, an Arabic version was prepared, with the Moroccan stars, Qibsī (as the hero) and Kulthūm (as the heroine). The film was shown not only locally, but exported to France, to be shown before Arab audiences there[606]. The local companies, who share the single film studio in Rabat, have been producing two to four Arabic-speaking films a year and hope to raise the number to six. The cinema halls—numbering in 1949 about a hundred, with a seating capacity of 65,000[607] could easily show more locally made films, were these available.

[602] *Al-Muṣawwar*, Nov. 14, 1951.
[603] *BE*, Aug. 23, 1952, p. 5.
[604] See the Belgian weekly *Ciné Revue*, Apr. 15, 1954, p. 30.
[605] Landau, in *MEA*, vol. IV, Nov., 1953, p. 358.
[606] See the Cairene weekly *al-Ghara'ib*, vol. I, Nov. 20, 1946, p. 14.
[607] UNESCO, *Press, film, radio*, vol. III, 1949, p. 170.

CHAPTER 2

Production and Acting

a. Distribution

THE SUCCESS of the Egyptian film in other lands is to be attributed, to an extent, to the great care bestowed on its distribution[608] both by the Egyptian government—interested, as it is, in the foreign currency attainable thereby[609]—and the producers. These, soon realizing the relationship between distribution in Egypt and abroad and their profits, became their own distributors, notwithstanding the work and fatigue involved[610]. While the Egyptian government naturally took into account the film industry's interests in its commercial treaties with other states (e.g., with Germany[611]), producers were more than worried about the growing number of foreign films imported yearly into Egypt (some 312 in the year 1953[612]). Therefore, they urged the Egyptian authorities, time and again, to protect this industry by higher tariffs, particularly after France had raised the custom duties on Egyptian films[613]. At the same time they busied themselves personally in distributing their films locally and abroad[614]. This in itself should not be taken to mean that the management of production took only a little of their time.

b. Production

The monopoly of the Egyptian film in the Arab Near East

608 In Arabic: *Tauzīʿ*.
609 See above, Third Part, ch. 1, the beginning of section c.
610 Article *al-Fīlm al-miṣrī fī'l-aqṭār al-sharqiyya*, in *AS*, Dec. 30, 1953.
611 *M*, July 14, 1952, p. 10.
612 *RY*, Feb. 15, 1954, p. 42.
613 *AJ*, Dec. 1, 1952, p. 8.
614 E.g., *al-Ḥayāt*, Feb. 22, 1953, p. 6. For a list of the main countries importing Egyptian films, see UNESCO, *Press, film, radio*, vol. III, 1949, pp. 163–164.

is beginning to attract even the attention of Hollywood financciers[615]. It reached its peak during the Second World War, due to lack of any competition from the Italian and German cinema. Despite war-time restrictions, six new studios began to function in the war years, bringing the total number to eighteen[616]. The number of producers[617], on both a great and a small scale,was over sixty[618]. Even if some of these had to close down, others took their place. Because of its inflated profits, the film industry became highly commercialized, attaching more importance to quantity than to quality. Seventy new films were shown in 1946[619], a number which has been maintained and sometimes surpassed[620]. It dropped slightly afterwards: thirty-three new films in 1948, fifty-eight in 1949, fifty-seven in 1950, fifty-three in 1951; since 1952 it has risen again to seventy[621]. Egypt still remains, along with the Argentine, tenth on the world film list (judging by the number of films it produces), and allegedly fourth on the list of exporters[622].

The film industry's income is considerable, especially when one considers the relatively low cost of living in Egypt. The larger companies, in particular, have been doing good business[623].

The total gross revenues of the film industry in 1952 amounted

[615] Mosharrafa, *op. cit.*, vol. II, p. 60.

[616] M. Saad El-Din, *Theatre and cinema*, in *B*, fasc. 12, May, 1947, p. 86.

[617] In Arabic: *muntijūn*.

[618] *AJ*, Nov. 24, 1952, p. 8.

[619] Saad El-Din, *op. cit.*, in *B*, May, 1947, p. 86. *Facts about the film industry in Egypt*, ibid., fasc. 9, Feb. 1947, p. 7. Contrast, however, UNESCO, *Press, film, radio*, vol. III, 1949, which gives slightly lower figures for these years.

[620] Fatḥī Abū' l-Faḍl, *al-Qiṣṣa fī ṣinā'at al-sīnimā'l-miṣriyya*, in *A*, June 9, 1952, p. 3, Cf. al-Aṭrash, ibid., Nov. 25, 1953, p. 5.

[621] *Annuaire de la fédération égyptienne de l'industrie 1952–1953* (1953), p. 157. Contrast, however, Ateek, *op. cit.*, in *B*, fasc. 51, Jan., 1951, p. 6; and UNESCO, *L'information à travers le monde*, relevant paragraphs reprinted in *PE*, Jan. 1, 1952, p. 5. The number allegedly fell to 62 in 1953 and rose to 84 in 1954—cf. *Variety* (N.Y.), Apr. 6, 1955.

[622] *PE*, ibid.

[623] *M*, June 3, 1952, p. 3, published a suggestive Profit-and-Loss sheet, pertaining to the Egyptian Company for Acting and Cinema (*Shirkat Miṣr li'l-tamthīl wa'l-sīnimā*), for the year 1951.

to £E2,150,000, and in 1953 they rose to £E2,700,000[624]. The film companies have, of course, to reckon also with great expenditure. The rather strange apportionment of this expenditure is another indication of what the public insists on. An Egyptian film hardly ever costs more than £E50,000, sometimes even less than £E25,000[625]. Of this amount, some £E250 to £E500 is paid to the script writer[626], generally[627], and another £E2,000 to the art director, and £E1,000 to the photography director[628]; while a large part of the rest of the expenses goes towards the salary of the actors. Only low-cost films pay their actors sums of from £E1,000 to £E4,000[629]. The more renowned stars, it is rumored, receive much more: Asmahān, up to £E10,000 per film[630], Lailā Murād, some £E10,000–12,000[631]; Umm Kulṯẖūm approximately £E15,000–18,000[632]; while others, like Muḥammad 'Abd al-Wahhāb, are paid £E18,000 or more per film[633] (or earn, like the late Camelia—Miss Lilian Cohen—some £E20,000 a year[634]). In other words a much greater percentage out of the total expenditure than is customary in the world film industry[635] goes to the actors. One can understand the attraction of the screen to the stage actors,

[624] *RY*, July 26, 1954, p. 33.
[625] UNESCO, *op. cit.*, vol. III, 1949, p. 164. Ph. Toynbee, *Egypt's Arabic film monopoly*, in *JP*, June 2, 1950, p.4.
[626] *AJ*, Aug. 4, 1952, p. 8; ibid., Dec. 8, 1952, p. 8; *al-Jail al-jadīd*, Dec. 7, 1953, p. 36.
[627] With very rare exceptions, such as that of Ṭaha Ḥusain, who received (true, after a suit of law) £E4,440—see *AS*, Dec. 30, 1953; cf. also *BE*, June 13, 1952, p. 3.
[628] *AJ*, Nov. 24, 1952, p. 8. For the exception, Muḥammad Karīm, who is said to take no less than £E4,000 for every film, see Jalīl al-Bundārī, *Azmat mukẖrijīn fī' l-sīnimā' l-miṣriyya*, in *AS*, Oct. 28, 1953, p. 26.
[629] *AJ*, July 28, 1952, p. 8; ibid., Aug. 4, 1952, p. 8.
[630] *A.N.A.*, in *JP*, July 3, 1944.
[631] *Facts about the film industry in Egypt*, in *B*, fasc. 9, Feb. 1947, p. 8. Toynbee, *op. cit.*, in *JP*, June 2, 1950, p. 4.
[632] *Facts*, ibid., ibid. Also *AS*, Dec. 30, 1953.
[633] Saad El-Din, *op. cit.*, in *B*, May, 1947, pp. 86–87; Toynbee, *op. cit.*, in *JP*, June 2, 1950, p. 4; Landau, in *MEA*, vol. IV, Nov., 1953, pp. 356–357.
[634] Colin Legum, *Miss Cohen from Cairo*, in *JP*, Feb. 10, 1950, p. 4.
[635] Cf. Prof. R. Maggi, *Filmindustria riflessi economici* (1934), ch. 3. On the whole problem see F. H. Ricketson, *The management of motion picture theatres* (1938).

many of whom still get paid, for instance, a paltry £E20 per month[636]! The double significance of this is clear: since the public hankers first and foremost for the stars, the latter obtain the lion's share of the film's budget; this means that the script writing, direction, decoration, lighting, photography, and all other elements of production inevitably suffer. It is only the largest film companies that are able, after facing all the expenditure, to devote a part of their gains to the acquisition of much-needed up-to-date machinery, some of it even for technicolor[637]. The greatest of these companies is *Studio Miṣr* which, founded in 1934[638], has withstood a terrible fire on its premises which ruined expensive equipment and some completely new finished or half-finished films[639]. The above studios really belong to the Egyptian Company for Acting and Cinema, but they filmed and sometimes distributed pictures for other companies as well. *Studio Miṣr* enjoyed this privilege because of its new photographic equipment and other modern apparatus, ably distributed throughout its many large filming studios[640]. Second only to it is the *Studio Jalāl* near Cairo, so-called after its founder. This last film company is said to be the proud possessor of modern equipment, specially suited for fine sound-recording[641].

c. Direction

Since so many producers manage both the production and distribution, they have had to leave the direction[642] of shooting the films to others, though previously they undertook the job themselves. The directors were at first foreigners—there is only

[636] *Al-Zamān*, Oct. 21, 1952, p. 4; cf. ibid., Aug. 29, 1952, p. 4. The directors of theatrical troupes get more, of course—cf. *RY*, Jan. 5, 1954, p. 42.
[637] Saad El-Din, *op. cit.*, in *B*, May, 1947, p. 86.
[638] See above, Third Part, ch. 1, section b.
[639] Details in *al-Muṣawwar*, June 13, 1951, p. 31.
[640] *AS*, Nov. 28, 1951, p. 13, cf. *AY*, Apr. 19, 1952. For a contradictory view see *RY*, May 31, 1954, p. 34.
[641] *Al-Muṣawwar*, July 23, 1954, p. 33.
[642] In Arabic: *Ikhrāj*.

a little literature in Arabic on production and direction[643]—but afterwards Egyptians. Of the foreigners, special mention should be made of André Vigneau, the technical director of *Studio Miṣr*, a Frenchman of great ability, who has shot some of the company's best documentaries[644]. Many of the Egyptian directors have had little, if any, particular training, being recruited from the ranks of the actors. Indeed, it was not uncommon for a producer to be his own art director and leading actor; and even nowadays one may hear of the director starring or, at least, acting in the film which is being shot at the time[645]. The strenuous, persistent demands of the cinema critics for specialization[646] have done but little to change this practice, since acting is a so much more fruitful source of income than art direction[647]. This attitude is one of the main retarding factors in the Egyptian film industry; it is, perhaps, to be observed best in the status of art direction (which apparently includes, in Egypt, all branches of direction).

At the end of the year 1953 there were about forty film directors in Egypt[648]. For a relatively long time they had tried their hand at directing various films, a good number of which were failures due to lack of proper artistic and technical advice. Nowadays, almost every director has cautiously specialized in one certain type of film (comedy, tragedy, melodrama), the choice depending upon his experience. Since it is the directors' duty to choose the script, they are in a great measure responsible for the development of the Arab cinema. Most of these directors have an insufficient knowledge of the problems involved as they have come to their work either from acting or from film criticism. Extremely few have had the benefit of special study.

643 Such as Muṣṭafā Ibrāhīm Ḥusain's handbook *Fann al-fīlm* (*M*, July 14, 1952, p. 10) or Ṭalba Raḍwān's *Ṣinā'at al-sīnimā* (ibid., May 19, 1952, p. 5; *A*, same date, p. 5),

644 M. Jacobs, *The cinema*, in *B*, fasc. 24, May 1948, p. 39.

645 *AJ*, Nov. 24, 1952, p. 8, for an example.

646 E.g., ibid., Aug. 4, 1952, p. 8.

647 See above, the previous Section.

648 Jalīl al-Bundārī, *op. cit.*, in *AS*, Oct. 28, 1953, p. 26.

Among these one should mention Yūsuf Wahbī, who studied in Italy; French-taught Aḥmad Badrkhān, a director of musical films: and German-taught Muḥammad Karīm. Most of the others are either auto-didacts or students who follow unwaveringly the patterns of their masters[649].

Although some directors may have a knowledge of music (an integral part of almost every Egyptian film), they have only a slight notion about the gestures and the tone required from the actors or about the proper background and decorations. Few are wise enough to secure the needed assistance of well-trained specialists in design[650] or costumes[651]. Thus anachronisms and incongruities[652] which might easily have been avoided find a place in a large number of Egyptian films. Unfortunately—possibly because many directors and *monteurs* do not have enough contacts with the day-to-day life of the people—[653] photography is frequently unimaginative. The camera is all too often employed inside the studio, using time and again the same decorations—economical devices, no doubt, but hardly praiseworthy. Even so, the pictures are sometimes inadequately cut[654].

When shooting a film, a variety of techniques is used, but not always accurately, for the resulting effect is often at the expense of the smoothness of continuity. The sequence of the film is thus sometimes stilted while the montage (mounting) is, now and then, done rather carelessly: very seldom are all available possibilities of montage considered in the light of their respective merits. The synchronization of the sound track is satisfactory, sometimes well-nigh perfect. However, discerning critics agree that production and direction stress music (of late, American music is being introduced) to such an extent that a majority of

649 Id., ibid.
650 Such as the able Aḥmad Khūrshīd—see *A*, Apr. 23, 1952, p. 8.
651 Such as Yvonne Māḍī (the actress Zōzō Māḍī's sister)— see *AY*, July 5, 1952, p. 8, cf. on these problems M. Verdone (ed.), *La moda e il costume nel film* (1950).
652 For instances see Rushdī Kāmil's *Inṭibā'āt etc.*, in *KM*, fasc. 12, Sep., 1946, p. 737. Id., *Ḥaul al-sīnimā' l-miṣriyya*, ibid., fasc. 26, Nov. 1947, pp. 291 *ss.*
653 Cf. *al-Taḥrīr* (organ of the Egyptian army), First issue, Sep. 17, 1952, p. 23.
654 Ph. Toynbee, *op. cit.*, in *JP*, June 2, 1950, p. 4.

the films are predominantly musical at the expense of the visual element and the plot. In other words, the blending of sight and sound, while technically elaborate, is not always pleasing to a trained audience[655]. The Arab public, however, likes it this way, in the same manner in which it expects their film stars to be primarily good singers.

d. Acting

Since the Arab film industry is particularly developed in Egypt, the most famous Arab stars[656] are found there. Often even the actors starring in films produced in Lebanon or elsewhere in the Near East are of Egyptian origin or have been trained there[657]. It is there, too, that the film actors' union[658] is most active. Having an educated membership, it finds no difficulty in safeguarding the working conditions and financial prerogatives which it considers its due. It includes not only theater and cinema actors[659] but also technical workers[660], including film directors[661] though not the script writers, who are a part of the union of writers and musicians[662]. The producers, also, have an opposing organization to look after their interests[663].

The actors' union is organized as are other trade-unions in Egypt, i.e., following the Western pattern of a council, headed by a president, a vice president, first and second secretaries and a treasurer[664]. The council, elected by a general assembly[665] strives to guard the union's professional standards and financial

[655] Landau, in *MEA*, vol. IV, Nov., 1953, pp. 353–354. On the required standards see K. London, *Film music* (London, 1936).
[656] In Arabic: *najm* or *munajjam*.
[657] For examples see Landau, in *MEA*, vol. IV, Nov., 1953, p. 356.
[658] In Arabic: *niqābat al-mumaththilīn*.
[659] *AJ* Sep. 28, 1952, p. 6. *Al-Zamān*, Oct. 22, 1952, p. 4. *RY*, June 7, 1954, p. 35.
[660] *AJ*, Nov. 24, 1952, p. 8.
[661] *Al-Zamān*, Sep. 12, 1952, p. 4.
[662] On which see ibid., Oct. 21, 1952, p. 4; *M*, June 16, 1952, p. 12.
[663] *AJ*, Dec. 22, 1952, p. 8.
[664] Ibid., Sep. 28, 1952, p. 6.
[665] *Al-Nidā'*, Apr. 8, 1952, p. 6. *Al-Kawākib*, Jan. 4, 1955, p. 20.

needs, by protesting against dismissals, preventing the competition of foreign or native actors and technicians (not affiliated with the union), arranging loans on easy terms, and granting pensions to the disabled and the old[666]. Therefore it finds little time, if any, to deal with the artistic or technical factors[667] which might have been an important common denominator for the members of this union.

The actors also need the moral backing of their union: conservative opinion, backed by propaganda deriving from orthodox Muslim circles, still regards the whole profession as disreputable and socially inferior. This campaign is more bitter than the campaign against the theater, since the impact of the cinema on the Arab masses is greater and reaches wider audiences. Many families would feel themselves dishonored, even today, should one of their daughters choose to be an actress[668]. It is perhaps this watchfulness by a not inconsiderable part of the public that makes actors and actresses wary of scandal. Thus, in contrast to Hollywood and the European film world, there is but little gossip about the Arab stars, and what there is, is relatively innocent. To give a few instances: Ṣabāḥ, a pretty Lebanese cabaret singer who became a film actress[669]—fondly called by her fans "Blackbird of the (Nile) Valley" (*S̲h̲uḥrūrat al-wādī*)—was reported[670] (falsely, it appears), to be about to marry a rich sheikh from Kuwait and leave the screen; one of the most talented film stars, Lailā Murād, was accused (wrongly) of aiding Israel in the Egypt-Israel war[671] and her films were banned, for a time, in Jordan[672], Syria, and in Egypt

[666] *M*, July 14, 1952, p. 10. *AJ*, July 21, 1952, p. 8.

[667] See 'Ut̲h̲mān al-'Antablī's referendum on *Hal addat niqābat al-sīnimā risālatahā*, in *M*, June 9, 1952, p. 8 and Ḥusain Ṣidqī's reaction to the various replies ibid., June 16, 1952, p. 12.

[668] Landau, in *MEA*, vol. IV, Nov. 1953, p. 356.

[669] Details see in the Lebanese daily *Kull s̲h̲ai'*, July 27, 1952, p. 6.

[670] *Al-Zamān*, Oct. 21, 1952, p. 4.

[671] Ibid., Oct. 21, 1952, p. 4; *PE*, Sep. 13, 1952, p. 6; *Teleg̲h̲rāph* (Beirut), Sep. 15–16, 1952, p. 2.

[672] *JP*, Oct. 6, 1952, based on Radio Ramallah.

itself[673]; an attractive belly-dancer turned film actress, Taḥiyya Kāriyōkā, was arrested as a Communist suspect[674]; the Egyptian film crooner, Farīd al-Aṭrash, allegedly seemed to be entertaining hopes (vain ones) of marrying nineteen-year-old ex-Queen Nārīmān[675]. An exception must be made, however, in the favor —or, rather, in the disfavor—of Sāmiya Jamāl, the Egyptian film actress who left her country to act in an American film and marry an American, a certain rich actor named Mr. King. In her case, every suggestion of scandal was bruited about in the Arabic press[676] and avidly gulped down by the public. The exception might have been caused either by wrath at her marrying a foreigner and a Christian at that, or, better still, by the envy of other stars and starlets. For in Egypt and other Arab countries, no less than in other lands, the competition between various stage and screen actors (with all its contiguous phenomena) is very bitter. Many are the actors, however renowned they may be, who compete for a part in various films[677].

If there are comparatively few "new faces,"[678] this is not due to lack of interest in the cinema. Young boys and girls, oblivious of future competition that awaits them, are attracted to the Arab cinema, not only by their desire for fame, but also by their craving for financial gain. Instances have already been given[679] to show that the cinema-acting profession in the Arab countries is highly remunerative. When one remembers that in most Arab countries the cost of living is fairly low—if compared, for

[673] Ibid., Oct. 15, 1952, based on A.P.

[674] Reported by U.P., in *JP*, Nov. 5, 1953, p. 3. See the impressions of the actress, after she had been set free, in *RY*, Mar. 22, 1954, p. 33.

[675] Reported by Reuter, in *JP*, Jan. 29, 1954, p. 1.

[676] E.g., *AJ*, Aug. 25, 1952, p. 8; *al-Jihād*, Mar. 5, 1956, p. 3; *AS*, May 20, 1953, pp. 24–25; *al-Ṣayyād*, June 3, 1954, p. 29. Her autobiography was serialized in the cinema weekly *al-Kawākib*, 1954–1955.

[677] See, e.g., *AY*, July 5, 1952, p. 8, for a three-sided competition.

[678] Leila Mourad, *A year of the Egyptian cinema*, in *The Arab World* (London), No. 21, Oct., 1954, p. 14.

[679] See above, p. 181.

example, with that in the United States, Great Britain, France, or Switzerland—and the income tax is reasonable, one can well understand why the film stars manage to live so luxuriously. It is this luxury which appeals to the many youths attracted to the film industry, some of whom have no true talent for it[680]. The fire of their hope is further fanned by the fact that only a few of the Arab actors of stage and screen were of aristocratic origin (which, traditionally, led social life in all its aspects). The greater part came from lowly families[681], like the aspirants themselves.

One of the main hindrances to the progress of the Arab cinema is the lack of specialization of these many young actors (and of many of the old ones, too). Egypt is the only Arab country that has a small Higher School for the Cinema (*Kulliyyat al-sīnimā*), supervised by the Ministry of Education, but this can train only a very limited number of students[682]. Many actors would like to study abroad, but are too poor to afford it (currency regulations are another, though less serious, obstacle). The various Arab governments have never spent much money on film actors' studies abroad; the Egyptian government did so[683], but stopped this financial aid a few years ago[684], apparently through lack of both interest in and funds for the purpose. It was only occasionally that Egyptian minor actors as well as assistant directors could participate in filming pictures abroad. When Yūsuf Wahbī was invited to act Pharaoh's part in a French film in 1952, he insisted on having Egyptian assistants take part[685].

[680] For such an instance cf. al-'Antablī, *op. cit.*, in *M.*, June 9, 1952, p. 8.

[681] Ḥusain Rifqī'l-Sharūnī, *al-Sīnimā fī'l-jaish*, in *Jaishunā*, Nos. 257–260 (undated), pp. 45–46.

[682] *M.*, Apr. 20, 1952, p. 5. This School's inadequateness probably prompted Muḥammad Ḥammāda to demand the foundation of an Institute for the Cinema, of an academic standard. Cf. his article *al-Sīnimā' l-miṣriyya fī khaṭar*, in *AS*, Apr. 15, 1953, p. 5.

[683] See, e.g., *BE*, May 31, 1949, p. 6.

[684] *M.*, June 30, 1952, p. 10.

[685] *Yūsuf Wahbī yataḥaddath 'an al-shu'ūn al-fanniyya*, in *al-Zamān*, Oct. 21, 1952, p. 4.

e. Some Arab Stars

The much-admired screen stars are mostly stage actors like Jūrj Abyaḍ, Yūsuf Wahbī, the late 'Alī'l-Kassār or Najīb al-Riḥānī, whose art has already been described[686], in addition to a few successful singers, famed for their opera performances[687]. Yūsuf Wahbī is probably the most renowned. He has forsaken the theater almost completely[688] spending large sums on producing and directing Arabic films, as well as much time on script writing and starring in his own films. Indeed his connection with the Arab cinema dates from its early infancy[689]. This indefatigable veteran, adored by his audiences, is one of the foremost protagonists of local themes and local actors as the mainstay of the Arab cinema, even though he holds that actors should, like himself, study and seek experience abroad. While so many Arab actors base their skill on the imitation of certain foreign stars, Wahbī has tried for years to develop a style based on the Egyptian character.

It is this prevalent lack of originality that makes it so difficult to point out any truly outstanding screen actors or actresses, who not only look kissable and can sing and dance (great assets, just as in the Arab theater), but also know how to act. Besides the above-named, some mention should be made of Muḥammad Salmān. A Lebanese from a poor villagers' family, Salmān left his country at the age of twenty-five, arriving in Cairo with a suitcase containing all his worldly possessions—a suit and pyjamas. Now he has become known for his sonorous voice and above-average acting in various Egyptian film melodramas. The Lebanese melodies he sings in his films (which have reached as far as Brazil) were considered such an important service to his native country that, in 1952, the Lebanese government

[686] See above, Second Part, Ch. 3.

[687] E.g., Umm Kulthūm. These are really operatic actors and as such should be the subject of a separate study.

[688] Cf. *al-Kawākib*, Jan. 18, 1955, pp. 8–9.

[689] See the preceding chapter.

decorated him[690]. Even more popular is the able comedian Ismā'īl Yāsīn, who has a charm all his own in rendering the most absurd situation lovably believable. One of his best creations is *Phantoms' House* (*Bait al-ashbāḥ*), in which he makes love to a gorilla[691]. Other younger actors hold some promise, but it is too early to judge whether they possess real talent.

Among the film actresses, besides Lailā Murād and the others already named[692], Shādiya deserves some mention. Born to a family of Turkish origin, she was a cabaret singer whose rise on the screen was meteoric: beginning in 1948 with a part in the film *The Mind on Vacation* (*al-'Aql fī ijāza*), Shādiya went from one success to another, playing in the next four years in forty films, in many of which she had the leading role[693]. Her great asset is the happy combination of a good voice, pretty face, and graceful acting. More character acting may be observed in the screen interpretations of the Lebanese actress, Nūr al-Hudā. She is not only possessed of an excellent voice for her singing parts, but she can act admirably the parts of suffering people, with both true-to-life pathos and restrained dignity. Her able interpretation of suffering humanity must be based, it seems, on her own knowledge of the common people with whom her childhood was spent. These experiences, however, seem to have left no external signs on her, for she is charmingly youthful, thus being eminently suited to act the traditional part of the innocent-looking, music-loving girl come to grips with life[694]. She succeeds, moreover, in adding a touchingly human element to every part she acts[695]. This is not the case of another innocent-looking Egyptian actress, Fātin Ḥamāma. Conscious of her success in the role of the innocent teen-ager falling in love for the

[690] *Kull shai'* July 27, 1952, p. 6; ibid., Aug. 3, 1952, p. 6.
[691] *A*, Oct. 27, 1951, p. 6; cf. *RY*, Oct. 30, 1951. Also the Syrian weekly *al-Dunyā*, Nov. 26, 1954, pp. 9, 14–15.
[692] See above, pp. 181–187.
[693] *Kull shai'*, Aug. 3, 1952, p. 6. Also *RY*, Mar. 15, 1954, pp. 32–33.
[694] M. Hairabèdian, *Une grande artiste du cinéma égyptien Nour-El-Houda* (ms., 6 pp.)
[695] For general material on the actors' interpretation in theater and cinema, see C. Tamberlani, *L'interpretazione nel teatro e nel cinema* (1941).

first time, she persists in acting this part alone[696]. This procedure is likely, in the long run, to diminish her popularity.

Summing up, one finds the following main traits in the Arab film industry:

1. Distribution is aided by the government, but many producers undertake this task themselves, both in their own country (Egypt) and abroad.

2. There is an emphasis on the quantity of production (about seventy films a year), rather than on its quality. This is brought about by the large profits of the film industry.

3. The film directors and their technical assistants lack a sufficient standard of specialization, which is often harmful to the montage of new films.

4. The visual element in the film is somewhat neglected, thus bowing to the music-loving public.

5. Actors and actresses, while under suspicion by the religious circles and always menaced with scandals (although less so than in the West), are amply compensated by large remuneration. This attracts many youngsters to the cinema.

6. While many screen actors and actresses still imitate great film stars, there are already a few original Arab actors and actresses who, besides a good voice and an ability to dance, have the knack for good character acting.

[696] See art. on Fātin Ḥamāma in *RY*, Jan. 11, 1954, p. 35. Cf. ibid., Apr. 4, 1954, p. 42, Apr. 12, 1954, p. 33, and May 3, 1954, p. 32, for her failure to act this part in real life.

CHAPTER 3

Themes of the Arab Cinema

a. Script Writing

One of the great drawbacks in the Arab cinema is the faulty script[697] writing. The lack of specialization is, perhaps, even more obvious in script writing—exclusively done by local authors—than in the technique of montage, where the local film industry has had the benefit of foreign guidance. With few exceptions, script writing in Egypt is done by people connected with the cinema in various ways, some of them directors or actors. A few of these write occasionally, others make a living at it. In the latter category ʿAlī'l-Zarqānī may be cited as a typical example: he allegedly manages to write some ten scripts a year, with almost clocklike regularity[698]. Another author boasts of writing a script—without the songs, it is true—in no more than three hours[699]. It is evident that at this rate the quality of the scripts is bound to suffer.

The result has been an amazing repetition of the practice customary in the nineteenth-century Arabic theater: The plots of diverse American and European films were adapted to Egyptian surroundings and new scripts were "created." As the name of the foreign film was often intentionally concealed[700], the original plot was many times quite unrecognizable in its Egyptianized form. Others, on the contrary, were so inefficiently patched up that the critics had no difficulty whatsoever in naming the original plot of the foreign film, which made a large part

[697] In Arabic: *sīnāriyō* (i.e., scenario).

[698] *Al-Jail al-jadīd*, Dec. 7, 1953, p. 36. See also *AY*, Dec. 25, 1948, p. 10 and Jan. 1, 1949, p. 10.

[699] 5 *kuttāb wa-5 ārā' fi'l-sīnimā*, in *AS*, Dec. 9, 1953.

[700] *Farīd al-Aṭrash yaṭlub fatḥ al-bāb ʿalā miṣrāʿaih*, ibid., Dec. 16, 1953, p. 9.

of the public feel that it had been cheated[701]. It appears that this doubtful practice was almost unknown before the Second World War. It apparently started[702] with the late Aḥmad Sālim's thinly veiled adaptation of *Random Harvest*. This was one of the Egyptian films presented at the Cannes Film Festival at the end of 1946[703]. Named *The Unknown Past* (*al-Māḍī'l-majhūl*) and starring the gifted Lailā Murād in Greer Garson's part[704], this Arabic film was such a success that it encouraged emulators in adaptation.

A smaller number of script writers get their inspiration from various foreign or local novels and stories. Most script writers, be they original minds, story plagiarists, or foreign-film adapters must however conform to certain rules. The usual procedure is for the producer to hire, first of all, his director and make a contract with some great star; then he asks for a script of a certain type to suit his stars. The following advertisement in the press[705] is fairly characteristic of the practice which subordinates the script writer's work to the actor's inclination:

"The 'Abd al-Wahhāb Film [Company] requests the honorable writers and authors to present a story, suitable for a cinematographic film starred by the musician 'Abd al-Wahhāb and directed by Muḥammad Karīm. The conditions are that the story be humane, or social, or patriotic, and that its events be modern (recent). Every writer should present a story with clear ideas and events, not longer than two foolscap pages. This should reach the 'Abd al-Wahhāb Film [Company], 25, Taufīq Street, Cairo, not later than September 15, 1952."

b. Types of Films

Since the greatest profits in the Arab film industry are de-

701 Faṭḥī Abū'l-Faḍl, *op. cit.*, in *A*, June 9, 1952.

702 Jalīl al-Bundārī, *Hal 'indanā kuttāb sīnāriyō* in *AS*, Oct. 21, 1953, p. 22.

703 *KM*, fasc. 13, Oct. 1946, p. 175.

704 Fully reviewed by Rushdī Kāmil, ibid., fasc. 8, May, 1946, pp. 706–708. Wgt (Gideon Weigert), in *JP*, Aug. 22, 1950, p. 2.

705 Transl. from *M*, Aug. 27, 1952, p. 5. For some ways to improve script writing, see, e.g., E. Vale, *The technique of screenplay writing* (1944).

rived from feature films with an interesting plot, both the producers and the public demand more of these from the script writers, who turn out, therefore, few original stories and many adaptations. This approach not only hampers the Arabic feature film[706] but also leaves little place for documentaries and instructional films[707].

Documentary films produced without governmental assistance are rare. It aided a newsreel (*Jarīdat Miṣr al-nāṭiqa*), showing pictures of life in Egypt and abroad; since sending its photographers abroad proved too expensive[708], most of the foreign parts of this newsreel were apparently obtained under an exchange system with four film companies (American, British, French, and Italian)[709]. Even though the government does not seem to aid financially the preparation of other documentaries (on the police organization[710] and the 1952 revolution[711]), reflecting the spirit of the times, it still places all the necessary facilities at the disposal of the producers and directors. The same applies to the private filming of pictures on religious subjects, aiming at diffusing better knowledge on religious matters in Arab lands. Among the best of these films is the one describing the pilgrimage to the Holy Places of Islam (*Al-ḥajj ilā bait Allāh al-ḥarām*), which, after being the cause of a diplomatic incident between Egypt and Saudi Arabia in 1936[712], was subsequently modified[713] and entered in the contest of the Venetian

[706] Cf. Ṭulaimāt's exposition of this problem in his *al-Qiṣṣa fī 'ālam al-sīnimā*, publ. in *K*, vol. I, fasc. 6, Apr. 1946, pp. 902–908.

[707] For documentaries and their place in the world film industry, see M. Herbier (ed.), *Intelligence du cinématographe* (1946), esp. ch. 5, pp. 403 *ss.*; and the miscellany *Cinéma d'aujourd'hui*, publ. by Congrès International du Cinéma à Bâle (1945), esp. pp. 163 *ss.*

[708] *AJ*, Dec. 1, 1952, p. 8.

[709] Of these, only the French company demands financial remuneration besides the exchange—see ibid., Dec. 22, 1952, p. 8. It seems that recently the production of this newsreel was discontinued, at least for the time being.

[710] Ibid., ibid.; *al-Akhbār*, Oct. 22, 1952, p. 8.

[711] *AS*, Dec. 30, 1953. Lately, the government itself produces documentaries.

[712] *OM*, vol. XVI, Apr. 1936, p. 237, based on the Egyptian press.

[713] Ibid., vol. XIX, Jan. 1939, p. 66, based on *Minbar al-sharq* of Cairo, Nov. 22, 1938.

Biennale[714]. Its success prompted others to follow[715], notwithstanding the delicate problem of religious opposition to the cinema in general.

The governments have undertaken however (in Egypt, particularly) the financing of several educational and political films. Even so, when compared to other film industries[716], only a small number of Arab films has been devoted to instructional aims. One feels that neither the government nor the film industry has fully grasped the need of the local populations for instructional films in Arabic.

During the Second World War, passive defense was explained to the population by film shows[717]. Several 16-mm. short documentaries have been prepared by the Egyptian Ministries of Health, Agriculture, and Social Affairs. The Ministry of Health strives to teach the peasants hygiene; that of Agriculture modern developments in fieldwork; and that of Social Affairs fuller co-operation[718]. The latter distributed, in 1951, two films on social activity in Egypt, the first dealing with the reforms carried out by social centers in rural areas, the second with the activities of private social organizations. These two films were produced, however, in French, primarily for propaganda purposes—so that they could be sent abroad[719]. The same purpose is evident in two other documentaries, *Sugar* and *The Pyramids*[720].

The Ministry of Education in Egypt, more than other ministries, has come under the fire of the critics, who have continually pointed out the danger of the cinema for the

714 See above, footnote 520.

715 *M*, June 29, 1952, p. 5; *AJ*, July 14, 1952, p. 8.

716 P. Thévenard & G. Tassel, *Le Cinéma scientifique français*.

717 *A.*, June 18, Nov. 3 & 4, 1941—summarized in *OM*, vol. XXI, Sep., 1941, p. 477 and vol. XXII, Jan., 1942, p. 23.

718 UNESCO, *Press, film, radio*, vol. III, 1949, p. 165.

719 *Al-Balāgh*, July 3, 1941, summarized ibid., vol. XXI, Oct., 1941, p. 530. *AL*, Dec. 7, 1951, p. 6. *JE*, Dec. 22, 1951. Landau, in *MEA*, vol. IV, Nov., 1953, p. 354.

720 M. Jacobs, *The Cinema*, in *B*, fasc. 24, May, 1948, p. 39.

younger generation[721]. Others have accused it of saving money by not using educational films in schools[722]. This is only partly true. The Ministry apparently has a special section dealing with audio-visual aids, including the film, in schools[723]; films are also used for instruction in the armed forces[724]. Too many of these however, are of foreign make, not fully suitable for the local public.

If the Arab governments were none too quick to grasp the educational and teaching value of the film, they were very quick indeed to sense its usefulness as propaganda. As early as 1937, the press was pointing out the possibilities of film propaganda[725]. Even in Iraq, where the film industry is only in its infancy, the authorities were planning in the year 1952 the preparation of a film describing Iraq's progress[726]. In this field too, however, Egypt was leading the way, as an outcome of its experience and potentialities. To give a few instances[727]: the Egyptian Minister for Propaganda laid plans for a documentary to show other countries the paintings of native children[728]; after the army revolution, a propaganda film about life in the Egyptian countryside was planned, in Arabic and French[729]; while other films, inspired and backed by the new regime, were to describe its new organization, the "Popular Front[730]." Negotiations were conducted with American film companies to prepare some propaganda documentaries for Egypt[731]. An American documentary on the plight of the Arab refugees was

[721] E.g., in *al-Muṣawwar*, June 29, 1951, p. 5.
[722] *M*, July 14, 1952, p. 10; *A*, Nov. 26, 1952.
[723] *A*, Sep. 20, 1952, p. 4.
[724] Ibid., May 10, 1952. For further details cf. UNESCO, *op. cit.*, vol. III (1949), pp. 163 *ss*.
[725] E.g., Aḥmad Kamāl Surūr, *al-Diʿāya li-Miṣr bi'l-sīnimā*, in *al-Rādyū'l-miṣrī*, Jan. 9, 1937, pp. 6, 11.
[726] *Al-Ahālī* (Baghdad), Oct. 22, 1952, p. 2.
[727] See also above, the documentaries, in French, on social life in Egypt.
[728] *A*, Apr. 9, 1952, p. 8.
[729] *Al-Zamān*, Aug. 29, 1952, p. 4; ibid., Oct. 21, 1952, p. 4.
[730] *AJ*, Mar. 2, 1953, p. 8.
[731] Ibid., ibid.

dubbed (post-synchronized) for Arabic and shown to overflowing audiences[732]. Furthermore, an Egyptian-produced propaganda film, *Bloody Palestine*, was reported in 1954 as nearing completion[733]; its aim seems to have been the vindication of the Arab defeat in Palestine six years before.

c. The Main Themes

The themes dealt with by the Arab cinema differ very little from those of the Arab theater[734] and therefore they will be accorded less space. A characteristic common to most feature films[735] is the musical part which sometimes gets the greatest attention[736]; this is even more evident than in the Arab theater. Suited as it is to the audience's taste, this often makes the film more pleasantly elaborate to the ear than to the eye. The musical score, although perfect in itself, is hardly ever given successfully as a background to the plot, even in the type of film that requires such an interplay[737]. One has too often the impression that one attends not a musical film, but, say, a photographed revue[738].

There seem to be two main currents of thematic interpretation in the Arab cinema. Firstly the realistic, which demands a true portrayal of everyday life[739] (chiefly in high society), even if this be exaggerated[740]. Secondly, the nonrealistic, which regards the cinema as an art, not photographic only, and wants it, as such, to describe even the most fantastic situations if they give food for thought. This difference of opinion is not new, nor

[732] Radio Cairo, Oct. 11, 1951, evening news bulletin; *AY*, June 14, 1952, p. 5.

[733] *JP*, Sep. 21, 1954, based on *Filasṭīn*. Lately, Egypt's army has produced many films.

[734] See above, Second Part, ch. 4.

[735] In many shorter films, too, such as those mentioned in *AJ*, July 28, 1952, p. 8.

[736] For a typical example see WGT in *JP*, Oct. 13, 1954.

[737] L. Chiarini (ed.), *La musica nel film* (1950) discusses these problems more fully.

[738] E.g., the film *The Circus Girl* (*Fatāt al-sīrk*)—cf. *al-Muṣawwar*, Sep. 21, 1951, p. 2.

[739] See, for this point of view (of the majority), Kamāl 'Aṭiyya, *al-Qiṣṣa al-sīnimā'iyya*, in *AJ*, Oct. 31, 1952, p. 8.

[740] E.g., always showing the Sudanese as waiters, janitors and hawkers—cf. the protest ibid., Dec. 22, 1952, p. 8.

is it confined to the Arab countries alone. In them, however, it seems that realistic films are preferred, possibly because their generally unsophisticated character lends itself more easily to understanding. Therefore the simple, lively film is attended by larger audiences, a fact appreciated of course by the business section of the film industry.

The themes of the Arabic feature films fall naturally into the following classification: the farce, the historical play, the melodrama, the drama, the comedy, and the political film.

1. *The Farce* This genre is as popular with the rural masses and the less educated urban class as the stage farce, possibly even more, because of its technical potentialities. A good example may be *The Woman's Play* (*La'bat al-sitt*), starring Taḥiyya Kāriyōkā, Bis̲h̲āra Wākīm, and the late Najīb al-Rīḥānī. This film was presented at the Cannes Film Festival late in the year 1946[741]. It describes the adventures of luckless Ḥasan (al-Rīḥānī) and his wife (Kāriyōkā) who becomes a film star. The comic effect, rather rough though it is, is obtained: i. by ambiguous situations, such as Ḥasan entering a room at night, not to seduce a girl, but to hunt for cigarette stubs; or the Lebanese suitor who mistakenly believes the girl to be unmarried. ii. by slapstick, such as Ḥasan trying to understand the wishes of a deaf-mute customer; the jilted man with the funny name of Balalaika, receiving a cream cake full in the face; a row in a cabaret, etc.[742]. Were it not for the slapstick, the film would have the elements of true comedy.

2. *Historical Films* There have not been many historical films worthy of the name. Lately the popularity of the historical film seems to be on the wane, since the public—whose nationalist aspirations, gathering new force from the historical film, have

[741] *KM*, fasc. 13, Oct., 1946, p. 175.

[742] For the details of the plot, see Rus̲h̲dī Kāmil, in *KM*, fasc. 7, Apr. 1946, pp. 523–524. Later, Kāmil considered this film as the only successful one in that season—cf. ibid., fasc. 12, Sep. 1946, p. 737.

been largely fulfilled—prefers films on modern topics. *'Antar and 'Abla*, starring Kōkā and Sirāj Munīr, treats of love and warfare in Pre-Islamic Arabia[743] in a way more suited to the life-like Oriental background than in certain Hollywood films on this subject[744]. Among other historical films[745], special mention should be made of the exquisite *Ḥabbāba*, admirable in its presentation of life and manners at the Court of the Caliph Yazīd II: Among the singing and dancing frolics at this Court, the film shows Ḥabbāba, the caliph's beloved, quietly going forward to her tragic end amid the endless rivalries of the ruler's family and courtiers[746]. Other noteworthy films, such as *Ṣalāḥ al-Dīn*, stress—with no little success—glorious epochs in Islamic history. Some historical films show deep interest in and sincere enthusiasm for the past.

3. *Melodramas* Melodramas are probably the best-liked films. In this category one does not necessarily count only musical films for there is hardly an Arab film which is not largely musical. The melodramatic film treats of an exciting trend of events, usually of an oversentimental quality, breath-taking and tear-jerking. The favorite themes are: the evil influence of games of chance, the young wife choking her aged husband whose wealth she plans to inherit, the youth attacking the poor girl after having made her drunk (all in *The Time of Wonders*[747]); the woman haunted by her own or her parents' past (*A Night of Love*[748]); and the girl suffering because of her father's drunkenness (*The Cup of Affliction*[749]). Other melodramas of the screen describe the criminal possibilities involved in the inheritance

[743] A topic dealt with in the Arabic theater, too, e.g., by Sh̲auqī—see above, Second Part, ch. 5, section a.

[744] M. Hairabèdian, *Les films égyptiens et ceux de Hollywood* (1950), pp. 28–29. Reviewed by Landau, in *HH*, vol. V, Winter 1954, pp. 145–146.

[745] Hairabèdian, ibid., pp. 22–23.

[746] Landau, in *MEA*, vol. IV, Nov., 1953, p. 355.

[747] *Zamān al-'ajā'ib*, starring Zōzō Nabīl—cf. *al-Nidā'*, July 22, 1952, p. 8.

[748] *Lailat g̲harām*—cf. *BE*, May 13, 1952, p. 5.

[749] *Ka's al-'ad̲h̲āb*, starring Fātin Ḥamāma and Muḥsin Sirḥān—cf. *M*, July 21, 1952, p. 5; *AJ*, Aug. 4, 1952, p. 8.

laws[750], how the unscrupulous woman breaks a home (*Master Ḥasan*[751]) and the disastrous impact of city life and luxury on the unsophisticated, simple rural life[752]. Such emotion-stirring effects are the only ones calculated to move the audience and increase the tension[753], since (until recently) one saw little caressing and even less kissing in the Arab film.

4. *Dramas* While many dramas tend to become melodramas, in a large measure because of the public clamor, there are still many good dramas shown on the screen; indeed, more than on the stage. Most of the themes are borrowed from contemporary family life and social relations in Egypt: a woman's jealousy of her husband, a physician who refuses to divulge his professional secrets to her (*Nāhid*[754]); the only son of a rich family, enamored of a poor neighbor whom he saves from the imminent danger of prostitution (*The Poor*[755]); the toil and misery of the working class (*The Locksmith's Son*[756]); and the exploitation by the rich feudal Pasha of his ignorant rural tenants (*My Father's Secret*[757]). Other topics portray in-law relations, the husband who suspects his wife unjustly of betrayal[758], the man falling in love with a married woman, the struggle of the girl who wants to choose her husband by herself, and the suffering of orphans, many of whom turn into criminals[759]. The social film, with its blatant

750 *Man al-jānī?*, starring Amīna Rizq—cf. W.G.T., in *The Palestine Post*, Sep. 23, 1948.

751 *Al-Usṭā Ḥasan*, starring Farīd S̲h̲auqī—cf. *A*, July 2, 1952, p. 10.

752 See also ibid., July 15, 1952, p. 5.

753 Bitterly critical of this tendency is 'Abd al-Laṭīf Ibrāhīm, *al-S̲h̲ās̲h̲a al-baiḍā' fī Miṣr*, in *KM*, fasc. 9, June, 1946, pp. 139–140.

754 *Nāhid*, starring Rāqiya Ibrāhīm and Yūsuf Wahbī—cf. *AL*, Apr. 1, 1952, p. 10.

755 *Al-Masākīn*, starring Taḥiyya Kāriyōkā, Maryam Fak̲h̲r al-Dīn and Ḥusain Ṣidqī—cf. *AJ*, July 14, 1952, p. 8.

756 *Ibn al-ḥaddād*, starring Yūsuf Wahbī—cf. W.G.T. in *JP*, Jan. 11, 1954, p. 2.

757 *Sirr abī*, starring Ṣabāḥ and Bis̲h̲āra Wākīm—cf. id., ibid., Apr. 19, 1954, p. 2. See also above, Third Part, ch. 1, section c.

758 *Kidtu ahdimu baitī*, starring Rāqiya Ibrāhīm and Muḥsin Sirḥān—cf. *RY*, Feb. 15, 1954, pp. 32–33.

759 See *A*, July 15, 1952, p. 5. *RY*, Mar. 15, 1954, pp. 32–33. For a fairly typical plot, see Rus̲h̲dī Kāmil, '*Audat al-qāfila*, in *KM*, fasc. 10, July, 1946, pp. 337–338; and W.G.T., in *JP*, Dec. 28, 1943.

call for reform (in no little measure the result of Wahbī's efforts), has become a great favorite with the masses. It is significant that modern Arab society encourages the social film, for it undoubtedly has an educational impact on the masses and considerable influence on social change.

5. *Comedies* It does happen, as is so often the case in the Arab theater, that a film comedy actually turns into a farce because of the slapstick involved. However, one feels that better progress in the comedy has been achieved in the Arab cinema than in the Arab theater. *Abū Ḥalmūs*, for instance, described the comic situations involved in the public and private life of a diplomat, this time a *chargé d'affaires*[760]. More charming, even though somewhat naïve, is the theme of the musical comedy, *'Anbar*. This is the story of a girl, back from school, who finds her aging father besieged by relatives, all trying to find where he has hidden his money; the girl, *'Anbar*, together with a young casino-owner in love with her, joins the search; this turns uproariously funny when it becomes known that the only map registering the treasure's hiding-place had been sewn in an old costume sold to the casino[761].

6. *Political Films* The tendency to use the stage[762] and screen for political purposes already evidenced in certain short documentaries[763], has entered the arena of the Arabic feature film, too. Not only was the showing of Cecil B. de Mille's *Samson and Delilah* forbidden in Egypt[764], probably because it showed a Jew victorious over his neighbors, but also the cinema took an active part, side by side with the theater, in Egypt's political struggle with Great Britain. In the years 1951–1952, for instance, the

[760] Starring Zōzō S̲h̲akīb, Najīb al-Rīḥānī and 'Abbās Fāris—cf. Hairabèdian, *Les films égyptiens etc.*, p. 22. Rus̲h̲dī Kāmil, *Abū Ḥalmūs*, in *KM*, fasc. 27, Dec., 1947, pp. 448–451.

[761] Starring Lailā Murād, Anwar Wajdī and the able comedian S̲h̲okōkō—reviewed at length by Ibn Zaidūn in *al-Muṣawwar*, Nov. 12, 1948, pp. 38–39.

[762] See above, pp. 120–122.

[763] See the present chapter, section b.

[761] Reported in the Hebrew weekly *Dĕvar ha-s̲h̲avū'a* (Tel-Aviv), Sep. 28, 1951.

military incidents were filmed[765]; and in addition the bitter anti-British film, *Danishwāi*, was revived[766]. Others were quickly filmed, such as the above *Juḥā's Nail* (*Mismār Juḥā*)[767] and another one, *Kīlū 99*, describing the bloody clashes at that spot[768].

In summing up the thematic problems of the Arab cinema, one notices the following characteristics:

1. The script writers, with a few exceptions, have seldom specialized in this branch; they write rapidly but seldom create new plots. They more often adapt stories from foreign films or foreign novels.

2. The script writers are further hampered by the demands being made of them to write scripts suiting only certain directors and actors.

3. The documentary film, whether educational or political in nature, is as yet in its infancy. Its possibilities have not been properly realized or fully utilized by the Arab governments.

4. The feature film is mainly musical, revue-like, even when music is integrally unnecessary. Love plays an important part (next to music), but without the sexy character predominant in the themes of many American films[769].

5. Though all types of films may be found, the sentimental melodrama and the farcical comedy generally predominate[770], since they are the ones that receive the widest acclaim.

765 Ḥilmī Raflah, the film director, in *AL*, Dec. 7, 1951, p. 2.
766 Ibid., Dec. 19, 1951, p. 2.
767 See above, footnote 412.
768 *AY*, Jan. 13, 1952, p. 8.
769 See, e.g., M. Wolfenstein & N. Leites, *An analysis of themes and plots*, in *The motion picture industry—Annals of the Amer. Acad. of Political and Social Science*, Nov., 1947, pp. 41–48.
770 This may be seen even by counting the plots of films summarized by Haira bèdian in his *Les films égyptiens etc.*

Conclusion

THIS STUDY has tried to describe the evolution and to trace the main characteristics of the theater and cinema in the Arab countries. It has been shown how the Passion plays, on one hand, got little enough hold on the Sunnite Arabs, but more acclaim among the Shiite ones. Shadow plays, on the other hand, although of foreign origin, soon became popular and served for ages, along with mimetic performances, as one of the main entertainments for the crowds. Their importance is more ethnographical than literary. Although not devoid, occasionally, of artistic merits, the main service of the shadow theater to posterity is in its preservation of the ancient mimetic humor for future generations and in the keeping alive of a certain interest in dramatic performances among the population.

The Arab theater, modern successor to the shadow play, although basically an imitation of European techniques, has worked out for itself a *modus vivendi* based on a synthesis of the foreign and the local. From its very beginnings, the Arab theater was headed towards finding a pleasing combination of the text and the music. This was contradistinct from the opera, in that the text was spoken and the music sung, separately. It was this approach that left its mark on both the musical and the popular (comic) theater, while its lack brought about the downfall of the champions of the classical theater.

These efforts to please the audience have hindered the Arab theater from reaching a higher artistic and literary level. Most actors and actresses—whose appearance on the stage was well-nigh a revolution—are content in reaping applause for their singing and do not cultivate seriously enough their acting technique. Many playwrights, too, lower their standards to suit the taste of their audiences, as regards both subject and treatment. The dramatic output of the very few, who let their personal outlook and creative genius direct their pens, is at best read, but hardly ever produced. This applies both to original and translated plays, the latter still having less success than the earlier, adapted ones which can be digested without any effort.

This attitude has lately cramped the activities of the theater considerably[771]. The new régime in Egypt has done but little to encourage the Arab theater, whose exponents are almost unanimously pessimistic as to its future. Personal misunderstandings have recently worsened the confusion. On one hand, plays that did not support openly the new régime have been stigmatized as being behind the times. On the other, those treating favorably the new social trends—and there are many such plays—have been described as fawning upon ʻAbd al-Nāṣir's régime as well as catering to the wishes of the masses. A Public Committee, appointed by the Government, included neither notable playwrights nor distinguished actors, so that it obtained but little cooperation and support from those it was designed to assist and advise. Recent reductions in entrance fees, probably intended to allow competition with the cinema, were hardly applauded by the actors. These regrettable conditions of the theater in Egypt are to be found at present, in varying degrees, elsewhere in the Arab countries.

Not less than the theater, the Arab cinema is centered in Egypt. The Egyptian film industry has passed through three main periods. It first shot experimental, amateurish films. During the Second World War it passed through a period of unrivaled prosperity, caused by the difficulty of importing foreign films into the Arab countries. Nowadays, in the post-War period, the import of American, European, and Indian films has forced the producers and directors to pay some attention to the quality of their films. The Arab cinema may be said to have passed from the silent film, first, to the musical, whose chief attraction was belly-dances; and, secondly, to feature

[771] As evidenced in the enlightening symposium on the contemporary theater in Egypt, publ. in *al-Muṣawwar*, Nov. 26, 1954, pp. 25–27.

films concerned with either Muslim history or social problems. Despite the great annual output of films, one feels that the high standard once achieved in the thematic field has not always been kept up in recent years. Notwithstanding its relatively good technical equipment, the general standard of the Arabic-speaking films remains low (with some notable exceptions, however). This is caused not only by inexperience and lack of specialization, but by the cinema's catering—as does the Arab theater—to popular demand for songs and dances. The naïveté of the Arabic film, which enables it to maintain an exceptionally close contact with the audience, hampers at the same time its progress.

Many drawbacks notwithstanding, the impact of the Arab stage and screen on the population is considerable. Not only are they a medium of influencing visibly their impressionable audiences but they serve, too, as the only inexpensive vehicle of communication (besides the radio) for the large illiterate sections of the population. As such, they have been one of the most widespread means for the penetration of Western customs and ideas. Their importance in molding the outlook of their audiences, past, present, and future, cannot be overestimated.

The future development of the Egyptian theater and cinema lies not only in buying better equipment for the stage and the studio, but also in lifting the artistic level of both actors and technicians and in enabling larger sections of the population to become acquainted better with the theater and cinema. A far greater number of halls ought to be erected in the countryside and the entrance fees reconsidered everywhere. These very necessary conditions for the progress of the Thespian arts may be fully achieved only through the whole-hearted support of the authorities. The governments of the Arab countries should not only defray a part of the costs for the specialization of the actors and technicians, but also subsidize the business people who are behind the theater and cinema. Only then will these arts be decommercialized and show improvement both in quality and in their truly artistic appeal to the large masses.

Bibliography

The following list includes only the more important works mentioned in the course of the book. For further details the reader is referred to the relevant footnotes.

MANUSCRIPTS

a. EUROPEAN LANGUAGES

1. Dablan, A., *Neuarabische Literatur.* Mimeographed. Haifa. n.d.
2. Hairabèdian, M., *Une grande artiste du cinéma égyptien Nour-el-Houda.* Typewritten. Paris, 1954; 6 pp.
3. Jacob, G., *Nachtrags-Bibliographie mit Excerpten als Annalen des Schattentheaters im Morgenland.* Typewritten. Kiel, 1936; 17 pp.
4. Orvieto, G. R., *La genesi del teatro arabo in Egitto.* Doctoral thesis, presented to the Univ. of Rome, 1948. Typewritten. [Rome]; 158 pp.
5. Public Record Office, London—archives of the Foreign Office.

b. ORIENTAL LANGUAGES

1. Al-Ṭuwairanī (?), Ḥasan Ḥusnī, *Fihrist al-inqilāb.* British Mus., Or. Ms. 9018 (prob. late 19th century; 60 leaves, all written on one side, except one written on both sides).

PRINTED WORKS IN EUROPEAN LANGUAGES

a. BOOKS

1. Abd-el-Jalil, J.-M., *Brève histoire de la littérature arabe.* 3rd ed., Paris, G. P. Maisonneuve, 1946; 308 pp.
2. Abdul Wahhab, Ahmed, *A thesis on the drama in the Arabic literture.* N.p. (Dacca?), publ. by the author, 1922; 112, II pp.
3. *Annuaire de la fédération égyptienne de l'industrie 1952–1953.* Cairo-Alexandria, 1953; 550 pp., illustrations.
4. Belzoni, G., *Narrative of the operations and recent discoveries in Egypt and Nubia.* London, 1820; XXII, 483 pp.
5. Bernard [Marius], *L'Algérie qui s'en va.* Paris, Plon, 1887; 385 pp.
6. Brockelmann, C., *Geschichte der arabischen Litteratur.* Esp. Suppl. II–III, Leiden, Brill, 1938–1942.
7. Cerbella, G. & Ageli, M., *Le feste musulmane in Tripoli appunti etnografici.* Tripoli, Barbiera, 1949; 90 pp.
8. Eberhardt, I., *Pages d'Islam.* Paris, Fasquelle, 1920; 340 pp.
9. Franck, D. S. (ed.), *Islam in the modern world.* Washington, The Middle East Institute, 1951; 76 pp.
10. Goretti, L., *Venti mesi in Soria.* Torino, Tip. Tarizzo, 1882; 324 pp.
11. Hairabèdian, M., *Les films égyptiens et ceux de Hollywood.* Paris, 1950; 40 pp.
12. Harry, M., *Tunis la blanche.* 17th ed., Paris, Fayard, n.d.; 319 pp.

13. Horovitz, J., *Spuren griechischer Mimen im Orient*. Berlin, Mayer & Müller, 1905; 104 pp.
14. Humières, Robert d', *Through isle and empire*, transl. by A. T. de Mattos. N.Y., Doubleday, 1905; IX, 300 pp.
15. Jacob, G., *Erwähnungen des Schattentheaters in der Welt-Litteratur*. 3rd ed., Berlin, Mayer, 1906; 49 pp.
16. Id., *Geschichte des Schattentheaters*. Berlin, Mayer & Mueller, 1907; VIII, 159 pp.
17. Id., *Der Leuchtturm von Alexandria ein arabisches Schattenspiel aus dem mittelalterlichen Ägypten*. Stuttgart, Kohlhammer, 1930; X, 94, 56 pp.
18. Id., *Al-Mutajjam, ein altarabisches Schauspiel für die Schattenbühne bestimmt von Muhammad Ibn Danijal. Erste Mitteilung über das Werk*. Erlangen, Mencke, 1901; 31 pp.
19. Id., *Das Schattentheater in seiner Wanderung vom Morgenland zum Abendland*. Berlin, Mayer & Müller, 1901; 22 pp.
20. Kern, Fr., *Innisâ'u-l-'Âlimât von Muḥammad Bey 'Osmân Galâl neuarabische Bearbeitung von Molière's Femmes Savantes transkribiert, übersetzt, eingeleitet und mit einem Glossar versehen*. Leipzig, Harrassowitz, 1898; 153 pp.
21. Kraft, I., *Plays, players, playhouses international drama of today*. N.Y., Dobsevage, 1928; XX, 265 pp.
22. Landau, J. M., *Shadow plays in the Near East*. Jerusalem, Palestine Institute of Folklore and Ethnology, 1948; English & Hebrew, 82 pp.
23. Lane, E. W., *An account of the manners and customs of the modern Egyptians, written in Egypt during the years* 1833, 34 *and* 35, *partly from notes made during a former visit to that country in the years* 1825, 26, 27 *and* 28. Vol. II, London, Nattali, 1846; VIII, 431 pp.
24. Littmann, E., *Arabische Schattenspiele*. Belin, Mayer & Müller, 1901; 83 pp.
25. Maltzan, H. von, *Reise in der Regentschaften Tunis und Tripolis*. Vol. I, Leipzig, Dyk, 1870; XVI, 404 pp., 8 tables of illustr.
26. Marinetti, F. T., *Il fascino dell'Egitto*. Verona, Mondadori, 1933; 179 pp.
27. Martinovitch, N. N., *The Turkish theatre*. N.Y., Theatre Arts, 1933; 125 pp.
28. Mosharrafa, M. M., *Cultural survey of modern Egypt*. 2 vols. London, Longmans, 1947–1948.
29. Pellat, Ch., *Langue et littérature arabes*. Paris, Ar. Colin, 1952; 224 pp.
30. Perolari-Malmignati, P., *Su e giù per la Siria note e schizzi*. Milano, Treves, 1878; 242 pp.
31. Prüfer, C., *Ein ägyptisches Schattenspiel*. Erlangen, Mencke, 1906; 23, 151 pp.
32. [Pückler-Muskau,] *Aus Mehemed Ali's Reich vom Verfasser der Briefe eines Verstorbenen*. Vol. I, Stuttgart, Hallberger, 1884; VI, 368 pp.
33. Id., *Semilasso in Afrika*. Vol. I, Stuttgart, Hallberger, 1836; XII, 275 pp.
34. Reich H., *Der Mimus ein litterar-entwicklungsgeschichtlicher Versuch*. Vol. I (2 parts), Berlin, Weidmann, 1903; 900 pp.
35. Ritter, H., *Karagös türkische Schattenspiele*. 3 vols., Istanbul-Wiesbaden, 1924–1941–1953.
36. Sladen, D., *Oriental Cairo*. London, Hurst & Blackett, 1911; XVI, 391 pp.
37. *Tournée officielle de la nouvelle troupe égyptienne sour la direction de Youssef Wahbi*. N.p., Société Orientale de Publicité, n.d. (1955?); 36 pp.
38. UNESCO, *Press, film, radio*. Vols. III–IV–V, Paris, 1949–1950–1951.
39. Virolleaud, Ch., *Le théâtre persan ou le drame de Kerbéla*. Paris, Adrien-Maisonneuve, 1950; IV, 143 pp.

40. Warner, C. D., *My winter on the Nile*. 18th ed., Boston, Houghton, Mifflin and Co., 1895; 496 pp.
41. Zetterstéen, K. V., *Henrik Ibsen, En Folkefiende och August Strindberg, Fadren pa arabiska*. Uppsala, Almqvist & Wiksells, 1949; 14 pp.

b. ARTICLES

1. 'Abd al-Raziq, M. H., *Arabic literature since the beginning of the nineteenth century, in BSOS*, vol. II, 1921–1922, pp. 249–265.
2. Arberry, A. J., *Ḥāfiẓ Ibrāhīm and Shawqī*, in *JRAS*, vol. XXXV, 1937, pp. 41–58.
3. Astre, G.-A., *Le théâtre philosophique de Tewfik El Hakim*, in *Critique* (Paris), fasc. 66, Nov., 1952, pp. 934–945.
4. Ateek, A. A., *The development of the cinema in Egypt*, in *B.*, fasc. 51, Jan., 1951, pp. 5–7.
5. Aubin, E., *Le chiisme et la nationalité persane*, in *RMM*, vol. IV. Mar., 1908, pp. 482–490.
6. Barbour, N., *The Arabic theatre in Egypt*, in *BSOS*, vol. VIII, 1935–1937, pp. 173–187, 991–1012.
7. Bencheneb, R., *Aspects du théâtre arabe en Algérie*, in *L'Islam et l'Occident, Cahiers du Sud*, 1947, pp. 271–276.
8. Id., *Rachid Ksentini (1887–1944) le père du théâtre arabe en Algérie*, in *Documents Algériens—Service d'information du Cabinet du Gouverneur Général de l'Algérie, Série Culturelle*, No. 16, Apr. 15, 1947.
9. Ben Cheneb, S., *Le théâtre arabe d'Alger*, in *Revue Africaine*, vol. LXXVII, 1935, pp. 72–85.
10. Bonjean, F. J., *Une renaissance égyptienne*, in *Europe*, vol. I, June and July, 1923, pp. 83–95, 199–217.
11. Brugsch, H., *Das morgenländische Theater*, in *Deutsche Revue*, vol. XII, 1887, part 3, pp. 25–34.
12. *Facts about the film industry in Egypt*, in *B.*, fasc. 9, Feb., 1947, pp. 7–8.
13. Fahmy, Skandar, *La renaissance du théâtre égyptien moderne*, in *RC*, vol. IV, 1940, pp. 107–112.
14. Gabrieli, Fr., *Maḥmūd Taimūr—Ibn Gialā*, in *OM*, vol. XXXI, July–Sep., 1951, p. 156.
15. (Id.) F. Ga. e U. Ri. (Rizzitano), *Teatro arabo*, in *Enciclopedia dello Spettacolo*, vol. I (Roma, 1954), pp. 769–774.
16. Guidi, M., *Le onoranze al poeta Egiziano Shawqī ed il lore significato politico*, in *OM*, vol. VII, 1927, pp. 346–353.
17. Jacob, G., *'Agīb ed-Dīn al-Wā'iẓ bei Ibn Danijāl*, in *Der Islam*, vol. IV, 1913, pp. 67–71.
18. Id., *Ein ägyptischer Jahrmarkt im 13. Jahrhundert*, in *Sitzungsber. Kön. Bay. Ak. d. Wiss., Philos.-philol. u. hist. Klasse*, 10 Abh., 1910; 42 pp.
19. Jacobs, M., *The Cairo opera house*, in *B.*, fasc. 33, Mar., 1949, pp. 17–18.
20. Id., *The cinema*, ibid., fasc. 24, May, 1948, pp. 39–40.
21. Id., *Egyptian stage actresses*, ibid., fasc. 22, Mar., 1948, pp. 15–17.
22. Id., *Neguib el-Rihani*, ibid., fasc. 18, Nov., 1947, pp. 16–18.
23. Kahle, P., *Islamische Schattenspielfiguren aus Egypten*, in *Der Islam*, vol. I, 1910, pp. 264 *ss.*, and vol. II, 1911, pp. 143 *ss.*
24. Id., *Das islamische Schattentheater in Aegypten*, in *OA*, vol. III, Apr., 1913, pp. 103–109.

25. Id., *Das Krokodilspiel*, in *Nachr. König. Gesellschaft d. Wiss. Gött., Phil.-hist. Klasse*, 1915–1920, pp. 277–359.
26. Id., *M. Ibn Dānijāl und sein zweites arabisches Schattenspiel*, in *Miscellanea Academica Berolinensis*, 1950, pp. 151–167.
27. Id., *Marktszene aus einem egyptischen Spiel*, in *ZA*, vol. XXVII, 1912, pp. 92–102.
28. Id., *Eine Zunftsprache der ägyptischen Schattenspieler*, in *Islamica*, vol. II, 1926, pp. 313–322.
29. Kampffmeyer, G., *Die Anfänge einer Geschichte der neueren arabischen Litteratur*, in *MSOS*, 1928, part 2, pp. 170–205.
30. *Id.*, *Arabische Dichter der Gegenwart. X: Ein wenig beachtetes Jugendwerk von Aḥmed Šauqī*, ibid., 1926, part 2, pp. 198–206.
30a. Kapeliuk, O., *The theater in Egypt*, in *New Outlook Middle East Monthly* (Tel-Aviv), vol. I, fasc. 4, Oct. 1957, pp. 32–38.
31. Kern, Fr., *Das egyptische Schattentheater*. App. to Horovitz, *Spuren griechischer Mimen* (see above, Bibl., Printed Works in European Languages, a, No. 13).
32. Kratschkowsky, Ign., *Modern Arabic literature, c. Drama*, in the *Encyclopaedia of Islam*, 1st ed., Suppl., *sub voce Arabia*.
33. Landau, J. M., *Abū Naḍḍāra, an Egyptian Jewish nationalist*, in *JJS*, vol. III, No. 1, 1952, pp. 30–44.
34. Id., *The Arab cinema*, in *MEA*, vol. IV, Nov., 1953, pp. 349–358.
35. Id., *The Arab theatre*, ibid., ibid., Mar., 1953, pp. 77–86.
36. Id., *Aziz Domet, d'origine araba, poeta, scrittore di romanzi e opere drammatiche di soggetto orientale in lingua tedesca (1890–1943)*, in *OM*, vol. XXXV, June, 1955, pp. 277–289.
37. Levy, K., *La'bät elhotä. Ein tunesisches Schattenspiel*, in *Festschrift für Kahle*, Leiden, 1935, pp. 119–124.
38. Littmann, E., *Ein arabisches Karagöz-Spiel*, in *ZDMG*, vol. LIV, 1900, pp. 661–680.
39. Id., *Eine neuarabische Posse aus Damascus*, in *ZDMG*, vol. LVI, 1902, pp. 86-97.
40. Id., *Das Malerspiel. Ein Schattenspiel aus Aleppo* in *Sitzungsber. d. Heidelberger Ak. d. Wiss., Philos.-Hist. Klasse*, Mar. 25, 1918; 50 pp.
41. L.V., *Le théâtre à Tunis (1932–1933)*, in *Revue des Etudes Islamiques*, vol. VI, 1932, pp. 537–544.
42. *The modern Egyptian theatre*, in *B.*, fasc. 2, July 1, 1946, pp. 10–11.
43. Mourad, Leila, *A year of the Egyptian cinema*, in *The Arab World* (London), fasc. 21, Oct., 1954, p. 14.
44. Moutran, Habib, *La troupe nationale égyptienne et Khalil Bey Moutran*, in *La Semaine Egyptienne* (Cairo), vol. XXII, Nos. 23–24, 1948, pp. 25–26.
45. Müller, W. M., *Zur Geschichte des arabischen Schattenspiels in Aegypten*, in *OLZ*, vol. XII, Aug., 1909, pp. 341–342.
46. Pérès, H., *Aḥmad Šawqî, années de jeunesse et de formation intellectuelle en Egypte et en France*, in *AIEOA*, vol. II, 1936, pp. 313–340.
47. Prüfer, C., *Drama, Arabic*, in *ERE*, vol. IV, 1911, pp. 872–878.
48. Id., *Das Schiffsspiel, Ein Schattenspiel aus Cairo*, in *Münchener Beitr. z. Kenntnis d. Orients*, vol. II, Feb., 1906, pp. 154–169.
49. Rachid, Fatma Nimet, *Une enquête sur l'avenir du théâtre oriental—III. Petit historique du théâtre arabe*, in *BE*, Mar. 23, 1939.
50. Rizzitano, U., "*L'albero del potere.*" *Commedia di satirica politica dell'Egiziano Taufīq al-Ḥakīm*, in *OM*, vol. XXIII, Oct., 1943, pp. 439–447.

51. Id., *Il simbolismo nelle opere di Taufīq al-Ḥakīm*, ibid., vol. XXVI, July–Dec., 1946, pp. 116–123.
52. Id., *Il teatro arabo in Egitto opere teatrali di Taufīq al-Ḥakīm*, ibid., vol. XXIII, June, 1943, pp. 247–266.
53. Saad El-Din, M., *Mahmoud Taimur*, in *B.*, fasc. 21, Feb., 1948, pp. 9–10.
54. Id., *Middle East playwrights*, ibid., fasc. 24, May, 1948, pp. 41–42.
55. Id., *Theatre and cinema*, ibid., fasc. 12, May, 1947, pp. 85–87.
56. Sadoul, G., *Le septième festival international du film de Cannes*, in *Les Lettres Françaises* (Paris), Apr. 8–15, 1954, p. 6.
57. Sanderson, John, *Shadow plays*, in *The Near East and India*, vol. XL, Oct. 8, 1931, pp. 387–388.
58. Saussey, E., *Une farce de Karagueuz en dialecte arabe de Damas*, in *Bulletin d'Études Orientales de Damas*, vols. VII–VIII, 1937–1938, p. 5–37.
59. Schoonover, K., *Contemporary Egyptian authors*, in *The Muslim World* (Hartford, Conn.), vol. XLV, 1955, pp. 26–36; and vol. XLVII, 1957, pp. 36–45.
60. Sidawi, E., *Le cinéma égyptien d'hier et d'aujourd'hui*, in *Le Monde Arabe* (Paris), fasc. 25, June 15, 1952, pp. 20–21.
61. Sidky, Abdel Rahman, *Le théâtre*, in *Cinquante ans de littérature égyptienne*, special issue of the *RC*, vol. XXXI, Feb., 1953, pp. 161–206.
62. Sobernheim, M., *Zur Metrik einiger in's Arabische übersetzter Dramen Molière's*, in *MSOS*, 1898, part 2, pp. 185–187.
63. Spies, O., *Tunesisches Schattentheater*, in *Public. d'hommage off. au P. W. Schmidt*, Vienna, 1928, pp. 693-702.
64. *Student of the drama*, in *B.*, fasc. 45, May–June, 1950, pp. 27–28.
65. *Le théâtre nord-africain à Paris*, in *Le Monde Arabe*, fasc., 12, Dec. 17, 1951, p. 10.
66. Tomiche-Dagher, N., *Représentations parisiennes du jeune théâtre algérien*, in *BE*, Aug., 30, 1952.
67. Toynbee, Ph., *Egypt's Arabic film monopoly*, in *JP*, June 2, 1950, p. 4.
68. Vollers, K., *Der neuarabische Tartuffe*, in *ZDMG*, vol. XLV, 1891, pp. 36–96.
69. Weigert, G., *Actor-playwright from Cairo*, in *JP*, Dec. 21, 1955, p. 4.
70. Worrell, W. H., *Kishkish: Arabic vaudeville in Cairo*, in *The Muslim World*, vol. X, 1920, pp. 134–137.
71. Zohny, S., *The development of the film industry*, in *B.*, fasc. 35, May–June, 1949, pp. 55–56.

PRINTED WORKS IN ORIENTAL LANGUAGES

(Arabic, Hebrew and Turkish)

a. BOOKS

1. Abū Sa'dī, Jibrā'īl, *Dars taḥlīlī 'alā riwāyat Qambīz li-amīr al-shu'arā' Aḥmad Shauqī*. Ṣaidā, Maṭb. al-rahbāniyya, 1942; 71 pp.
2. Abū Shādī, Aḥmad Zakī, *Masraḥ al-adab*. Cairo, al-Mu'ayyad, n.d.; 252 pp.
2a. Ahmet, Refik, *Türk tiyatrosu tarihi*, vol. I. Istanbul, Kanaat, 1934; 132 pp.
3. Al-'Aqqād, 'Abbās Maḥmūd, *Riwāyat Qambīz fī' l-mīzān*. Cairo, Maṭb. al-majalla al-jadīda, n.d. (1930?); 88 pp.
4. Al-Bustānī, Buṭrus, *Udabā' al-'Arab fī'l-Andalus wa-'aṣr al-inbi'āth*. 3rd ed., Beirut, Maktabat Ṣādir, 1937; 330 pp.
5. Dāghir, Yūsuf As'ad, *Maṣādir al-dirāsa al-adabiyya*, vol. II, part 1. Beirut, Manshūrāt jam'iyyat ahl al-qalam, 1956; XXII, 864 pp.

6. Edham, Ismā'īl & Nājī, Ibrāhīm, *Taufīq al-Ḥakīm*. Cairo, Sa'd, 1945; 238 pp.
7. Fahmī, Zakī, *Ṣafwat al-'aṣr fī ta'rīkh wa-rusūm mashāhīr rijāl Miṣr*. Vol. 1, Cairo, al-I'timād, 1926; IV, 735 pp.
8. *Faraḥ Anṭūn ḥayātuh wa-ta'bīnuh wa-mukhtārātuh*. Cairo, Suppl. to *Majallat al-sayyidāt wa'l-rijāl*, 1923; 144, 62 pp.
9. Farrūkh, 'Umar, *Kalima fī Aḥmad Shauqī*. 2nd ed., Beirut, Maimana, 1950; 64 pp.
10. Gerçek, Selim Nüzhet, *Türk temaşası meddah karagöz ortaoyunu*. Istanbul, Kanaat Kitabevi, 1942; 159 pp.
11. Ḥusain, Ṭaha, *Ḥāfiẓ wa-Shauqī*. Cairo, al-I'timād, 1933; X, 224 pp.
11a. Najm, Muḥammad Yūsuf, *al-Masraḥiyya fī'l-adab al-'arabī'l-ḥadīth* (1847–1914). Beirut, Dār Bairūt li'l-ṭibā'a wa'l-nashr, 1956; 511 pp.
12. Al-Nashshāshībī, Muḥammad Is'āf, *al-'Arabiyya wa-shā'iruhā'l-akbar Aḥmad Shauqī*. Cairo, Najīb Mitrī, 1928; 52 pp.
13. Id., *al-Baṭal al- khālid Ṣalāḥ al-Dīn wa'l-shā'ir al-khālid Aḥmad Shauqī*. Jerusalem, Maṭb. Bait al-maqdis, 1932; 110 pp.
14. al-Qabbānī, Sulaimān Ḥasan, *Bughyat al-mumaththilīn*. Alexandria, Gharzūzī, n.d. (prob. 1912–1914); 184 pp.
15. Shaukat, Maḥmūd Ḥāmid, *al-Masraḥiyya fī shi'r Shauqī*. N.p., Maṭb. al-Muqtaṭaf, 1947; 144 pp.
16. Taimūr, Muḥammad, *Mu'allafāt*. Vol. II, Cairo, Maṭb. al-I'timād, 1922; 461 pp.
17. Zaidān, Jurjī, *Tarājim mashāhīr al-sharq fī'l qarn al-tāsi' 'ashar*. 2nd ed., 2 vols., Cairo, al-Hilāl, 1910–1911.
18. Id., *Ta'rīkh ādāb al-lugha al-'arabiyya*. Vol. IV, Cairo, al-Hilāl, 1914; 328 pp.
19. Al-Zayyāt, Aḥmad Ḥasan, *Ta'rīkh al-adab al-'arabī li'l-madāris al-thānawiyya wa'l-'ulyā*. 10th ed., Cairo, al-Risāla, n.d.; VIII, 521 pp.

b. ARTICLES

1. Abū'l-Faḍl, Fatḥī, *al-Qiṣṣa fī ṣinā'at al-sīnimā'l-miṣriyya*, in *A.*, June 9, 1952, p. 3.
2. 'Abbūd, Mārūn, *Adīb Isḥāq*, in *K.*, vol. III, Feb., 1948, pp. 271–283.
3. Id., *Faraḥ Anṭūn*, ibid., vol. II, Nov., 1947, pp. 1736–1747.
4. 'Aid, 'Azīz, *Risālat al-fann al-masraḥī hiya ta'mīm al-thaqāfa al-'ulyā*, in *H.*, vol. XLV, Mar. 1, 1937, pp. 561–563.
5. Amīn, Muṣṭafā, *Ḥaḍart al-maulid*, in *AS.* Dec. 29, 1954, pp. 16–17.
6. Al-'Antablī, 'Uthmān, *Hal addat niqābat al-sīnimā risālatahā*, in *M.*, June 9, 1952, p. 8.
7. Id., *al-Masraḥ al-miṣrī yamūt*, ibid., Dec. 8, 1952.
8. Id., *al-Sīnimā'l-miṣriyya fī'l-'ahd al-jadīd*, ibid., Aug. 18, 1952.
9. 'Aql, Sa'īd, *al-Ittijāhāt al-jadīda fī'l-adab al-'arabī—al-marsaḥ*, in *Ma.*, vol. XXXV, 1937, pp. 41–52.
10. 'Aṭiyya, Kamāl, *al-Qiṣṣa al-sīnimā'iyya*, in *AJ*, Oct. 31, 1952, p. 8.
11. Al-Bārūdī, 'Abd al-Fattāḥ, *al-Mausim al-masraḥī*, in *K.*, vol. VII, June, 1952, pp. 753–755.
12. Id., *al-Mausim al-ṣaifī*, ibid., Oct., 1952, pp. 1003–1005.
13. Bāz, Jurjī Niqūlā, *al-Shaikh Iskandar al-'Āzār*, in *H.*, vol. XXVII, Apr. 1, 1919, pp. 644–646.
14. Al-Bundārī, Jalīl, *Azmat mukhrijīn fī'l-sīnimā'l-miṣriyya*, in *AS*, Oct. 28, 1953, p. 26.

15. Id., *Hal 'indanā kuttāb sīnāriyō?* ibid., Oct. 21, 1953, pp. 22–23.
16. Al-Bustānī, Fu'ād Ifrām, *Shakhṣiyyat Aḥmad Shauqī*, in *Ma.*, vol. XXXIV, 1936, pp. 67–75.
16a. Dāghir, Yūsuf As'ad, *Fann al-tamthīl fī khilāl qarn*, in *Ma.*, vol, XLII, 1948, pp. 434–460; vol. XLIII, 1949, pp. 118–139, 271–296.
17. al-Diwahjī, Sa'īd, *Ibn Dāniyāl al-Mauṣilī*, in *K.*, June, 1951, pp. 611–617.
18. *Dhikrā Mulyīr wa-riwāyātih fī'l-lugha al-'arabiyya*, in *H.*, vol. XXX, Mar. 1, 1922, pp. 555–558.
19. Dhuhnī, Ṣalāḥ, *al-Firqa al-miṣriyya fī 'ām*, in *K.*, vol. II, July 1947, pp. 1418–1422.
20. *Al-Fann fī Tūnis*, in *RY*, May 24, 1954, p. 34.
21. *Farīd al-Aṭrash yaṭlub fatḥ al-bāb 'alā miṣrā'aih*, in *AS*, Dec. 16, 1953, p. 9.
22. Fāris, Bishr, *Fī' l-ta'līf al-masraḥī*, in *al-Thaqāfa*, Mar. 7, 1939, pp. 44–45.
23. Fu'ād, Ḥasan, *Fann al-Riḥānī aulā bi'l-takrīm*, in *RY*, June 14, 1954, p. 31.
24. Ghānim, Fatḥī, *al-Sīnimā'l-miṣriyya laisat fī khaṭar*, in *AS*, Dec. 29, 1954, pp. 46–47.
25. Ḥabīb, Taufīq, *Shiksbīr fī Miṣr*, in *H.*, vol. XXXVI, Dec. 1, 1927, pp. 201–204.
26. Al-Ḥakīm, As'ad, *Shauqī wa'l-masraḥ al-'arabī*, in Aḥmad 'Ubaid, *Dhikrā'l-shā-'irain shā'ir al-Nīl wa-amīr al-shu'arā'*. Damascus, 1953, pp. 339–344.
27. Ḥammāda, Muḥammad, *al-Sīnimā'l-miṣriyya fī khaṭar*, in *AS*, Apr. 15, 1953, p. 5.
28. Ḥaqqī, Yaḥyā, *Masraḥ al-Riḥānī*, in *al-Adīb* (Beirut), Apr. 1954, pp. 14–18.
29. Ḥassūna, Muḥammad Amīn, *al-Masraḥ al-miṣrī*, in *al-Sharq al-adnā* (Cyprus), Oct. 7, 1951, pp. 16, 17, 34.
30. Ḥubaiqa, Najīb, *Fann al-tamthīl*, in *Ma.*, vol. II, 1899, pp. 20–23, 71–74, 156–160, 250–257, 341–345, 501–507.
31. Ḥunain, Edwār, *Shauqī 'alā'l-masraḥ*, ibid., vol. XXXII, 1934, pp. 563–580; XXXIII, 1935, pp. 68–92, 273–288, 394–427. Repr. sep., Beirut, al-Maṭb. al-kāthūlīkiyya, 1936; XII, 94 pp.
32. Ḥusain, Ṭaha, *Silāḥ al-yaum, in KM*, fasc. 8, May, 1946, pp. 704–705.
33. Ibn Zaidūn, *'Anbar*, in *al-Muṣawwar*, Nov. 12, 1948, pp. 38–39.
34. Ibrāhīm, 'Abd al-Laṭīf, *al-Shāsha al-baiḍā' fī Miṣr*, in *KM*, Fasc. 9, June, 1946, pp. 139–140.
35. Ilyās, Ilyās Maqdisī, *Nawāḥī'l-naqṣ fī'l-fīlm al-miṣrī*, in *Dunyā'l-kawākib*, Sep. 15, 1952, p. 25.
36. *Ittijāh al-ta'līf*, in *K.*, vol. I, Jan., 1946, pp. 392–414; vol. II, Jan., 1947, pp. 463–489; vol. III, Jan., 1948, pp. 165–199; vol. IV, Jan., 1949, pp. 138–166.
37. *Jauq Abyaḍ*, in *H.*, vol. XXI, Nov. 1, 1912, pp. 125–126.
38. Al-Jauzī, Naṣrī, *Kaifa nanhaḍ bi'l-masraḥ al-Filasṭīnī?* in *al-Hadaf*, Apr. 21, 1946, p. 11.
39. Kāmil, Rushdī, *Ḥaul al-sīnimā'l-miṣriyya*, in *KM.*, fasc. 26, Nov., 1947, pp. 291–295.
40. Id., *Inṭibā'āt min al-sīnimā'l-miṣriyya*, ibid., fasc. 12, Sep., 1946, pp. 736–738.
41. Id., *Shahriyyat al-masraḥ*, ibid., fasc. 9, June, 1946, pp. 139–140.
42. Id., *Shahriyyat al-sīnimā*, ibid., fasc., 17, Feb., 1947, pp. 162–164.
43. Khashaba, Durainī, *Fauq jabal al-Ūlimb*, in *K.*, vol. IV, Oct. 1947, pp. 1630–1641.
44. *5 kuttāb wa-5 ārā' fī'l-sīnimā*, in *AS*. Dec. 9, 1953.

45. Landau, J. M., *'Al ha-teiaṭrōn etsel ha-'aravīm*, in *Bamah* quarterly (Tel-Aviv), fasc. 47, Jan., 1946, pp. 48–53; fasc. 48, June, 1946, pp. 65–75; fasc. 49, Sep., 1946, pp. 48–60; fasc. 50, Jan., 1947, pp. 107–115.
46. Id., *Drama ḥevratīt-ḥinnūkhīt bĕ-'aravīt*, ibid., fasc. 51, May, 1947, pp. 33–34.
47. Id., *Dramaṭūrgiyya mitsrīt—A. Shauqī*, in *Bamōt* (Jerusalem), vol. I, Mar., 1953, pp. 305–309.
48. Id., *Dramōt 'araviyyōt bĕ-tirgūm tsarfatī*, in *HH*, vol. III, Autumn, 1951, p. 101.
49. Id., *ha-Armenī she-haqar et ha-qolnō'a ha-'aravī*, in *Zĕmannīm* (Jerusalem), Mar. 18, 1955, p. 5.
50. Id., *ha-Nos'īm ba-qolnō'a ha-mitsrī*, *HH*, vol. V, Winter 1954, pp. 145–146.
51. Id., *ha-Teiaṭrōn ha-'aravī bĕ-Erets Isra'el ba-shana ha-aḥarōna*, in *Bamah*, fasc. 52, Dec., 1947, p. 43.
52. Id., *Li-shĕ'elat reshītō shel ha-teiaṭrōn bĕ-Mitsrayīm*, in *HH*, vol. II, July, 1951, pp. 389–391.
53. Id., *Shauqī vĕ-yĕtsīratō bĕ-aspaqlaryah 'aravīt*. ibid, vol. III, Autumn, 1951, p. 101.
54. Id., *Turkī kōtev 'al qaragöz*, ibid., vol. V, Summer, 1954, p. 322.
55. Al-Maqdisī, Anīs, *Naẓra 'āmma fī Maṣra' Kliyūpātra baḥth intiqādī fī'l-riwāya-'llatī akhrajahā ḥadīthan Aḥmad Shauqī Bek*, in *Mu.*, vol. LXXV, Oct. 1, 1929, pp. 285–292.
56. *Al-Masraḥ au al-marzaḥ*, ibid,. vol. LXIX, Aug. 1, 1926, pp. 223–224.
57. *Al-Masraḥ wa-mustaqbaluh wa-mā huwa ḥaẓẓunā minh*, in *H.*, vol. XXXVI, Dec. 1, 1927, pp. 175–176.
58. Muṭrān, Khalīl, *al-Tamthīl al-'arabī wa-nahḍatuh al-jadīda*, ibid, vol. XXIX, Feb. 1, 1921, pp. 465–472.
59. Al-Najjār, 'Abd al-Wahhāb, *al-Sīnimā wa'l-islām*, in *Majallat al-shubbān al-muslimīn*, Ramaḍan 1348 (Feb. 1930), pp. 356–357.
60. Najm, Muḥammad Yūsuf, *Aḥmad Abū Khalīl al-Qabbānī*, in *al-Adīb*, vol. XXVII, Jan., 1955, pp. 19–22; Feb., 1955, pp. 17–21.
61. Id., *Madrasat Mārūn al-Naqqāsh*, ibid., Mar., 1955, pp. 24–26.
62. Quṭb, Sayyid, *al-'Abbāsa masraḥiyya shi'riyya ta'līf 'Azīz Abāẓa*. in *KM*, fasc., 4, Jan., 1946, pp. 588–594.
63. Ramzī, Ḥasan, *Ghurfat al-sīnimā tas'ā li-yakūn al-fīlm al-miṣrī 'ālamiyyan*, in *RY*, May 24, 1954, p. 34
64. Al-Rīḥānī, Najīb, *Ta'rīkh ḥayātihim bi-aqlāmihim*, in *Dunyā'l-fann*, Nov. 19, 1946, p. 13.
65. Surūr, Aḥmad Kamāl, *al-Di'āya li-Miṣr bi'l-sīnimā*, in *al-Rādyū'l-miṣrī*, Jan. 9, 1937, pp. 6, 11.
66. Swanson, J., *Mudhakkarāt mu'assis ṣinā'at al-sīnimā fī Miṣr*, serial in *Dunyā' l-kawākib*, 1953–1954.
67. Ṣidqī, 'Abd al-Raḥmān, *Mawāsim al-tamthīl al-miṣriyya wa'l-ajnabiyya, in K.*, vol. VII, Jan., 1952, pp. 94–98.
68. Id., *Shahriyyat al-masraḥ*, in *KM*, fasc. 15, Dec., 1946, pp. 540–544.
69. Ṣidqī, Ḥusain, *Tastaṭī' niqābat al-sīnimā'iyyīn idā' risālatihā*, in *M.*, June 16, 1952, p. 12.
70. Al-Ṣirafī,* Ḥasan Kāmil, *Bījmālyūn fī'l-adab al-'arabī*, in *Mu.*, vol. CII, Jan. 1, 1943, pp. 87–92.

*It appears that he himself spells his name thus (not al-Ṣairafī)—cf. *GAL*, Suppl. III, p. 165, n. 1.

71. Shamūsh, I., *Be'ayat ha-safa ba-sippūr ha-'aravī ha-mōdernī*, in *Tarbītz*, vol. XXIII, 1952, pp. 231–235.
72. Al-Sharūnī, Ḥusain Rifqī, *al-Sīnimā fī'l-jaish*, in *Jaishunā*, Nos. 257–260 (undated), pp. 45–46.
73. *Al-Tamthīl al-'arabī*, in *H.*, vol. XIV, Dec. 1, 1905, pp. 141–149; ibid., vol. XV, Nov. 1, 1906, pp. 117–118 (additions and corrections).
74. *Al-Tamthīl al-'arabī māḍīh wa-mustaqbaluh*, a referendum, in *H.*, vol. XXXII, 1924, pp. 481–484, 638–641, 751–753.
75. *Al-Tamthīl al-'arabī. Nahḍatuh al-akhīra 'alā yad al-janāb al-'ālī*, ibid., vol. XVIII, May 1, 1910, pp. 464–472; ibid., June 1, 1910, pp. 545–547 (additions).
76. *Al-Tamthīl fī Miṣr. Jauq Jūrj Abyaḍ*, ibid., vol. XX, Apr. 1, 1912, pp. 436–438.
77. *Al-Tamthīl fī Miṣr nahḍatuh al-jadīda*, ibid., vol. XXXIII, Nov. 1, 1924, pp. 185–186.
78. *Taufīq al-Ḥakīm yataḥaddath*, in *al-Thaqāfa*, Jan. 5, 1953, pp. 6–7, 16.
79. Ṭannūs, Jūrj, *al-Shaikh Salāma Ḥijāzī*, in *H.*, vol. XXVI, Nov. 1, 1917, pp. 186–189.
80. Ṭulaimāt, Zakī, *Kaifa dakhal al-tamthīl bilād al-sharq*, in *K.*, vol. I, Feb., 1946, pp. 581–587.
81. Id., *Khaiṭ min al-fann al-sīnimā'ī fī Miṣr*, ibid., Jan., 1946, pp. 415–422.
82. Id., *al-Masraḥ al-miṣrī fī 'ām*, ibid., July, 1946, pp. 481–488.
83. Id., *al-Qiṣṣa fī 'ālam al-sīnimā*, ibid., Apr., 1946, pp. 902–908.
84. Id., *al-Riwāya al-tamthīliyya wa-limādhā lam yu'ālijhā'l-'arab*, ibid., Nov., 1945, pp. 101–108.
85. Wahbī, Yūsuf, *Qīmat al-masraḥ al-ijtimā'iyya fī'l-sharq*, in *al-Yaum*, July 8, 1955, pp. 2–3.
86. *Yūsuf Wahbī yataḥaddath 'an al-shu'ūn al-fanniyya*, in *al-Zamān*, Oct. 21, 1952, p. 4.

APPENDIX

A List of Some Arabic Plays, 1848–1956

Principles guiding the List:

1. Plays are listed in two sections, original and translated.
2. Plays are listed alphabetically under the author's known last name (the particle *al* is not taken into consideration in the alphabetical sequence).
3. Anonymous plays are listed under first word of title.
4. If a play has had more than one translation into Arabic, it is listed under author's name and arranged by the alphabetical order of the translators' names.
5. References in parentheses indicate sources for additional information, if any, about a play.

1. ORIGINAL PLAYS

1. Abāẓa, 'Azīz, *al-'Abbāsa*, an historical play in literary Arabic verse (*K.*, vol. I, Dec., 1945, pp. 223–230; *KM*, vol. I, Jan., 1946, pp. 588–594).
2. Id., *'Alā hāmish al-jāmi'a al-'arabiyya*, a 1-act play, presenting poets from various Arab countries. Prod. before Fārūq, 1946. Publ. in *K.*, vol. I, Apr., 1946, pp. 858–864.
3. Id., *Anāt ḥā'ira* (*KM*, fasc. 4, Jan., 1946, p. 588).
4. Id., *Ghurūb al-Andalus*, a 5-act hist. play in lit. Ar. verse—the story of the last of the "Mulūk al-ṭawā'if." Cairo, Maṭb. Miṣr. n.d. (1952?); XVI, 120 pp. (*al-Zamān*, Oct. 21, 1952, p. 4; *AJ*, Oct. 27, 1952; *A.*, Dec. 3, 1952). First named *Suqūṭ al-Andalus* (*M.*, June 30, 1952, p. 10). With an introd. by Ṭaha Ḥusain.
5. Id., *al-Nāṣir* (*A.*, Dec. 3, 1952, p. 5).
6. Id., *Qais wa-Lubnā*. A 5-act drama in lit. Ar. verse, describing fiery love in the early days of the Umayyad dynasty. With an introd. by 'Abbās Maḥmūd al-'Aqqād. N.p. (Cairo?), al-Firqa al-miṣriyya li'l-tamthīl wa'l-mūsīqā, n.d.; 174 pp. First prod. in Egypt, 1943 (*KM*, vol. I, Jan., 1946, p. 588; *RC*, Feb. 1953, p. 181).
7. Id., *Shajarat al-Durr*. A 4-act hist. drama in lit. Ar. verse, tracing the career of the famous woman who ruled Egypt in mid-13th century (*A.*, Dec. 3, 1952, p. 5; *RC*, Feb., 1953, pp. 196–206).
8. 'Abbās, 'Abd al-Ḥamīd, *Mathalunā'l-a'lā*, apparently a moral-play for schools. Baghdad, Government Press, prob. 1934 (*Mu.*, vol. LXXXV, Oct. 1, 1934, p. 256).
9. 'Abbās al-Azharī, Aḥmad, *Dhī Qār* (Dāghir, p. 587).
10. Id., *Fatāt al-ghār* (ibid).
11. Id., *al-Samau'al wa'l-sibāq* (ibid.).
12. *'Abbāsiyya*. In the répertoire of the al-Riḥānī troupe (*A.*, July 27, 1952, p. 7).

12a. 'Abbūd, Mārūn, *al-Akhras al-mutakallim*. Publ. 1925; 32 pp. (*Ma.*, XLII, 1948, p. 438).

12b. Id., *Ashbāḥ al-qarn al-sābi' 'ashar*. 1924; 80 pp. (ibid., p. 440).

12c. Id., *Maghāwir al-jinn.* Beirut, Maṭābi' Qūzmā, 1926; 92 pp. (ibid. XLIII, 1949, p. 286).

13. al-'Abbūshī, Burhān al-Dīn, *Waṭan al-shahīd.* A 5-act political play in lit. Ar. verse, calling for united Arab action against Jewish activities in Palestine. Jerusalem, al-Maṭb. al-iqtiṣādiyya, 1947; II, 86 pp.

14. 'Abd Allāh, Ṣūfī, *Kasbunā'l-brīmō.* A play in the colloquial Arabic of Egypt. Prod. in 1951–1952 (*K.*, vol. VII, June, 1952, p. 753).
'Abd al-'Azīz, 'Umar, see: List of Ar. Plays, Transl.—Prévost.

15. 'Abd al-'Aẓīm, 'Alī, *al-Wallāda.* An hist. play in verse. Prob. 1948 (ibid., vol. IV, Jan., 1949, pp. 153–154).
'Abd al-Fādī, Ibrāhīm, see: List of Ar. Plays, Transl.—Maeterlinck.

15a. 'Abd al-Fattāḥ, Muḥammad, *Lailā.* Prod. in Egypt (Najm, *al-Masraḥiyya etc.*, p. 84).
'Abd al-Hādī, Raḍwān, see: List of Arabic Plays, Transl.—Shakespeare.

15b. 'Abd al-Ḥamīd, Muḥammad, *al-Rāqiṣa.* A 3-act play. Cairo, Maṭb al-Ismā'īliyya al-kubrā, 1947; 117 pp. (*Ma.*, XLIII, 1949, p. 120).
'Abd al-Ḥamīd, Muḥammad Munīr, see: List of Ar. Plays, Transl.—Sheridan.
'Abd al-Malik, Iskandar Jirjis, see: List of Ar. Plays, Transl.—Shakespeare.

16. 'Abd al-Mun'im, Ismā'īl, *'Amr bnu al-'Āṣṣ.* An hist. play, followed by a list of Arabic technical terms of the theater. Cairo, Maṭb. al-Qāhira, 1925 (?) (*Fihris*, IV, p. 68).

16a. 'Abd al-Muṭṭalib, Muḥammad & Mar'ī, Muḥammad 'Abd al-Muṭī', *Ḥayāt Imri' al-Qais bni Ḥujr.* 1911 (Najm, *al-Masraḥiyya etc.*, pp. 324–325).

16b. Id. & Id., *Ḥayāt al-Muhalhil bni Rabī'a au ḥarb al-Basūs*, 1911 (ibid., pp. 321–324).

16c. 'Abd al-Nūr, Jabbūr, *al-Ḥubb yantaqim* (*Ma.*, XLII, 1948, p. 455).
'Abduh, Ṭānyūs, see: List of Ar. Plays, Transl.—Schiller; Shakespeare.

17. Abīla, Shārl, *Ibn Wā'il.* A 3-act hist. tragedy in lit. Ar. prose. 2nd ed., Beirut, 1925; 45 pp. (Sarkīs, *Jāmi'*, I, No. 1096).

17a. Abū'l-'Azm, Muḥammad 'Abd al-Ḥamīd, *Tauliyat Muḥammad 'Alī Bāshā.* An hist. play for prod. in schools. Cairo, Maṭb. al-ma'ārif, n.d., prob. 1941; 32 pp.

18. Abū Fāḍil, Farīd Shāhīn, *al-Ḥasnā' al-'arabiyya Zainab bint Isḥāq.* A 3-act play on the controversy between Mu'āwiya and Ḥusain. Antioch, Maṭb. al-Riyāḍ, prob. 1934; 62 pp. (*Mu.*, vol. LXXXV, Oct. 1, 1934, p. 256).

19. Abū Fāḍil, Waḍī', *Tammūz wa-Ba'la au Adūnīs wa-'Ashtarūt.* Tells in lit. Ar. verse the love story of the ancient Canaanite Gods, with nationalist implications. N.p. (Cairo?), Maṭb. Waḍī' Abū Fāḍil, n.d., prob. 1937 (*Mu.*, vol. XCI, June 1, 1937, p. 127; *GAL*, Suppl. III, pp. 417–418).

19a. Abū Fāris, Jirjis, *Ilā'l-dair.* A 5-act play. Daura (Lebanon), Maṭb. Fāḍil wa-Jamīl; 80 pp. (*Ma.*, XLII, 1948, p. 442).

20. Abū Hanā, Niqūlā, *al-'Afw 'ind al-maqdara au al-Ma'mūn wa-'ammuh Ibrāhīm bnu al-Mahdī.* A 4-act hist. play in lit. Ar. prose and verse. Ṣaidā, Maṭb Dair al-Mukhliṣ, 1928; 120 pp. (*Ma.*, vol. XXVI, 1928, p. 554; *Majallat al-majma' al-'ilmī'l-'arabī*, vol. VIII, 1928, p. 766. *GAL*, S. III, p. 417, reads author's name Niqūlā Ḥannā.

21. Abū Ḥadīd, Muḥammad Farīd, *'Abd al-shaiṭān.* A 3-act play in lit. Ar. prose, on the theme of *Faust*: the poet who is so poor and so frustrated in his love that he agrees to sell his soul to the Devil. N.p., Dār al-ma'ārif, 1945; 148 pp.

22. Id., *Maisūn al-ghajariyya*. Cairo, 1928 (*GAL*, S. III, p. 227).
22a. Abū Nādir, Ilyās Jurjī Shibl, *al-Thaura al-Durziyya fī'l-arāḍī'l-lubnāniyya*. N.Y., 1926; 62 pp. (*Ma.*, XLII, 1948, p. 452.)
22b. Abū Nādir, Jirjis, *Istiqlāl Lubnān*. A 5-act hist. play. Beirut, Maṭb. al-Daura-al-Nahr, 1947; 56 pp. (ibid., p. 440).
Abū Naḍḍāra, see: List of Ar. Plays, Orig. Plays—Ṣanū'.
22c. Abū'l-Naṣr,' Umar, *al-Baṭal lā yamūt*. Beirut (*Ma.*, XLII, 1948, p. 448).
22d. Id., *al-Imtiḥān*. Beirut (ibid., p. 442).
22e. Id., *al-Umm*. Beirut (ibid., ibid.).
22f. Abū Qaus, 'Abd al-Raḥmān, *Bākhūs* (i.e., *Bacchus*). A play based on the Pygmalion story. Aleppo, 1943; 124 pp. (ibid., p. 446).
22g. Id., *Ṭilsim al-ḥayāt*. Aleppo, 1941 (ibid., XLIII, 1949, p. 132).
22h. Id., *Thaurat al-'abīd*. Verse. Aleppo, al-Maṭb. al-'aṣriyya, 1937; 61 pp. (ibid., XLII, 1948, p. 453).
22i. Abū Rīsha, 'Umar, *Dhī Qār*. A 4-act play in verse. Aleppo, 1932 (ibid., XLIII, 1949, p. 119).
22j. Abū Sulaimān, Yūsuf Shiblī, *Abdālūnīm malik Ṣīdūn*. A 5-act hist. drama in lit. Ar. prose and verse. Prod. 1901. Publ. al-Ḥadath, 1903; 92 pp. (ibid., XLII, 1948, p. 435).
22k. Id., *Wadī'at al-īmān fī ḍawāḥī Lubnān*. A 3-act hist. play. Beirut, al-Maṭb. al-kāthūlikiyya, 1899; 72 pp. (ibid., XLIII, 1949, p. 294).
See also: List of Ar. Plays, Transl.—Delaporte.
22l. 'Abū'l-Su'ūd, 'Abd al-Wahhāb, *Khaulat bint al-uzūr*. An hist. play. Damascus, Dār al-yaqẓa al-'arabiyya, 1944; together with Nos. 22n and 22o, 158 pp. (*Ma.*, XLII, 1948, p. 459).
22m. Id., *Shuhadā' al-intiqām*. A 5-act play. Damascus, al-Maṭb al-'arabiyya, A.H. 1332; 71 pp. (ibid., XLIII, 1949, p. 129).
22n. Id., *Tatwīj Faiṣal*. Damascus, 1944. Publ. together with Nos. 22l and 22o (ibid., XLII, 1948, p. 450).
22o. Id., *Wa-mu'taṣimāh*. Publ. together with Nos. 22l & 22n, above (ibid.).
22p. Id., *al-Waṭan*. Damascus, Dār al-yaqẓa al-'arabiyya, 1944; 158 pp. (ibid., XLIII, 1949, p. 294).
23. Abū'l-Su'ūd, Muḥammad Labīb, *Riwāyat al-mayyit al-ḥayy*. A play in lit. Ar. 1st ed., Cairo, Maṭb al-Nīl, 1903; 40 pp. 2nd ed., Cairo, Maṭb. al-iṣlāḥ, 1911. Prod. in Egypt early in the 20th century
(*Fihris*, IV, p. 127; *Mu.*, vol. XXIX, Jan. 1, 1904, p. 90; *H.*, vol. XX, Jan. 1, 1912, p. 256).
24. Abū Shabaka, Ilyās, *al-Rawā'i'*. Beirut, Mak. Ṣādir, 1930; 120 pp. (*GAL*, S. III, p. 367. Dāghir, p. 69, reads *al-Riwā'ī* and claims the play is transl. from English).
See also: List of Ar. Plays, Transl.—Ghanem; Karr; Molière; Rostand.
25. Abū Shādī, Aḥmad Zakī, *Akhnatun Fir'aun Miṣr*. A 3-act hist. opera about one of the greatest Pharaohs. Cairo, Dār al-'uṣūr li'l-ṭab' wa'l-nashr, n.d., prob. 1931; 62, 20 pp. (*GAL*, S. III, p. 115).
26. Id., *al-Āliha*. A 3-act symbolical opera in lit. Ar. verse, tracing the spiritual struggle of a poet who must choose between the Goddesses of Lust and Power and those of Beauty and Love. Cairo, Dār al-'uṣūr li'l-ṭab' wa'l-nashr, n.d. (introd, signed Aug. 1927); 100, 36 pp. (ibid., p. 114; *H.*, vol. XXXVIII, Jan. 1, 1930, p. 372; *Mu*, vol. LXXVI, Feb. 1, 1930, pp. 227–228).

27. Id., *Ardashīr wa-ḥayāt al-nufūs*. A 4-act opera in lit. Ar. verse, based on the tale of Prince Ardashīr in the *Arabian Nights*. Alexandria, al-Maṭb. al-salafiyya, 1928, 155 (?) pp. (*GAL*, ibid., pp. 113–114; *H.*, vol. XXXVI, Feb. 1, 1928, p. 500; *Mu.*, vol. LXXII, Mar. 1, 1928, p. 348).
28. Id., *Bint al-ṣaḥrā'* (Barbour, in *BSOS*, vol. VII, 1935, p. 182, n. 1).
29. Id., *Iḥsān*. A 3-act opera in lit. Ar. verse about an Egyptian officer and his girl who dies of longing when she receives the false news of her fiancé's death. Cairo, al-Maṭb. al-salafiyya, 1927; 160 pp., of which the opera proper is on pp. 37–64 only (*GAL*, S. III, p. 113; *H.*, vol. XXXVI, Dec. 1, 1927, p. 241; *Mu.*, vol. LXXII, Mar. 1, 1928, p. 349; Sarkīs, *Jāmi'*, II, No. 202; *Fihris*, IV, pp. 4–5).
30. Id., *al-Zabbā' malikat Tadmur*. A 4-act hist. opera in lit. Ar. verse, descr. the might of Queen Zenobia of Palmyra and her defeat and imprisonment by the Romans. Cairo, al-Maṭb. al-salafiyya, n.d. (1927); 88 pp. (*GAL*, ibid., pp. 114–115; Sarkīs, ibid., No. 218; *H.*, vol. XXXVI, Jan. 1, 1928, p. 378; *Fihris*, IV, p. 43).
See also: List of Ar. Plays, Transl.—Shakespeare.
Abū Shūsha, 'Abbās, see: List of Ar. Plays, Transl.—Schiller.
31. Adham, 'Abd al-Wahhāb, *al-Sayyid Ḥāṭūm*. A 4-act comedy in lit. Ar. prose and a few verses. It pokes fun at a youngster, his attempts at learning and at social behavior. Damascus, Maṭb. Bābil, 1930; 79, 1 pp.
32. 'Afīf, Ḥusain, *Suhair*. A play in lit. Ar. blank verse. Cairo, Maṭb. Ḥijāzī, prob. 1938; 185 pp. (*H.*, vol. XLVI, July 1, 1938, p. 1080).
33. Id., *Waḥīd au qalb fannān*. A play in lit. Ar. blank verse. Maṭb. Ḥijāzī, 1936; 191 pp.
34. 'Afīfī, 'Abd Allāh, *al-Hādī*. An hist. play in lit. Ar., set in the reign of that Caliph. Cairo, Maṭb. al-Ma'ārif, n.d. (*BSOS*, vol. VIII, 1935–1937, p. 999).
35. al-Aḥdab, Ibrāhīm, *'Abd al-Salām al-ma'rūf bi-Dīk al-Jinn ma' zaujatih Ward* (Dāghir, p. 86).
36. Id., *Abū Nu'ās ma' Jinān jāriyat Thaqīf* (ibid.).
37. Id., *Jamīl Buthaina* (ibid.).
38. Id., *Kuthair 'Azza* (ibid.).
39. Id., *Majnūn Lailā* (ibid.).
40. Id., *Mazdak* (ibid.).
41. Id., *Muḥammad bnu Ḥāmid al-Khāqānī wa-'Arīb* (ibid.).
42. Id., *al-Munkhul al-Yashkarī ma' al-Mutajarrida zaujat al-malik al-Nu'mān* (ibid.).
43. Id., *al-Mu'tamid bnu 'Ibād* (ibid., reads mistakenly *'Iyād*).
43a. Id., *Nā'ila malikat al-ḥaḍar ma' Jadhīma malik al-'arab*. Prod. 1879 (Najm, *al-Masraḥiyya*, p. 55).
44. Id., *Qais wa-Lubnā* (Dāghir, p. 86).
45. Id., *Sa'īd bnu Ḥāmid wa-faḍl al-shā'ira* (ibid).
46. Id., *al-Saif wa'l-qalam* (ibid.).
47. Id., *al-Tuḥfa al-rushdiyya*. Beirut, 1868; 89 pp. (From Dāghir, ibid., p. 85, it would appear that this is not a play—contrast however Ḥunain, *Shauqī 'alā'l-masraḥ*, repr., p. 18).
48. Id., *'Urwa bnu Ḥuzām ma' maḥbūbatih 'Afrā'* (Dāghir, ibid., p. 86).
49. Id., *Wallāda bint al-Mustakfī ma' al-wazīr Ibn Zaidūn*. Prose and verse (ibid.).
50. Id., *Washy al-yarā'a fī 'ulūm al-balāgha wa'l-barā'a*. Beirut, 1870; 86 pp. (Ibid.; Ḥunain, *op. cit.*, repr., p. 18, reads *Washy al-barā'a* and gives publ. date as 1869).

51. Id., *Yazīd bnu 'Abd al-Malik ma' jāriyataih Ḥabbāba wa-Salāma* (Dāghir, ibid.). See also: List of Ar. Plays, Transl.—Racine.
Aḥmad, Ma'rūf, see below: al-Arnā'ūṭ, Ma'rūf Aḥmad.
51a. 'Aid, 'Azīz, *al-Kābūrāl Sīmūn.* A 5-act play. Damascus, Maṭb. Ibn Zaidūn, 1939; 98 pp. (*Ma.*, XLIII, 1949, p. 276).
See also: List of Ar. Plays, Transl.—Feydeau.
51b. 'Ajlān, Kāmil Muḥammad, *Ghādat al-haudaj.* A 4-act play. Mak. Miṣr; 68 pp. (ibid., p. 138).
51c. Id., *'Ushshāq al-'arab.* A collection of five short plays by this author. Lajnat al-nashr li'l-jāmi'iyyīn; 144 pp. (ibid., p. 135).
51d. Id., *al-Zahra.* A hist. melodrama. Lajnat al-nashr li'l-jāmi'iyyīn (ibid., p. 123).
52. Āl Nāṣir al-Dīn, Amīn, *Jazā' al-khiyāna.* A play, publ. (Dāghir, p. 39).
53. Id., *Gharā'ib al-ẓulm.* A ms. play in verse (ibid.).
54. 'Alā' al-Dīn, Muḥammad Ḥasan, *al-Marsaḥiyya al-shi'riyya Imru' al-Qais bnu Ḥujr.* A 4-act hist. play, in pedantic lit. Ar. verse, descr. the life and death of a famous pre-Islamic poet. Jerusalem, al-Maṭb. al-tijāriyya, 1946; 111 pp.
55. al-'Alā'ilī, Jamīla Muḥammad, *al-Mar'a al-raḥīma.* Appar. broadcast in the Arabic program at Radio Bari (*GAL*, S. III, pp. 175, 1321).
56. al-Alfī, Barsūm Bāsilī, *Riwāyat tarbiyat al-banāt.* A 3-act play, calling for the education of the Arab woman. Cairo (?), prob. 1899 (*H.*, vol. VIII, Dec. 15, 1899, pp. 191–192).
57. Id., *Sulṭān al-hawā.* A play descr. the Cairene night-life and criticizing it. Prob. 1900 (ibid., Aug. 15, 1900, p. 703).
58. 'Alī, 'Abd al-Raḥmān 'Uthmān, *Ma'sāt al-taqālīd.* Alex., Maṭb. al-taqaddum, prob. 1933 (*H.*, vol. XLII, Feb. 1, 1934, p. 506).
59. 'Alī, Ḥasan, *Riwāyat Draifūs.* In preparation, 1899 (ibid., vol. VIII, Oct. 1, 1899, p. 31).
60. 'Alī, Muḥammad Kāmil, *Shaikh al-ḥāra.* A 5-act libretto for an opéra comique, in lit. Ar. mixed with coll. Ar. Prob. 1928; 95 pp. (ibid., vol. XXXVII, Feb. 1, 1929, p. 500).
61. 'Allālū, *'Antar al-ḥashā'ishī.* A 3-act comedy about the misadventures of a hashish-smoking cobbler. First prod. in Alger, 1930 (*Revue Africaine*, Quarterly, Alger, vol. LXXVII, 1935, p. 80).
62. Id., & Daḥmūn, *Jeḥa.* A 2-act comedy of manners in coll. Ar. First prod. in Alger, 1926, often repeated (ibid., pp. 76–78).
63. 'Allām, 'Abbās, *'Abd al-Raḥmān al-Nāṣir.* A 5-act hist. drama in lit. Ar. prose, treating of the exploits, of the renowned Spanish Caliph. Cairo, Mak. al-wafd, n.d., prob. 1933–4; 8, 225 pp. Written for the inauguration of the Azbakiyya Gardens Theater and prod. there for the first time, 1921.
64. Id., *Ah yā ḥarāmī.* A 3-act opera-bouffe inspired by the English *Pick-pocket.* First prod. in Egypt, 1922 ('Allām, *'Abd al-Raḥmān al-Nāṣir*, bibl. app., No. 8).
65. Id., *Alā mōd* (i.e., *À la mode*). A 3-act comedy. First prod. 1921 (ibid., No. 6).
66. Id., *Bism al-qānūn.* A 3-act comedy. First prod. by Abyaḍ in Cairo, 1924 (ibid., No. 10).
67. Id., *Illī y'īsh yamma yshūf.* A 2-act comedy in coll. Ar. First prod. 1917 (ibid., No. 3).
68. Id., *Malik wa-shaiṭān.* A 4-act comedy. First prod. by amateurs in Port Said, 1915, then in Cairo repeatedly (ibid., No. 1).

69. Id., *Safīnat Nūḥ*. A 3-act comedy. First prod. by Abyaḍ in Cairo, 1924 (Ibid., No. 9).
70. Id., *Sihām*. A 4-act comedy. Written in reply to Georges Feydeau's vaudeville *La dame de chez Maxime*. First prod. 1926 (ibid., No. 12).
71. Id., *S̲h̲aqā' al-'ā'ilāt*. A 5-act *pièce*. First prod. by Salāma Ḥijāzī in Cairo, 1916 (ibid., No. 2).
72. Id., *al-S̲h̲arīṭ al-aḥmar*. A 5-act *comédie dramatique*. First prod. by Ḥijāzī, 1917 (ibid., No. 4).
73. Id., *Ṭōṭō*. A 4-act comedy. First prod. in 1933 by the troupe of Fāṭima Rus̲h̲dī (ibid., No. 17).
74. Id., *Zahrat al-s̲h̲āi*. A 3-act drama. First prod. 1926 (ibid., No. 13).
75. Id., *al-Zauba'a*. A 3-act comédie dramatique, inspired by Gaston Devore's *La conscience de l'enfant*. First prod. 1921 (ibid., No. 7).
76. Id., *al-Zauja al-'ad̲h̲rā'*. A 4-act comedy inspired by Alfred Savoir's *La huitième femme de Barbe Bleue*. First prod. 1933 (ibid., No. 16).
See also: List of Ar. Plays, Transl.—Bernstein; Lorde; Mayo.
76a. Amīn, 'Iṣām Sāmī, *al-Muwazzaf*. A 4-act play. Beirut, Maṭb. al-Inṣāf, 1946; 78 pp. (*Ma.*, XLIII, 1949, p. 289).
Amīn, 'Umar 'Abd al-'Azīz, see: List of Ar. Plays, Transl.—Shakespeare.
77. 'Āmir, 'Affān, *Bū Nāja* (?) (*BE*, Nov. 1, 1952, p. 3).
'Ammārī, see: List of Ar. Plays, Orig. Plays—Ṭūrī.
78. Andrā'us, Ḥannā, *Ṭāriq bnu Ziyād*. An hist. drama (Muḥammad Taimūr, Mu'allafāt, vol. II, art on Āl 'Ukkās̲h̲a).
79. 'Anḥūrī, Salīm, *Riwāyat As̲h̲īl*. A 5-act tragedy in lit. Ar. prose & verse, treating of Achilles' exploits. Prod. in Damascus, 1899, then in Beirut. Publ. prob. 1904 (*H.*, vol. XIII, Feb. 1, 1905, p. 320. Sarkīs, *Mu'jam*, p. 1388, and *GAL*, S. III, p. 341, give full author's name as Salīm b. Rufā'īl Jirjis 'Anḥūrī, but make no mention of this play. Dāg̲h̲ir, p. 615, says this play was adapted from the French and is still in ms.).
80. Id., *Riwāyat Hind wa-'Iṣām*. Prose and verse. Appar. still in ms. (Dāg̲h̲ir, ibid.).
81. al-'Ānī, Yūsuf, *Harmal wa-ḥabbet sōda*. A drama in coll. Ar. (of Iraq) prose, concerning the conflict between the older and younger generations. Publ. together with the following two plays. Baghdad, Mans̲h̲ūrāt al-t̲h̲aqāfa al-jadīda, 1954–1955; 94 pp. (*al-Adīb*, vol. XXVII, Mar. 1955, pp. 59–62).
82. Id., *Ra's il-S̲h̲elīla*. A drama in coll. Ar. (of Iraq) prose about some defects in the Iraqi public service. Publ. together with Nos. 81 & 83 (ibid.).
83. Id., *Tu'mur bek*. A satirical play in coll. Ar. (of Iraq) prose, directed against the non-working aristocracy. Publ. together with the preceding two plays (ibid.).
84. Anṭūn, Faraḥ, *Abū'l-Hūl yataḥarrak au al-Farā'ina sāhirūn*. An hist. musical, appar. still in ms. (*H.*, vol. XXXI, Feb. 1, 1923, p. 528).
85. Id., *Banāt al-s̲h̲awāri' au banāt al-k̲h̲udūr*. An operatic comedy (*Faraḥ Anṭūn wa-ḥayātuh wa-ta'bīnuh wa-muk̲h̲tārātuh*, 1923, p. 133).
86. Id., *al-Burj al-hā'il*. A 5-act hist. play, inspired by A. Dumas (père). Prod. in Alexandria and Cairo. Publ. Alex., al-Mak. al-k̲h̲adyawiyya, prob. 1898 (*H.*, vol. VII, Jan. 1, 1899, p. 253. *GAL*, S. III, p. 193, gives date of publ. as 1904. Dāg̲h̲ir, p. 150, gives al-Maṭb. al-'Ut̲h̲māniyya as publisher).
87. Id., *al-Fatāt al-ḥasnā' Graziella*. A vaudeville inspired by Louis de Lamartine. Lit. Ar., mixed with the coll. Ar. of Syria (*GAL*, S. III, p. 194).

88. Id., *Miṣr al-jadīda wa-Miṣr al-qadīma*. A musical. Often prod. since 1913. (*GAL*, ibid., p. 193).
89. Id., *al-Mutaṣarrif fī'l-'ibād*. Appar. an adapted operetta (*Mu.*, vol. LXI, Aug. 1, 1922, p. 265).
90. Id., *Ṣalāḥ al-Dīn au fatḥ Bait al-Maqdis*. Cairo, 1923; 63 pp. (ibid., *H.*, vol. XXXI, Feb. 1, 1923, p. 528; *GAL*, S. III, p. 193; Dāghir, p. 150).
91. Id., *al-Sulṭān Ṣalāḥ al-Dīn wa-mamlakat Urushalīm*. A 4-act hist. play, with political hints, in lit. Ar. prose. Written 1914. Cairo, Suppl. to *Majallat al-Sayyidāt wa'l-rijāl*, 1923; 62 pp. (*Mu*, vol. LXIV, Feb. 1, 1924, p 221; vol. II, Nov. 1947, p. 1738; *Fihris*, IV, p. 48).
See also: List of Ar. Plays, Transl.—Dumas; France; Gallet; Meilhac; Sardou; Sophocles; *Zaza*.
Anṭūn, Rabbāṭ, see: Rabbāṭ, Anṭūn.
91a. Anwar, 'Alī, *Shahāmat al-'arab*. A play about 'Antara (Najm, *al-Masraḥiyya etc.*, p. 380).
92. 'Aql, Sa'īd, *Bint Yaftāḥ*. A play, prob. based on the Biblical story (Judges, 11) of Jephthah's daughter. 2 acts of lit. Ar. verse. 64 pp.
92a. Id., *Qadmūs*. A 3-act tragedy. Beirut, 1941. (*Ma.*, XLIII, 1949, p. 275).
93. 'Aql, Shadīd Wadī', *Firsinjitūrīks*. An hist. play about Vercingetorix (Dāghir, p. 609).
94. Id., *Istishhād al-qiddīs Tūmās Bākīt*. A 3-act hist. play about Thomas Becket's martyrdom. Ba'abdā, al-Maṭb. al-Lubnāniyya, 1905; 48 pp. (ibid.).
95. Id., *al-Lubnānī'l-muhājir* (ibid.).
96. Id., *Maghārat al-luṣūṣ* (ibid.).
al-'Aqqād, Maḥmūd Aḥmad, see: List of Ar. Plays, Transl.—Shakespeare.
97. 'Arafāt, Anwar 'Amr, *Wa-lakum fī'l-qiṣaṣ ḥayāt*. Beirut, Maṭb. al-wafā', prob. 1934; 75 pp. (*H.*, vol. XLII, Aug. 1, 1934, p. 1267).
98. 'Arīḍa, Nasīb, *Riwāyat al-shā'ir 'Abd al-Salām bni Raghbān. A* 4-act play. N.Y., 1923 (*GAL*, S. III, p. 445).
99. al-Arnā'ūṭ, Ma'rūf Aḥmad, *'Amr bnu al-'Āṣṣ fī Ṭarablus al-gharb* (Dāghir, p. 109).
100. Id., *al-Rujū' ilā Ederna*. Damascus, Maṭb. al-Nafā'is, 1913; 90 pp. (ibid.).
See also: List of Ar. Plays, Transl.—Coppée; Dennery; Dumas.
100a. Id., *al-Sharīf*. Damascus (*Ma.*, XLIII, 1949, p. 128).
101. Arslān, Amīn, *Asrār al-quṣūr*. A play about some 19th century Turkish Sultans and their Court. Publ. in South America (?), al-Maṭb. al-Jamāliyya, 1900 (*Fihris*, IV, p. 8. Cf. *GAL*, S. III, p. 229). Prod. in Egypt, 1951–2 (*K.*, vol. VII, June, 1952, p. 753).
101a. al-Asīr, Yūsuf, *Saif al-naṣr*. 1875 (Najm, *al-Masraḥiyya etc.*, p. 58).
102. 'Āṣim, Ismā'īl, *Ḥusn al-'awāqib*. A musical play in coll. Ar. (*GAL*, ibid., p. 112, n. 1).
102a. Id., *Ṣidq al-ikhā'*. A social drama. 1894 (Najm, *al-Masraḥiyya etc.*, pp. 402–405).
102b. al-Ashqar, Buṭrus, *al-Amīra al-naṣrāniyya fī 'aṣr al-jāhiliyya*. Bait Shabāb, Maṭb. al-'alam, 1935; 128 pp. (*Ma.*, XLII, 1948, p. 444).
102c. Id., *Jamāl Bāshā fī Lubnān* (ibid., p. 454).
103. al-Ashqar, Fā'iz Sam'ān, *al-Amīra Fīnīs*. Mak. al-hilāl (?), prob. 1907 (*H.*, vol. XVI, Nov. 1, 1907, p. 127).
103a. al-Ashqar, Ilyās Manṣūr, *al-Ḥayāt fidā' al-gharām*. A 3-act play. Beirut, Maṭb. al-ijtihād, 1908; 40 pp. (*Ma.*, XLII, 1948, p. 458).

103b. 'Aṭā' Allāh, Amīn, *Ṣabaḥ il-kheir.* A comedy, in coll. Ar.; 15 pp. (ibid., XLIII, 1949, p. 130).

104. Id., *Shuhadā' al-gharām.* A parody of Shakespeare's *Romeo and Juliet.* Lit. Ar. verse. Prod. by Ḥijāzī, 1906 (*H.*, vol. XXXVI, Dec. 1, 1927, p. 204). See also: List of Ar. Plays, Orig. Plays—al-Khūrī, Amīn; List of Ar. Plays, Transl.—Molière.

'Aṭā' Allāh (al-Lubnānī), Rashīd, see: List of Ar. Plays, Orig. Plays.—Fīktōr.

'Aṭiyya, 'Alī Imām, see: List of Ar. Plays, Transl.—Shakespeare.

105. 'Aṭiyya, Rashīd al-Ḥājj, *Tabri'at al-muttaham au jazā' al-makr.* A 4-act drama in lit. Ar. verse. Ba'abdā, al-Maṭb. al-'uthmāniyya, 1897; 68 pp. (Ḥunain, *Shauqī 'alā'l-masraḥ*, p. 18).

106 'Aṭiyya, Shāhīn, *'Āqibat sū' al-tarbiya* (Shaikhū, *Ta'rīkh al-ādāb al-'arabiyya fī'l-rub' al-awwal min al-qarn al-'ishrīn*, p. 70).

107. Id., *Ḥukm Sulaimān* (ibid.).

108. Avierino, Alexandra de, *Shaqā' al-ummahāt.* A drama (*GAL*, S. III, p. 259).

'Awwād, As'ad, see: List of Ar. Plays, Transl.—Voltaire.

109. al-'Ayyād, Būlus, *Ṭifl al-midhwad.* A religious play in prose. Prob. 1948 (*K.*, vol. IV, Jan. 1949, p. 141).

110. 'Ayyāsh, 'Abd al-Raḥmān, *al-Ḥajjāj.* Retells the story of the great Umayyad soldier and administrator. Ḥamāt, Maṭb. Abū'l-Fidā', 1946; 81 pp. (ibid., vol. I, Jan. 1947, p. 488, and vol. II, Feb. 1947, p. 627).

111. Ayyūb, Muḥammad, *Bahmān Shāh.* An hist. play about Persia. Alex., al-Maṭb. al-miṣriyya, 1899 (*H.*, vol. VIII, Oct. 15, 1899, p. 63; *Fihris*, IV, p. 19).

Ayyūb, Nadīm Anṭūnyūs, see: List of Ar. Plays, Transl.—Racine.

al-'Āzār, Augustinus, see: List of Ar. Plays, Transl.—Racine.

112. al-'Azār, Iskandar, *Ḥarb al-Basūs.* An hist. play, written in 1869 (*H.*, vol. XXVII, Apr. 1, 1919, p. 644. Dāghir, p. 585, suggests publ. date 1870?).

113. Id., *Majā'a Rūmiyya.* Prod. a few times in Beirut for charity purposes (*H.*, ibid., pp. 644–645. Written during or after 1878, cf. Dāghir, p. 585).

114. Id., *Min ashqā'l-azwāj* (*H.*, ibid., p. 645. Acc. to Dāghir, p. 585, the ms. text is lost).

115. Id., *Rasm Suriyā au man rāma mu'ānadat al-unthā fal-ya'tī li-tudmagh jabhatuh.* A play calling for the education of women. Written in 1875 and prod. in Beirut the same year for charity purposes (*H.*, ibid., p. 644).

'Azmī, Fatḥī, see: List of Ar. Plays, Transl.—Ḥāmid.

115a. al-'Āzār, Nasīm, *Arwāḥ al-aḥrār.* A 4-act play. Publ. 1908–1909 (Najm, *al-Masraḥiyya etc.*, pp. 343–345; contrast *Ma.*, XLII, 1948, p. 439).

'Āzār, Shākir, see: List of Ar. Plays, Transl.—Corneille.

116. 'Azīz, Najīb, *Riwāyat 'adl al-mulūk.* An hist. drama in lit. Ar. prose and verse, descr. the love affairs of Alexis the son of the Czar Peter the Great. Prob. 1896 (*Mu.*, vol. XX, Dec. 1, 1896, p. 934).

116a. 'Azūz, Muḥammad 'Alī, *Maḥasin al-zuhūr.* Prod. in Alexandria, May 1896 (Najm, *al-Masraḥiyya etc.*, p. 179).

116b. al-'Aẓm, 'Abduh Sulaimān, *Faẓā'i' Jamāl fī Sūriyā wa-Lubnān.* Beirut, Maṭb. al-Salām, 1938; 79 pp. (ibid., XLIII, 1949, p. 273).

117. Badawī, Maḥmūd, *al-'Abbāsa ukht Hārūn al-Rashīd.* An hist. play in lit. Ar about the fall of the Barmakids. Cairo, 1931 (*BSOS*, vol. VIII, 1935–1937, pp. 998–999; *GAL*, S. III, p. 279).

118. Id., *S̲hajarat al-Durr.* An hist. play in lit. Ar., following closely the known run-of-events in 13th century Egypt. Prod. by the Ramses troupe, 1932–3. Publ. Cairo, 1933 (*GAL*, ibid., pp. 279–280).
118a. Badī', Muḥammad, *al-Ṣayyādūn al-it̲hnā 'as̲har.* Cairo (*Ma.*, XLIII, 1949, p. 131).
119. Badī', Muṣṭafā, *al-K̲hidā'.* Prod. on the stage of the Opera at Alger, 1945 (*Le Monde Arabe*, Paris, fasc. 12, Dec. 17, 1951, p. 10).
Badrān, Muḥammad, see: List of Ar. Plays, Transl.—Molière.
119a. Bahīt, Yūsuf, *Intiqāl al-'ad̲hrā'.* A one-act play with music. Deir al-Muk̲hliṣ, 1936 (*Ma.*, XLII, 1948, p. 444).
al-Bahnasāwī, Kāmil, see: List of Ar. Plays, Transl.—Dumas (fils).
120. al-Baḥrī, Jamīl Ḥabīb, *Fī sabīl al-s̲haraf.* A 5-act tragedy. Haifa, 1926; 76 pp. (Sarkīs, *Jāmi'*, I, No. 1151; *GAL*, S. III, p. 417, based on *Ma.*, vol. XXIV, p. 417.)
121. Id., *Fī'l-sijn* (S̲haik̲hū, *Ta'rīk̲h . . . fī'l-rub' al-awwal etc.*, p. 168).
122. Id., *al-Hujūm 'alā'l-Beljīk* (ibid.).
123. Id., *al-Ḥaqīqa al-mu'lima* (ibid.).
124. Id., *al-Ik̲htifā' al-g̲harīb* (ibid.).
125. Id., *al-K̲hā'in.* A 3-act tragedy. Haifa, al-Mak. al-waṭaniyya, n.d., prob. 1924 (*Mu*, vol. LXIV, Mar. 1, 1924, p. 348; *H.*, vol. XXXII, June 1, 1924, p. 997; *GAL*, S. III, p. 417; Sarkīs, *Jāmi'*, I, No. 1118).
126. Id., *Qātil ak̲hīh.* A 3-act tragedy, possibly adapted from the French. Haifa, prob. 1919 (*H.*, vol. XXVIII, Oct. 1–Nov. 1, 1919, p. 174; and vol. XXXII, Dec. 1, 1923, p. 325. *GAL*, S. III, p. 417, gives 1923 and 1927 as the dates of publ.; *BSOS*, vol. VIII, 1935–1937, suggests 1927).
127. Id., *Sajīn al-qaṣr.* A 5-act tragedy, adapted from the French (?). Ḥariṣā (Lebanon), prob. 1920 (*H.*, vol. XXVIII, May 1, 1920, p. 752. *GAL*, S. III, p. 417, presumably mentions another ed., Haifa, 1927).
128. Id., *Suqūṭ Bag̲hdād* (S̲haik̲hū, *Ta'rīk̲h . . . fī'l-rub' al-awwal etc.*, p. 168).
129. Id., *al-Waṭan al-maḥbūb.* Cairo, 1923 (ibid., *GAL*, S. III, p. 417).
130. Id., *al-Zahra al-ḥamrā'* (S̲haik̲hū, ibid.).
131. Id., *Ẓulm al-wālid* (ibid.).
131a. Bāk̲hūs, K̲halīl, *Dīmitriyūs*, 1887 (ibid., p. 110; *Ma.*, XLIII, 1949, p. 118).
132. Bāk̲hūs, K̲halīl Ṭannūs, *al-Ḥārit̲h malik Najrān.* A 3-act hist. play in lit. Ar. verse. 1st ed., 1887, 2nd ed., Jisr Nahr Bairūt, Maṭb. al-ḥuqūq, 1910; 66 pp. (S̲haik̲hū, p. 110; Ḥunain, *S̲hauqī 'alā'l-masraḥ*, repr. p. 18).
133. Bāk̲hūs, al-K̲hūrī Ni'mat Allāh, & others, *Ḥulm fa-yaqẓa.* A prologue and 3-act play in lit. Ar. prose and verse. Adapted from the French, it tells of court-intrigues in Florence. Beirut, al-Maṭb. al-lubnāniyya, 1913; 138 pp.
134. Bākt̲hīr, 'Alī Aḥmad, *Ak̲hnātūn wa-Nafartītī.* A 4-act play in lit. Ar. free verse. It descr. life and love in ancient Egypt. Cairo, Mak. Miṣr, prob. 1940; 8, 216 pp. (*Mu.*, vol. XCVII, Nov. 1940, p. 446).
134a. Id., *'Audat al-firdaus au istiqlāl Indūnīsiyā.* A 4-act play. Cairo, Mak. al-K̲hānjī, 1946; 156 pp. (*Ma.*, XLIII, 1949, p. 138).
134b. Id., *al-Duktūr Ḥāzim.* A social drama in 7 scenes. Cairo, Lajnat al-nas̲hr li'l-jāmi'iyyīn; 142 pp. (*Ma.*, XLII, 1948, p. 460).
135. Id., *Fāris al-balqā' Abū Miḥjan al-T̲haqafī*, A 2-act play in lit. Ar. prose and verse, descr. the wars between Arabs and Persians in the days of the Caliph 'Umar. Publ. together with Nos. 137 & 143 under the title *Ibrāhīm Bās̲hā masraḥiyya fī t̲halāt̲h fuṣūl wa-masraḥiyyatān uk̲hrayān.* [Cairo], Dār al-fikr al-

'arabī, n.d., prob. 1944–1945; pp. 115–157 (*K.*, vol. IV, Jan., 1949, p. 141).

135a. Id., *al-Fir'aun al-mau'ūd.* A 6-scene play. Cairo, Lajnat al-nashr li'l-jāmi'iyyīn; 95 pp. (*Ma.*, XLIII, 1949, p.273).

136. Id., *Humām au fī 'āṣimat al-aḥqāf.* A drama in lit. Ar. verse, campaigning against the ignorance of the Arab woman. Cairo, al-Maṭb. al-salafiyya, prob. 1934 (*Mu.*, vol. LXXXV, Oct. 1, 1934, p. 256, which gives the author's name as Bākīr).

137. Id., *Ibrāhīm Bāshā rasūl al-waḥda al-'arabiyya.* A 3-act play in lit. Ar. prose, descr. Ibrāhīm's feats of valor in Syria and Turkey; intended as a call for Arab unity. Publ. together with Nos. 135 & 143. [Cairo], Dār al-fikr al-'arabī, n.d., prob. 1944–1945; pp. 3–91.

138. Id., *Ma'sāt Ūdīb.* A 3-act tragedy in lit. Ar. prose, inspired from the Greek legend of Oedip. Cairo, Dār al-kitāb al-'arabī, n.d.; 186 pp.

139. Id., *Mismār Juḥā.* A play descr. the adventures of Juḥā, the popular wise-guy of the Near East. Prod. in Egypt, 1951–2 (*al-Muṣawwar*, Nov. 14, 1951; *M.*, June 5, 1952, p. 5).

140. Id., *Qaṣr al-haudaj.* A 3-act & epilogue musical play, in lit. Ar. verse (with occ. prose), about the love of the desert Beduins. Cairo, Maṭb. Miṣr, n.d., prob. 1944; 77 pp.

141. Id., *Sirr al-Ḥākim bi-amr Allāh au lughz al-ta'rīkh.* A 6-scene hist. drama in lit. Ar. prose and a few verses. Tells the story of the famous, unfortunate Fatimid Caliph. [Cairo,] Dār al-fikr al-'arabī, n.d.; 151 pp.

142. Id., *Shailūk al-jadīd* is made of two plays, both in lit. Ar. prose: the 4-act *al-Mushkila* and the 3-act *al-Ḥall.* Together they form one single political play, with a strong anti-Zionist bias. Cairo, Mak. Miṣr. n.d., prob. 1945; 164 pp. (*Bamah*, Quarterly, Tel-Aviv, fasc. 50, Jan., 1947, pp. 111–112).

143. Id., *'Umar al-Mukhtār.* A 2-act play in lit. Ar. prose and verse. This is a eulogy of the Tripolitanians' war against Badoglio's Italians. Publ. together with Nos. 135 & 137. [Cairo,] Dār al-fikr al-'arabī, n.d., prob. 1944–1945; pp. 93–114.
See also: List of Ar. Plays, Transl.—Shakespeare.
Balīṭ, Jūrjī, see: List of Ar. Plays, Transl.—Racine.

144. Barakāt, Ibrāhīm, *Badr al-dujā.* A 4-act play about a girl who was to marry an old man while she was in love with a younger one. Cairo, 1901 (*H.*, vol. IX, Feb., 1901, p. 311).
al-Bārūdī, Ḥasan, see: List of Ar. Plays, Transl.—Aicard.

144a. Baṣbūṣ, Ḥannā Ṭannūs, *Amīr al-Arz.* An hist. play in prose and verse, with music. 1928; 96 pp. (*Ma.*, XLII, 1948, p. 443).

145. Baṣīr, Muḥammad Mahdī, *Daulat al-bukhalā'.* A 5-act play. Baghdad, Maṭb. Dār al-Salām, 1924 (*Fihris*, IV, p. 37).

145a. Baṣra, Muḥammad, *Hind bint al-malik al-Nu'mān bint al-Mundhir malik al-'arab.* An hist. play (Najm, *al-Masraḥiyya etc.*, p. 332).

145b. Bash'alānī, Jūrj, *al-Amīr Fakhr 'al-Dīn ḥākim Lubnān.* A play in prose and verse (*Ma.* QXLII, 1948, p. 443).

145c. Baṭṭī, Salīm, *Taqrī' al-ḍamīr.* Baghdad, Maṭb. J. J. al-Isrā'īliyya, 1931 (ibid., p. 451).
Ben Ḥalla, 'Abd al-Ḥamīd, see: List of Ar. Plays, Transl.—Romains.
al-Bijānī, 'Abbās Abū Nukhūl, see: List of Ar. Plays, Transl.—Marmontel.

145d. al-Bijānī, Ni'mat Allāh, *Yūsuf al-ḥasan.* A 2-act religious play. Publ., 32 pp. (*Ma.* XLIII, 1949, p. 296).

146. *Bint al-hawā*. Prod. in Egypt, 1951–1952 (*K.*, vol. VII, June, 1952, p. 753).
146a. Buḥairī, 'Alī Muḥammad, *Khālid bnu al-Walīd*. A 5-act hist. play in verse. Mak. Miṣr, 1945; 108 pp. (*Ma.*, XLII, 1948, p. 459).
146b. Buḥairī, 'Āmir Muḥammad, *al-Amīn wa'l-Ma'mūn*. An hist. play (ibid., p. 444).
al-Bunnī, Raslān 'Abd al-Ghanī, see: List of Ar. Plays, Transl.—Bennett.
147. al-Bustānī, 'Abd Allāh, *Brūtūs ayyām Tarkwīn al-ẓālim*. An hist. play in verse (Dāghir, p. 194).
148. Id., *al-Ḥukm 'alā ibn Hīrūdis*. An hist. play in verse (ibid., p. 193).
149. Id., *Imru' al-Qais fī ḥarb Banī Asad*. An hist. play in prose (ibid., p. 194).
150. Id., *Jassās qātil Kulaib*. An hist. play in prose (ibid.).
151. Id., *Maqtal Hīrūdis li-waladaih*. A 5-act hist. drama in lit. Ar. verse. Beirut, al-Maṭb. al-adabiyya, 1889; 87 pp. (*Ma.*, vol. XXV, 1927, p. 624. *GAL*, S. III, p. 416. Dāghir, p. 194, mentions 84 pp.).
152. Id., *al-Samau'al au wafā' al-'arab*. An hist. play in prose (Dāghir, p. 194).
153. Id., *Riwāyat al-wardatain*. A play in lit. Ar. verse about the Wars of the Roses (*Ma.*, vol. XXV, 1927, p. 624).
154. Id., *'Umar al-Ḥimyarī, akhū Ḥasan*. An hist. play in prose (Dāghir, p. 194).
155. Id., *Yūsuf bnu Ya'qūb*. A play in verse (ibid.).
See also: List of Ar. Plays, Transl.—Shakespeare.
156. al-Bustānī, Būlus, *Fatāt al-Nāṣira*. A 4-act religious play, descr. Jesus' birth and life until the death of Herodes. Beirut, al-Maṭb. al-kāthūlikiyya, 1925; 72 pp. (*GAL*, S. III, p. 416, based on *Ma.*, vol. XXXIII, 1935, p. 55; Sarkīs, *Jāmi'*, I, No. 1147).
See also: List of Ar. Plays, Transl.—Bornier.
156a. al-Bustānī, Buṭrus, *Dā'ud al-malik*. A 5-act hist. play in verse. 1906; 128 pp. (*Ma.*, XLII, 1948, p. 460).
157. al-Bustānī, Fu'ād Ifrām, *Balāṭ al-amīr*. A 2-act hist. play in prose and verse. First prod. Beirut, 1946 (ibid., p. 448).
al-Bustānī, Nabīl, see: List of Ar. Plays, Transl.—Schmid.
al-Bustānī, Sa'd Allāh, see: List of Ar. Plays, Transl.—Fénelon.
158. al-Bustānī, Sa'īd, *Dhāt al-khidr* (Shaikhū, *Ta'rīkh . . . fī'l-rub' al-awwal etc.*, p. 24).
159. Id., *Samīr al-amīr* (ibid.).
160. al-Bustānī, Salīm Buṭrus, *al-Iskandar*. Prod. in Syria. In ms.? (Dāghir, p. 186).
161. Id., *Qais wa-Lailā*. Prod. in Syria. In ms.? (ibid).
162. Id., *Yūsuf wa-Iṣṭāk*. Prod. in Syria. In ms.? (ibid.).
al-Bustānī, Wadī', see: List of Ar. Plays, Transl.—Kālidāsa.
Cohen, see below: Kūhin.
Dablan, Amīn, see: List of Ar. Plays, Transl.—Domet.
162a. Dādā, Jūrj, *al-Akh al-ẓālim* (*Ma.*, XLII, 1948, p. 438).
162b. al-Daḥdāḥ, Edwār, *al-Jāsūs*. A 1-act play, publ. in *al-Makshūf*, No. 274 (ibid., p. 453).
162c. Id., *Qais bnu 'Āṣim*. A 3-act play. Beirut, Maṭb. Ṣaiqalī, 1945; 88 pp. (ibid., XLIII, 1949, p. 276).
163. al-Daḥdāḥ, Khaṭṭār, *Yūsuf al-Ḥasan*. A play for prod. in schools, prob. still in ms. (Shaikhū, *Ta'rīkh . . . fī'l-rub' al-awwal etc.*, p. 112).
See also: List of Ar. Plays, Transl.—Corneille; Racine.
Daḥmūn. see: List of Ar. Plays, Orig. Plays.—'Allāllū.
163a. al-Dairānī, Ifrām Ḥunain, *Ḥikmat Sulaimān*. Verse. Beirut, al-Maṭb. al-kāthūlīkiyya (*Ma.*, XLII, 1948, p. 457).

164. Id., *al-Ibn al-ṣhāṭir.* A 5-act tragedy for production in Catholic schools. Beirut, al-Maṭb. al-kāṯẖulikiyya, prob. 1923 (*H.*, vol. XXXI, Apr. 1, 1923, p. 779).
164a. al-Dairānī, Mubārak Ṯẖābit, *Karīma al-lubnāniyya fī Ḥaurān.* A 2-act play. Beirut, Maṭb. al-ijtihād, 1925; 33 pp. (*Ma.*, XLIII, 1949, p. 277).
164b. Id., *Man minhumā'bnatī.* A 2-act comedy. Beirut, Maṭb. al-ittiḥād, 1925; 24 pp. (ibid., p. 289).
164c. Id., *Riwāyat al-qiddīsain Būlā wa-Anṭūnyūs* (ibid., p. 275).
164d. Dakẖūl (?), Jūrj, *al-Mu'allim al-ta'īs.* A farce about a luckless teacher (Najm, *al-Masraḥiyya etc.*, pp. 438–440).
164e. Dallāl, Mīkẖā'īl, *al-Fatāt al-kẖarsā'.* In ms. (*Ma.*, XLIII, 1949, p. 272).
164f. Id., *Iḥsān al-insān.* Prod. in Lebanon (ibid., XLII, 1948, p. 438).
164g. Id., *al-Nafḥ al-'āṭir fī'l-fatā'l-muhājir.* Prod. at a Lebanese school. In ms. (ibid., XLIII, 1949, p. 291).
Dammūs, Ḥalīm, see: List of Ar. Plays, Transl.—Coppée.
165. Damyān, Rāgẖib, *'Ajā'ib al-ḥadaṯẖān.* A play of love and war, inc. a few songs. Prob. 1898 (*H.*, Apr. 15, 1898, p. 632).
165a. Darwīsẖ, Sẖālōm, *Ba'd maut akẖīh.* A 1-act play. Baghdad, Maṭb. al-Ḥāṣid, 1931 (*Ma.*, XLII, 1948, p. 448).
Dasūqī, Maḥmūd Ibrāhīm, see: List of Ar. Plays, Transl.—Goethe; Shaw.
166. Dā'ud, Mikẖā'īl Bisẖāra, *Nabī'l-Farā'ina.* An hist. play about a Pharaoh who lived in the 14th century B.C. Cairo, Maṭb. al-muḥīṭ, 1915 (*Fihris*, IV, p. 128).
167. Dayyah, Anīs, *al-Igẖwā'.* A 3-act drama, in lit. Ar. prose, descr. the social consequences of carnal sins. Beirut, Maṭb. jarīdat al-kaukab, n.d.; 66 pp.
168. Id., *Ma'sāt al-ṣanaubar.* A 3-act social drama. Beirut, Maṭb. al-umma, prob. 1932; 34 pp. (*H.*, vol. XLI, Dec. 1, 1932, p. 270).
169. Dību, Jurjī, *Riwāyat al-malikain Shā'ūl wa-Dā'ud.* A 3-act tragedy in lit. Ar. rhymed prose and verse, based on the Biblical story. Prod. a few times in Tripoli (Syria), then publ. N.p., n.d.; 56 pp. (Sẖaikẖū, *Ta'rīkẖ . . . fī'l-rub' al-awwal etc.*, p. 77, names the author Mīkẖā'īl Jirjis Dību, and mentions other works, without specifying, however, if they are plays.)
al-Dimasẖqī, Adīb, see: List of Ar. Plays, Orig. Plays.—Isḥāq, Adīb.
170. al-Dīwānī, Muḥammad Zakī, *Kẖiyānat al-wuzarā'.* Prob. 1905 (*H.*, vol. XIII, Aug. 1, 1905, p. 567).
171. Dūlār, 'Abd al-Ḥalīm, *Na'īm bnu Ḥāzim* (Muḥammad Taimūr, *Mu'allafāt*, vol. II, art. on Āl 'Ukkāsẖa).
See also: List of Ar. Plays, Transl.—Charles Hugo.
172. *al-Dunyā lammā tiḍḥak.* Appar. an opéra ballet, in the répertoire of al-Rīḥānī troupe (*A.*, June 30, 1952, p. 7; July 20, 1952, p. 7; July 27, 1952, p. 7).
173. al-Ḏẖahabī, 'Adnān, *Maṣra' Sẖahrazād.* A 3-act symbolical play (ready for publ., acc. to List on p. 88 of the following play).
174. Id., *Nasẖīd al-ansẖād.* A 2-act symbolical play in lit. Ar. prose, based on the Biblical *Song of Songs.* Dedicated to Prof. L. Massignon. Cairo, Dār al-fikr al-'arabī, n.d. (1947?); 87 pp.
174a. Eddeh, Kẖalīl, *Wafā' al-Samau'al.* Prod. 1887 (Najm, *al-Masraḥiyya etc.*, p. 54).
Fahmī, 'Abd al-Raḥmān, see: List of Ar. Plays, Transl.—Shakespeare.
174b. Fahmī, Maḥmūd, & Taufīq, Muḥammad, *Anbā' al-zamān fī ḥarb al-daula wa'l-Yūnān.* 1909 (ibid., pp. 347–350).
174c. Fahmī, Muḥammad, *Dumū'.* Cairo, Maṭb. Bābil, 1933; 172 pp. (*Ma.*, XLIII, 1949, p. 118).

Fā'id, Muṣṭafā Kamāl, see: List of Ar. Plays, Transl.—Freytag.

175. al-Fākhūrī, Nakhla, *Riwāya fī dhimmat al-'arab*. A 4-act hist. drama, in lit. Ar. verse, about the Arab king al-Nu'mān bnu al-Mundhir and his times. Acre, al-Maṭb. al-waṭaniyya, n.d.; 66 pp.

176. al-Fākhūrī, Yūsuf, *al-Burj al-shimālī*. A 3-act play, inspired from *Soirées Littéraires*. Prod. in 1897, 1898, 1926. Publ. Ḥarīṣā, by *Majallat al-masarra*, 1926; 68 pp. (Shaikhū, *Ta'rīkh . . . fī'l-rub' al-awwal etc.*, p. 177; Sarkīs, *Jāmi'*, II, No. 206).

177. Id., *Jān Hāshīt*. An hist. play about the 15th century French heroine, Jeanne Hachette. Dedicated to Gen. Weygand. Lit. Ar. prose and verse. Ḥarīṣā, Maṭb. Būlus, 1924; 64 pp. (Shaikhū, ibid.; *H.*, vol. XXXII, June 1, 1924, pp. 996–997).

178. Id., *Rajā' wa-ya's*. A prologue and 3-act tragedy in verse and prose, set in 15th century Bavaria. Ḥarīṣā, Maṭb. al-Qiddīs Būlus, 1927; 98 pp. (Shaikhū, ibid.; *Mu.*, vol. LXX, June 1, 1927, p. 630; Sarkīs, *Jāmi'*, II, No. 212).

179. Faltā'us, Ḥabīb, *Riwāyat al-qā'id al-mughram au quwwād Miṣr*. A 5-act hist. drama in lit. Ar. prose & verse, set in the times of Psametich. N.p., al-Kutubī, n.d.; 32 pp.

179a. Faraḥ, Iskandar, *Kliyūbātra*. An hist. play. 1888 (Najm, *al-Masraḥiyya etc.*, p. 353).

179b. Faraḥ, Niqūlā Amīn, *Taḥrīr Amīrikā au Wāshinṭūn* (*Ma.*, XLII, 1948, p. 450).

179c. Faraḥāt, Estefān, *Shimshūn*. Beirut, 1948 (ibid., XLIII, 1949, p. 128).

179d. Id., *Wājib al-auṭān fauq al-'āṭifa*. 1930 (ibid., p. 293).

180. Fāris, Aḥmad, *al-Muṣalliḥ*. A play in lit. Ar. First prod. in Alger, 1923 (*Revue Africaine*, vol. LXXVII, 1935, p. 75).

181. Fāris, Bishr, *Mafriq al-ṭarīq*. A 1-act symbolical play, based on a dialogue between "he" and "she." Lit. Ar. prose. Publ. as a suppl. to *Mu.*, Mar., 1938; 37 pp. 2nd ed., Cairo, Maṭb. al-ma'ārif, 1938; 40 pp., French title page—*Quand les chemins divergent* (*Mu.*, vol. XCII, Apr. 1, 1938, pp. 477–478; *H.*, vol. XLVI, July 1, 1938, p. 1077; *GAL*, S. III, pp. 168–169). Transl. into French (?).

181a. Fāris, Ḥalīm, *al-Muhājir al-lubnānī*. Beirut, 1947 (*Ma.*, XLIII, 1949, p. 289).

181b. Id., *Rujū' al-muhājir*. 1907 (ibid., p. 120).

181c. Id., *Unshūdat al-hudā*. Lebanon, 1907 (ibid., XLII, 1948, p. 444).

182. *al-Faṣl al-rābi' 'ashar min al-fuṣūl al-hazliyya al-muḍḥika wa-huwa faṣl lōkandat Bārīz*. A 1-act farce in coll. Ar. of Damascus about some troubles and misunderstandings in a hotel. Prod. in Beirut, 1899. Publ. from a ms., in Arabic with a German transl. by Littmann in *ZDMG*, vol. LVI, 1902, pp. 88–97.

Fatḥī, Muḥammad, see: List of Ar. Plays, Transl.—Shaw.

Fattāl, Kaddūr, see: List of Ar. Plays, Transl.—Shakespeare.

182a. Fauq al-'āda, Anwar (pseudonym?), *al-Mutaḥarrī'l-ṣaghīr fī kashf al-sariqāt*. Damascus, Maṭb. Zaidūn; 31 pp. (*Ma.*, XLIII, 1949, p. 281).

183. Fauzī, Khaṭība Muḥammad, *Bint ḥaẓẓ*. Appar. a revue. Prod. in Egypt, 1948 (*A.*, Oct. 26, 1948, p. 2).

184. Fawwāz, Zainab, *Riwāyat al-hawā wa'l-wafā'*. A 4-act drama about marriage problems, set in Baghdad. Cairo, Maṭb. al-jāmi'a, 1892 (*H.*, vol. I, Mar., 1893, p. 246; *Fihris*, IV, p. 133. *GAL*, S. III, p. 280, reads *Riwāyat al-hanā' etc.*; ibid., p. 175, reads correctly, but considers it a novel. For authoress' full name see Sarkīs, *Mu'jam*, p. 989).

185. Fayyāḍ, Ilyās, *Firās al-Bunduqiyya*. A 5-act drama about Venetian history. 1911 (*GAL*, ibid., p. 362, reads *al-Bandaqiyya*).
186. Id., *'Ibrat al-abkār* (Dāghir, p. 641).
187. Id., *al-Zauja al-khā'ina*. Prod. in Beirut, 1903 (ibid.; *Ma.*, XLIII, 1949, p. 123).
See also: List of Ar. Plays, Transl.—Berton; Delavigne; Dennery; Hugo; Sardou.
Fayyāḍ, Najīb Farj Allāh, see: List of Ar. Plays, Transl.—Voltaire.
Fayyāḍ, Niqūlā, see: List of Ar. Plays, Transl.—Schiller.
188. *Fī sabīl al-waṭan*. A 2-act drama. First prod. in Alger, 1922 (*Revue Africaine*, vol. LXXVII, 1935, p. 75).
188a. Fikrī, 'Abd Allāh, *al-Hanā' ba'd al-'anā'*. Cairo, 1913(?) (*Ma.*, XLIII, 1949, p. 293).
189. Fīktōr, Sārūfīm, (Séraphim Victor), *al-Dhikrā'l-khālida*. A collection of four comedies. Beirut, al-Maṭb. al-kāthūlīkiyya, 1927; 167 pp. (Sarkīs, *Jāmi'*, II, No. 211).
Filasṭīn, Wadī', see: List of Ar. Plays, Transl.—Strindberg.
190. Fīlīmūn (Philemon?), *Ādām wa-Ḥawā'*. A religious play in prose and verse. Prod. in Tyre, 1903. Publ. 1903 (*H.*, vol. XII, Oct. 1, 1903, p. 64).
Fuḍalā', Muḥammad Ṭāhir, see: List of Ar. Plays, Transl.—Rostand.
191. Gardener, *Riwāyat Yūsuf al-ṣiddīq wa-ikhwatih mahība ramziyya tamthīliyya*. A 4-act drama, in lit. Ar. prose and verse, based on the story in Genesis. First prod. in Cairo, at an English school, Dec. 1920. Publ. Cairo, al-Jam'iyya al-usqufiyya, Maṭb. Ra'amsīs, 1921; 4, 102 pp., 10 illust. hors-texte.
191a. Id., *Shā'ul al-Ṭarsūsī*. A 4-act play about Paulus of Tarsus. Cairo, 111 pp. (*Ma.*, XLIII, 1949, p. 127).
191b. Ghabrīl, Mīkhā'īl, *al-Durra al-farīda fī Afdūkiyā'l-shahīda*. A 5-act play. al-Ḥadath, al-Maṭb. al-sharqiyya; 161 pp. (ibid., XLII, 1948, p. 460).
192. Id., *al-Sa'āda fī'l-shahāda*. Beirut, al-Maṭb. al-kāthūlīkiyya, 1891; 96 pp. (Ḥunain, *Shauqī 'alā'l-masraḥ*, repr., p. 18).
193. al-Ghaḍbān, 'Ādil, *Aḥmus al-awwal au ṭard al-ru'āt*. A play in lit. Ar. prose. It treats of the expulsion of the Hyksos from Egypt. Cairo, al-Maṭb. al-'aṣriyya, 1933; 103 pp. (*BSOS*, vol. VIII, 1935–1937, p. 999. *GAL*, S. III, pp. 274-275, corrects title to *Aḥmas etc.*).
193a. Ghālib, Ḥannā, *al-Rajul al-musāfir*. A 1-act play. Beirut, 1938; 14 pp. (*Ma.*, XLIII, 1949, p. 120).
193b. Id., *Rusul al-silm*. A 5-scene play. Beirut, 1937; 15 pp. (ibid., p. 121).
193c. Ghānim, 'Abd Allāh, *Shaiṭān al-rīḥ*. Beirut, 1930; 61 pp. (ibid., p. 130).
193d. Gharfīnī, Na'ūm Ni'ma, *al-Riyāl al-muzayyaf*. A 2-act play. 28 pp. (ibid., p. 122).
194. al-Gharīb, Yūsuf Ilyās, *Ḥasnā' al-basātīn*. Tokoman, prob. 1924–1925; 102 pp. (*H.*, vol. XXXIII, Mar. 1, 1925, p. 653).
194a. Ghaṣūb, Yūsuf, *Qabaḍai*. A 1-act comedy (in coll. Ar.?). 1931 (*Ma.*, XLIII, 1949, p. 275).
194b. Ghazāla, Sulaimān, *al-Ḥaqq wa'l-'adāla*. Verse. Baghdad, Dār al-ṭibā'a al-ḥadītha, 1929; 64 pp. (ibid., XLII, 1948, p. 457).
195. Id., *Lahjat al-abṭal*. 1911 (Ḥunain, *Shauqī 'alā'l-masraḥ*, repr., p. 18).
195a. Ghuṣn, Mārūn, *Heraql au intiṣār al-ṣalīb*. Beirut, 1926 (*Ma.*, XLIII, 1949, p. 292).
196. Id., *al-Kāhin au intiqām sharīf*. A play consisting of a prologue and 3 acts.

Publ. by Majallat al-s̲h̲arq, 1926 (Sarkīs, *Jāmi'*, II, No. 227. Authorship established by mention on back cover of No. 198, below).

197. Id., *Riwāyat al-malikain.* A 1-act opera, with music by Wadī' Ṣabrā. Beirut, al Maṭb. al-kāt̲h̲ūlīkiyya, 1927; 30 pp. (*GAL*, S. III, p. 389, based on Sarkīs, *Jāmi'*, II, No. 217).

198. Id., *al-S̲h̲abaḥ al-hā'il au inqād̲h̲ al-amīr.* A 3-act hist. drama, adapted from the French, Lit. Ar. prose & verse. Appar. first publ. in the periodical *Risālat al-salām*, then Beirut, Maṭb. Jad'ūn, n.d.; 48, 1 pp. (Sarkīs, ibid., No. 221, reads—mistakenly—*al-S̲h̲aik̲h̲ al-habal etc.*).

199. Hānī, Yūsuf, *Mir'āt al-wafā'.* Prob. 1897 (*H.*, Dec. 1, 1897, p. 280).

199a. al-Harāwī, Muḥammad, *'Awāṭif al-banīn.* Prod. in Egypt, 1929 (*Ma.*, XLIII, 1949, p. 137).

199b. Hārūn, Mīs̲h̲āl, *Riwāyat Majnūn.* Beirut, 1944 (ibid., p. 282).

200. Hilāl, Maḥmūd Muḥammad Bakr, *Filasṭīn.* A play in lit. (?) Ar. verse. Prob. 1949 (*K.*, vol. IV, May, 1949, p. 756).

201. *Hīlāna al-jamīla.* An Arabic rendering of the famous operette *The Beautiful Helen*, in 3 acts. Cairo, Būlāq, A.H. 1285 (*Fihris*, IV, p. 134).

202. Hindāwī, K̲h̲alīl, *Fitna.* A 1-act play in lit. Ar., telling in well-chosen words the story about the quarrel of the apple and the judgment of Paris. Beirut, Mans̲h̲ūrāt al-adīb, 1945.

203. Id., *Jazīra bi-lā rajul.* A 1-act play in lit. Ar. prose descr. the adventures of Ulysses. Beirut, Mans̲h̲ūrāt al-adīb, 1945.

204. Id., *al-Laḥn al-tā'ih.* A 1-act play in lit. Ar. prose, descr. Mozart's last moments. Beirut, Mans̲h̲ūrāt al-adīb, 1945.

205. Id., *Mailā'.* A 1-act play in lit. Ar. verse, treating of passionate love among the Beduins. Beirut, Mans̲h̲ūrāt al-adīb, 1945.

206. Id., *al-Mat̲h̲t̲h̲āl al-tā'ih.* A 1-act play in lit. Ar. prose, telling how the real Galathea took the statue's place in Pygmalion's studio. Publ. in *Mu.*, vol. CI, Aug. 1, 1942, pp. 229–240, repr. Beirut, Mans̲h̲ūrāt al-adīb, 1945.

207. Id., *Phryné.* A 1-act play in lit. Ar., being the tale of Phryné, the embodiment of womanly beauty who was acquitted by the Athenian judges, on account of her beauty, of the crime of having cursed the Gods. Publ. in *Mu.*, vol. C, May 1, 1942, pp. 450–459.

208. Id., *Psyché.* A 1-act play in lit. Ar., descr. the love of Cupid and Psyché, which triumphs notwithstanding the intrigues of Venus. Publ. ibid., vol. CII, Apr. 1, 1943, pp. 377–391.

209. Id., *Sāriq al-nār.* A 1-act play in lit. Ar., sketching the story of Prometheus' theft of the fire and his punishment. This title was given to Hindāwī's collection of six plays (above, Nos. 202, 203, 204, 205, 206, 208), publ. together, Beirut, Mans̲h̲ūrāt al-adīb, 1945.
See also: List of Ar. Plays, Transl.—Valéry.

209a. Hindī, Ḥannā K̲h̲alīl, *al-S̲h̲ahīd al-'arabī* (*Ma.*, XLIII, 1949, p. 129).

210. Hindī, Yūsuf, *al-Hanā' ba'd al-'anā'.* A 5-act play. Port Said, Maḥbūb al-Kutubī, prob. 1901 (*H.*, vol. IX, June 15, 1901, p. 528).

210a. Hunūd, Fīlīp, *Tājir al-'abīd* (*Ma.*, XLII, 1948, p. 450).

210b. Ḥabas̲h̲ī, Fahīm, *al-Māl wa'l-banūn.* A 4-act play. Prod. in Egypt (ibid., XLIII, 1949, p. 281).

210c. Id., *Ṭabīb al-mu'jizāt.* Prod. in Egypt (ibid., p. 132).
Ḥabīb, Muṣṭafā Ṭaha, see: List of Ar. Plays, Transl.—Shaw.
al-Ḥaddād, Amīn, see: List of Ar. Plays, Transl.—Shakespeare.

Ḥaddād, Hārūn, see: List of Ar. Plays, Transl.—Frondaie.
Ḥaddād, Ilyās Naṣr Allāh, see: List of Ar. Plays, Transl.—Lessing.

211. Ḥaddād, Mīs̲h̲īl (Michel), & Qaʿwār, Jamāl, *Ẓalām wa-nūr*. A 4-act school play, in lit. Ar. prose & verse, about life in the State of Israel. Nazareth, Mak. al-aḥdāt̲h̲ wa'l-s̲h̲abība, 1954; 47 pp.

212. Ḥaddād, Najīb, *ʿAmr bnu ʿAdī au ḥifẓ al-ʿuhūd*. A 3-act musical tragedy in lit. Ar. verse. Set in Arabia during the 2nd century A.D. Alex., al-Maṭb. al-tijāriyya, 1902; 110 pp. (*Mu.*, vol. XXVIII, Feb. 1, 1903, p. 179. Dāg̲h̲ir, p. 302).

213. Id., *al-Mahdī* (or *Riwāyat al-Mahdī*). An hist. play about the Sudanese Mahdi in the late 19th century (*H.*, vol. VII, Feb. 15, 1899, p. 291. Dāg̲h̲ir, p. 302).

214. Id., *al-Rajā' baʿd al-ya's*. A 5-act hist. drama in lit. Ar. prose & verse, inspired by the Greek tragedians. 1st ed., Cairo, Maṭb. al-tamaddun, 1902. 2nd ed., Alex., Maṭb. G̲h̲arzūzī, 1904; 94 pp. (*H.*, vol. XI, Oct. 1902, p. 63; *Fihris*, IV, p. 38. Dāg̲h̲ir, p. 301, mentions another ed., Cairo, al-Maṭb. al-Yūsufiyya, 48 pp.).

215. Id., *Ṣalāḥ al-Dīn al-Ayyūbī*. A 5-act hist. drama in lit. Ar. prose & verse, inspired by Scott's *Talisman*. 1st ed., Alex., 1898. 2nd ed., Cairo, Maṭb. al-maʿārif, 1902; 80 pp. (*H.*, vol. X, May 15, 1902, p. 516; *GAL*, S. III, p. 268. Dāg̲h̲ir, p. 301, mentions two later editions, 1904 and 1921, the latter in 64 pp.).
See also: List of Ar. Plays, Transl.—Corneille; Hugo; Molière; Racine; Shakespeare; Voltaire.

216. al-Ḥaddād, Niqūlā, *al-Mamlūk al-s̲h̲ārid*. A play based on Jurjī Zaidān's novel of the same title. Appar. never prod. (*H.*, vol. XVIII, June 1, 1910, p. 546).

217. Id., *Ṣalāḥ al-Dīn al-Ayyūbī* (see *GAL*, S. III, p. 227).

218. al-Ḥaddād, Niqūlā Ilyās, *al-Ḥubb al-d̲h̲ahabī*. Appar. still in ms. (Dāg̲h̲ir, p. 309).

219. Id., *K̲h̲ālid ibn al-Walīd*. Appar. still in ms. (ibid.).
al-Ḥaddād, S̲h̲adīd Bāz, see: List of Ar. Plays, Transl.—Goethe; Schiller.

220. Ḥaddād, Yuḥannā, *Iblīs*. An hist. play in verse. 32 pp. (*Ma.*, XLII, 1948, p. 436).

221. al-Ḥaddād, Yūsuf, *al-As̲h̲bāḥ*. An hist. drama, set in the times of Emir Bas̲h̲īr. Appar. still in ms. (Dāg̲h̲ir, p. 311).

222. Id., *al-Lubnāniyya*. Rio de Janeiro, Maṭb. al-ṣawāb, 1933; 84 pp. (ibid.).

223. Id., *Riwāyat Art̲h̲ūr dūq Barīṭāniya*. Adapted (?) Beirut, 1913 (ibid.; S̲h̲aik̲h̲ū, *Ta'rīk̲h̲ . . . fī'l-rubʿ al-awwal etc.*, p. 148).

224. Ḥāfiẓ, Muḥammad Ras̲h̲ād, *Samīra*. Although this play won the competition of the Egyptian Ministry of Education in 1932, no troupe accepted it at first (*GAL*, S. III, pp. 274, 280); when prod. in 1933, it had but a short run. Publ. Cairo, Maṭb. al-ṣabāḥ, n.d. (*BSOS*, vol. VIII, 1935–1937, p. 1000).

225. al-Ḥā'ik, Mīs̲h̲āl Yūsuf, *Baṭal Lubnān*. A 5-act nationalist drama. Beirut, Maṭb. al-ijtihād, 1922; 96 pp. (*GAL*, S. III, p. 416).

225a. Id., *Fatāt al-arz*. Cairo, al-Maṭb. al-tijāriyya, 1912; 95 pp. (*Ma.*, XLIII, 1949, p. 272).

225b. al-Ḥā'ik, Yūsuf, *ʿAd̲h̲rā' Yaftāḥ*. A 3-act play. 1936 (ibid., p. 134).

225c. Id., *Amīrat G̲h̲assān*. A 3-act play. Maṭb. al-itqān, 1933; 64 pp. (ibid., XLII, 1948, p. 460).

225d. Id., *Ḥanna ibnat Fransīs al-t̲h̲ānī waliyyat ʿahd Barīṭāniya*. A 4-act hist. play. Maṭb. al-itqān, 1931; 37 pp. (ibid., p. 458).

226. Id. *Lailā ibnat al-malik al-Nu'mān wa'l-aqāṣira.* A 5-act hist. play. in lit. Ar. prose & verse, descr. the wars between the Persians and the ever-victorious Arabs of the kingdom of al-Ḥīra. Bait Shabāb, Maṭb. al-'alam, 1932; 90 pp.

226a. Id., *al-Qiddīsa Jān Dark.* A 5-act play. 2nd ed., Bait Shabāb, Maṭb. jarīdat al-'alam, 1930; 85 pp. (*Ma.*, XLIII, 1949, p. 275).

227. Id., *Thurayya al-amīra al-hindiyya.* A 3-act semi-hist. play in lit. Ar. prose. Beirut, Mak. Ṣādir, n.d. (1951?); 64 pp.

al-Ḥājj, Lūyīs, see: List of Ar. Plays, Transl.—Pirandello.

228. al-Ḥakīm, Taufīq, *'Aduww Iblīs.* A 1-scene play in lit. Ar. prose, records a dialogue between the angel Azrael, who had just taken Muḥammad's soul, and the Devil. Publ. in al-Ḥakīm's collection *'Ahd al-shaiṭān,* Cairo, Mak. al-ādāb, 1942, pp. 147–163.

229. Id., *Ahl al-kahf.* A drama in lit. Ar. prose—the legend of three men and their dog, who awake in a cave after a three-centuries sleep. 1st ed., Cairo, Maṭb. Miṣr, 1933; 117 pp. (*H.*, vol. XLI, May 1, 1933, p. 988). 2nd ed., Maṭb. al-i'timād, 1933; 117 pp. (*GAL*, S. III, pp. 243–244). 3rd ed., Lajnat al-ta'līf wa'l-tarjama wa'l-nashr, 1940. 4th ed., Cairo, Mak. al-ādāb, 1945; 176 pp. Transl. into French, 1939, by A. Khédry, in *RC*, vol. III, Dec. 1939–Mar., 1940, repr. in Khédry & Costandi, *Théâtre arabe*, as *La caverne des songes.* Transl. into Italian, Rome, 1940 (*Muslim World*, vol. XLV, 1955, p. 29). Transl. into English by P. J. Vatikiotis; first act publ. in *Islamic Literature* (Lahore), Mar. 1955, other acts to follow.

230. Id., *il-Aidī'l-nā'ima.* A play in coll. Ar. Publ. Cairo, prob. 1954–1955 (*al-Yaum*, Jaffa, Feb. 11, 1955).

231. Id., *'Alī Bābā.* A youth attempt of the author, appar. still in ms. (Rizzitano, in *OM*, vol. XXIII, June, 1943, p. 256).

232. Id., *al-'Arīs.* A youth attempt of the author, appar. still in ms. (ibid., p. 255).

233. Id., *Bain al-ḥulm wa'l-ḥaqīqa.* A 1-scene play in lit. Ar. prose, being the dialogue of an ancient Egyptian painter with his wife who is jealous of a statue. Publ. in the author's *'Ahd al-shaiṭān*, Cairo, Mak. al-ādāb, 1942, pp. 127–145.

234. Id., *al-Malik Ūdīb.* A play which descr. the intrigues at the court of Thebes, centred around Oedip. Cairo, 1949. Transl. into French by Khédry in Khédry & Costandi, *op. cit.*, as *Oedipe Roi* (*Muslim World*, vol. XLV, 1955, p. 29, reads title as *Udaib*).

235. Id., *al-Mar'a al-jadīda.* One of the author's first attempts. Still in ms.? (*OM* vol. XXIII, June, 1943, p. 255).

236. Id., *Masraḥ al-mujtama'*, being a collection of al-Ḥakīm's later plays—mainly social—21 in number, written in lit. Ar. prose. Cairo, Mak. al-ādāb, 1950; 788 pp. In order of publication, they are:

(1) *Bain yaum wa-laila.* 2 scenes.

(2) *Urīd an aqtul,* 1 act. Transl. by Khédry, in his *Théâtre multicolore* (1954), as *Je veux tuer.*

(3) *al-Nā'iba al-muḥtarama.* 2 scenes. Transl. by id., ibid., as *Madame politique.*

(4) *Aṣḥāb al-sa'āda al-zaujiyya.* 1 act.

(5) *Maulid baṭal.* 2 scenes, relating the war in Palestine.

(6) *al-Liṣṣ.* 4 acts.

(7) *Urīd hādhā'l-rajul.* 1 act.

(8) *'Araf kaifa yamūt.* 1 act. Transl. by Khédry, in Khédry & Costandi, *op. cit.*, as *L'art de mourir.*

(9) *al-Mukhrij.* 1 act. Transl. by Khédry, ibid., as *Le metteur en scène.*
(10) *'Imārat al-mu'allim Kandūz.* 1 act.
(11) *al-Kanz.* 1 act. Transl. by Khédry, in *Théâtre multicolore*, as *Le trésor.*
(12) Bait al-naml. 1 act. Transl. by Khédry, in Khédry & Costandi, *op. cit.*, as *La maison des fourmis.*
(13) *A'māl ḥurra.* 1 act.
(14) *Sāḥira.* 1 act. Transl. by Khédry, in *Théâtre multicolore*, as *Sorcière.*
(15) *al-Ḥubb al-'udhrī.* 1 act.
(16) *al-Jiyā'.* 1 act.
(17) *al-'Ushsh al-hādi'.* 4 acts. Transl. by Khédry, in *Théâtre multicolore*, as *Un nid tranquille.*
(18) *Miftāḥ al-najāḥ.* 1 act.
(19) *al-Rajul alladhī ṣamad.* 1 act.
(20) *Lau 'araf al-shabāb.* 4 acts.
(21) *Ughniyat al-maut.* 1 act. Transl. by Khédry in *Théâtre multicolore*, as *Chant de la mort.*

237. Id., *Masraḥiyyāt*, being a collection of the author's earlier plays, publ. in two vols. of 4 plays each. Cairo, Mak. al-nahḍa al-miṣriyya, 1937: vol. I, 298 pp.; vol. II, 312 pp. (*GAL*, S. III, p. 247.) In order of publication, they are:

(1) *Ba'd al-maut*, renamed *Sirr al-muntaḥira* by the National Troupe. A 4-act drama in lit. Ar. prose, telling the story of a physician who becomes a woman-chaser, after the suicide of a patient who was in love with him (vol. I, pp. 7–123).
(2) *Nahr al-junūn.* A 1-act symbolical play, in lit. Ar. prose, telling the story of a king and his vizier, who, too, drank out of the "River of Madness" after all their subjects had done so (I, 125–144). Transl. into French by Khédry, in Khédry & Costandi, *op. cit.*, as *Le fleuve de la folie.*
(3) *Raṣāṣa fī'l-qalb.* A 3-act comedy in coll. Ar. prose, descr. playfully the eternal triangle, this time between a girl, a physician and his penniless friend. Written approx. in 1932 (I, 145–270).
(4) *Jinsunā'l-laṭīf.* A 1-act comedy in coll. Ar. prose, written at the request of the feminist leader, Hudā Sha'rāwī. It shows the luckless husband of a woman pilot being forced by her friends, all career women, to join his wife on her flight (I, 271–298).
(5) *al-Khurūj min al-janna.* A 3-act semi-symbolical play in lit. Ar. prose, descr. a wife driving away her husband in order to reawaken in him the poetical flame (II, 1–110).
(6) *Devant son guichet.* A 1-act play, written in Paris, 1926; later transl. into lit. Ar. prose by Aḥmad al-Ṣāwī Muḥammad. It is dedicated to Emma Durand, prob. the name of the pretty cashier at the Odéon, with whom the hero of the play leads a lively dialogue ending in a date (II, 111–129).
(7) *al-Zammār.* A 1-act comedy in coll. Ar. prose & verse, descr. the misadventures of luckless Sālim, a medical orderly overfond of music. Written in 1930, first publ. in al-Ḥakīm's *Ahl al-fann*, 1934 (*Muslim World*, vol. XLV, 1955, p. 29), then republ. (II, 131–192). Transl. into French by N. Costandi, in Khédry & Costandi, *op. cit.*, as *Le joueur de flute*; and into Hebrew by M. Kapelyūk as *Boqer bĕ-mirpa'at maḥlaqat ha-brī'ūt.*
(8) *Ḥayāt taḥaṭṭamat.* A 4-act tragi-comedy in coll. Ar. prose, forms a sequel to the former. Excellent portrayal of the rural background (II, 194–312).

238. Id., *Muḥammad.* An hist. play in lit. Ar. prose, divided into a prologue, 3 acts and an epilogue. Treats of the Prophet's life from birth to death, in a wealthy imagery of detail. Obviously intended for reading only. N.p., Lajnat al-ta'līf wa'l-tarjama wa'l-nashr, 1936; 485 pp. (*GAL*, S. III, pp. 244–245). 2nd ed. (?), Maṭb. al-ma'ārif, 1936 (*Muslim World*, vol. XLV, 1955, p. 30, mentions another 1st (?) ed., n.d.). The last scene transl. into English by W. R. Polk, in *New Directions*, No. 15 (Meridian Books, M 18, N.Y., 1955), pp. 277–283.

239. Id., *Pijmālyūn.* A 4-act drama in lit. Ar. prose, gives a new twist to Shaw's comedy, by setting it in ancient Greece and hinting at the frailties of those Gods who meddle in human affairs. Cairo, Mak. al-ādāb, 1942; 197 pp. (*Mu*, vol. CII, Jan. 1, 1943, pp. 87–92). Transl. into French by Khédry, in Khédry & Costandi, *op. cit.*, as *Pygmalion.*

240. Id., *Prāksā au mushkilat al-ḥukm.* A comedy inspired from Aristophanes, about the rule of Greek women. Cairo, Maṭb. al-tawakkul, 1939 (*GAL*, S. III, p. 250). Transl. by Khédry, in *Théâtre multicolore*, as *Le problème du pouvoir.*

241. Id., *Rāqiṣat al-ma'bad.* Cairo, Maṭb. al-tawakkul, prob. 1939 (*GAL*, ibid.).

242. Id., *Sulaimān al-ḥakīm.* A 7-scene hist. drama in lit. Ar. prose. Based on legends in the Pentateuch, the Koran and the tales of the *Arabian Nights.* Cairo, Mak. al-ādāb, 1943; 196 pp. Transl. into French by N. Costandi, in Khédry & Costandi, *op. cit.*, as *Salomon le sage.* Possibly a reissue of the ms. play *Khātim Sulaimān*, mentioned in *OM*, vol. XXIII, June, 1943, p. 255?

243. Id., *Ṣāḥibat al-jalāla.* A play about ex-King Fārūq's erstwhile doings. Publ. serially in *AY*, 1954–1955 (*al-Yaum*, Feb. 13, 1955).

244. Id., *Shahrazād.* A 7-scene semi-symbolical drama in lit. Ar. prose, treating of the loves and conversations of Shehrezade and her king-husband, outside the Royal palace. 1st ed., Cairo, Dār al-kutub, 1934; 162 pp. 2nd ed., Cairo, Mak. al-ādāb, 1944 (*H.*, vol. XLII, May 1, 1934, p. 887; *Mu.*, vol. LXXXIV, June 1, 1934, p. 773; *OM*, vol. XXV, 1945, p. 57, n. 1; ibid., vol. XXVI, 1946, p. 119, n. 1; *RC*, Feb. 1953, pp. 183–189; *GAL*, S. III, pp. 245–246). Transl. into French by Khédry in 1936, repr. in Khédry & Costandi, *op. cit.*, as *Schéhérezade.* First prod. in French by the Comédie Française, in Paris, 1955 (*Yĕdī'ōt aḥarōnōt*, Tel-Aviv, Nov. 21, 1955, p. 2).

245. Id., *Shajarat al-ḥukm.* A 1-act political satire, in lit. (?) Ar. Transl. into Italian by U. Rizzitano, as *L'albero del potere*, in *OM*, vol. XXIII, Oct., 1943, pp. 440–447.

245a. al-Ḥalabī, Muḥammad 'Alī, *'Umar bnu al-Khaṭṭāb fī'l-jāhiliyya wa'l-islām.* Beirut, 1935; 64 pp. (*Ma.*, XLIII, 1949, pp. 136–137).

245b. Ḥallāq, 'Abd Allāh, *Mayyit yatakallam.* Aleppo, 1936 (ibid., p. 289).

al-Ḥalwī, Ḥasīb, see: List of Ar. Plays, Transl.—Molière; Racine.

245c. al-Ḥāmātī, Sam'ān, *al-Jāliya wa'l-ṣaḥāfa.* A 3-act comedy. Tokoman, 1918; 30 pp. (ibid., XLII, 1948, p. 453).

246. Ḥamdī, Ibrāhīm Najīb, *Riwāyat al-burj al-hā'il.* A 5-act hist. drama in lit. Ar. prose with a few verses, set in France. Inspired by Dumas (père). Cairo, Maṭb. al-ṣidq, n.d. (1904); 79 pp.

246a. Ḥāmid, Badr al-Dīn, *Maisalūn.* A 5-act play. Ḥamāt, Maṭābi' Abī'l-Fidā', 1946; 168 pp. (*Ma.*, XLIII, 1949, p. 289).

Ḥamdī, Muḥammad, see: List of Ar. Plays, Transl.—Shakespeare.

Ḥannā, Niqūlā, see: List of Ar. Plays, Orig. Plays.—Abū Hanā, Niqūlā.

246b. Ḥassūn, Salīm, *Istishhād Mār Ṭarsīsyūs.* Mosul, Dominican Press (*Ma.*, XLII, 1948, p. 440).

246c. Ḥaṣlab, Khalīl, *al-Iskandar dhū'l-qarnain* (ibid., ibid.).
246d. Ḥashīma, 'Abd Allāh, *'Āṣifa fī'l-qarya* (ibid., XLIII, 1949, p. 133).
246e. Id., *Lailā* (ibid., p. 280).
247. al-Ḥilwu, Yuḥannā, *Riwāyat kitāb Kalīla wa-Dimna.* A 3-act hist. drama in lit. Ar. prose. Detroit (Michigan), Mak. al-Dalīl, 1945; 73 pp.
247a. Ḥubaiqa, Buṭrus, *al-Fitya al-thalātha.* A 1-act play. Beirut, al-Maṭb. al-kāthūlīkiyya, 1936; 28 pp. (*Ma.*, XLIII, 1949, p. 273).
247b. Id., *Istishhād Būlus al-rasūl.* A 3-act religious play. Beirut, al-Maṭb. al-kāthūlīkiyya, 1935; 62 pp. (ibid., XLII, 1948, p. 439).
247c. Ḥubaiqa, Najīb, *al-Fāris al-aswad* (Najm, *al-Masraḥiyya etc.*, p. 54).
247d. Id., *al-Ibn al-ākhar.* Prod. repeatedly in Beirut (*Ma.*, XLII, 1948, p. 436).
247e. Id., *Ibn al-khā'in* (Najm, *al-Masraḥiyya etc.*, p. 54).
248. Id., *Luṣūṣ al-ghāb* (*GAL*, S. II, p. 763).
248a. Id., *Makā'id al-qaṣr* (*Ma.*, XLIII, 1949, p. 286).
249. Id., *Shahīd al-wafā'* (ibid. Dāghir, p. 296, thinks—prob. rightly—this is an adaptation).
250. Id., *al-Shaqīqatān* (Dāghir, ibid.).
See also: List of Ar. Plays, Transl.—Camille.
250a. al-Ḥurr, Ṭannūs, *al-Shābb al-jāhil al-sikkīr.* A social drama. First prod. in Beirut, 1863 (Najm, *al-Masraḥiyya etc.*, pp. 57, 397).
251. Ḥusain, 'Abd Allāh, *Ghādat al-'arab.* Zagazig (?), prob. 1902 (*H.*, vol. XI, Nov. 1, 1902, p. 94).
251a. Ḥusain, Muḥammad Ḥājj, *Milād Abī'l-'Alā'.* Publ. Ladhiqiyya, 1943 (*Ma.*, XLIII, 1949, p. 290).
251b. Id., *Ṣabāḥiyyāt 'Umar.* Publ. Ladhiqiyya, 1943 (ibid., p. 130).
Ḥusain, Ṭaha, see: List of Ar. Plays, Transl.—Gide; Racine; Sophocles.
Ḥusnī, Ḥasan, see: List of Ar. Plays, Orig. Plays—al-Ṭuwairānī, Ḥasan Ḥusnī.
252. Ḥusnī, Muḥammad, *Riwāyat Ba'jar* (*GAL*, S. III, p. 280).
253. al-Ḥuwaik, Ilyās Ṭannūs, *Mir'āt al-qurūn al-mutawassiṭa.* 1909 (Ḥunain, *Shauqī 'alā'l-masraḥ*, p. 18. *Ma.*, XLIII, 1949, p. 283, reads author's name Ilyās Anṭūn al-Ḥuwaik).
See also: List of Ar. Plays, Transl.—Racine.
253a. al-'Ibādī, Muḥammad, *Muqātil Miṣr Aḥmad 'Urābī.* 1897 (Najm, *al-Masraḥiyya etc.*, pp. 336–339).
254. *Ibnat ḥāris al-ṣaid.* A social drama in which a profligate becomes the rival-in-love of his illegitimate, unrecognized son. Prod. by Iskandar Faraḥ's troupe (*al-Jāmi'a*, N.Y., vol. V, July 1, 1906, pp. 47–48). Inspired by Al. Dumas' *Les gardes forestiers*? (*Ma.*, XLII, 1948, p. 437, suggests I. Faraḥ as the author).
Ibrāhīm, 'Abd al-Malik, see: List of Ar. Plays, Transl.—Shakespeare.
Ibrāhīm, Ḥāfiẓ, see: List of Ar. Plays, Transl.—Shakespeare.
255. Ibrāhīm, Ḥāfiẓ & Ṣabrī, Ismā'īl, *al-Manẓūma al-tamthīliyya.* A 1-act tragedy in lit. Ar. verse, about the dying hours of a patriot from Beirut. First prod. in Cairo, March 1912. Publ. in Sulaimān Ḥasan al-Qabbānī's *Bughyat al-mumaththilīn*, Alex., Gharzūzī, n.d. (prob. 1912–1914); pp. 118–125.
Ibrāhīm, Muḥammad 'Awaḍ,* see: List of Ar. Plays, Transl.—Goethe; Shaw; Shakespeare.
'Iffat, Muḥammad, see: List of Ar. Plays, Transl.—Shakespeare.
'Iffat, Muḥammad Khalīl, see: List of Ar. Plays, Transl.—Voltaire.

*GAL, S. III, p. 233, wrongly reads his name as Muḥammad 'Iwaḍ Muḥammad. Cf. ibid., p. 1322: M. 'Auḍ M.

256. Ilyās, Niqūlā, *Riwāyat ḥarb al-'uthmān ma' al-yūnān.* A 3-act semi-hist. drama in lit. Ar. prose & verse about battles against the Turks and Greeks. Cairo, Maṭb. al-ma'ārif, n.d. (prob. early 20th century); 51 pp.
al-'Inānī, 'Alī, see: List of Ar. Plays, Transl.—Schiller.
'Īsā, see: List of Ar. Plays, Transl.—Botril.
256a. Isḥāq, 'Abd Allāh, *Fī sabīl al-sharaf* (*Ma.*, XLIII, 1949, p. 274).
Isḥāq al-Dimashqī, Adīb, see: List of Ar. Plays, Transl.—d'Ache; *Charlemagne;* Racine.
Iskandar, Būlus, see: List of Ar. Plays, Transl.—Shakespeare.
Iskandar, Ya'qūb, see: List of Ar. Plays, Transl.—Shakespeare.
al-Iskandarī, Muṣṭafā Shafīq, see: List of Ar. Plays, Orig. Plays—al-Sikandarī, Muṣṭafā Shafīq.
257. Ismā'īl, Ibrāhīm 'Izz al-Dīn, *Tamthīliyyāt Kalīla wa-Dimna,* vol. I, 5 short school-plays, in lit. Ar. prose, adapted from the stories of *Kalīla wa-Dimna.* Cairo, Dār al-kutub al-ahliyya, n.d.; 224 pp. The author announces on p. 213 the future publ. of vol. II.
257a. Ismā'īl, Zakariyā Ḥamūda, *al-Mustaqbal.* A 4-act play. Damanhūr, Maṭb. al-sha'b, 1933; 144 pp. (*Ma.*, XLIII, 1949, p. 284).
258. 'Iwaḍ, Maḥmūd, *Ṣirā' il-nafs nūr 'alā nūr aḍā'a fī'l-qarn il-'ishrīn.* A 3-act social drama in coll. Ar. prose (of Egypt). N.p. (Cairo?), Maṭb. lajnat al-bayān al-'arabī, 1950; 69 pp.
259. al-Iyādī, Muḥammad al-Sikandarī, *Riwāyat Abī'l-Futūḥ al-malik al-Nāṣir.* A 5-act semi-hist. drama in lit. Ar. about some wars between the Arabs and the Persians, caused by court intrigues and personal ambition. Alex., n.d. (*GAL*, S. III, p. 266, suggests 1880?).
260. al-Jabalāwī, Muḥammad Ṭāhir, *Dīk al-Jinn al-Ḥimṣī.* A play in lit. Ar. verse. It tells of a poet's love and jealousy. Minyā (?), Maṭb. Ṣādiq, prob. 1935; 131 pp. (*H.*, vol. XLIV, Feb. 1, 1936, pp. 474–475).
260a. Id., *al-Riwāya al-ḍā'i'a* (*Ma.*, XLIII, 1949, p. 121).
260b. Jābir, Anīs, *Bi-tamaddun aghniyā'inā au al-ghanī al-mutamaddin.* A 1-act comedy. 'Āliya (Lebanon); 10 pp. (ibid, XLII, 1948, p. 446).
260c. Id., *al-Ghanī' l-muqtaṣid* (ibid., XLIII, 1949, p. 139).
Jahshān, Najīb, see: List of Ar. Plays, Transl.—Racine.
261. Jalāl, Muḥammad 'Uthmān, *al-Mukhaddimīn* (inner title page: *al-Khaddāmīn wa'l-mukhaddamīn*). A 2-act comedy of manners in modern Egyptian society. Coll. Ar. verse (of Egypt). Adapted (?). Cairo, Maṭb. al-Nīl, 1904; 24 pp. (*Fihris.* IV, p. 112).
See also: List of Ar. Plays, Transl.—Corneille; Molière; Racine.
261a. Jāmātī, Ḥabīb, *'Antara.* A 4-act hist. play. Prod. in Egypt (*Ma.*, XLIII, 1949, p. 137). See also: List of Ar. Plays, Transl.—Prévost; Sardou.
262. Jamī'ī (Jumai'ī?), 'Umar, *Abnā' al-arāmil.* A 3-act social drama, revolving around life in the countryside. Lit. Ar. prose. Cairo, Dār al-kitāb al-'arabī, 1947; IV, 155 pp.
263. Id., *Fajr jadīd.* A 3-act social drama in lit. Ar. prose. The author deals ably, even though too sentimentally, with the problem of prostitution, and pleads boldly for sex education. Cairo, Maṭb. 'Aṭāyā, n.d., prob. 1947; 110 pp. (*Bamah*, fasc. 51, May 1947, pp. 33–34; *K.*, vol. III, Jan., 1948, p. 168).
264. Id., *Na'īsh marra wāḥida.* A collection of short plays (mentioned on p. 112 of No. 263, above, as awaiting publication).
265. Id., *Thaub al-'arūs.* A 3-act play (mentioned ibid., awaiting publ.).

266. al-Jarnūsī, Ḵẖālid, *al-Fātiḥ*. A 5-act play in lit. Ar. verse, descr. Ibn al-Walīd's conquest of Mecca. Publ. in *M.*, June–July, 1952. Jaudat, Ṣāliḥ, see: List of Ar. Plays, Transl.–Brieux.

267. al-Jauzī, Naṣrī, *al-'Adl asās al-mulk* (*al-Jihād*, Mar. 12, 1956, p. 3).

268. Id., *'Air al-jalā'* (ibid).

269. Id., *Bidnā reidyō*. A 1-act sketch in the coll. Ar. prose of Palestine, treats of the humorous quarrels in a middle-class Arab family, whose younger generation wants, and gets, a radio. Broadcast, then ed. by Prof. S. D. Goitein, with notes in Hebrew, Jerusalem, Mass, 1944; 44 pp.

270. Id., *al-Dunyā umm* (*al-Jihād*, Mar. 12, 1956, p. 3).

271. Id., *Ḏẖakā' al-qāḍī*. A children-play in lit. Ar. prose, descr. a famous trial before the Caliph Hārūn al-Rasẖīd. Jerusalem, al-Maṭb. al-tijāriyya, n.d., prob. 1945–1946; 32 pp.

272. Id., *Fu'ād wa-Lailā* (*al-Jihād*, Mar. 12, 1956, p. 3).

273. Id., *al-Ḥaqq ya'lū* (ibid.).

274. Id., *Sẖabḥ al-aḥrār*. Prod. at the YMCA in Jerusalem (ibid.).

275. Id., *al-Sẖumū' al-muḥtariqa*. A prologue and 4-act social drama in lit. Ar. prose, moralizing on the suffering of children for their father's unhealthy lust. Jerusalem, Maṭb. Bait al-Maqdis, 1937 (?); 69 pp. (*Bamah*, fasc. 50, 1947, p. 110).

276. Id., *Ṣuwar min al-māḍī*. An hist. play for children, prob. in lit. Ar. (announced as ready for publ. in No. 271, above).

277. Id., *Turāṯẖ al-ābā'*. A 2-act children-play in lit. Ar. prose, set in the days of the Caliph al-Ma'mūn and extolling the virtues of keeping the ancestors' lands. Prob. indirect propaganda against selling land in Palestine to the Jews. Jerusalem, Maṭb. Bait al-Maqdis, n.d. (1946?); 31 pp. (*Hed ha-ḥinnūḵẖ*, Tel-Aviv, vol. XXI, Sīwān-Tammūz 5707, pp. 44–45).

278. Jazānah, Muḥammad Ḥalīm, *Jaḏẖima wa'l-Ẕabbā'*. The story of Zenobia Queen of Palmyra. Prob. 1901 (*H.*, vol. X, Oct. 15, 1901, p. 67; *Mu.*, vol. XXVI, Nov. 1, 1901, pp. 1042–1043).

279. al-Jiddī (al-Jundī?), Salīm, *Riwāyat jazā' al-sẖahāma*. A 5-act drama of love and intrigue. Lit. Ar. prose & verse. Publ. in *Muntaḵẖabāt Salīm al-Jiddī* (?), n.p., Maṭb. al-Rāwī, n.d.; pp. 5–97.

280. al-Jilālī, 'Abd al-Raḥmān, *Annibāl*. Appar. an hist. play (*Le Monde Arabe*, fasc. 3, Sep. 21, 1951, p. 14. Should be corrected to read al-Jalālī?).

281. Id., *Maulid* (ibid.).

282. al-Jilālī, Kātib, *L'opéré fi'l-opéra* (*BE*, Nov. 1, 1952, p. 3).

283. Jirjis, 'Īsā, *al-Rīfiyya al-ḥasnā'*. A play (?). Prob. 1934 (*H.*, vol. XLII, July 1, 1934, p. 1145). Jirjis, Yūsuf Iskandar, see: List of Ar. Plays, Transl.—Shakespeare.

284. Jum'a, Muḥammad Luṭfī, *Nīrūn*. Appar. an hist. play about Nero, the Roman Emperor (*GAL*, S. III, p. 276).

285. Id., *Qalb al-mar'a*. A 5-act psychological play. Written in 1915 (acc. to *Fihris*, IV, p. 101, still in ms. Dāgẖir, p. 275, does not say whether published). See also: List of Ar. Plays, Transl.—Shakespeare.

286. al-Jumayyil, Anṭūn, *Abṭāl al-ḥurriyya*. A 5-scene drama, in lit. Ar. prose. descr. in pompous words the Young Turk revolution of 1908. First prod. in Cairo, 1908, at a ceremony in honor of the new Turkish constitution. Publ. in the booklet descr. the ceremony, of same name, Cairo, Mak. al-ma'ārif, n.d., prob. 1909; pp. 31–44. French sub-title: *Les héros de la liberté par A.-J. Gemayel* (Sarkīs, *Mu'jam*, p. 713; Dāgẖir, p. 277).

287. Id., *Riwāyat al-Samau'al au wafā' al-'arab*. A 4-act hist. play about the faithfulness of a famous Jewish chieftain before Islam. Cairo, Maṭb. al-ahrām, 1909; 95 pp. (*H.*, vol. XVII, July 1, 1909, p. 615; and vol. XVIII, May 1, 1910, p. 472. Dāghir, p. 277).
al-Jundī, Muḥammad 'Abd al-Salām, see: List of Ar. Plays, Transl.—Rostand.
al-Juraidīnī, Sāmī, see: List of Ar. Plays, Transl.—Shakespeare.
Jūrjī, Yūsuf Iskandar, see: List of Ar. Plays, Transl.—Barrie.
288. Kāmil, 'Ādil, *Waika 'Antar*. A 3-act social comedy in lit. Ar. prose. Cairo, Lajnat al-nashr li'l-jāmi'iyyīn, prob. 1941; 165 pp. (*Mu.*, vol. XCIX, Nov. 1, 1941, pp. 419–420).
Kāmil, Aḥmad, see: List of Ar. Plays, Transl.—Piave.
289. Kāmil, Khalīl, *Maẓālim al-ābā'*. A 5-act social drama. Prod. a few times in Egypt, Publ. prob. 1897 (*H.*, vol. V, May 15, 1897, p. 720).
290. Kāmil, Maḥmūd, *Fāṭima*. Prod. in 1931. Publ. Cairo, Maṭb. jarīdat al-ṣabāḥ, n.d. (*BSOS*, vol. VIII, 1935–1937, p. 1000. *GAL*, S. III, p. 280, presumably mentions another ed., Maṭb. al-siyāsa, n.d.).
290a. Id., *al-Wuḥūsh*. First prod. in Cairo, 1926 (*Ma.*, XLIII, 1949, p. 294).
See also: List of Ar. Plays, Transl.—Daudet.
290b. Kāmil, Muḥammad, *Shaikh al-ḥāra*. A 5-act opéra-comique in lit. & coll. Ar. Cairo, 1928; 95 pp. (*Ma.*, p. 129).
291. Kāmil, Muṣṭafā, *Fatḥ al-Andalus*. Lit. Ar. prose. 1st ed., 1894, of which 6,000 copies were reportedly distributed. 2nd ed., repr. in 'Alī Kāmil, *Muṣṭafā Kāmil fī 24 rabī'*, vol. II, 1908, pp. 167–192 (cf. *GAL*, S. III, 164–166. Also *H.*, vol. XVI, Mar. 1, 1908, p. 327; *Fihris*, IV, p. 76).
291a. Kan'ān, Najīb, *Fatāt al-dustūr*. A 5-act play. Cairo, 1908; 105 pp. (*Ma.*, XLIII, 1949, p. 272).
See also: List of Ar. Plays, Transl.—Verne.
Kan'ān, Taufīq, see: List of Ar. Plays, Transl.—Dumas.
Karam, E., see: List of Ar. Plays, Transl.—Voltaire.
292. Kātseflīs, William, *Riwāyat shaqā' al-tāj au ḥaras jalālatihā*. A prologue and 4-act hist. play about Marie Antoinette and her Court. Lit. Ar. prose. N.Y., Maṭb. mir'āt al-gharb, 1912; 67 pp. (*Mu.*, vol. XL, May 1, 1912, p. 509; *Fihris*, IV, p. 53. *GAL*, S. III, p. 1325—correcting p. 439, n. 3—suggests this reading of author's name, acc. to information given by Kračkovsky).
292a. Kattānī, Sulaimān, *Amal wa-ya's*. A symbolical play. Bait Shabāb, Maṭb. al-'alam; 28 pp. (*Ma.*, XLII, 1948, p. 443).
293. *Kifāḥ al-sha'b*. A 4-act play descr. Egypt until Kléber's assassination. Prod. in 1952 (*al-Zamān*, Oct. 21, 1952, p. 4; *al-Akhbār*, Oct. 22, 1952, p. 8).
Kilāb, Fāris, see: List of Ar. Plays, Transl.—Voltaire.
al-Kīlānī, Ibrāhīm, see: List of Ar. Plays, Transl.—Romains.
al-Kīlānī, Kāmil, see: List of Ar. Plays, Transl.—Hervieu; Sarment.
294. Ksenṭīnī, Rashīd, *Bū Borma*. A 3-act comedy of social manners. First prod. in Alger, 1928 (*Revue Africaine*, vol. LXXVII, 1935, p. 82; *Cahiers du Sud*, 1947, pp. 271–276).
295. Id., *Lunja al-Andalusiyya*. A 5-act comedy set in Spain. First prod. in Alger, 1930 (*Revue Africaine*, ibid., pp. 79–80. Documents Algériens, Série Culturelle, No. 16, Apr. 15, 1947).
296. Id., *Mon cousin de Stamboul*. 1928 (*Cahiers du Sud*, 1947, pp. 271–276).
297. Id., *al-Mōrstān*. A comedy (ibid.).

298. Id., *Shawītō wa-Z̲riribān*. A 3-act comedy. First prod. in Alger, 1929 (*Revue Africaine*, vol. LXXVII, 1935, p. 82; Doc. Algériens, Série Culturelle, No. 16, Apr. 15, 1947).

299. Id., *Un trou parterre*. A comedy. 1931 (Doc. Algériens, ibid.).

300. Id., *Zīd ʿaleih*. A comedy. 1933 (*Cahiers du Sud*, 1947, pp. 271–276).

301. Kūhin (Cohen), Salīm Zakī, *Riwāyat al-musrif*. Prod. at the Jewish school in Beirut, 1895 (*H.*, vol. IV, Oct. 1, 1895, p. 116).
    Khabbāz, Ḥannā, see: List of Ar. Plays, Transl.—Shakespeare.

301a. Khair Allāh, Amīn Z̲āhir, *al-Ardfī'l-samā'* (*Ma.*, XLII, 1948, p. 431).

301b.Id., *al-Bayān al-ṣarāh ʿan nadhar Yaftāḥ*. Damascus, 1923; 104 pp. (ibid., p. 449).

301c.Id., *Maryam al-Majdaliyya*. A 4-act play. 1913 (ibid., XLIII, 1949, p. 284).

301d.Id., *Naghamāt al-ʿandalīb fī istirjāʿ ʿūd al-ṣalīb*. Beirut, Maṭb. al-ijtihād, 1929; 56 pp. (ibid., p. 291).

302. Id., *Riwāyat al-Samauʾal*. Verse. Prob. lit. Ar. (Sẖaikẖū, *Ta'rīkẖ . . . fī'l-rubʿ al-awwal etc.*, p. 161).

303. Khair Allāh, Muḥammad Munjī, *Mā baʿd al-dawāra illā'l-kẖasāra*. A 3-act tragedy in lit. Ar. prose & verse, set in modern Egypt. 2nd ed., Alex., Maṭb. al-ṣidq, A.H. 1322; 39 pp .(*H.*, vol. VI, Dec. 1, 1897, p. 279).

304. Id., *Riwāyat Majnūn Lailā*. A 6-act drama, in lit. Ar. prose & verse, about this early poet. N.p., Maṭb. al-Raqīb, 1898; 112 pp. Another ed.—Alex., 1904? (ibid., vol. VI, 1898, p. 934; *OLZ*, vol. II, Feb., 1899, p. 57; *GAL*, S. III, p. 229).

305. Id., *Riwāyat makr al-nisā' wa'l-rijāl*. A 5-act melodrama in lit. Ar., naively woven around several intricately crossing pairs of lovers, part of whom die or commit suicide, while the others arrive at a happy marriage. Alex., Maṭb. al-najāḥ, n.d., prob. 1900; 68 pp. (*H.*, vol. IX, Dec. 1, 1900, p. 159).

306. Khairī, Badīʿ, *Ḥasan wa-Morqoṣ wa-Cohen*. A comedy of manners about a ring of dishonest people. Often prod. by al-Rīḥānī troupe (e.g., *A.*, July 27, 1952, p. 7).

307. Id., *Laqzat Injlīzī*. A political satire (?). Prod. in Egypt in 1951 (*AY*, Dec. 22, 1951, p. 7).

308. Id., *Maqlab ḥarīmī*. Prod. by al-Rīḥānī troupe in Egypt, 1952 (*A.*, Mar. 29, 1952, p. 3.).

309. Id., & al-Rīḥānī, Najīb, *Yā mā kān fī nafsī*. Prod. by al-Rīḥānī troupe in Egypt, 1949–1952 (*AY*, Jan. 29, 1949, p. 10; *A.*, July 15, 1952, p. 7).
    See also: List of Ar. Plays, Orig. Plays—al-Tūnisī, Bairam & Khairī, Badīʿ.

310. al-Khāl, Yūsuf, *Hīrōdiya*. A 3-act hist. play about Herod and his family. Lit. Ar. verse. N.Y., 1954; 88 pp.

311. *Khālid bnu al-Walīd*. A play descr. the battle of Badr. Prod. by the Association of Muslim Youths, 1952 (*M.*, June 6, 1952, p. 5).

311a.Khalīfa, Yuḥannā, *Rīsẖilyū*. A play about Richelieu, 1947 (*Ma.*, XLIII, 1949, p. 122).

311b.Id., *Semīrāmīs*. A 4-act hist. play. Maṭb. al-mursalīn al-lubnāniyyīn, 1947; 48 pp. (ibid., p. 126).
    Khalīl, Naẓmī, see: List of Ar. Plays, Transl.—Schiller.
    Khāliṣ, Ṣalāḥ, see: List of Ar. Plays, Transl.—Cocteau.

312. al-Khaṭīb, Fu'ād, *Fatḥ al-Andalus*. A 3-act hist. play in lit. Ar. verse, descr. the conquest of Spain by the Muslim forces led by Ṭāriq. Damascus, Maṭb. Ibn Zaidūn, 1931; 94 pp. (*Mu.*, vol. LXXXI, Oct. 1, 1932, pp. 370–371).

313. Khawwām, Rizq Allāh, *Yūsuf bnu Ya'qūb*. A 2-act hist. religious play, prod. in Aleppo, then printed. Aleppo, al-Maṭb. al-mārūniyya, prob. 1926 (*Mu.*, vol. LXIX, Nov. 1, 1926, p. 338; Sarkīs, *Jāmi'*, I, No. 1172).
al-Khayyāṭ, Muḥī'l-Dīn, see: List of Ar. Plays, Transl.—Kemal.

314. al-Khūrī, Amīn, *Riwāyat 'Abd al-Ḥamīd wa'l-dustūr*. A 4-act hist. drama in lit. Ar. prose & verse, descr. 'Abd al-Ḥamīd's attempt and failure to overthrow, in 1909, the Turkish constitution. Ed. by Amīn 'Aṭā' Allāh. N.p. (Beirut, Maṭb. al-ādāb?), n.d. (prob. 1909); 48 pp.

314a. Id., *Riwāyat Nābulyūn Būnābārt*. An hist. play about Napoleon I (Najm, *al-Masraḥiyya etc.*, pp. 339–341).
See also: List of Ar. Plays, Transl.—Voltaire.

315. al-Khūrī, Qaiṣar, *Ḥizb al-ightirāb wa'l-iqtirāb fī ḥubb al-waṭan*. N.Y., 1904; 40 pp. (Ḥunain, *Shauqī 'alā'l-masraḥ*, repr., p. 18; *Ma.*, XLII, 1948, p. 456, reads title *Ḥarb etc.*)

316. Khūrī, Raṣīf, *Thaurat Baidabā masraḥiyya shi'riyya*. A 7-act hist. play in lit. Ar. verse, tracing—in approved Communist style—the tyranny of an Indian King and his assassination by the mutinous populace. Beirut, Maṭb. al-funūn, n.d.; 6, 92, 2 pp.
al-Khūrī, Salīm, see: Shaḥḥāda, Salīm.

316a. al-Khūrī, Shukrī, *Yā ḥasratī 'alaika yā Zu'aitar*. Sao Paolo, Maṭb. Abū'l-Haul, 1911; 183 pp. (*Ma.*, XLIII, 1949, p. 295.)

317. al-Khūrī, Yūsuf Murād, *Tanaṣṣur al-Nu'mān*. 1903 (Ḥunain, *Shauqī 'alā'l-masraḥ*, repr. p. 18).

318. Khurshīd, Muḥammad, *Qulūb al-hawānim*. A social drama about a couple who decide to end their forced marriage by separation. Cairo, 1933 (*BSOS*, vol. VIII, 1935–1937, p. 999; *GAL*, S. III, p. 280).

318a. Khuwaiḍ, Farīd, *'Alā madhhab al-khiyāna*. Prod. in Beirut, 1948 (*Ma.*, XLIII, 1949, p. 136).
Labīb, Muḥammad, see: List of Ar. Plays, Orig. Plays—Abū'l-Su'ūd, Muḥammad Labīb.

319. Laḥūd, Adīb, *Bishr ibn 'Awāna*. A 4-act play of Arab love, war and hunting. 78 pp. (*Ma.*, vol. XLVIII, 1954, p. 223).

320. Id., *Imru' al-Qais wa'l-fatāt al-ṭā'iyya*. A 3-act play about the wit of the celebrated poet. 64 pp. (ibid.).

320a. Id., *al-Qiddīsa Barbāra al-shahīda*. 'Umshait, 1910 (ibid., XLIII, 1949, p. 275).

321. Id., *al-Shahāma wa'l-sharaf*. A 5-act hist. play in lit. Ar. prose and verse, treating of tragic love. Beirut, Mak. Ṣādir, 1952; 95 pp. (ibid., vol. XLVIII, 1954, p. 223).

322. Id., *al-Zabbā' malikat Jazīrat al-'arab*. A 4-act hist. play about the life and times of Zenobia, Queen of Palmyra. Beirut, Ṣādir, 1952; 85 pp. (ibid., pp. 222–223).
See also: List of Ar. Plays, Orig. Plays—'Ubaid, Bishāra & Laḥūd, Adīb.
Lūqā, Nashīd, see: List of Ar. Plays, Transl.—Shakespeare.

322a. Luṭf Allāh, Ilyās, *al-Ibn al-ḍāll*. Alexandria (*Ma.*, XLII, 1948, p. 436).

322b. Id., *Ma'sāt Ayyūb al-ṣiddīq*. Publ. Jerusalem, 1889 (ibid. ,p. 446; ibid., XLIII, 1949, p. 280).

322c. al-Madanī, Hāshim al-Defterdār, *Ilā Gharnāṭa*. An hist. play. Maṭb. al-Inṣāf, 1941; 94 pp. (ibid., XLII, 1948, p. 442).

323. al-Madrasa al-markaziyya li'l-banāt, *al-Fatāt al-'irāqiyya*. A 5-act play for

school-children, in simple language. Baghdad (?), prob. 1925; 26 pp. (*H.*, vol. XLII, Jan. 1, 1934, p. 378).

al-Maghribī, 'Abd al-Qādir, see: List of Ar. Plays, Transl.—Dumas.

323a. al-Maghribī, Muḥammad, *Gharām wa-intiqām.* A 5-act comedy. 32 pp. (*Ma.*, XLIII, 1949, p. 139).

324. Id., *Riwāyat maghāriz al-'ajā'iz.* A 3-act social comedy in coll. Ar. prose and verse (of Egypt), descr. love intrigues in modern Egypt, prob. Alexandria. N.p., al-Maṭb. al-'āmira al-sharafiyya, A.H. 1321; 32 pp.

Maghzilī, Muḥammad, see: List of Ar. Plays, Transl.—Musset.

324a. Maḥfūẓ, Najīb, *Rādūbīs.* Cairo, Lajnat al-nashr li'l-jāmi'iyyīn, 1943 (*Ma.* XLIII, 1949, p. 119).

324b. Maḥjūb, Muḥammad Yūsuf, *Balāl.* Cairo, Mak. Miṣr; 24 pp. (ibid., XLII, 1948, p. 448).

324c. Id., *al-Fīl wa'l-islām.* Cairo, Mak. Miṣr; 15 pp. (ibid., XLIII, 1949, p. 274).

324d. Id., *al-Hijra al-ūlā.* Cairo, Mak. Miṣr; 24 pp. (ibid., p. 292).

324e. Id., *'Umar wa'l-'ajūz.* Cairo, Mak. Miṣr; 24 pp. (ibid., p. 137).

Maḥmūd, Maḥmūd, see: List of Ar. Plays, Transl.—Euripides.

324f. al-Majdalānī, Nāṣīf, *Fī sabīl al-waṭan.* Beirut, 1932 (*Ma.*, XLIII, 1949, p. 274).

325. Makkī, Aḥmad, *al-'Āṣifa.* A symbolical play in lit. Ar., it descr. the alternation of hope and despair in a couple's hearts while trapped in a cave beset by the rising tide of the sea. Beirut, Manshūrāt al-makshūf, 1937 (*GAL*, S. III, p. 418).

326. Id., *Lailat al-qadr.* A symbolical play in lit. Ar., descr. the temptations offered a monk by an attractive girl and his yielding to them. This is the title of the collection of Makki's three plays (Nos. 325, 326, 327), publ. Beirut, Manshūrāt al-makshūf, 1937; 151 pp. No. 326 shows the influence of A. France's *Thais?*

327. Id., *al-Sarāb.* The best of Makkī's three symbolical plays. Tells, in lit. Ar., the story of various groups of a caravan, dying of thirst in the desert, and the reaction of two spirits (a numerical restriction of the Greek chorus) to their behavior. Obviously the vain search for luck. Beirut, Manshūrāt al-makshūf, 1937.*

328. Mallāṭ, Shiblī, *Riwāyat Alfred al-kabīr.* An hist. play. 1st ed., Ba'abdā, al-Maṭb. al-lubnāniyya, 1905; 2nd ed., Beirut, Mak. al-taufīq, prob. 1924; 84 pp.

See also: List of Ar. Plays, Transl.—Dubois.

329. Mallūl, Nasīm, *Riwāyat shahāmat al-'arab au al-Samau'al wa-Imru' al-Qais.* An 8-act hist. drama, for school usage, idealizing the famous Jewish Arab chieftain and poet. Baghdad, Maṭb. Dār al-Salām, 1928 (*GAL*, S. III, p. 490).

330. Ma'lūf, Fauzī 'Īsā, *Ibn Ḥamīd au suqūṭ Gharnāṭa.* A 5-act hist. play based on Florian's *Gonzalve de Cordoue.* Publ. by Majallat al-'uṣba al-andalusiyya, 1952; 117 pp. Prod. in Zahle, Damascus and Brazil (ibid., p. 451. Dāghir, p. 721).

331. Ma'lūf, Mīshāl Ibrāhīm, *Sajīn al-ẓulm.* A 5-act detective play, set in the era of Turkish constitutional reforms. Zahle, Maṭb. al-muhadhdhab; 102 pp. (*Fihris*, IV, p. 46).

*Both Makkī and *GAL*, S. III, p. 418, err in attributing the motto of this play ("vanitas vanitatum omnia vanitas") to the Psalms. It is from Ecclesiastes I, 2.

332. Mamīsh, Muḥammad, *al-Asīr*. Amman, al-Maṭb. al-waṭaniyya, prob. 1933; 33 pp. (*H.*, vol. XLII, Jan. 1, 1934, p. 378).
al-Manfalūṭī, Muṣṭafā Luṭfī, see: List of Ar. Plays, Transl.—Rostand.
333. Manṣūr, Ibrāhīm Yūsuf, *Ādām*. A 4-act symbolical drama, in lit. Ar. prose. descr. the social struggle between old and new. Written 1950, rewritten 1953, still in ms. (information supplied by the author, Nov. 1955).
334. Id., *Muqāmarat al-ziwāj*. A 4-act social drama about modern Iraq. Lit. Ar. prose. Baghdad, Maṭb. al-ma'ārif, 1954. First prod. in Baghdad, 1954 (same source).
334a. al-Maqdisī, Anīs al-Khūrī, *Ilā'l-Ḥamrā'*. An hist. play about the fall of Granada (*Ma.*, XLII, 1948, p. 442).
334b. Mardam, 'Adnān, *Maṣra' al-Ḥusain* (ibid., XLIII, 1949, p. 285).
334c. Mar'ī, Edwār, *Afkār fī'l-jaḥīm* (ibid., XLII, 1948, p. 441).
335. Mar'ī, Ḥasan, *Ḥādithat Dānishwāi*. A 4-act political play in lit. Ar. prose. It descr. the punishment meted out by the British to some Egyptian villagers. Production on the stage forbidden by the British authorities. Cairo, publ. by the author (?), n.d. (1907); 45, 3 pp. (*RMM*, vol. III, 1907, pp. 504–509; *GAL*, S. III, p. 34, n. 1).
Mar'ī, Muḥammad 'Abd al-Muṭī', see above: 'Abd al-Muṭṭalib.
335a. Mārūn, Kāmil, *Fajr al-naṣr fī Kristūf Kūlumb* (*Ma.*, XLIII, 1949, p. 273).
335b. Mas'ad, Amīn, *Dāniyāl al-nabī*. 1901 (ibid., XLII, 1948, p. 460).
Mas'ūd, Muḥammad, see: List of Ar. Plays, Transl.—Molière.
336. al-Mashʻalānī, Buṭrus al-Khūrī Yuḥannā, *al-Asīra*. A 5-act hist. drama in lit. Ar. verse, treating of love and warfare between the Romans and the Macedonians circa 200 B.C. al-Ḥadath (Lebanon), al-Maṭb. al-sharqiyya, 1903; 70 pp.
337. Mashʻalānī, Salīm, *Malikat Saba'*. A 5-act semi-hist. play, in lit. Ar. prose with a few verses. Based on a novel of the same name by Amīn Zaidān, it descr. the intrigues around King Salomon and the Queen of Sheba. N.Y., Maṭb. jarīdat al-hudā, n.d. (1927?); 64 pp. First prod. at the Academy of music in Brooklyn, N.Y., Mar. 19, 1927.
Maṭar, Jūrj, see: List of Ar. Plays, Transl.—Richepin.
338. al-Māzinī, Ibrāhīm 'Abd al-Qādir, *Gharīzat al-mar'a au ḥukm al-ṭā'a*. Prod. in 1931. Publ. Cairo, Maṭb. al-siyāsa, n.d., prob. 1931. 2nd ed., Maṭb. jarīdat al-ṣabāḥ; 80 pp. (*BSOS*, vol. VIII, 1935–1937. *GAL*, S. III, p. 280. Dāghir, p. 685).
338a. Id., *Thalāthat rijāl wa-imra'a*. Lajnat al-nashr li'l-jāmi'iyyīn, 1944 (*Ma.*, XLII, 1948, p. 452).
338b. Maẓhar, Ibrāhīm Sāmī, *Baṭal Tesālyā Ibrāhīm Bāshā*. A 5-act hist. play. Cairo, Maṭb. al-ikhlāṣ, 1897; 60 pp. (ibid., p. 448).
338c. Mīkhā'īl, Najīb, *al-Malik al-Nu'mān* (Najm, *al-Masraḥiyya etc.*, p. 332).
339. *Milyūn ḍaḥka*. Prod. in Egypt, 1951–1952 (*K.*, vol. VII, June 1952, p. 753).
340. al-Minyāwī al-Miṣrī, Maḥmūd Najīb, *Riwāyat al-ṣafā' ba'd al-'anā'*. A 5-act hist. play, in lit. Ar. prose, set in the days of Charlemagne. Cairo, Maṭb. al-taufīq, n.d.; 90 pp.
341. Mīrzā, Zuhair, *Kāfir*. Lit. Ar. verse. Prob. 1949 (*K.*, vol. IV, May, 1949, p. 756).
342. al-Miṣrī, Ibrāhīm, *al-Anāniyya*. A social drama in coll. Ar., descr. the reactions of a westernized Muslim family to their father's wish to bring home

a third wife. First prod. 1923. Publ. at the end of al-Miṣrī's *al-Adab al-ḥayy*, Cairo, 1928–1930 (*GAL*, S. III, pp. 232, 279. *BSOS*, vol. VIII, 1935–1937, p. 1000, says the play is written in lit. Ar.).

342a. Id., *al-Farīsa*. First prod. in Cairo, 1928 (*Ma.*, XLIII, 1949, p. 273).

343. Id., *Naḥwa al-nūr*. A social drama, gloomier than the previous one. It descr. the emotions and actions of a journalist who discovers his wife's faithlessness, and decides thereupon to sacrifice his career. Publ. in the author's *al-Fikr wa'l-'ālam*, Cairo, 1933 (*GAL*, S. III, p. 279; *BSOS*, VIII, pp. 1000–1001).

Mōyāl, Estīr, see: List of Ar. Plays, Transl.—Musset.

Mu'awwaḍ, Muḥammad 'Abd al-Ḥāfiẓ, see: List of Ar. Plays, Orig. Plays—Badrān, Muḥammad.

343a. Mudawwar, Farīd, *Fauq al-intiqām*. Beirut, 1931; 109 pp. (*Ma.*, XLIII, 1949, p. 273).

343b. Id., *Gharīb hādhā*. Beirut; 84 pp. (ibid., p. 139).

343c. Id., *Hākadhā anā*. Beirut, al-Jāmi'a al-Amīrikiyya; 69 pp. (ibid., p. 292).

343d. Id., *Kidhbeh yā abī*. Coll. Ar. (?). Beirut, al-Jāmi'a al-Amīrikiyya; 72 pp. (ibid., p. 277).

Muḥammad, 'Abd al-Laṭīf, see: List of Ar. Plays, Transl.—Shakespeare.

344. Muḥammad, Aḥmad Ṣādiq, *Thamarat al-ghawāya*. A 5-act social drama, Alex., Maṭb. al-Iskandariyya, 1900 (*Fihris*, IV, p. 23. *H.*, vol. IX, Feb. 1, 1901, p. 288, reads drama's title as *Thaurat etc.*).

Muḥammad, Aḥmad al-Ṣāwī, see: List of Ar. Plays, Orig. Plays—al-Ḥakīm, *Devant son guichet*.

344a. Muḥarram, Ḥusain, *'Awāṭif il-zauja*. A 3-act play in coll. Ar. of Egypt (*Ma.*, XLIII, 1949, p. 137).

345. Muḥī'l-Dīn, Bāshṭarzī, *Amara est juste* (*Cahiers du Sud*, 1947, pp. 271–276).

346. Id., *Après l'ivresse* (ibid.).

347. Id., *Ash Kalū* (?) (ibid.).

348. Id., *Benī oui-oui* (ibid.).

349. Id., *Bū shenshāna* (ibid.).

350. Id., *Bū Kernūna* (?) (ibid.).

351. Id., *La cocaïne* (ibid.).

352. Id., *Dār Bībī* (?) (ibid.).

353. Id., *Dār el-maḥābel* (ibid).

354. Id., *al-Ennīf* (?) (ibid.).

355. Id., *Fe'l-qahwa* (ibid.).

356. Id., *Les femmes* (ibid.).

357. Id., *Ḥājj Ḥlīma* (ibid.).

358. Id., *el-Ḥebāl* (ibid.).

359. Id., *Ḥubb el-nisā'* (ibid.).

360. Id., *Juḥā et l'usurier* (ibid.).

361. Id., *el-Kheddā'īn* (ibid.).

362. Id., *Qalb min ḥadīd* (*BE*, Nov. 1, 1952, p. 3).

363. Id., *Sī Mezyān* (?) (*Cahiers du Sud*, 1947, pp. 271–276).

364. Id., *el-Ṭbīb e-sqūllī* (ibid.).

365. Id., *Un marriage par téléphone* (ibid.).

366. Id., *Yā sa'adī* (ibid.).

367. Id., *Zēd Ayett* (?) (ibid.).

368. Id. & Rūyāl, Bashīr, *Qā'id Ḥansā'* (*BE*, Nov. 1, 1952, p. 3).

See also: List of Ar. Plays, Transl.—Molière.

369. Mumtāz, Ibrāhīm, *Tāj al-mulūk*. A 5-act play, Mak. al-hilāl (?), prob. 1904 (*H.*, vol. XII, May 1, 1904, p. 479).

369a. Mundhir, Ibrāhīm, *Bain al-qaṣr wa'l-qafr*. Beirut, 1948; 67 pp. (*Ma.*, XLII, 1948, p. 449).

370. al-Muqanna' (pseudonym), *Abū'l-'Alā' al-Ma'arrī*. A 2-act play. 1931 (?) (*GAL*, S. III, p. 419).

370a. Murād, Jūrj, *Bairūt 'alā'l-marsaḥ au arba' sanawāt al-ḥarb*. A 4-act play. Beirut, al-Maṭb. al-lubnāniyya, 1920; 88 pp. (*Ma.*, XLII, 1948, p, 449).

371. Muruwwa, Adīb, *'Anākib al-sharq*. A 1-act symbolical drama in lit. Ar. prose, termed by its author "a legend of our present age." The whole play is a conversation between the mind, conscience and heart of a sleeping youth. Publ. in Muruwwa's *Masāriḥ wa-abṭāl*, Beirut, Dār al-'ilm li'l-malāyīn, 1951; pp. 131–138.

372. Id., *al-Baṭal*. A 2-act drama in lit. Ar. prose, about an author looking for an imaginative hero in Paris. Ibid.; pp. 15–30.

373. Id., *al-Dunyā 'iyāda*. A 1-act comedy in lit. Ar. prose about a few persons in the waiting room of an eye-specialist. Ibid.; pp. 95–113.

374. Id., *Ḥubb kīmāwī*. A 1-act lovers' quarrel in lit. Ar. prose. Ibid.; pp. 123–130.

375. Id., *Mashrū' qubla*. A 2-act comedy in lit. Ar. prose about a young couple in an elevator. Ibid.; pp. 47–59.

376. Id., *Taubat Shahrazād*. A 2-act semi-symbolical play in lit. Ar. prose, about Shehrezad who renounces her claim to eternity in order to gather knowledge on the outer side of the fortress of history. Ibid.; pp. 81–94.

377. Mūsā, Nabawiyya, *Nūt-ḥotep au al-faḍīla al-muḍṭahada*. A play in lit. Ar. prose & verse, set in ancient Egypt in the days of the 17th and 18th dynasties. Cairo, Maṭb. al-muqtaṭaf, prob. 1939; 70 pp. (*Mu.*, vol. XLVII, July 1, 1939, p. 957).

378. Muṣauba', Rashīd, *Salāṭinat al-Azhar*. Mak. al-hilāl (?), prob. 1899 (*H.*, vol. VIII, Jan. 15, 1900, p. 253. *GAL*, S. III, p. 340, and Sarkīs, *Mu'jam*, p. 1757, give author's full name as Muṣauba' Rashīd Ḥannā'l-Lubnānī, but make no mention of this play).

378a. Muṣṭafā, Ṣafā', *Kātrīn*. Beirut, Maṭb. al-kashshāf, 1939; 171 pp. (*Ma.*, XLIII, 1949. p. 277).

al-Mushīr, Muḥammad, see: List of Ar. Plays, Transl.—Tolstoy.

379. *Mu'tamar al-abālīs*. A 1-act political play (anti-Communist propaganda). Lit. Ar. prose. Jaffa, Maṭb. Dugma, n.d. (1955); 14 pp.

Muṭrān, Khalīl, see: List of Ar. Plays, Transl.—Corneille; Knochblauch; Schiller; Shakespeare.

379a. Mūyāl, Shim'ūn, *Qurrat al-'uyūn au 'alā'l-bāghī tadūr al-dawā'ir*. Beirut, al-Maṭb. al-lubnāniyya, 1885; 56 pp. (*Ma.*, XLIII, 1949, p. 275).

380. al-Nabbūt, Khalīl Ibrāhīm, *Wathbat al-'arab*. An hist. drama in lit. Ar. prose & verse about Faiṣal, the son of Ḥusain, and his exploits in Syria. Buenos Ayres, al-Maṭb. al-tijāriyya, prob. 1936; 65 pp. (*H.*, vol. XLV, Jan. 1, 1937, p. 354. *Mu.*, vol. XCI, Oct. 1, 1937, p. 375).

381. Nadīm, 'Abd Allāh, *al-'Arab*. Prod. for charity purposes by Nadīm and his pupils in Alexandria, approx. in 1880 (*H.*, vol. V, Feb. 1, 1897, pp. 404, 408).

382. Id., *al-Waṭan*. Prod. on the same occasion as the preceding play.

382a. Nadīm, Muḥammad, *al-Fatāt al-'Irāqiyya*. A 5-act play. Baghdad, Maṭb. al-fallāḥ, 1925; 26 pp. (*Ma.*, XLIII, 1949, p. 272).

382b. Nādir, Jibrā'īl, *Ghādat al-tur'a au Jamāl Bāshā wa'l-tur'a*, 1928; 64 pp. (ibid., p. 138).

al-Naḥḥās, Muḥammad Kāmil, see: List of Ar. Plays, Transl.—Shaw.

383. Nājī, Ibrāhīm, *al-Maut fī ijāza*. A play adapted from the English. Prod. in Egypt, 1946–1947 (*K.*, vol. II, July 1947, p. 1421).

384. Najīb, Sulaimān, *Awwal bakhtī*. A 3-act play in the coll. Ar. of Egypt. Its hero is a man who divorces his wife for another woman and then returns to his first wife. Prod. in Egypt, 1946 (*KM*, fasc. 9, June 1946, pp. 150–151).
See also: List of Ar. Plays, Transl.—Coward.

384a. al-Najjār, Mīkhā'īl Isḥāq, *Asīrat al-wafā'*. A 5-act play. 55 pp. (*Ma.*, XLII, 1948, p. 440).

385. Najm, Fransīs, *Shahīd al-dīn wa-abṭāl al-muruwwa*, A 3-act play. Beirut, Maṭb. Ṣādir, 1921; 53 pp. (Shaikhū, *Ta'rīkh . . . fī'l-rub' al-awwal etc.*, p. 180).

386. Nāqil, A., *al-Kāhina* (*BE*, Nov. 1, 1952, p. 3).

387. Naqqāsh, Ḥannā Luṭf Allāh, *al-Failasūf al-ghayūr*. A comedy. Prob. 1897 (*H.* vol. VI, Dec. 1, 1897, p. 279).

388. al-Naqqāsh, Mārūn, *Riwāyat Abī'l-Ḥasan al-mughaffal au riwāyat Hārūn al-Rashīd*. A 3-act comedy in lit. Ar. verse and rhymed prose, about the man who became Caliph-for-a-day. Publ. together with two adaptations from Molière in his *Arzat Lubnān*, Beirut, al-Maṭb. al-'umūmiyya, 1869; pp. 108–172.
See also: List of Ar. Plays, Transl.—Molière.

389. al-Naqqāsh, Salīm Khalīl, *al-Muqāmir* (Khalīl Muṭrān in *H.*, vol. XXIX, Feb. 1, 1921, p. 470).

390. Id., *Riwāyat al-ẓalūm*. A 5-act drama in lit. Ar. prose and verse, treating of Court intrigue and romance. First prod. by the troupe of Yūsuf al-Khayyāṭ at the Opera House in Cairo, 1878. 1st ed., Cairo, al-Mak. al-sa'īdiyya, n.d.; 48 pp. 2nd ed., Alexandria, al-Maṭb. al-tijāriyya, 1902; 76 pp. (*H.*, vol. XV, Nov. 1, 1906, p. 117; ibid. vol. XVIII, May 1, 1910, p. 470).
See also: List of Ar. Plays, Transl.—Corneille; Ghislanzoni; Racine.

Nāṣif, 'Iṣām al-Dīn ibn Ḥafnī, see: List of Ar. Plays, Transl.—Tolstoy.

Naṣīf, Narjis, see: List of Ar. Plays, Transl.—Shaw.

391. Nāṣir al-Dīn, Amīn, *al-Jāhil*. 1908 (*Ma.*, XLII, 1948, p. 453).

391a. Id., *Jazā' al-khiyāna*. 1908 (ibid., p. 454).

391b. Naṣr, Nasīm Ḥannā, *Ikhlāṣ al-'adhārā*. 96 pp. (ibid., p. 438).

392. Naṣṣār, Najīb, *Shamām al-'arab*. Lit. Ar. (?), Haifa, Maṭb. al-Karmil, 1914 (*Fihris*, IV, p. 54).

392a. Nashāṭī, Futūḥ, *Miṣr al-khālida* (*Ma.*, XLIII, 1949, p. 285).
See also: List of Ar. Plays, Transl.—Maeterlinck.

393. Nīqūlā'ūs, Naṣīf, *Nakbat al-Barāmika*. A 5-act tragedy in lit. Ar., treating of the fall of the Barmakids, and ending in the death of the chief actors. Tanta, Maṭb. al-sharq, prob. 1922 (*H.*, vol. XXX, June 1, 1922, p. 882; *Mu.*, vol. LXI, June 1, 1922, pp. 90–91; Sarkīs, *Jāmi'*, I, No. 1167; *Fihris*, IV, p. 130).

394. Nu'aima, Mīkhā'īl, *al-Ābā' wa'l-banūn*. A 4-act social drama in lit. Ar. prose about relations between the older and the younger generation in modern Arab society. First publ. in *Majallat al-funūn*, then repr. N.Y., Shirkat al-funūn, 1917; 116 pp. (*H.*, vol. XXXVI, July 1, 1918, p. 823; *GAL*, S. III, pp. 472–473; *Fihris*, IV, p. 1).

395. Id., *al-Waraqa al-akhīra*. A 1-act play of family life, with some symbolical hints. Publ. in *K.*, vol. VII, Jan., 1952, pp. 62–72.

al-Numair, Fahmī Ḥannā, see: List of Ar. Plays, Transl.—Drinkwater.

395a. Nu'mān, Mitrī, *al-Amān*. Ḥarīṣā, Maṭb. al-Ābā' al-Būlusiyyīn; 40 pp. (*Ma.*, XLII, 1948, p. 442).

395b. Id., *Fī sabīl al-tha'r*. A 5-act play in verse. Ḥarīṣā, Maṭb. al-ābā', 1937; 200 pp. (ibid., XLIII, 1949, p. 174).

395c. Id., *al-Khauf min al-dair*. Ḥarīṣā, Maṭb. al-ābā' al-Būlusiyyīn; 40 pp. (ibid., XLII, 1948, p. 442).

395d. Id., *al-Talāqī ba'd al-firāq*. A 3-act play in verse. 1933 (ibid., p. 451).

395e. Nūr, 'Alī, *Shuhadā' al-ikhlāṣ*. A.H. 1322 (ibid., XLIII, 1949, p. 129).

Nūr al-Dīn, Fu'ād, see: List of Ar. Plays, Transl.—Molière.

396. al-Qabbānī, Abū Khalīl, *'Abd al-Salām al-Ḥimṣī* (Dāghir, p. 644).

397. Id., *'Afīfa wa'l-amīr 'Alī* (ibid., p. 645).

398. Id., *al-Amīr 'Alī* (ibid., p. 644).

399. Id., *al-Amīr Maḥmūd wa-zahr al-riyāḍ* (ibid.).

400. Id., *al-Amīr Yaḥyā* (ibid.).

401. Id., *'Āqibat al-ṣiyāna wa-ghā'ilat al-khiyāna* (ibid.).

402. Id., *Asad al-sharā* (ibid.).

403. Id., *Ḥamzah al-muḥtāl*. Prod. in Egypt, 1884, by al-Qabbānī himself (*al-Adīb*, vol. XXVII, Feb., 1955, pp. 18–19).

404. Id., *Ḥiyal al-nisā' al-shahīra bi-Lusiya* (?) (Dāghir, p. 645).

405. Id., *Jamīl wa-Jamīla* (ibid.).

406. Id., *Majnūn Lailā* (ibid., pp. 644, 645).

407. Id., *Nafḥ al-rubā* (ibid., p. 644).

408. Id., *Nākir al-jamīl* (ibid., p. 645, refers appar. to the same play as *Nākirat al-jamīl*).

409. Id., *Riwāyat al-amīr Maḥmūd najl shāh al-'Ajam*. A 5-act semi-hist. play (with music), in lit. Ar. prose & verse. Cairo, al-Maṭb. al-'umūmiyya, A.H. 1318; 39 pp.

410. Id., *Riwāyat 'Antar*. A 4-act hist. play (with music), in lit. Ar. prose & verse about a pre-Islamic poet and warrior. Cairo, al-Maṭb. al-'umūmiyya, A.H. 1318; 48 pp.

411. Id., *Riwāyat Hārūn al-Rashīd ma' al-amīr Ghānim*. A 5-act semi-hist. play (with music), in lit. Ar. prose & verse. Cairo, al-Maṭb. al-'umūmiyya, A.H. 1318; 32 pp.

412. Id., *al-Sulṭān Ḥasan* (Dāghir, p. 645).

413. Id., *al-Shaikh Daḥdāḥ* (ibid.).

414. Id., *al-Shaikh Miṣbāḥ wa-Qūt al-arwāḥ* (ibid. Najm, *al-Masraḥiyya etc.*, p. 116, reads *al-Shaikh Waḍḍāh wa-Miṣbāḥ etc.*).

415. Id., *Uns al-jalīs* (Dāghir. ibid., p. 644).

416. Id., *Wallāda au 'iffat al-muḥibbīn* (ibid., p. 645).

See also: List of Ar. Plays, Transl.—Ghislanzoni; Racine.

417. Qalfāṭ, Nakhla, *Ḍarar al-ḍarratain*. A 4-act play. Cairo, Maṭb. al-islām (*Fihris*, IV, p. 59).

418. Qarāllī, Naṣr Allāh, *Kamāl al-jamāl fī ḥaqā'iq al-aḥwāl*. A 4-act play for schools explaining the physical phenomena (?). Prob. 1897 (*H.*, vol. VI, Dec. 1, 1897, p. 279).

419. Qardāḥī, Yu'ākīm, *'Awāqib al-'ishra al-radī'a*. Haifa (Shaikhū, *Ta'rīkh . . . fī'l-rub' al-awwal etc.*, p. 177).

Qa'wār, Jamāl, see: List of Ar. Plays, Orig. Plays—Ḥaddād, Mīshīl.

Qīqānō, Anṭūn, see: List of Ar. Plays, Transl.—Corneille.

al-Qirabī, Aḥmad 'Uthmān, see: List of Ar. Plays, Transl.—Shakespeare.

Qunṣul, Ilyās, see: List of Ar. Plays, Transl.—Coppée.

419a. Qunṣul, Zakī, *al-Thaura al-sūriyya.* 1936. (*Ma.*, XLII, 1948, p. 453).
al-Qurashī, Muṣṭafā 'Azīz, see: List of Ar. Plays, Transl.—Shakespeare.

420. al-Quṣṭī, Ḥasan, a play whose title is transl. as *Acortezza di mente* by P. Perolari-Malmignati, who saw it produced in Beirut, 1875 (his *Su e giù per la Siria*, pp. 153–160).

421. Rabbāṭ, Anṭūn, *al-Rashīd wa'l-Barāmika.* A 5-act hist. play in lit. Ar. prose and verse, by a Jesuit priest. Beirut, al-Maṭb. al-kāthūlīkiyya, 1910 (*H.*, vol. XIX, Oct. 1, 1910, p. 63. *Ma.*, vol. XXV, 1927, p. 623; *Fihris*, IV, p. 39; *GAL*, S. III, p. 416; ibid., p. 382, however, wrongly defines this an hist. novel. *Ma.*, XLIII, 1949, p. 121, mentions a 2nd ed., 1924; 109 pp.)

422. al-Rāḍī, 'Abd al-Ḥamīd, *Thaurāt al-'arab al-kubrā.* A 3-act drama in lit. Ar. verse, descr. the main events in the life of Ḥusain, Sharif of Mecca. Baghdad, Maṭb. al-Jazīra, 1936 (*GAL*, S. III, pp. 490–491).

422a. Rāḍī, Rashād, *Jamīl Buthaina.* Verse. Cairo, Maṭb. Wādī'l-mulūk; 175 pp. (*Ma.*, XLII, 1948, p. 454).

423. al-Rāfi'ī, Muṣṭafā, *Riwāyat Ḥusām al-Dīn al-Andalusī.* A 6-act semi-hist. play on the glories of the Arabs in Andalusia. Lit. Ar. rhymed prose & verse. 3rd ed. Cairo, Maṭb. al-wā'iẓ, 1905; 96 pp.

423a. al-Rāfi'ī, Sa'īd, *Natījat al-maisir au dhilla fī'l-ḥayāt.* A 6-act play. Prod. in Cairo (*Ma.*, XLIII, 1949, p. 290).

424. al-Rāfi'ī, Taufīq [Sa'īd], *Mamlakat al-shayāṭīn.* A 5-act play about the decline of Muslim power. Cairo (?), prob. 1918 (*H.*, vol. XXVI, Mar. 1, 1918, p. 534).

425. Id., *Maṣra' al-ẓālimīn.* An hist. play in lit. Ar. With an introd., by the author, on theater arts. Cairo, al-Maṭb. al-Jamāliyya, 1910 (*Fihris*, IV, p. 121).

426. Id., *Riwāyat ḍaḥiyyat al-wājib.* A 6-act social drama in lit. Ar. prose, treating of family life and problems. Alex., Gharzūzī, 1913; 128 pp.

427. Id., *Ẓalla fī'l-ḥayāt.* A play, based on a French novel, about the fate of a girl who grows companionlessly, but still finds her way in society when she enters it as an adult. Prob. 1918 (*H.*, vol. XXVII, Nov. 1, 1918, p. 190; *Mu.*, Dec. 1, 1918, p. 599).

428. al-Raḥīmī, Khalīl, *Danishwāi al-ḥamrā'.* An anti-British (?) play. Prod. in Egypt, 1951–2 (*AL*, Nov. 30, 1951, p. 6; *AS*, Dec. 12, 1951, p. 8; *A.*, Jan. 19, 1952, p. 3).

429. al-Raḥmānī, Ḥannā, *Ghufrān al-amīr.* A 4-act hist. drama, in lit. Ar. prose and verse. descr. the wars and intrigues between the Arabian kingdoms of Ghassān and al-Ḥīra, approx. in 491 A.D. 1st ed. in *Ma.* 2nd rev. ed., Beirut, al-Maṭb. al-kāthūlikiyya, 1927; 48 pp. French title: *Le pardon du prince de Ghassan par l'Abbé Jean Rahmani.*
Raḥmī, Maḥmūd, see: List of Ar. Plays, Transl.—Ghislanzoni.

430. Raḥmī, Muḥammad Ḥusnī, *al-Akhras.* A play whose events are set near the Rhone river in 1845. Adapted from the French (?). Cairo, Maṭb. al-iqtiṣād, 1915 (*Fihris*, IV, p. 5).

430a. Ramaḍān, 'Abd al-Ghanī, *al-Riwāya al-adabiyya fī'l-khid'a al-surūjiyya.* A.H. 1284. (*Ma.*, XLIII, 1949, p. 121).

431. Rāmī, Aḥmad, *Gharām al-shu'arā'* (mentioned by Nu'aima in his play, see above No. 394).

432. Id., *Samīrāmīs.* A 4-act tragedy in lit. Ar. prose, descr. the warlike exploits and unhappy love of the great Assyrian queen. Cairo, Mak. al-ahrām, n.d.; 96 pp. (*GAL*, S. III, p. 129).
See also: List of Ar. Plays, Transl.—Rostand.

432a. Ramzī, Ḥasan, *al-Badawiyya* (*Ma.*, XLII, 1948, p. 447 but see No. 437).
432b. Ramzī, Ḥusain, *al-Amīr Salīm* (ibid., p. 443 but see No. 435).
432c. Id., *al-Ḍaḥāyā*. Prod. in Egypt (ibid., XLIII, 1949, p. 131).
432d. Id., *Ṭarīdat al-usra*. Prod. in Egypt (ibid., p. 132).
433. Ramzī, Ibrāhīm, *Abṭāl al-Manṣūra*. Lit. Ar. (*BSOS*, vol. VIII, 1935–1937, p. 998; *GAL*, S. III, p. 276).
434. Id., *Abū Khawandah* (Dāghir, p. 403).
435. Id., *al-Amīr Shalīm* (*GAL*, S. III, p. 276).
436. Id., *'Azza bint al-khalīfa*. Cairo, Maṭb. al-raghā'ib, 1916 (Dāghir, p. 403; *Fihris*, IV, p. 65).
437. Id., *al-Badawiyya*. A play in lit. Ar. descr. the carrying off of a Beduin girl by the Caliph al-Āmir bi-aḥkām Allāh. First prod. in Egypt, 1918. Publ. Cairo, Maṭb. al-sufūr, 1922 (*GAL*, S. III, pp. 276, 1323; *Fihris*, IV, p. 19; *BSOS*, vol. VIII, 1937, p. 998).
438. Id., *Bint al-Ikhshīd*. Cairo, Maṭb. al-ma'ārif (Dāghir, p. 402).
439. Id., *Bint al-yaum* (ibid., p. 403).
440. Id., *Dukhūl el-ḥammām mush zaī khurūguh*. A play in coll. Ar. (of Egypt). First prod., 1917. Publ. Cairo, Maṭb. al-salafiyya, 1924 (*GAL*, S. III, p.276; *BSOS*, vol. VIII, 1937, p. 998).
441. Id., *al-Durra al-yatīma* (Dāghir, p. 403).
442. Id., *al-Fajr al-ṣādiq* (ibid.).
443. Id., *al-Huwārī*. A 1-act opéra comique, with music by Sayyid Darwīsh. Written 1918, prod. same year by Abyaḍ and his troupe. Publ. Cairo, Maṭb. al-sufūr, 1922 (*GAL*, S. III, p. 276; *Fihris*, IV, p. 133).
444. Id., *Ḥanjal Būbū* (*GAL*, ibid.).
445. Id., *Ismā'īl al-Fātiḥ* (Dāghir, p. 403).
446. Id., *Richelieu* (*GAL*, S. III, p. 276. Acc. to Dāghir, p. 403, adapted).
447. Id., *Riwāyat al-Ḥākim bi-amr Allāh*. A play about the famous Fatimid Caliph. Prod. in Egypt. Publ. Cairo, Maṭb. al-shəbāb, 1915 (*GAL*, ibid., pp. 276, 1323; *H.*, vol. XXV, Nov. 1, 1916, p. 176; *Mu.*, vol. LI, July 1, 1917, p. 91; *Fihris*, IV, p. 27. *Ma.*, XLII, 1948, p. 455, mentions a 1917 ed.).
448. Id., *Riwāyat al-Mu'tamid bni 'Ibād*. A play about this unfortunate Spanish Caliph. Cairo, 1891 (*Mu.*, vol. XVI, Apr. 1, 1892, p. 497).
449. Id., *Ṣarkhat al-ṭifl* (Dāghir, p. 403).
450. Id., *'Uqbāl el-ḥabāyeb* (ibid.).
See also: List of Ar. Plays, Transl.—Ibsen; Shakespeare; Shaw.
451. Rāshid, Maḥmūd Khalīl, *Salāma wa-Salmā*. A musical play in lit. Ar., descr. love and rivalry among early Arab poets. 2nd ed., Alex., Maṭb. al-Rashād, 1922 (*GAL*, S. III, p. 277).
452. Rashīdī, Aḥmad Ḥamdī, *Fukāhat al-zamān deh riwāyat hāt lī min de*. A 2-act comedy in coll. Ar. (of Egypt) zajal verse. Cairo, 1907; 80 pp. (ibid., p. 280).
452a. al-Rashīdī, Jirjis Murquṣ, *al-Liqā' al-ma'nūs fī ḥarb al-Basūs*, 1897 (Najm, *al-Masraḥiyya etc.*, pp. 314–315).
453. al-Rifā'ī, Nasīb, *Lan ta'ūdī yā Faransā*. Damascus, 1947 (*K.*, Jan. 1948, p. 191).
454. Rif'at, 'Abd al-Fattāḥ, *Riwāyat al-thaura al-'Urābiyya*. A 5-act hist. play, in lit. Ar. prose & verse, about the 'Urābī (Arabi) revolution of 1879–1882. Cairo, Maṭb. al-hilāl, 1897; 73 pp. (*H.*, vol. V, June 1, 1897, p. 759; cf. ibid., vol. VI, Nov. 15, 1897, p. 230).
455. al-Rīḥānī, Amīn, *Dhikrā'l-Firdausī wafā' al-zamān*. A 2-act hist. drama, in lit.

Ar. prose, treating of Firdausī's literary achievement and nobleness of character. Beirut, Jarīdat al-balāg͟h, 1934; 48 pp. Publ. in commemoration of the millenium of Firdausī's death, the drama was immediately transl. into Persian by Muṣṭafā Ṭabāṭabā'ī.

456. Id., *al-Sujanā' au 'Abd al-Ḥamīd fī Atīnī* (Athens). The author's first drama. Prod. in Beirut, 1909, appar. still in ms. (*GAL*, S. III, pp. 399–400).

457. al-Rīhānī, Najīb, *Kis͟h-kis͟h bek*. A vaudeville play (ibid., p. 281).

458. Id. (?), *Silāḥ al-yaum*. A play about friendship betrayed through an official's intrigues (*KM*, fasc. 8, May, 1946, pp. 704–705).
See also: List of Ar. Plays, Orig. Plays—K͟hairī, Badī' & al-Rīhānī, Najīb.

459. *Riwāyat Ādām wa-Ḥawā'*. A play, appar. in lit. Ar. verse, about the banishment of man from Paradise. Prob. 1903 (*Mu.*, vol. XXVIII, Nov. 1, 1903, p. 972).

460. *Riwāyat Maisalūn*. A play descr. the bloody events in Syria during 1920. Prob. 1946 (*K.*, vol. II, Jan., 1947, p. 487).

461. *Riwāyat Yūsuf al-ṣiddīq*. A 5-act play in lit. Ar. rhymed prose, with verses (esp. Zajals). The contents follow closely the Biblical story, without any hint at Talmudic or Koranic legends (Christian authorship?). Cairo, Muḥammad al-Kutubī, n.d. (prob. 1897); 38 pp. (*H.*, vol. V, Mar. 1, 1897, p. 517; ibid., vol. X, June 1, 1902, p. 548; Sarkīs, *Jāmi'*, I, No. 1177).

462. *Riwāyat al-zawāg bi'l-nabbūt wa'l-bak͟hīl al-'akrūt*. A 1-act farce in coll. Ar. (of Egypt) prose. N.p. (Cairo?), n.d.; 22, 2 pp. (*GAL*, S. III, pp. 280–281, reads *ba'd al-nabbūt wa'l-bak͟hīl al-'akrūt*).

Riyāḍ, Fā'iq, see: List of Ar. Plays, Transl.—Schiller.

al-Riyās͟hī, Iskandar, see: List of Ar. Plays, Transl.—Rostand.

Rizq Allāh, Niqūlā, see: List of Ar. Plays, Transl.—Hugo; Shapespeare.

462a. Rus͟hdī, 'Abd al-Raḥmān, *al-Ma'mūn*. Cairo (*Ma.*, XLIII, 1949, p. 281).

462b. Id., *Taḥt al-'alam*. Cairo (ibid., XLII, 1948, p. 450).
See also: List of Ar. Plays, Transl.—Daudet.

463. Rus͟hdī, Ḥasan, *Ḥisān al-'arabī*. A 6-act play about the customs of the Arab nomads in Nejd. Prob. 1900; 168 pp. (*H.*, vol. IX, Feb. 2, 1901, p. 311).

Rus͟hdī, 'Umar, see: List of Ar. Plays, Transl.—Frondaie.

Rūyāl, Bas͟hīr, see: List of Ar. Plays, Orig. Plays—Muḥī'l-Dīn.

464. Sa'āda, Yūsuf, *Ibnat al-arz*. Beirut, al-Maṭb. al-kāt͟hūlikiyya, 1934; 100 pp. (*GAL*, S. III, p. 419).

464a. al-Sa'ātī, 'Abd al-Raḥmān, *Abṭāl al-Manṣūriyya*. An hist. play. Cairo; 32 pp. (*Ma.*, XLII, 1948, p. 436).

464b. Id., *Haul aswār al-Fusṭāṭ*. Cairo, Dār al-ṭibā'a li'l-ik͟hwān al-muslimīn; 33 pp. (ibid., p. 458).

464c. Id., *al-Mu'izz li-Dīn Allāh*. Prod. in Cairo (ibid., XLIII, 1949, p. 286).

465. Sābā, 'Īsā Mīk͟hā'īl, *Amīrat al-'afāf*. A 4-act drama. Beirut, Mak. al-taufīq, prob. 1924; 60 pp. (*H.*, vol. XXXIII, Feb. 1, 1925, p. 563).

465a. Id., *Hākad͟hā qadat al-aḥwāl*. A 4-act play. Beirut, Maṭb. al-wafā', 1934; 40 pp. (*Ma.*, XLIII, 1949, p. 292).

465b. Id., *Mu'āwiya bnu Marwān bni al-Ḥakam*. A 3-act play. Beirut, 1932 (ibid., p. 286).

465c. Id., *T͟ha'labat al-jāḥid au ittaqi s͟harr man aḥsanta ilaihi*. A 4-act play. Bait S͟habāb, Maṭb. al-'alam, 1921; 48 pp. (ibid., XLII, 1948, p. 452).

465d. Sa'd, Jirjis, *Bulūg͟h al-amal*. Prod. in Alexandria, 1897 (Najm, *al-Masraḥiyya etc.*, p. 179).

Sa'd, Salīm, see: List of Ar. Plays, Transl.—Maugham.
Sa'da, Salīm (same person?), see: List of Ar. Plays, Transl.—Valéry.
Saḥḥār, Na'ūm Fatḥ Allāh, see: List of Ar. Plays, Transl.—Beauvoir.

466. Sa'īd, Aḥmad Khairī, *Bain al-ka's wa'l-ṭa's.* A play in coll. Ar., prod. by Abyaḍ in 1916 (*GAL*, S. III, p. 276).

467. Id., *Issā'.* A play in coll. Ar. (*GAL*, ibid., pp. 276, 1323, reads *Asā*).
Sa'īd, 'Alī, see: List of Ar. Plays, Transl.—Lorca.

467a. Sa'īd, Nuṣrat, *Lūyīs al-sābi' 'ashar.* A 3-act play. Aleppo, 1933 (*Ma.*, XLIII, 1949, p. 280).

468. Sa'īd, Nuṣrat 'Abd al-Karīm, *Maṣra' al-baghī wakhīm.* A 3-act tragedy. Aleppo (?), al-Maṭb. al-mārūniyya, 1929 (ibid., p. 417, based on *RAAD*, vol. IX, 1929, p. 768).

469. Sa'īd, Shukrī, *al-Mīlād al-majīd.* A play intended to be prod. for Christmas 1955 (appar. descr. the birth of Jesus). 1955 (*al-Jihād*, Dec. 25, 1955, p. 3).

469a. Sālim, Aughusṭīn, *Fī wujūb al-ṭā'a li'l-wālidain.* Beirut, Maṭb. Jad'ūn, 1926; 40 pp. (*Ma.*, XLIII, 1949, pp. 274, 294).

469b. Salīm, Fu'ād, *Waḥy Iblīs.* Ḥamāt, Maṭb. al-iṣlāḥ, 1947; 132 pp. (ibid., p. 294).
See also: List of Ar. Plays, Transl.—Sardou.

470. al-Sam'ānī, Būlus, *al-Sarādīb.* A 5-act hist. drama in lit. Ar. prose with a few verses, descr. the religious conflict in Rome, A.D. 389. Jerusalem, Jam'iyyat al-īmān, 1924; 6, 110 pp.
Sanua, James, see: List of Ar. Plays, Orig. Plays—Ṣanū', Ya'qūb.

471. Sārah, Ḥannā, *Riwāyat al-inqilāb al-'uthmānī.* Adapted into a play from Jurjī Zaidān's novel of the same title. Appar. still in ms., written prob. 1911 (*H.*, vol. XX, Jan. 1, 1912, p. 248).
al-Saranjāwī, 'Abd al-Fattāḥ, see: List of Ar. Plays, Transl.—Shakespeare.
Sarāyā, 'Abd al-Ḥamīd, see: List of Ar. Plays, Transl.—Ibsen.
al-Sibā'ī, Muḥammad, see: List of Ar. Plays, Transl.—Shakespeare.

472. al-Sibā'ī, Yūsuf, *Warā' al-sitār.* A 3-act comedy in lit. Ar. prose about the life and adventures of writers, printers and others. N.p., Nādī'l-qiṣṣa—al-kitāb al-dhahabī, Aug., 1952; 167 pp.
Sifīn, Nāshid, see: List of Ar. Plays, Transl.—Shakespeare.

473. Sifta (?), Aḥmad, *Barbarūs* (i.e., Barbarosse) (*BE*, Nov. 1, 1952, p. 3).
See also: List of Ar. Plays, Transl.—Sophocles.

474. al-Sikandarī, Muṣṭafā Shafīq, *Faṣl mizrāb al-hawā.* A 5-scene farce, in lit. Ar. prose & verse, about life in modern Egypt. First prod. in 1898. 2nd ed., N.p., Khurdajī, n.d. (early 20th century); 24 pp.

475. Sirrī, 'Abd al-Qādir, *Khātim al-'aqīq.* Prob. 1895. (*H.*, vol. IV, Dec. 1, 1895, p. 274).

476. Sulaimān, 'Azīz, *Jā'a al-ḥaqq.* A play in coll. Ar. (of Egypt), prod. in 1953 in Muḥammad Najīb's honor by prison inmates (*al-Muṣawwar*, Apr. 24, 1953, pp. 50–51).

477. Surūr, 'Alī, *Yathrib fī intiẓār al-rasūl.* A play in verse. Prob. 1948 (*K.*, vol. IV, Jan., 1949, p. 154).

477a. Ṣa'b, William, *al-Ajniḥa al-mutakassira.* A 5-act play inspired by Jubrān's novel bearing the same title. Beirut, al-Maṭb. al-ḥadītha, 1943; 32 pp. (*Ma.*, XLII, 1948, p. 437).

478. Ṣabrī, Aḥmad, *Kāhin Āmūn masraḥiyya Fir'auniyya.* A 4-act hist. tragedy in lit. Ar. prose. It traces the intrigues of a warlike priest in ancient Egypt against

his peace-loving king, the husband of beautiful Nafartītī. Cairo, Mak. al-nahḍa al-miṣriyya, n.d., prob. 1938; 14, 141 pp. (*GAL*, S. III, p. 280).
Ṣabrī, Ismā'īl, see: List of Ar. Plays, Orig. Plays—Ibrāhīm, Ḥāfiẓ & Ṣabrī, Ismā'īl.

479. Ṣabrī, 'Uṯẖmān, *Sẖabābunā fī Ūrubba*. A 4-act comedy about an Egyptian student who married a French girl against his father's wishes. Cairo, al-Maṭb. al-salafiyya, 1922 (*H.*, vol. XXXII, Dec. 1, 1923, p. 324; *Mu.*, vol. LXV, Jan. 1, 1924, p. 100; *GAL*, S. III, pp. 278–279; Sarkīs, *Jāmi'*, I, No. 1125; *Fihris*, IV, p. 111. *Ma.*, XLIII, 1949, p. 127, says this was publ. 1923; 140 pp.
Ṣādiq, Aḥmad, see: List of Ar. Plays, Orig. Plays—Muḥammad, Aḥmad Ṣādiq.

480. Ṣādiq, Ḥasan, *al-Qiṣaṣ*, vol. I, Appar. a collection of seven (?) plays. Cairo, al-Mak. al-Raḥmāniyya, 1924 (*Fihris*, IV, p. 98).
See also: List of Ar. Plays, Transl.—Schiller.

481. al-Ṣafadī, Muḥī'l-Dīn al-Ḥājj 'Īsā, *Maṣra' Kulaib*. A 5-act hist. drama in lit. Ar. verse. It retells the story of the battles of Kulaib bnu Rabī'a, the poet who lived in the fifth century A.D. Cairo, Maṭb. dār al-kutub al-'arabiyya, 1947; 160 pp. 11 illustr. in text.

481a. Ṣafīr, Buṭrus Faraj, *al-Ibna al-bikr*. An hist. play about King Clovis. Publ. in *Risālat al-salām*, vol. II (*Ma.*, XLII, 1948, p. 437).

481b. Ṣafīr, Ya'qūb, *Fī ẓill rāyat al-arz*. 1918 (ibid., XLIII, 1949, p. 274).

482. al-Ṣagẖīr, 'Alī, *Margarīt*. A play in verse. Prob. 1948 (*K.*, vol. IV, Jan., 1949, p. 163).

482a. Ṣaḥnāwī, Albīr (Albert), *Daḥāyā'l-mujtama'*. A 5-act play. Ḥarīṣā, al-Maṭb. al-Būlusiyya, 1938; 119 pp. (*Ma.*, XLIII, 1949, p. 131).

482b. Ṣaidāwī, Ilyās, *al-Sirr al-maktūm fī'l-ẓālim wa'l-maẓlūm*. 1885 (ibid., p. 125).

482c. al-Ṣā'igẖ, Sulaimān, *al-Amīr al-Ḥamadānī*. A 3-act hist. play. Publ. in *al-Najm* (Mosul), vol. VIII (ibid., XLII, 1948, p. 443).

482d. Id., *al-Ẓabbā'*. Prod. in Mosul (ibid., XLIII, 1949, pp. 122–123).
al-Ṣaiqalī, Iskandar, see: List of Ar. Plays, Transl.—Molière.

483. *al-Ṣalīb wa'l-hilāl*. A love story between Muslims and Copts, banned by the Egyptian censors (*GAL*, S. III, p. 281.)

483a. Ṣalībā, Amīn Ẓāhir Kẖair Allāh, *Urainab bint Isḥāq* (*Ma.*, XLII, 1948, p. 439).

483b. Ṣalībā, Bartolomā'us, *al-Gẖadr al-ḏẖamīm*. A 3-act play. 1911; 77 pp. (ibid., XLIII, 1949, p. 139).

483c. Id., *al-Kẖādim al-ablah*. A comedy. 1932 (ibid., XLII, 1948, p. 459).

483d. Id., *al-Qadr*. A 3-act play. 77 pp. (ibid., XLIII, 1949, p. 275).
Ṣāliḥ, Aḥmad Muḥammad, see: List of Ar. Plays, Transl.—Shakespeare.

484. Ṣāliḥ, Zakī, *Īzīs*. A play, appar. about metempsychosis. Cairo, Maṭb. al-niẓām, prob. 1934 (*Mu.*, vol. LXXXV, Oct. 1, 1934, p. 256).

485. Ṣanū', Ya'qūb (James), *al-Akẖawāt al-latīniyya*. Prose & verse in various languages. Paris, 1905 (Dāgẖir, p. 550).

486. Id., *Ānisa 'alā mōḍa*. Coll. Ar. (?) (ibid.).

487. Id., *al-Barbarī* (ibid.).

488. Id., *al-Būrṣa* (ibid.).

489. Id., *al-Ḍarratān* (ibid. Summarized in Najm, *al-Masraḥiyya etc.*, pp. 86–87).

490. Id., *Fāṭima*. A 3-act comedy, first written in Italian by Ṣ., 1869–1870, then transl. by him into Ar. and French (Dāgẖir, ibid., p. 551).

491. Id., *Gẖandūr Miṣr* (ibid.).

492. Id., *Gẖazwat Ra's Tōr*. A satire on betting (ibid. Last word means "oxhead"?).

493. Id., *al-Ḥashshāsh* (ibid., p. 550).
494. Id., *Mulyīr Miṣr wa-mā yuqāsih.* A comedy in coll. Ar. (of Egypt) about the joys and troubles of a theater director. Publ. Beirut, al-Maṭb. al-adabiyya, 1912 (*GAL*, S. III, p. 265; *Fihris*, IV, p. 127; *JJS*, vol. III, 1952, pp. 32–33).
495. Id., *Rāstōr wa-shaikh al-balad* (Dāghir, p. 551. For first word, see above, play No. 492).
496. Id., *al-Salāsil al-muḥaṭṭama.* A pro-Turkish drama. Paris, 1911 (ibid., p. 550).
497. Id., *al-Ṣadāqa* (ibid.).
498. Id., *Shaikh al-balad* (ibid.).
499. Id., *al-Waṭan wa'l-ḥurriyya* (ibid., p. 551).
500. Id., *Zaujat al-ab.* A satire on old men who marry young girls (ibid., p. 550).
501. Id., *Zubaida.* A satire on the imitation of Western women by the Oriental girls (ibid.).
501a. Ṣaqqāl, Jūrj, *Mār Ifrām.* Prod. in Lebanon, 1900 (*Ma.*, XLIII, 1949, p. 280).
Ṣawāyā, Jūrj, see: List of Ar. Plays, Transl.—Daudet.
502. Ṣidqī, Amīn, *Ḥimār wa-ḥalāwa.* A farce starring Najīb al-Rīḥānī (Worrell, in the *Muslim World*, vol. X, 1920, p. 136, reads *Ḥamār etc.*, transl. by him as "red cheeks").
Ṣubḥī, Ibrāhīm, see: List of Ar. Plays, Transl.—Molière.
502a. Shābbī, 'Abd Allāh Aḥmad, *Ḥayāt 'Umar bni al-Khaṭṭāb awwal ḥākim dīmuqrāṭī fī'l-islām.* Tripoli, Maṭb. jam'iyyat is'āf al-muḥtājīn, A.H. 1344; 36 pp. (*Ma.*, XLII, 1948, p. 458).
503. Shafīq, Muḥammad, *Faṣl al-bakhīl.* A farce (*GAL*, S. III, p. 281).
503a. Shāhīn, Ḥanna Khūrī, *Jazā' al-faḍīla.* Beirut, al-Maṭb. al-amīrikiyya, 1930; 71 pp. (*Ma.*, XLII, 1948, p. 454).
503b. Shāhīn, Muḥammad 'Alī 'Afīfī, *Ḍiyā'*, Cairo, 1929; 55 pp. (ibid., XLIII, 1949, p. 131).
503c. Shaḥḥāda, 'Abd Allāh, *Buthaina wa-Jamīl* (ibid., XLII, 1948, p. 446).
503d. Shaḥḥāda, Salīm, & al-Khūrī, Salīm, *Umarā' Lubnān.* Prod. 1870 (Najm, *al-Masraḥiyya*, etc., p. 55).
503e. Shalfūn, Buṭrus, *'Ajā'ib al-qadr.* Prod. in Cairo, approx. 1888 (ibid., p. 185).
504. Shalfūn, Iskandar, *Ma'bad al-nīrān.* A play, prob. adapted from the French. Publ. in the author's magazine *Rauḍat al-Balābil* (?) (Dāghir, p. 492).
505. Id., *al-Sabāyā.* A musical play, in prose & verse, about ancient Rome. Cairo, Maṭb. Ra'amsīs, 1912 (*Mu.*, vol. LXIII, Aug. 1, 1923, p. 188; *H.*, vol. XXXII, Dec. 1, 1923, p. 325; *Fihris*, IV, p. 46. *GAL*, S. III, p. 1322, wrongly reads author's name as Shaffūn. *Ma.*, XLIII, 1949, pp. 124–125, mentions a 1923 ed.
Shalhūb, Buṭrus, see: List of Ar. Plays, Transl.—Bisson.
505a. Shammās, Ḥabīb, *al-Ḥajjāj bnu Yūsuf.* Ḥarīṣā, Maṭb. al-Qiddīs Būlus (*Ma.*, XLII, 1948, p. 456).
505b. Id., *Kisrā wa'l-'arab.* Prod. in Beirut, 1899 (ibid., XLIII, 1949, p. 277).
506. Sharaf al-Dīn, Muḥammad al-Riḍā, *al-Ḥusain 'alaih al-salām.* An 8-act hist. play, in lit. Ar. verse, treating of the last days of Ḥusain ibn 'Alī. Baghdad, Maṭb. al-najāḥ, 1933; XII, 240 pp. (*H.*, vol. XLII, Jan. 1, 1934, p. 378).
507. *al-Sharaf al-yābānī.* Prod. by the Egyptian troupe in Egypt, 1948 (*A.*, Oct. 26, 1948, p. 6).
508. *Shāri' al-bahlawān raqm 777.* A vaudeville, directed by Zakī Ṭulaimāt and prod. by the Egyptian troupe at the Opera House in Cairo, 1944 (*Mu.*, vol. CVI, Jan. 1, 1945, pp. 74–75).

509. S̲harīf, Ṭāhir 'Alī, *Badī'*. A 3-act tragedy (melodrama?) about the vices of alcoholism. First prod. in Alger, 1924 (*Revue Africaine*, vol. LXXVII, 1935, p. 74).
510. Id., *K̲hadī'at al-g̲harām*. A 4-act tragedy (continuation of No. 511, below). First prod. in Alger, 1923 (ibid.).
511. Id., *al-S̲hifā' ba'd al-'anā'*. A 1-act play in lit. Ar. prose, with songs. Treats of the agonies of a drunkard. First prod. in Alger, 1921 (ibid.).
512. S̲harqī, Jurjī, *al-'Iẓa*. A 5-act play. Tanta, Maṭb. al-s̲ha'b, 1932 (*H.*, vol. XLI, May 1, 1933, p. 990; *GAL*, S. III, p. 280).
S̲hā'ūl, Anwar, see: List of Ar. Plays, Transl.—Schiller.
513. S̲hauqī, Aḥmad, *'Alī bek al-kabīr au daulat al-mamālīk*. A 3-act hist. drama, in lit. Ar. verse, about early 18th century Egypt. 1st ed., Cairo, Maṭb. al-Muhandis, A. H. 1311 (1894). 2nd ed., Cairo, Maṭb. Miṣr, 1932; 3, 174 pp. Prod. in Egypt since 1932 (*Mu.*, vol. XVIII, Mar. 1, 1894, p. 420; *Fihris*, IV, p. 67; *GAL*, S. III, pp. 43–44).
514. Id., *Amīrat al-Andalus*. A 5-act hist. drama, in lit. Ar. prose, about the last Caliphs in Spain. Cairo (?), Dār al-kutub al-miṣriyya, 1932; 157 pp. Often prod. (*H.*, vol. XLI, Dec. 1, 1932, pp. 265–266; *GAL*, S. III, p. 47).
515. Id., *'Antara*. A 4-act hist. drama in lit. Ar. verse, retelling the story of this pre-Islamic fighter and poet. Cairo (?), Dār al-kutub al-miṣriyya, 1932; 139 pp. Some extracts repr. in *Apōllō*, Dec., 1932, pp. 346–350 (*GAL*, ibid.).
516. Id., *al-Bak̲hīla*. A drama, appar. in ms. (?) (ibid.).
517. Id., *Majnūn Lailā*. A 5-act tragedy, in lit. Ar. verse, descr. the unhappy love of an early Arab poet. 1st ed., Cairo, 1916; 4, 153 pp. 2nd ed., Cairo (?), Maṭb. Miṣr, 1931; 4, 153 pp. (*H.*, vol. XXXIX, Mar. 1, 1931, pp. 776–777; *GAL*, S. III, p. 44). Transl. into English by Prof. A. J. Arberry, Cairo, Lencioni, 1933; 61 pp.
518. Id., *Maṣra' Kliyūpātrā*. A 4-act tragedy in lit. Ar. verse, descr. Cleopatra's fall and tragic end. Cairo (?), Maṭb. Miṣr, 1929; 5, 151 pp. Repr. by Maṭb. al-istiqāma and Maṭb. al-ma'ārif (*H.*, vol. XXXVII, Aug. 1, 1929, p. 1265; *GAL*, S. III, pp. 44–45). Often prod. (*al-Balāg̲h al-usbū'ī*, Jan. 8, 1930, p. 21; *RY*, Apr. 24, 1947, p. 26). Appar. transl. into English by Mrs. Ruskin (N. Barbour, in *Dunyā'l-fann*, Nov. 19, 1946, p. 19).
519. Id., *Qambīz*. A 3-act tragedy, in lit. Ar. verse, descr. Cambyses' rule and misdeeds in Egypt. Cairo (?), Maṭb. Miṣr, 1931; 4, 160 pp. (*GAL*, S. III, pp. 45–47).
520. Id., *al-Sitt Hudā*. A comedy in lit. Ar. verse, appar. still in ms. Partly publ. in *H.*, vol. XLV, Dec. 1, 1936, pp. 157–164. Prepared for broadcasting in 1952 (*al-Nidā'*, June 23, 1952, p. 8; cf. *AJ*, June 20, 1952, p. 8. *GAL*, S. III, p. 47, wrongly reads *Alasta hudā*, while Buṭrūs al-Bustānī, *Udabā' al-'arab fī'l-Andalus wa-'aṣr al-inbi'āt̲h*, p. 213, reads *al-Sayyida Hudā*).
521. S̲hawā, Zuhair, *Jais̲hunā'l-sūrī*. Prob. 1945 (*K.*, vol. I, Jan. 1946, p. 407).
522. Id., *Labaiki Filasṭīn*. An anti-Zionist play. Damascus, 1947 (ibid., vol. III, Jan., 1948, p. 191).
523. *al-S̲hyāṭīn al-sūd*. Prod. in Egypt by the Ramses troupe.
524. S̲hiftāsī, Fransīs, *Ibnat al-s̲hams*. A play about ancient Egypt; it won the second prize in the playwriting competition of the Ministry of education in 1932, but appar. was never prod. Publ. Cairo, al-Maṭb. al-amīriyya, prob. 1934; 165 pp. (*GAL*, S. III, p. 274. *H.*, vol. XLII, June 1, 1934, pp. 1017–1018, which reads author's name as Siftas̲hī).

524a. al-Shimālī, Estefān, *Yūsuf al-Ḥasan bnu Ya'qūb*. Prod. in Lebanon, 1869 (*Ma.*, XLIII, 1949, p. 296).

Shihāb, Fakhrī, see: List of Ar. Plays, Transl.—Tagore.

524b. Shuḥaibar, Anṭūn, *Intiṣār al-faḍīla au ḥāditḥat al-ibna al-isrā'īliyya*. Prod. 1879 (Najm, *al-Masraḥiyya etc.*, p. 52).

525. Shukrī, 'Abd al-Raḥmān, *al-Ḥallāq al-majnūn*. A drama about a psychopathic barber, who cuts a customer's neck with his razor, believing that he has a mutton head before him (*GAL*, S. III, p. 126).

526. Shukrī, Maḥmūd, *Riwāyat makārim al-akhlāq*. Cairo, 1929 (ibid., p. 280).

527. Id., *al-Ṣadīq al-waḥīd*. A social drama about an unfortunate girl, cast alone in a strange land. Cairo, Maṭb. al-Jamāliyya, 1917 (*Fihris*, IV, p. 56).

527a. Shukrī, Muḥammad, *'Uthmān fī'l-Hind*. Prod. by 'Alī'l-Kassār in Alexandria (*Ma.*, XLIII, 1949, p. 134).

528. Shumayyil, Amīn, *al-Ẓifāf al-siyāsī*. A semi-symbolical drama about politics during the Russo-Turkish war of 1877 (Dāghir, p. 495).

529. Shumayyil, Shiblī, *al-Ma'sāt al-kubrā*. A 5-act play about the First World War. First publ. in *al-Baṣīr*, 1915. Repr. prob. 1915; 115 pp. (*Mu.*, vol. XLVIII, Feb. 1, 1916, p. 194). Transl. into French by playwright's nephew, Mariyūs Shumail, prob. in 1917 (cf. ibid., vol. LII, Feb. 1, 1918, p. 134).

529a. Shuqair, Shākir, *al-'Āshiq al-mastūr*. Beirut, Mak. Ṣādir (*Ma.*, XLIII, 1949, p. 133).

529b. Id., *Burqu' al-hawā* (ibid., XLII, 1948, p. 447).

529c. Id., *Siḥr al-'uyūn* (ibid., XLIII, 1949, p. 125).

529d. Id., *al-Summ fī'l-dasam*. Beirut, Mak. Ṣādir (ibid., p. 126).

529e. Id., *Sūsān*. Beirut, Mak. Ṣādir (ibid, p. 127).

530. Shuqair, Shākir Mughāmis, *al- 'Aila al-muhadhdhaba*. Prod. in a Lebanese girls' school, 1872 (Dāghir, p. 490).

530a. al-Shuwairī, Dā'ud Mar'ī, *Afkār fī'l-jaḥīm fī'l-zamān al-qadīm*. A religious educational play. 1897. (Najm, *al-Masraḥiyya etc.*, p. 384).

531. Taimūr, 'Ā'isha 'Iṣmet, *Riwāyat al-liqā' ba'd al-shaqā'*. A play about the love adventures of Caliph al-Manṣūr's son.

532. Taimūr, Maḥmūd, *Abū Shūsha*. A 1-act social drama about the Egyptian village. 1st ed., in coll. Ar. (of Egypt) prose, Cairo, Majallat al-ḥawādith, 1941; 2nd ed., in lit. Ar. prose, Damascus, Maṭb. al-taraqqī, 1943; together with No. 542, below; pp. 15–66. Introd. by Zakī Ṭulaimāt, pp. 4–14 (*Mu.*, vol. CIV, Mar. 1, 1944, p. 300).

533. Id., *'Arūs al-Nīl*. A 3-act musical play, in coll. Ar. (of Egypt) prose, telling the story of a Pharaoh who cheated the Nile of its yearly bride, by substituting a statue for his sister. Cairo, Muḥammad Ḥamdī, 1941; 76 pp. Prod. in Egypt, 1942 (*Mu.*, vol. C, Mar. 1, 1942, pp. 302–303).

533a. Id., *Ashtar min iblīs*. 1953. (*Muslim World*, vol. XLVII, Jan. 1957, p. 42).

534. Id., *'Awālī*. A 3-act drama in lit. Ar. prose, telling the story of a brave Arab woman in some past age, who hunts with the men and is determined to choose her husband by herself, even if she has to refuse the Caliph's proposal. Cairo, al-Mak. al-tijāriyya al-kubrā, 1942; 149 pp. (*Mu.*, vol. CI, Nov. 1, 1942, pp. 441–443).

535. Id., *Fidā'* (mentioned in playwright's No. 538, below).

536. Id., *Ḥaflat shāi*. A 1-act comedy in lit. Ar. prose. A satire of the emptiness of French-inspired snobbery. Cairo, Dār al-kutub al-ahliyya, 1943; together with No. 543, below; pp. 85–151 (*Mu.*, vol. CIII, June 1, 1943, pp. 102–103).

537. Id., *Ḥawwā' al-khālida.* A 6-act hist. play, in lit. Ar. prose, descr. the love of 'Antar and 'Abla. Cairo, Dār Sa'd Miṣr li'l-ṭibā'a wa'l-nashr, 1945; 174 pp. First prod. in 1946 (*KM*, fasc. 15, Dec. 1946, pp. 543–544; *K.*, vol. II, Jan. 1947, p. 465, and July, 1947, pp. 1418–1419; *RC*, Feb., 1953, p. 181).

538. Id., *Ibn Jalā.* Traces the story of the able fighter and governor al-Ḥajjāj. Cairo, Dār al-ma'ārif, 1951; 270, 1 pp. (*OM*, vol. XXXI, July–Sep., 1951, p. 156).

539. Id., *al-Infijār qiṭ'a tamthīliyya li'l-qirā'a.* A 1-scene pièce, intended for reading, not acting (fear of offending the morals?). It descr. the flirt of a girl and boy in the cinema and in a taxi. Publ. in Taimūr's *al-Ḥājj Shalabī wa-qiṣaṣ ukhrā*, Cairo, Maṭb. al-i'timād, 1930; pp. 229–237.

540. Id., *Kidb fī kidb.* A social comedy in coll. Ar. (of Egypt) prose, about the results of a forced falsehood. Prod. in Egypt, 1952, under Zakī Ṭulaimāt's direction (*A.*, Apr. 4, 1952, p. 5; *al-Nidā'*, Apr. 8, 1952, p. 6; *K.*, vol. VII, June, 1952, p. 753).

541. Id., *al-Makhba' raqm 13.* A 3-act comedy in coll. Ar. (of Egypt) prose. Descr. the emotions and reactions of a set of men and women, of different social standing, when trapped together in an air-raid shelter. Cairo, Majallat al-ḥawādith, 1941; 141 pp. (*Mu.*, vol. C, Jan. 1, 1942, pp. 106–108, and Mar. 1, 1942, pp. 300–301). Appar. was publ. in lit. Ar. as well, acc. to No. 547, below, p. 271.

542. Id., *al-Maukib.* A 1-act comedy about a family from the countryside, who had settled in Cairo. 1st ed., in coll. Ar. prose (of Egypt), Cairo, Majallat al-ḥawādith, 1941. 2nd ed., in lit. Ar. prose, Damascus, Maṭb. al-taraqqī, 1943, together with No. 532, above; pp. 67–104 (*Mu.*, vol. CIV, Mar. 1, 1944, p. 300).

543. Id., *al-Munqidha.* A 1-act drama of love and war in Mamluk Egypt. Prod. 1942, in coll. Ar. (of Egypt), then publ. in lit. Ar. prose, Cairo, Dār al-kutub al-ahliyya, 1943, together with No. 536, above; pp. 7–83 (ibid., vol. CIII, June 1, 1943, pp. 102–103; *K.*, vol. IV, Mar., 1949, p. 477).

544. Id., *Qanābil.* A 3-act comedy in lit. Ar. prose, descr. some town-dwellers who flee to the countryside during the war, but fall into trouble there too. Cairo, Lajnat al-nashr li'l-jāmi'iyyīn, 1943; 189 pp. (*Mu.*, vol. CIV, Feb. 1, 1944, pp. 196–197).

545. Id., *Suhād au al-laḥn al-tā'ih.* A 3-act hist. play, in lit. Ar. prose. Tells the story of an unsuccessful suitor—in the early days of Islam—who changes from a musician into a warrior. [Cairo], Mak. 'Īsā'l-Bābī'l-Ḥalabī, 1942; 116, 4 pp. (ibid., vol. CII, Jan. 1, 1943, pp. 105–106).

546. Id., *al-Ṣu'lūk.* A 1-act play, in coll. Ar. (of Egypt) prose, about a gold-digging, luxury-loving lady. Cairo, Majallat al-ḥawādith, prob. 1941 (*Mu.*, vol. XCIX, Nov. 1, 1941, pp. 417–418). Prod. in Egypt, 1949 (*K.*, vol. IV, Mar., 1949, p. 477).

546a. Id., *Shafāh ghalīẓa.* Cairo, 1946 (*Ma.*, XLIII, 1949, p. 128).

547. Id., *al-Yaum khamr.* A 6-act hist. play in lit. Ar. prose, retelling the adventures and loves of the early Arab poet Imru' al-Qais, in the desert of the Ar. Peninsula and in Constantinople. Cairo, Dār al-ma'ārif, 1949; 270, 1 pp. (*RC*, Feb., 1953, pp. 190–195).

548. Taimūr, Muḥammad, *al-Hāwiya.* A 4-act comedy in coll. Ar. (of Egypt) prose. This is a social satire on the drug addict who is prepared to sell his honor and his property. First prod. 1921, then publ. in playwright's *Mu'alla-*

fāt, vol. II, Cairo, Maṭb. al-i'timād, 1922; pp. 331–451 (*GAL*, S. III, pp. 272–273; *Fihris*, IV, p. 34).

549. Id., *Riwāyat 'Abd al-Sattār Efendī*. A 4-act comedy in coll. Ar. (of Egypt) prose. Descr. skillfully a middle-class Egyptian family, in the throes of double intrigue, making and unmaking marriage plans. First prod. 1918, then publ. in playwright's *Mu'allafāt*, vol. III, Cairo, al-Maṭb. al-salafiyya, A. H. 1341 (*GAL*, ibid., p. 272; *Fihris*, IV, p. 120).

550. Id., *Riwāyat al-'iṣhra al-ṭayyiba*. A 4-act opéra bouffe, in coll. Ar. (of Egypt) prose & verse. This is the story of an aristocratic girl educated in the countryside, in the Mamluk period. Inspired from *Bluebeard*. First prod. in 1920, then publ. ibid. (*Fihris*, ibid. *GAL*, S. III, p. 172, reads '*aṣhara*. See also *BSOS*, vol. VIII, 1937, p. 996).

551. Id., *Riwāyat al-'uṣfūr fī'l-qafaṣ*. A 4-act comedy, first written in coll. Ar. (of Egypt), then rewritten and publ, in lit. Ar. It traces the story of a youth who falls in love with a French *bonne*, thus defying the authority of his domineering father. First prod. in 1918, then publ. ibid., pp. 1–254 (*Fihris*, ibid.; *GAL*, ibid., p. 271).
See also: List of Ar. Plays, Transl.—Aicard.

552. Taqī'l-Dīn, Aḥmad, *al-Ghurūr*. A 4-act drama. Damascus, Maṭb. al-i'tidāl, prob. 1932; 94 pp. (*H.*, vol. XLI, Dec. 1, 1932, p. 269).

553. Id., *Laqīṭ al-ṣaḥrā'*. A drama, Prob. 1932 (ibid., p. 270).

554. Taqī'l-Dīn, Sa'īd, *Ḥafnat rīḥ*. A 1-act comedy. Beirut, Dār al-'ilm li'l-malāyīn, prob. 1947 (*KM*, fasc. 29, Feb., 1948, p. 154; *K.*, vol. IV, Jan., 1949, p. 158).

555. Id., *Laulā' l-muḥāmī*. A play descr. Syrian society during the First World War. Introd. by Khalīl Muṭrān. Beirut, 1924 (*H.*, vol. XXXIII, Apr. 1, 1925, p. 787; *GAL*, S. III, p. 416, based upon *Ma.*, vol. XXXIII, p. 236).

555a. Id., *Nakhb al-'aduww*. A 3-act play. Beirut, Mak. al-Kashshāf, 1947 (*Ma.*, XLIII, 1949, p. 290.)
Taqlā, Salīm, see: List of Ar. Plays, Transl.—Racine.

556. Taufīq, Aḥmad, *Riwāyat shams al-dunyā*. A 5-act drama in lit. Ar. prose & verse. Cairo, al-Maṭb. al-sharafiyya, n.d.; 59 pp.
Taufīq, Muḥammad, see above: Fahmī, Muḥammad.

557. al-Tūnisī, Bairam & Khairī, Badī', *al-'Ishra al-ṭayyiba*. A drama, with music by Sayyid Darwīsh. Prod. in Egypt, 1946–7 (*K.*, vol. II, July 1947, pp. 1420–1421). Was this influenced by Muḥammad Taimūr's opéra bouffe (above, No. 550)?
al-Tūnisī, Maḥmūd Bairam, see: List of Ar. Plays, Transl.—Knochblauch.
Ṭabāṭabā'ī, Muṣṭafā, see: List of Ar. Plays, Orig. Plays—al-Rīḥānī, Amīn.

557a. al-Ṭabīb, Ibrāhīm, *il-Juhalā' il-mudda'īn bi'l-'ilm au hāt il-kāwī yā Sa'īd*. A 3-act comedy in coll. Ar. Beirut, al-Maṭb. al-'ilmiyya, 1897 (*Ma.*, XLII, 1948, p. 455. Najm, *al-Masraḥiyya etc.*, p. 435, gives 1884 as date of publ.).

558. Ṭaha, 'Alī Maḥmūd, *Arwāḥ wa-ashbāḥ*. A pot-pourri of dramatic dialogues, in lit. Ar. verse, between Thais and others. Cairo, Shirkat fann al-ṭibā'a, 1942; 86 pp., plates.

558a. Id., *Ughniyat al-arwāḥ al-arba'*. Cairo, 'Īsā'l-Bābī'l-Ḥalabī, 132 pp. (*Ma.*, XLII, 1948, p. 440).
al-Ṭahar, 'Alī Sharīf, see: List of Ar. Plays, Orig. Plays—Sharīf, Ṭāhir 'Alī.

558b. Ṭal'at, Munīr, *al-Maghfara au al-gharām al-muzayyaf*. Alexandria, Maṭb. al-salām; 55 pp. (*Ma.*, XLIII, 1949, p. 286).

559. Ṭal'at, Munīra, *Ḍaḥāyā'l-shaqā'*. Alexandria (?), prob. 1932; 48 pp. (*H.*, vol. XLI, Dec. 1, 1932, p. 270).

560. Id., *Riwāyat al-bā'isa.* A 5-act drama about social conditions in Egypt. Alex., Maṭb. al-mustaqbal, prob. 1930; 54 pp. (ibid., vol. XXXIX, Feb. 1, 1931, p. 621).
561. Ṭannūs, Yuḥannā Ṭūbī, *al-'Imrān.* A play about pre-Islamic times (*Ma.*, vol. XXV, 1927, p. 623. *GAL*, S. III, p. 416, reads *al-'Amrānī*).
562. Id., *al-Baṭriyark Jibrā'īl Ḥajjūlā'l-s̱hahīd.* Beirut, 1923; 66 pp. (S̱haik̲h̲ū, *Ta'rīk̲h̲ . . .fī'l-rub' al-awwal etc.*, p. 143).
563. Id., *Dāḥis wa'l-G̱habrā'.* A play set in pre-Islamic times (*Ma.*, vol. XXV, 1927, p. 623; *GAL*, S. III, p. 416).
564. Id., *Kulaib wa'l-Muhalhil.* A play set in pre-Islamic times (*Ma.*, ibid.; *GAL*, ibid.).
565. Id., *al-Nu'mān malik al-Ḥīra fī S̱haibān.* A 4-act play. Beirut, Maṭb. al-ittiḥād, 1924 (*Ma.*, ibid., and vol. XXXIII, 1935, p. 315; *GAL*, ibid.; Sarkīs, *Jāmi'*, I, No. 1166).
565a. Ṭarzāwī, Martīnūs Ilyās, *al-Fidā'.* 1931 (*Ma.*, XLIII, 1949, p. 273).
Ṭrād, Najīb Nasīm, see: List of Ar. Plays, Transl.—Schiller.
566. al-Ṭūbī, Asmā, *Maṣra' qaiṣar Rūsiya wa-'ā'ilatih.* A 5-act tragedy. Acre, al-Maṭb. al-waṭaniyya, 1925; 68 pp. (*GAL*, ibid., p. 417; Sarkīs, *Jāmi'*, I, No. 1164, II, No. 216; *H.*, vol. XXXIV, Feb. 1, 1926, p. 549).
567. Ṭūrī, Muḥammad & 'Ammārī, *Ak̲h̲ā Mezeg̲h̲īs̲h̲* (?) (*BE*, Nov. 1, 1952, p. 3).
568. Ṭuwair, 'Abd Allāh, *Wāqi'at al-Barāmika.* An hist. drama in lit. Ar. about the fall of the Barmakids. Cairo, Maṭb. Būlāq, A.H. 1307 (*Fihris*, IV, p. 134).
569. al-Ṭuwairānī (?), Ḥasan Ḥusnī, *Fihrist al-inqilāb.* An unfinished hist. drama in lit. Ar. prose & verse, treating of the intricate intrigues of the anti-Turkish Arab nationalists. British Mus., Ms. Or. 9018. Prob. late 19th century, 60 leaves, all written on one side, except one written on both sides (for the author, whose name is given only as Ḥasan Ḥusnī, cf. *GAL*, S. III, pp. 83–84, 228; Sarkīs, *Mu'jam*, pp. 1253–1254).
570. Id., *Mudhis̲h̲āt al-qadr* (Dāg̲h̲ir, p. 581).
571. T̲h̲., A., *Abū Muslim al-K̲h̲urasānī.* A 3-act hist. tragedy, in prose & verse. Haifa, al-Zahra, prob. 1923 (*H.*, vol. XXXI, Apr. 1, 1923, p. 779; *Mu.*, vol. LXIII, July 1, 1923, p. 92).
T̲h̲ābit, Ḥasan, see: List of Ar. Plays, Transl.—Bernstein.
T̲h̲ābit, Louis G̲h̲annām, see: List of Ar. Plays, Transl.—Shakespeare.
T̲h̲ābit, Maḥmūd Luṭfī, see: List of Ar. Plays, Transl.—Shakespeare.
572. 'Ubaid, Bis̲h̲āra & Laḥūd, Adīb, *Lubnān 'alā'l-masraḥ* (S̱haik̲h̲ū, *Ta'rīk̲h̲ . . . fī'l-rub' al-awwal etc.*, p. 175; ibid., p. 178, mentions the same play as *Lubnān 'alā'l-masāriḥ*).
573. al-'Ums̲h̲ailī, Yūsuf, *al-Amīrān al-asīrān.* A 3-act psuedo-hist. drama, in lit. Ar. prose & verse, adapted from French sources for presentation in Catholic schools. First publ. in *Ma.*, then Beirut, al-Maṭb. al-kāt̲h̲ūlīkiyya, 1927; 57 pp. (*Ma.*, XLII, 1948, p. 443, reads author's name al-'Ums̲h̲aiṭī).
573a. 'Urfī, Widād, *al-Imbirāṭūr G̱hilyūm* (*Ma.*, XLII, 1948, p. 442).
573b. Id., *Maḥmūd al-fātiḥ* (ibid.).
573c. Id., *al-Sulṭān 'Abd al-Ḥamīd* (ibid.).
Victor, see: List of Ar. Plays, Orig. Plays—Fīktōr.
574. Wahbī, Ismā'īl, *al-'Arā'is.* A musical play inspired by P. Wolf (*GAL*, S. III, p. 271).
575. Id., *al-D̲h̲ahab.* An adaptation .Prod., with Yūsuf Wahbī in the lead, at the Cairo Opera House, 1951–2 (*AY*, Nov. 24, 1951, p. 6; *A.*, Feb. 14, 1952, p. 3).

576. Wahbī, Muḥammad Taufīq, *Hāḏẖā janā' abī* (*al-Muṣawwar*, Mar. 5, 1954, p. 28).
577. Id., *al-Tauba al-ṣādiqa* (ibid.).
578. Id., *Widād* (ibid.).
578a.Wahbī, Tādrus, *Buṭrus al-akbar*. Cairo, 1884 (Najm, *al-Masraḥiyya etc.*, p. 185).
579. Wahbī, Yūsuf, *Asrār al-quṣūr*. Prod. in Egypt in 1951–2, by the Egyptian troupe (*AΥ*, Dec. 29, 1951, p. 9; *A.*, Dec. 29, 1951, p. 3; ibid., Jan. 3, 1952 p. 3).
579a.Id., *Aulād al-ḏẖawāt*. Coll. Ar. Prod. in Egypt (*Ma.*, XLII, 1948, p. 445).
580. Id., *Aulād al-fuqarā'*. A melodrama in coll. Ar. (of Egypt) about Egyptian seducers, drug addicts and prostitutes (*BSOS*, vol. VIII, 1937, pp. 996–997).
580a.Id., *Aulād al-sẖawāri'*. Prod. in Egypt (*Ma.*, XLII, 1948, p. 445).
581. Id., *Ayyām al-ḥarb*, appar. a comedy. Prod. in Egypt in 1952 by the Egyptian troupe (*A.*, Apr. 28, 1952, p. 5).
582. Id., *Ayyām zamān*. A drama presented by the New Egyptian troupe (*Tournée officielle de la nouvelle troupe égyptienne sous la direction de Youssef Wahbi*).
583. Id., *Banāt al-rīf*. A 4-act drama. Presented by the same troupe (ibid.).
584. Id., *Bayūmī Efendī*. A 4-act play. Presented by the same troupe (ibid.).
585. Id., *Ḥadaṯẖa ḏẖāta yaum*. A 3-act play. Presented by the same troupe (ibid.).
586. Id., *Kursī'l-i'tirāf*. A 4-act play. Presented by the same troupe (ibid.).
587. Id., *al-Mā'ida al-ẖaḍrā'*. A 4-act social drama. Presented by the same troupe (ibid).
588. Id., *al-Majnūn*. Based on two French plays—*Le système du docteur Goudron et du Professeur Plume* and *Au téléphone*. Wahbī's first play, with which the Ramses troupe started its career (*RC*, vol. III, 1940, p. 109).
589. Id., *Nasībtī muṣībtī*. A 3-act comedy, prob. adapted. Coll. Ar. (?). Presented by the New Egyptian troupe (*Tournée officielle etc.*).
590. Id., *Qalb kabīr*. A 3-act social drama. Presented by the same troupe (ibid.).
591. Id., *Ragel el-sā'a*. A play in coll. Ar. (?). Presented by the same troupe (ibid.).
592. Id., *Rāsbūtīn*. A 4-act hist. drama about the Russian courtier. Partly adapted. Presented by the same troupe (ibid.).
593. Id., *70 sana*. A revue in 15 scenes, tracing the course of modern Egyptian history. Prod. in Egypt, 1952 (*M.*, Jan. 17, 1952).
594. Id., *al-Ṣaḥrā'*.
595. Id., *al-Sẖahīda*. A 3-act melodrama. Presented by the New Egyptian troupe (*Tournée officielle etc.*).
Wākīm, Bisẖāra, see: List of Ar. Plays, Transl.—Richepin.
596. Wanīsẖ, Muḥammad, *Munīb*. A 3-act play (*BE*, Nov. 1, 1952, p. 3).
597. Wāṣif, Maḥmūd, *'Ajā'ib al-aqdār*. A 5-act semi-hist. play, in lit. Ar. prose & verse, about the Persian Wars. Cairo, Maṭb. Turk, n.d.; 78 pp.
598. Id., *Riwāyat Hārūn al-Rasẖīd wa-Qūṭ al-qulūb wa-ẖalīfat al-ṣayyād*. A 5-act musical play in lit. Ar. prose (rhymed, sometimes), grouping together various characters from popular legend. Cairo, al-Mak. al-Azhariyya, A.H. 1318; 48 pp.
599. Id., *Riwāyat maḥāsin al-ṣudaf*. A 5-act drama of Muslim court-life and court-love, in lit. Ar. verse & rhymed prose. Cairo, al-Maṭb. al-'umūmiyya, A.H. 1318; 40 pp.
600. Id., *Riwāyat al-murū'a wa'l-wafā'ma' al-ẖaliyyain al-wafiyyain*. A 5-act drama of war and intrigue between the French principalities of the Middle Ages. Cairo, al-Maṭb. al-'umūmiyya, A.H. 1318; 52 pp.

601. Ya'qūb, Ṭannūs Jūrj, *Riwāyat al-akhawain Munfārdī*. Prod. at a school in Brazil. Prob. 1920 (*H.*, vol. XXIX, May 1, 1921, p. 815).

602. Yazbak, Anṭūn, *'Āṣifa fī'l-beit*. A musical play in coll. Ar. (*GAL*, S. III, p. 112, n. 1).

602a. Id., *al-'Awāṣif*. Prod. in Cairo (*Ma.*, XLIII, 1949, p. 137).

603. Id., *al-Dhabā'iḥ*. A 4-act tragedy about social problems, written in coll. Ar. (of Egypt) prose. Often prod. Publ. Cairo, Shirkat al-qirṭās, n.d., prob. 1927; 76 pp. (Sarkīs, *Jāmi'*, II, No. 210).

al-Yāzijī, Ḥabīb, see: List of Ar. Plays, Transl.—Gide.

604. al-Yāzijī, Khalīl, *al-Khansā' au kaid al-nisā'*. Publ. (?) in lit. Ar. verse, 1877 (*K.*, Jan. 1951, p. 135).

605. Id., *Riwāyat al-murū'a wa'l-wafā' au al-faraj ba'd al-ḍīq*. Descr. in lit. Ar. the feuds of the Arab tribes before Islam. Written in 1876, first prod. in Beirut, 1878. 1st ed., Beirut, al-Maṭb. al-adabiyya, 1884. 2nd ed., Cairo, Maṭb. al-ma'ārif, 1902; 6, 121 pp. (*Mu.*, vol. XXVII, Sep. 1, 1902, pp. 910–911; *Fihris* IV, p. 115; Sarkīs, *Mu'jam*, pp. 1932–1933; *GAL*, S. II, p. 767).

Yūnān, Ramsīs, see: List of Ar. Plays, Transl.—Camus.

606. Yūsuf, 'Azīz, *Murr al-firāq wa-ḥulw al-ṭalāq*. A play in prose & verse, inspired by *Hoffmanns Erzaehlungen*. Cairo, Maṭb. al-ta'līf, 1891 (*Fihris*, IV, p. 114).

606a. Yūsuf, Mīshāl, *Yūsuf Bek Karam*. Publ. (*Ma.*, XLIII, 1949, p. 296).

Yūsuf, Muṣṭafā Ḥasan, see: List of Ar. Plays, Transl.—Shaw.

607. al-Zahāwī, Jamīl Ṣidqī, *Riwāyat Lailā wa-Samīr* (French title: *Leilâ et Samir drame ottoman constitutionnel*). A 6-act drama in lit. Ar. Its subject is love and political intrigue in Baghdad, early in the 20th century, where the hero dreams of Arab home rule and of Arabic as the official language. Baghdad, Maṭb. al-aitām li'l-ābā' al-karmiliyyīn al-mursalīn, 1927; 32 pp. (acc. to *GAL*, S. III, p. 487, also publ. in *Lughat al-'arab*, vol. V, 1928, pp. 577–608).

608. Zain, Zain, *Muḥammad 'Alī Bāshā'l-kabīr*. A 5-act hist. play. Cairo, al-Mak. al-sharqiyya, prob. 1900 (*H.*, vol. IX, Nov. 1900, p. 127).

Zain al-Dīn, Ḥusain, see: List of Ar. Plays, Transl.—Schiller.

608a. Zaitūn, Maḥmūd Maḥmūd, *Waḥdat al-wādī*. Cairo, 1947 (*Ma.*, XLIII, 1949, p. 294).

609. Zaitūn, Maḥmūd Muḥammad, *Mīlād al-nabī*. A play in verse. Prob. 1948 (*K.*, vol. IV, Jan., 1949, p. 154).

Zakī, Aḥmad, see: List of Ar. Plays, Transl.—Shaw.

Zakī, Najīb, see: List of Ar. Plays, Transl.—Corneille.

Zalzal, Najīb, see: List of Ar. Plays, Transl.—Corneille.

Zayyā, Ḥannā, see: List of Ar. Plays, Transl.—Racine.

al-Zayyāt, 'Abduh Ḥasan, see: List of Ar. Plays, Transl.—Schiller.

610. al-Zayyāt, Aḥmad 'Abd al-Waḥīd, *Ṣadr al-baghāsha*. Cairo, n.d. (*GAL*, S. III, p. 281).

II TRANSLATED PLAYS

1. Ache (?), Le Comte d', *La belle Parisienne*, transl. by Adīb Isḥāq as *al-Bārīsiyya al-ḥasnā' au gharā'ib al-ittifāq*. Beirut, 1884 (*GAL*, S. II, p. 759. Sarkīs, *Mu'jam*, p. 419, mentions a Cairene ed. Dāghir, p. 114, considers the above two separate works).

1a. Aicard, J., *Le père Lebonnard*, adapted by Ḥasan al-Bārūdī as *Bayūmī Efendī*. Prod. by the Ramses troupe in 1932–3 (*BSOS*, vol. VIII, 1937, p. 992.

Influenced one of Yūsuf Wahbī's plays?—see List of Ar. Plays, Orig. Plays, No. 584).

1b. Id., *Le père Lebonnard*, transl. by Muḥammad Taimūr (*Ma.*, XLII, 1948, p. 435).

2. Banville, Th. de, *Gringoire*, transl. in 1933 (?) (*BSOS*, vol. VIII, 1937, p. 992).

Bauche, H., see: List of Ar. Plays, Transl.—Lorde, An. & Bauche, H.

2a. Barrie, J. M., *The admirable Crichton*, transl. by Yūsuf Iskandar Jurjī as *Krītūn al-mubdi'*. Cairo, Mak. al-Hilāl; 138 pp. (*Ma.*, XLIII, 1949, p. 277).

3. Beauvoir, Madame de (pseud. of A. L. B. Robineau), *Fanfan et Colas*, adapted by Na'ūm Fatḥ Allāh Saḥḥār (who transcr. his name Naoum Sahhar), as *Riwāyat Laṭīf wa-Khōshābā*, in coll. Ar. (of Iraq) prose. Mosul, Dair al-ābā' al-dūminiqiyyīn, 1893; 83 pp.

4. Bennett, E. Ar., *The great adventure*, transl. by Edwārd M. Sulaimān as *al-Mughāmara al-kubrā*, in lit. Ar. prose. School ed. Cairo, al-Mak. al-mulūkiyya, 1934–5; 111 pp.

5. Id., *Milestones*, transl. by Raslān 'Abd al-Ghanī al-Bunnī as *'Alāmāt al-amyāl*. Lit. Ar. prose. Cairo, al-Mak. al-mulūkiyya, n.d.; 112 pp.

6. Bernard, Tr., *Le petit café*, adapted by Stephan Rustī (*RC*, vol. III, 1940, p. 110).

7. Bernstein, H., *Le voleur*, adapted by 'Abbās 'Allām as *Kauthar*, First prod. in 1926 (bibl. notice at the end of 'Allām's *'Abd al-Raḥmān al-Nāṣir*, see List of Ar. Plays, Orig. Plays, No. 63).

7a. Id., *Le voleur*, transl. by Ḥasan Thābit as *al-Sāriq*. Cairo (*Ma.*, XLIII, 1949, p. 124).

8. Berton, P., *Napoléon*, transl. by Ilyās Fayyāḍ as *Nābūlyūn* (Dāghir, p. 641).

9. Bisson, Alexandre, *Madame X*, transl. by Buṭrus Shalhūb as *Madām Īks riwāya 'an maḥabbat al-umm*. Lit. Ar. mixed with coll. Ar. N.Y., 1930; 63 pp.

10. Bornier, Henri de, *La fille de Roland*, transl. by Būlus al-Bustānī as *Qudwat al-ḥiṣān au ibnat Rōlān*. Beirut, Maṭb. Ṣabrā 1912 (*Fihris*, IV, p. 83. Shaikhū, *Ta'rīkh . . . fī'l-rub' al-awwal etc.*, p. 141, reports play's name prob. rightly as *Qudwat al-ḥiṣān fī ibnat Rōlān*).

11. Botrel, Th., *La nuit rouge* (?), adapted by 'Īsā in lit. Ar. prose. 2 acts instead of the original one. Prod. in Jerusalem, 1902. Jerusalem (?), 41 pp. (Title page missing from my copy).

12. Brieux, E., *La foi*, transl. by Ṣāliḥ Jaudat as *al-Īmān*. Prod. by Jūrj Abyaḍ. Cairo, Mak. al-ma'ārif, 1914 (*H.*, vol. XXII, June 1, 1914, p. 719; *Fihris*, IV, p. 16).

13. Camille (le Jésuite), *L'homme de la forêt noire*, *Le roi des oubliettes* and *Le solitaire des tombeaux*, all three adapted by Najīb Ḥubaiqa into one 5-act tragedy in lit. Ar. prose, as *al-Fāris al-aswad*. Ba'abdā, al-Maṭb. al-'uthmāniyya, 1899; 147 pp. (*Ma.*, vol. II, Oct. 1, 1899, p. 907. Dāghir, p. 297).

14. Camus, A., *Caligula*, transl. by Ramsīs Yūnān as *Kālījūlā*, in lit. Ar. prose. Cairo, Dar al-kitāb al-'arabī, n.d., prob. 1947; 95 pp.

15. *Charlemagne*, adapted by Adīb Isḥāq as *Shārlmān*, in 4 acts of lit. Ar. prose and verse. Publ. in the posthumous collection *al-Durar* by 'Aunī Isḥāq, Beirut, al-Maṭb. al-adabiyya, 1909; pp. 572–616 (Dāghir, p. 113).

16. Cocteau, J., *Antigone*, transl. by Ṣalāḥ Khāliṣ as *Antījūnā*. Baghdad, Mak. Jāmi'at Baghdad, prob. 1955 (*al-Adīb*, Apr., 1955, p. 66).

17. Id., *L'école des veuves*, transl. by the same as *Madrasat al-arāmil*. Together with No. 16, above, and No. 18, below (ibid.).

18. Id., *Le pauvre matelot,* transl. by the same as *al-Baḥḥār al-bā'is.* Together with Nos. 16 and 17, above (ibid.).
19. Coppée, Fr. E. J., *Guerre de 100 ans,* transl. by Ma'rūf Aḥmad al-Arnā'ūṭ as *Ḥarb al-mi'a* (Dāghir, p. 109).
20. Id., *Pour la couronne,* transl. by Ḥalīm Dammūs as *Fī sabīl al-tāj.* Lit. Ar. prose & verse. Beirut, al-Maṭb. al-kāthūlīkiyya, 1926; VIII, 71, 21 pp. (*H.*, vol. XXXIV, July 1, 1926, p. 1112; Sarkīs, *Jāmi'*, I, No. 1150. *GAL*, S. III, p. 347, wrongly gives translator's full name as Ḥalīm Dammūs Ibrāhīm. *Fihris*, IV, p. 81, and Dāghir, p. 731, mention another transl. by Muṣṭafā Luṭfī 'l-Manfalūṭī, but this seems to have been written in the form of a novel).
21. Id., *Pour le drapeau* (?), transl. by Ilyās Qunṣul as *Fī sabīl al-ḥurriyya,* appar. in an abbreviated form. Buenos Ayres, al-Maṭb. al-sūriyya al-lubnāniyya, prob. 1934 (*Mu.*, vol. LXXXV, Oct. 1, 1934, p. 256).
22. Corneille, P., *Le Cid.*, transl. by Shākir 'Āzār and Najīb Zalzal as *Tanāzu' al-sharaf wa'l-gharām.* Ba'abdā, al-Maṭb. al-'uthmāniyya, 1898 (Ḥunain, *Shauqī 'alā'l-masraḥ,* repr. p. 18).
23. Id., *Le Cid,* transl. by Najīb al-Ḥaddād as *Riwāyat al-Sīd au gharām wa-intiqām.* Lit. Ar. rhymed prose and verse. Some changes. 1st ed., N.p. Maṭb. al-taufīq, n.d., prob. 1900. 2nd ed. Alex., Gharzūzī, 1904; 112 pp. (*H.*, vol. IX, Jan. 1, 1901, p. 224. Dāghir, p. 301).
24. Id., *Le Cid,* adapted by Muḥammad 'Uthmān Jalāl.
25. Id., *Le Cid,* transl. by Khalīl Muṭrān as *al-Sīd,* in lit. Ar. Transl. approx. in 1932. First prod. in Cairo, 1936. Publ. in Lebanon, al-Maṭb. al-Būlusiyya, prob. 1952 (*A.*, Feb. 16, 1952, p. 6).
25a. Id., *Le Cid.*, transl. by Anṭūn Qīqānō as *Ḥabībī 'aduwwī au al-muntaqim li-abīh.* 96 pp. (*Ma.*, XLII, 1948, p. 455).
26. Id., *Cinna,* transl. by Khaṭṭār al-Daḥdāḥ as *Ughūsṭūs.* Prob. still in ms. (Shaikhū, *Ta'rīkh . . . fī'l-rub' al-awwal etc.*, p. 112).
27. Id., *Cinna,* transl. by Najīb al-Ḥaddād as *Ḥilm al-mulūk.* Lit. Ar. prose & verse. Cairo, al-Mak. al-sa'īdiyya, n.d.; 48 pp. Another (?) ed. Cairo, Maṭb. al-tamaddun, 1901 (?) (*H.*, vol. X, Feb. 15, 1901, p. 322; *Fihris,* IV, p. 33. Dāghir, p. 302, mentions still another ed., Alex., Gharzūzī, 1904). Some additions.
28. Id., *Les trois Horaces et les trois Curiaces,* adapted by Muḥammad 'Uthmān Jalāl.
28a. Id., *Les trois Horaces et les trois Curiaces,* adapted by Salīm Khalīl al-Naqqāsh as *Mayy au Hūrās.* 1868 (Najm, *al-Masraḥiyya etc.*, pp 95, 204–206).
29. Coward, N., *Blithe Spirit,* adapted by Sulaimān Najīb as *'Ifrīt mar'atī.* Prod. in Egypt, under Zakī Ṭulaimāt's direction in 1946 (*al-Sīnimā,* Nov. 21, 1946, p. 30; *KM,* fasc. 15, Dec., 1946, pp. 542–543; *K.*, vol. II, July, 1947, p. 1419).
29a. Daudet, A., *L'Arlésienne,* transl. by 'Abd al-Raḥmān Rushdī as *Arlīziyya* (*Ma.*, XLII, 1948, p. 439).
30. Id., *L'Arlésienne,* transl. by Jūrj Ṣawāyā as *al-Arlizyāna.* Buenos Ayres, Majallat al-iṣlāḥ, prob. 1932; 59 pp. (*Mu.*, vol. LXXXV, Oct. 1, 1934, p. 256. *GAL*, S. III, p. 454, which does not mention this play, reads translator's name as Jūrjī Ṣuwāyā). This play had been prod. in Egypt previously, appar. in another transl. (Muḥammad Taimūr, *Mu'allafāt,* vol. II, art. on 'Abd al-Raḥmān Rushdī).
30a. Id., *Sapho,* transl. by Maḥmūd Kāmil as *Sāfū.* First prod., Cairo, 1935 (*Ma.*, XLIII, 1949, p. 124).

31. Delaporte, R.P., *Louis de Gonzague*, transl. by Yūsuf Shiblī Abū Sulaimān as *Lūyis dī Ghūnzāghā*. Lit Ar. verse. Beirut, al-Maṭb. al-kāthūlīkiyya, 1903; 32 pp. (Ḥunain, *Shauqī 'alā'l-masraḥ*, repr., p. 18).
32. Delavigne, C., *Louis XI*, transl. by Ilyās Fayyāḍ as *Lūyīs al-ḥādī 'ashar*. Prod. in Egypt, 1911, by Abyaḍ (*H.*, vol. XX, Apr. 1, 1912, pp. 436–437).
33. Dennery, A. Ph., *Diane*, transl. by Maḥmūd Aḥmad al-Arnā'ūṭ as *Diyānā* (Dāghir, p. 109).
34. Id. & Tarbé des Sablons, E. J. L., *Martyre*, adapted by Ilyās Fayyāḍ as *Riwāyat al-shahīda au 'awāṭif al-banīn*, in lit. Ar. prose. First prod. by Salāma Ḥijāzī's troupe in Cairo, 1908. Alex., Gharzūzī, 1909; 170 pp.
35. Dickens, Ch., *David Copperfield*, adapted into a play as *al-Dhahab*. Prod. in Egypt, 1951 (*K.*, vol. VII, Jan., 1952, p. 96; ibid., June, 1952, p. 753).
36. Id., *A tale of two cities*, adapted into a play as *Qiṣṣat al-madīnatain*. Prod. in Egypt, 1951–2 (ibid., June, 1952, p. 753).
37. Domet, Aziz, *Der letzte Omajade*, transl. by playwright's brother, Amīn Dablan, as *Ākhir banī Umayya*. Lit. Ar. Cairo, 'Īsā'l-Bābī'l-Ḥalabī, 1933; 160 pp. First prod. in Arabic in Haifa, Jerusalem, Cairo—1933 (*OM*, vol. XXXV, 1955, pp. 282, 288).
38. Drinkwater, J., *Abraham Lincoln*, transl. by Fahmī Ḥannā al-Numair & L. N. Niyol (?), as *Abrāhām Linkūln*, in lit. Ar. prose. Cairo, Maṭb. Ḥijāzī, 1935–6; 110 pp. (*Ma.*, XLII, 1948, p. 435, & XLIII, 1949, p. 278, mention other translations).
38a. Dubois, F., *Le reliquaire*, transl. by Shiblī Mallāṭ as *al-Dhakhīra*. Beirut, 1906; 86 pp. (*Ma.*, XLIII, 1949, p. 119).
39. Dumas, Al. (fils), *La dame aux camélias*, adapted by Faraḥ Anṭūn into a musical play named *Dhāt al-wurūd* (*Mu.*, vol. LXI, Aug. 1, 1922, p. 265. Dāghir, p. 151, reads *Dhāt al-ward*).
39a. Id., *La dame aux camélias*, transl. by 'Abd al-Qādir al-Maghribī as *Ghādat al-Kāmīliyā*. Cairo, 1905 (*Ma.*, XLIII, 1949, p. 138, which also mentions two other translations).
40. Id., *Denise*, transl. by Kāmil al-Bahnasāwī as *Tāj al-mar'a*. Cairo, Angelo, 1947; 167 pp. (*KM*, fasc. 8, May, 1946, pp. 705–706; *K.*, vol. III, Jan., 1948, p. 169, and Feb., 1948, pp. 328–329).
41. Dumas, Al. (père), *Catherine Howard*, adapted with abbreviations and many changes by Taufīq Kan'ān as *Maṭāmi' al-nisā'*. 6 acts, lit. Ar. prose & verse. Cairo, Maṭb. al-Nīl, n.d.; 99 pp.
42. Id., *La dame de Monsoreau*, transl. by Ma'rūf Aḥmad al-Arnā'ūṭ as *Lā dām dī Mūnrū* (?) (Dāghir, p. 109).
43. Id., *Le fils du peuple*, transl. by Faraḥ Anṭūn as *Ibn al-sha'b al-latīn* (Dāghir, p. 150. *Mu.*, vol. LXI, Aug. 1, 1922, p. 265. *GAL*, S. III, p. 193, reads *al-shi'b*).
44. Euripides, *Plays*, transl. from the English by Maḥmūd Maḥmūd. Cairo, Lajnat al-nashr li'l-jāmi'iyyīn, 1946; 222 pp. (*K.*, vol. II, Jan., 1947, p. 466).
44a. Fénelon, F., *Télémaque*, adapted into a play by Sa'd Allāh al-Bustānī as *Tilīmāk*. First prod. July 1869. Publ. Cairo, al-Mak. al-Sa'diyya; 48 pp. (*Ma.*, XLII, 1948, p. 451).
45. Feydeau, E., *La puce à l'oreille*, adapted by 'Azīz 'Aid (*RC*, vol. III, 1940, p. 110).
45a. France, A., *Thais*, adapted into a musical play by Faraḥ Anṭūn. Prod. in Egypt (*Ma.*, XLII, 1948, p. 450).

46. Freytag, G., *Die Journalisten*, transl. by Muṣṭafā Kamāl Fā'id as *al-Ṣuḥufiyyūn*, in lit. Ar. prose. Cairo, al-Nāshir al-miṣrī, n.d.; 148 pp.
47. Frondaie, P., *L'homme qui assassina*. Partly transl. by Hārūn Ḥaddād as *al-Rajul alladhī qatal*, in lit. Ar. prose, in *al-Nidā'*, July 22, 1952, p. 10. Fully transl. by 'Umar Rushdī, same title, in lit. Ar. prose. Cairo, Maṭb. Majallatī, 1936; 136 pp.
48. Gallet, *Thais*, libretto adapted by Faraḥ Anṭūn as *Tāyīs* (Dāghir, p. 150).
49. Ghanem, Choukri, *Antar*, transl. from the French by Ilyās Abū Shabaka as *'Antar*, in 5 acts. Beirut, Mak. al-taufīq, 1926 (*Mu.*, vol. LXIX, Nov. 1, 1926, p. 338; *GAL*, S. III, p. 367; Sarkīs, *Jāmi'*, II, No. 1142).
50. Ghislanzoni, *Aida* (the libretto), adapted by Salīm Khalīl al-Naqqāsh, as *Riwāyat 'Āyīda al-shahīra*, 5 acts of lit. Ar. prose & verse. Cairo, al-Mak. al-sa'īdiyya, n.d.; 39 pp. (*GAL*, S. III, p. 266, n. 1, gives 1875 as the year of publ.).
51. Id., *Aida*, transl. by Abū Khalīl al-Qabbānī as *'Ā'ida* (Dāghir, p. 645).
51a. Id., *Aida*, adapted by Maḥmūd Raḥmī. Cairo (*Ma.*, XLIII, 1949, p. 132).
52. Gide, An., *Oedipe*, transl. by Ṭaha Ḥusain as *Ūdīb*, in lit. Ar. prose, following the original closely, in Ḥusain's *André Jīd min abṭāl al-asāṭīr al-yūnāniyya, Ūdīb—Thisiyus*. Dār al-kātib al-miṣrī, 1946; 8, 310 pp.; pp. 57–177.
53. Id., *Oedipe*, transl. by Ḥabīb al-Yāzijī as *al-Malik Ūdīb*. Buenos Ayres, al-Maṭb. al-tijāriyya, prob. 1932; 38 pp. (*H.*, vol. XLI, Jan. 1, 1933, p. 412).
54. Goethe, W. A. von, *Egmont*, transl. by Maḥmūd Ibrāhīm al-Dasūqī. Cairo, Maṭb. al-nahḍa al-miṣriyya, 1946; 165 pp. together with No. 57, below (*K.*, vol. I, June, 1946, pp. 315–316, and vol. II, Jan., 1947, p. 466).
55. Id., *Faust*, transl. by Muḥammad 'Awaḍ Ibrāhīm as *Fā'ust*, in lit. Ar. prose. Inc. part I of *Faust*, although the *Prelude upon the stage* is missing. Tries to follow the original closely. Cairo, Maṭb. al-i'timād, 1929; 20, 208 pp. (*H.*, vol. XXXVIII, Nov. 1, 1929, pp. 113–114; *Mu.*, vol. LXXV, Dec. 1, 1929, p. 588).
56. Id., *Goetz von Berlichingen*, transl. by Shadīd Bāz al-Ḥaddād as *Ghats fun Barlīshinghin dhū'l-yad al-ḥadīdiyya*. 'Ubayya (Lebanon), Maṭb. al-ṣafā', prob. 1923 (*H.*, vol. XXXI, Feb. 1, 1923, p. 551; *Mu.*, vol. LXVIII, Mar. 1, 1926, p. 343. *Fihris*, IV, p. 70. *Ma.*, XLIII, 1949, p. 119, mentions a Beirut, 1922, ed.).
57. Id., *Iphigenie auf Tauris*. Transl. & publ. together with No. 54, above.
Halévy, Ludovic, see below: Meilhac, Henry & Halévy, Ludovic.
57a. Ḥāmid, 'Abdulḥaqq, *Ṭāriq bnu Ziyād*. Transl. (from the Turkish ?) by Fatḥī 'Azmī, under the same title. Prod. in Egypt, Feb. 1905 (Najm, p. 180).
Hart, Moss, see below: Kaufman, George & Hart, Moss.
58. Hervieu, Paul, *Les paroles restent*, transl. by Kāmil Kīlānī as *al-Qaul yabqā*, in lit. Ar. prose with a few verses, publ. in Kīlānī's *Rawā'i' min qiṣaṣ al-gharb*, Cairo, 'Īsā'l-Bābī'l-Ḥalabī, 1933; pp. 489–574.
59. Howard, Sidney, *The silver cord*, transl. together with Nos. 68, 103, 211. Ed. by Ḥasan Maḥmūd, introd. by Taufīq al-Ḥakīm. Cairo, 1954 (*Muslim World*, vol. XLVI, Apr., 1956, p. 174).
60. Hugo, Ch. *Les Misérables*, transl. by 'Abd al-Ḥalīm Dūlār as *al-Bu'asā'*. Cairo, 'Abd al-Muta'āl, prob. 1906 (*H.*, vol. XIV, July 1, 1906, p. 611). Prod. in Egypt, 1951–2 (*K.*, vol. VII, June, 1952, p. 753).
60a. Hugo, V., *Les Burgraves*, adapted with abbreviations by Najīb al-Ḥaddād as *Tha'rāt al-'arab*. Lit. Ar. prose & verse. Cairo, Maṭb. al-tamaddun, 1902;

58 pp. (*H.*, vol. X, July 15, 1902, pp. 610–611; *Fihris*, IV, p. 22. Dāghir, p. 301, mentions another ed., Alexandria, Gharzūzī, 1904).

61. Id., *Hernani*, transl. by Najīb al-Ḥaddād as *Riwāyat Ḥamdān*. Lit. Ar. prose & verse. Cairo, al-Mak. al-sa'īdiyya, n.d., prob. 1901; 56 pp. 2nd ed. (?), n.p. (Cairo), Maṭb. al-tamaddun, n.d.; 90 pp. (*H.*, vol. IX, June 1, 1901, p. 503. *Fihris*, IV, p. 33, gives 1902 as date of publ. Cf. also Dāghir, p. 302).

62. Id., *Marie Tudor*, transl. by Ilyās Fayyāḍ as *Mārī Tīdūr* (Dāghir, p. 641).

63. Id., *Le roi s'amuse*, transl. by the same as *Mudhik al-malik*. Prod. in Egypt by Abyaḍ (Muḥammad Taimūr, *Mu'allafāt*, vol. II, art. on Jūrj Abyaḍ, pp. 131–143. Dāghir, p. 641).

64. Id., *Ruy Blas*, transl. by Niqūlā Rizq Allāh as *Rūy Blās*. Prod. by Abyaḍ, 1914 (*H.*, vol. XXII, Apr. 1, 1914, p. 559).

65. Ibsen, H., *An enemy of the people*, transl. by Ibrāhīm Ramzī as *'Aduww al-sha'b*. Cairo, Dār al-ṭibā'a al-ahliyya, 1932; 219 pp. (Dāghir, p. 403).

66. Id., *The ghosts*, transl. by 'Abd al-Ḥamīd Sarāyā as *al-Ashbāḥ*, was to be prod. in 1953 (*AS*, Oct. 21, 1953).

67. Kālidāsa, *Shakuntalā*, transl. by Wadī' al-Bustānī. Appar. still in ms. (Dāghir, p. 198).

68. Kaufman, George & Hart, Moss, *You can't take it with you*, transl. together with Nos. 59, 103 & 211. Ed. by Ḥasan Maḥmūd, introd. by Taufīq al-Ḥakīm. Cairo, 1954 (*Muslim World*, vol. XLVI, Apr. 1956, p. 174).

69. Karr, Al., *Madeleine*, adapted by Ilyās Abū Shabaka as a 5-act social drama named *Mājdūlīn*. Beirut, prob. 1925; 67 pp. (*H.*, vol. XXXIV, Jan. 1, 1926, p. 438; *Mu.*, vol. LXVIII, Jan. 1, 1926, p. 99. *GAL*, S. III, p. 367, sees in this adaptation the influence of Fr. Coppée).

70. Kemal, Namik, *Vatan ve Silistra*, transl. by Muḥī'l-Dīn al-Khayyāṭ as *al-Waṭan au Silistra*. Lit. Ar. prose & verse. Beirut, al-Maṭb. al-ahliyya, A.H. 1326; VIII, 142 pp. (*H.*, vol. XVII, Mar. 1, 1909, p. 383).

71. Knochblauch (?), Ed., *Kismet*, transl. by Khalīl Muṭrān, as *al-Qaḍā' wa'l-qadr*, from Jules Lemaitre's French version (Muḥammad Taimūr, *Mu'-allafāt*, vol. II, art. on Āl 'Ukkāsha). Barbour mentions appar. another adaptation by Maḥmūd Bairam al-Tūnisī as *Laila min alf laila*, prod. by Fāṭima Rushdī's troupe (*BSOS*, vol. VIII, 1937, pp. 992–993).

72. Lessing, G. E., *Nathan der Weise*, transl. by Ilyās Naṣr Allāh Ḥaddād as *Nāthān al-ḥakīm*. Lit. Ar. prose, tries to follow the original closely. Jerusalem, Maṭb. Dār al-aitām al-sūriyya, 1932; 84 pp. (*H.*, vol. XL, Aug. 1, 1932, p. 1482; *Mu.*, vol. LXXXI, Oct. 1, 1932, p. 371).

73. Lorca, F. Garcia, *Bodas de sangre*, transl. by 'Alī Sa'īd as *'Urs al-dam*, in lit. Ar. verse (?). Beirut, Dār al-mu'jam al-'arabī, 1954–5 (*al-Adīb*, vol. XXVII, Mar., 1955, p. 60).

74. Lorde, An. & Bauche, H., *La grande épouvante*, adapted by 'Abbās 'Allām as *al-Sāḥir*. First prod., 1927 (bibl. notice at the end of 'Allām's *'Abd al-Raḥmān al-Nāṣir*, see List of Ar. Plays, Orig. Plays, No. 63).

75. Maeterlinck, M. *L'intruse* (?), transl. by Futūḥ Nashāṭī as *Fī dākhil al-dār*, in lit. Ar. prose. Publ. in *K.*, vol. IV, Apr., 1949, pp. 623–636.

75a. Id., *Marie Magdeleine*, adapted with some abbreviations and additions by Ibrāhīm 'Abd al-Fādī as *Maryam al-Majdaliyya*. Lit. Ar. prose. Cairo, Mak. jam'iyyat al-maḥabba al-qibṭiyya, n.d. (prob. 1936); 96 pp.

75b. Marmontel, J.-F., *Bélisaire*, transl. by 'Abbās Abū Nukhūl al-Bijānī. Sao Paolo, 1903; 183 pp. (*Ma.*, XLII, 1948, p. 448).

75c. Maugham, S., *The letter*, transl. by Salīm Sa'd as *al-Khiṭāb*. Prod. in Cairo (ibid., p. 459).

76. Mayo, M., *Baby mine*, adapted by 'Abbās 'Allām as *al-Mar'a al-kadhdhāba*. First prod. in 1927 (bibl. notice at the end of 'Allām's '*Abd al-Raḥmān al-Nāṣir*, see List of Ar. Plays, Orig. Plays, No. 63).

77. Meilhac, Henry & Halévy, Ludovic, *Carmen*, libretto adapted by Faraḥ Anṭūn as *Karmin* (Dāghir, p. 150).

78. Molière, J. B. Poquelin, *L'avare*, transl. by Ilyās Abū Shabaka as *al-Bakhīl*. 1st ed., Beirut, Maṭb. Ṣādir, prob. 1932–3; 104 pp. 2nd ed., Beirut, Maṭb. Ṣādir, n.d. (1951?); 123 pp. (*H.*, vol. XLI, July 1, 1933, p. 1276; *Mu.*, vol. LXXXIII, Nov. 1, 1933, p. 495).

79. Id., *L'avare*, transl. by Najīb al-Ḥaddād as *Riwāyat al-bakhīl*. Lit. Ar. prose (*H.*, vol. XXX, Mar. 1, 1922, p. 556. Dāghir, p. 301).

80. Id., *L'avare*, partly transl. by Dā'ud Kurdī as *Arbājūn* (i.e., Harpagon), *au bakhīl Mulyīr*, in lit. Ar. Publ. in *al-Urdunn*, July 2, 1952, p. 3.

81. Id., *L'avare*, adapted into a 3-act play by Muḥī'l-Dīn, as *el-Meshēkha* (*Cahiers du Sud*, 1947, pp. 271–276).

82. Id., *L'avare*, adapted by Mārūn al-Naqqāsh as *Riwāyat al-bakhīl*, into a 5-act musical comedy in lit. Ar. verse. First prod. in 1848. Publ. in the playwright's *Arzat Lubnān*, Beirut, al-Maṭb. al-'umūmiyya, 1869, pp. 29–107.

83. Id., *Le bourgeois gentilhomme*, transl. by Ilyās Abū Shabaka as *al-Muthrī'l-nabīl*, in lit. Ar. prose. 1st ed., Beirut, Maṭb. Ṣādir, 1932; 80 pp. 2nd ed., Beirut, Mak. Ṣādir, n.d. (1951?); 104 pp. (*Mu.*, vol. LXXXI, Oct. 1, 1932, p. 371; *H.*, vol. XLI, Jan. 1, 1933, p. 412).

83a. Id., *Le bourgeois gentilhomme*, transl. by Fu'ād Nūr al-Dīn as *al-'Āmmī'l-nabīl*. 1934; 250 pp. (*Ma.*, XLIII, 1949, p. 133).

84. Id., *Don Juan*, transl. as *el-Kāfer bi'llāh*, in the coll. Ar. of Algeria. Prod. in Alger, 1954 (*L'Algérie libre*, Oct. 23, 1954, p. 2).

85. Id., *L'école des femmes*, adapted by Muḥammad 'Uthmān Jalāl as *Madraset il-nisā'*. Coll. Ar. (of Egypt) verse. Cairo, al-Maṭb. al-sharafiyya, A.H. 1307 (1889–1890); pp. 189–240 (Sarkīs, *Mu'jam*, p. 1307).

86. Id., *L'école des maris*, adapted by the same as *Madraset il-azwāg*. Coll. Ar. (of Egypt) verse. Cairo, al-Maṭb. al-sharafiyya, A.H. 1307 (1889–1890); pp. 147–188 (ibid). Repr. in Latin transcr. with introd. & notes by M. Sobernheim, Berlin, Cavalry, 1896; 129 pp.

87. Id., *Les fâcheux*, adapted by the same as *il-Thuqalā'*. Coll. Ar. (of Egypt) verse. Cairo, al-Maṭb. al-sharafiyya, A.H. 1314 (1896–1897); 31 pp. (ibid.; *Fihris*, IV, p. 23).

87a. Id., *Les femmes savantes*, transl. by Ḥasīb al-Ḥalwī as *al-Nisā' al-'ālimāt* (Najm, *al-Masraḥiyya etc.*, p. 290).

88. Id., *Les femmes savantes*, adapted by Jalāl as *il-Nisā' il-'ālimāt*. Coll. Ar. (of Egypt) rajaz verse. Cairo, al-Maṭb. al-sharafiyya, A.H. 1307 (1889–1890); pp. 79–145. Repr. in Latin transcr. and notes by Fr. Kern, Leipzig, Harrassowitz, 1898; 153 pp.

89. Id., *Le malade imaginaire*, transl. by Ilyās Abū Shabaka as *Marīḍ al-wahm*, in lit. Ar. prose. Beirut, Maṭb. Ṣādir, 1932; 83 pp. (*H.*, vol. XLI, Mar. 1, 1933, pp. 702–703; *Mu.*, vol. LXXXII, May 1, 1933, p. 624).

90. Id., *Le malade imaginaire*, adapted by Muḥī'l-Dīn into a 2-act play *as Slīmān al-Lūk* (?) (*Cahiers du Sud*, 1947, pp. 271–276).

91. Id., *Le médecin malgré lui*, transl. by Ilyās Abū S̱h̲abaka as *al-Ṭabīb rag̲h̲m 'anhu*. Lit. Ar. prose. 1st ed., Beirut, Maṭb. Ṣādir, 1932–3. 2nd ed., renamed *al-Ṭabīb 'alā'l-rag̲h̲m minhu*, Beirut, Mak. Ṣādir, 1951 (?); 63 pp. (*H.*, vol. XLI, Mar. 1, 1933, pp. 702–703).

92. Id., *Le médecin malgré lui*, transl. by Najīb al-Ḥaddād as *al-Ṭabīb al-murg̲h̲am* (Dāg̲h̲ir, p. 302. *BSOS*, vol. II, 1921–1923, considers this an original play).

93. Id., *Le médecin malgré lui*, transl. by Muḥammad Mas'ūd as *al-Jāhil al-mutaṭabbib*. Rhymed prose. Alex., al-Maṭb. al-Ibrāhīmiyya, prob. 1889. (*Mu.*, vol. XIII, May 1, 1889, p. 576).

94. Id., *Le médecin malgré lui*, transl. by Iskandar al-Ṣaiqalī as *Riwāyat al-ṭabīb al-mag̲h̲ṣūb*, in lit. Ar. prose. Prod. in Alexandria and Beirut; then adapted into an operetta (which flopped) by Amīn 'Aṭā' Allāh (*H.*, vol. XXX, Mar. 1, 1922, p. 506).

95. Id., *Le médecin malgré lui*, transl. as *Ṭabīb bi-rag̲h̲m anfih*. Prod. in Egypt, 1951–2 (*K.*, vol. VII, June, 1952, p. 753).

96. Id., *Le médecin volant*, transl. by Ibrāhīm Ṣubḥī as *Riwāyat al-ḥakīm al-ṭayyār*, in lit. Ar. rhymed prose. Alex., al-Maṭb. al-Ibrāhīmiyya, prob. 1889 (*Mu.*, vol. XIII, May 1, 1889, p. 576).

97. Id., *Le misanthrope*, transl. by Muḥammad Badrān & Muḥammad 'Abd al-Ḥāfiẓ Mu'awwaḍ, in lit. Ar. prose. Cairo, Maṭb. al-ta'līf wa'l-tarjama wa'l-nas̲h̲r, 1949; 144 pp. (*K.*, vol. IV, Apr., 1949, p. 621).

97a. Id., *Tartuffe*, transl. by Ḥasīb al-Ḥalwī as *Ṭarṭūf* (Najm, *al-Masraḥiyya etc.*, p. 290).

98. Id., *Tartuffe*, adapted by Muḥammad 'Ut̲h̲mān Jalāl, as *il-S̲h̲eik̲h̲ Matlūf*. Coll. Ar. (of Egypt) prose & verse. 1st ed., Cairo, A.H. 1290 (1873); 87 pp. 2nd ed., Cairo, al-Maṭb. al-s̲h̲arafiyya, A.H. 1307 (1889–1890); 77 pp. 3rd ed., Cairo, al-Maṭb. al-Jamāliyya, 1912. Repr. in Latin transcr. by Vollers, in *ZDMG*, vol. XLV, 1891, pp. 36 *ss.* (*Fihris*, IV, p. 55. Sarkīs, *Mu'jam*, p. 1307, reads *S̲h̲lūf*).

99. Id., *Tartuffe*, adapted by Mārūn al-Naqqās̲h̲ as *Riwāyat al-salīṭ al-ḥasūd*, in a 3-act musical comedy in lit. Ar. verse & rhymed prose. Publ. in playwright's *Arzat Lubnān*, Beirut, al-Maṭb. al-'umūmiyya, 1869; pp. 273–429.

100. Id., *Tartuffe*, transl. as *Matlūf*. Prod. in Egypt, 1952 (*K.*, vol. VII, Oct., 1952, p. 1004).

101. Musset, Alfred de, (?), adapted by Muḥammad al-Mag̲h̲zilī as *al-K̲h̲ill al-wafī*. Prod. by al-Qabbānī's troupe in Egypt, 1884 (*al-Adīb*, vol. XXVII, Feb., 1955, pp. 17–18).

101a. Id., (?), transl. by Estīr Mōyāl as *Durrat al-'ifāf*. Beirut, Maṭb. jarīdat al-naṣr, 1911 (?); 65 pp. (*Ma.*, XLII, 1948, p. 460).

102. *Napoléon*, transl. as *K̲h̲alīfat al-dam*. Prod. in Egypt by Abyaḍ (Muḥammad Taimūr, *Mu'allafāt*, vol. II, pp. 131–143).

103. O'Neill, Eugene, *Beyond the horizon*, transl. together with Nos. 59, 68, above, and 211, below. Ed. by Ḥasan Maḥmūd, introd. by Taufīq al-Ḥakīm. Cairo, 1954 (*Muslim World*, vol. XLVI, Apr., 1956, p. 174).

104. Piave, F. M., *Rigoletto*, adapted by Aḥmad Kāmil as *al-Malik al-mutalāhī*. Prod. in Cairo, Nov. 1904 (Najm, *al-Masraḥiyya etc.*, p. 180).

104a. Pirandello, L., *L'imbecille*, transl. by Lūyīs əl-Ḥajj as *al-Ablah*. Publ. in *al-Maks̲h̲ūf*, Nos. 83–85 (*Ma.*, XLII, 1948, p. 436).

104b. Prévost d'Exiles, l'Abbé, *Manon Lescaut*, adapted by 'Umar 'Abd al-'Azīz as *Mānūn Liskū au qalb fī 'āṣifa* (ibid., XLIII, 1949, p. 281).

104c. Id., *Manon Lescaut*, adapted by Ḥabīb Jāmātī. Prod. in Egypt (ibid.).

105. Racine, Jean, *Alexandre le grand*, transl. by Ibrāhīm al-Aḥdab as *al-Iskandar al-Maqdūnī* (Dāghir, p. 86.)

106. Id., *Alexandre le grand*, adapted by Muḥammad 'Uthmān Jalāl as *Iskandar al-akbar*, in verse written in coll. Ar. (of Egypt). Publ. together with Nos. 112 & 115, below, in Jalāl's *al-Riwāyāt al-mufīda fī 'ilm al-trajīda*, Cairo, al-Maṭb. al-sharafiyya, A.H. 1311 (1893–1894); pp. 91–130 (*Fihris*, IV, p. 42).

107. Id., *Andromaque*, transl. by Ṭaha Ḥusain as *Andrūmāk*, in 5 acts of lit. Ar. prose, Cairo, al-Maṭb. al-amīriyya, prob. 1935; 73 pp. (*H.*, vol. XLIV, Jan. 1, 1936, pp. 354–355).

108. Id., *Andromaque*, adapted by Adīb Isḥāq as *Andrūmāk*, in 5 acts of lit. Ar. prose & verse. Written approx. 1875. Publ. by 'Aunī Isḥāq in Adīb Isḥāq's posthumous collection *al-Durar*, Beirut, al-Maṭb. al-adabiyya, 1909, pp. 533–571; and separately, n.d.; 44 pp. (Dāghir, p. 113).

109. Id., *Athalie*, transl. by Najīb Jahshān as *'Athalyā*. 1896 (Shaikhū, *Ta'rīkh . . . fī'l-rub' al-awwal etc.*, p. 170).

110. Id., *Bérénice*, transl. by Najīb al-Ḥaddād as *Bīrīnīs* (Dāghir, p. 302).

110a. Id., *Britannicus*, transl. by Jūrjī Balīṭ in lit. Ar. verse (*Ma.*, XLII, 1948, p. 447).

110b. Id., *Esther*, transl. by Nadīm Anṭūnyūs Ayyūb. Aleppo, 1933 (ibid., p. 440).

111. Id., *Esther*, transl. by Khaṭṭār al-Daḥdāḥ as *Estīr*. Prob. still in ms. (Shaikhū, *Ta'rīkh . . . fī'l-rub' al-awwal etc.*, p. 112).

111a. Id., *Esther*, transl. into lit. Ar. by Ilyās Ṭannūs al-Ḥuwaik. Ba'abdā, al-Maṭb. al-lubnāniyya, 1907; 63 pp. (*Ma.*, XLII, 1948, p. 440).

112. Id., *Esther*, adapted by Muḥammad 'Uthmān Jalāl, as *Estīr* in coll. Ar. (of Egypt) verse. Publ. together with Nos. 106, above, & 115, below; pp. 2–38 (*Fihris*, IV, p. 42).

113. Id., *Iphigénie*, transl. by Augustinus 'Āzār. Prod. in a Maronite school at Aleppo, approx. 1882. Appar. still in ms. (*H.*, vol. XXV, May 1, 1917, p. 689).

114. Id., *Iphigénie*, transl. by Khaṭṭār al-Daḥdāḥ as *Fiyūjīniya*. Prob. still in ms. (Shaikhū, *Ta'rīkh . . . fī'l-rub' al-awwal etc.*, p. 112).

115. Id., *Iphigénie*, adapted by Muḥammad 'Uthmān Jalāl, in coll. Ar. (of Egypt) verse, Publ. together with Nos. 106 & 112, above; pp. 39–50 (*Fihris*, IV, p. 42).

116. Id., *Iphigénie*, transl. by Shiblī Shumayyil as *Ifījīnī*, in lit. Ar. verse. Prob. 1916 (*H.*, vol. XXV, Feb. 1, 1917, p. 424).

116a. Id., *Mithridate*, adapted by Salīm al-Naqqāsh as *Mītrīdāt* (Najm, *al-Masraḥiyya etc.*, p. 95).

117. Id., *Mithridate*, adapted by Abū Khalīl al-Qabbānī as *Lubāb al-gharām au Mitrīdāt*, and prod. in Egypt by his troupe (*al-Adīb*, vol. XXVII, Feb. 1945, pp. 18–19. Alternatively Salīm Taqlā's adaptation was used, appar. still in ms.?—mentioned by Dāghir, p. 221).

118. Id., *Phèdre*, transl. by Ibrāhīm al-Aḥdab as *Fidrā'* (Dāghir, p. 86).

119. Id., *Phèdre*, transl. by Najīb al-Ḥaddād as *Fīdr* (ibid., p. 302).

119a. Id., *Phèdre*, transl. by Ḥasīb al-Ḥalwī (Najm, *al-Masraḥiyya etc.*, p. 334).

119b. Id., *Phèdre*, transl. by Ḥannā Zayyā as *'Āqibat al-gharām*. Publ. 1897 (*Ma.*, XLIII, 1949, p. 133).

119c. Id., *La Thébaide ou les frères ennemis*, adapted as *al-Akhawān al-mutaḥāribān*. Prod. in Alexandria, Oct. 1878 (Najm, *al-Masraḥiyya etc.*, p. 104).

119d. Richepin, J., *Par le glaive*, transl. by Jūrj Maṭar and Bishāra Wākīm as *Bi-ḥadd al-saif.* 1928 (*Ma.*, XLII, 1948, p. 446).
Robineau, A. L. B., see: List of Ar. Plays, Transl.—Beauvoir.
120. Romains, J., *Knock*, transl. by 'Abd al-Ḥamīd ben Ḥalla (*BE*, Nov. 1, 1952, p. 3).
121. Id., *Knock*, transl. by Ibrāhīm al-Kīlānī, Damascus, prob. 1945; 209 pp. (*K.*, vol. II, Jan., 1947, p. 488).
122. Rostand, Ed., *L'Aiglon*, transl. by Aḥmad Rāmī as *al-Nasr al-ṣaghīr*. Prod. by Wahbī's Egyptian troupe in 1951 (*AS*, Nov. 28, 1951, p. 7; *K.*, vol. VII, Jan., 1952, p. 96).
123. Id., *Cyrano de Bergerac*, transl. by Ilyās Abū Shabaka as *al-Shā'ir au Sīrānū dī Birjirāk*. Lit. Ar. prose. Beirut, Mak. al-'adl, n.d.; 136 pp. (*GAL*, S. III, p. 367).
124. Id., *Cyrano de Bergerac*, transl. by Muḥammad Ṭāhir Fuḍalā' (*BE*, Nov. 1, 1952, p. 3).
125. Id., *Cyrano de Bergerac*, transl. by Muḥammad 'Abd al-Salām al-Jundī as *al-Shā'ir au Sīrānū dī Birjirāk*. Lit. Ar. With the cooperation of Muṣṭafā Luṭfī'l-Manfalūṭī (?). Cairo (?), al-Mak. al-tijāriyya, prob. 1921 (*H.*, vol. XXIX, July 1, 1921, pp. 988—989; *Mu.*, vol. LIX, Aug. 1, 1921, p. 189).
125a. Id., *La Samaritaine*, transl. by Iskandar al-Riyāshī as *al-Sāmiriyya wa-Yasū'*. Zahle, Maṭb. al-Ṣaḥāfī' l-tā'ih (*Ma.*, XLIII, 1949, p. 124).
126. Sardou, V., *Fernande*, transl. by Ilyās Fayyāḍ as *Dūq Fernānd* (Dāghir, p. 641).
126a. Id., *Patrie*, transl. by Fu'ād Salīm & Ḥabīb Jāmātī as *al-Waṭan*. Prod. in Egypt (*Ma.*, XLIII, 1949, p. 294).
127. Id., *La sorcière*, transl. by Faraḥ Anṭūn as *al-Sāḥira*. Prod. in Egypt by Abyaḍ (*Mu.*, vol. LXI, Aug. 1, 1922, p. 265).
128. Sarment, J., *Le pêcheur d'ombres*, transl. by Kāmil Kīlānī, as *Ṣayyād al-khayāl*, in lit. Ar. prose with a few verses, in Kīlānī's *Rawā'i' min qiṣaṣ al-gharb*, Cairo, 'Isā'l-Bābī'l-Ḥalabī, 1933; pp. 5–149.
129. Schiller, Fr. *Die Jungfrau von Orleans*, transl. by [Shadīd] Bāz al-Ḥaddād as *Jān Dārk au 'adhrā' Urliyyān*. Publ. by Majallat al-maurid al-ṣāfī, prob. 1928; 110 pp. (*H.*, vol. XXXVII, Feb. 1, 1929, p. 500).
130. Id., *Die Jungfrau von Orleans*, partly transl. by Naẓmī Khalīl, as *'Adhrā' Urliyyān*, in lit. Ar. prose. Publ. in *H.*, vol. XLIV, Feb. 1, 1936, pp. 430–439.
131. Id., *Kabale und Liebe*, transl. by Ṭānyūs 'Abduh as *Riwāyat gharām wa-iḥtiyāl*, in prose and verse. Some changes in the dialogue. Cairo, al-Maṭb. al-'umūmiyya, n.d. (*GAL*, S. III, p. 269, n.1; *Fihris*, IV, p. 71).
132. Id., *Kabale und Liebe*, transl. by Niqūlā Fayyāḍ & Najīb Nasīm Ṭrād as *al-Khidā' wa'l-ḥubb*, in lit. Ar. Prod. in Beirut, 1900 (?). Publ. Beirut, Jarīdat al-maḥabba, prob. 1900; 100 pp. (*H.*, vol. VIII, Sep. 15, 1900, p. 749).
133. Id., *Kabale und Liebe*, transl. by Khalīl Muṭrān as *al-Ḥubb wa'l-dasīsa*. Prob. 1927 (*GAL*, S. III, p. 95).
134. Id., *Kabale und Liebe*, transl. by Ḥasan Ṣādiq as *al-Ḥubb wa'l-dasīsa*, in lit. Ar. Cairo, Maṭb. al-i'timād, prob. 1936; 168 pp. (*Mu.*, vol. LXXXVIII, Apr. 1, 1936, p. 557; *H.*, vol. XLIV, May 1, 1936, p. 845).
135. Id., *Die Räuber*, transl. by Fā'iq Riyāḍ as *al-Ṭāghiya*. Cairo, Dār al-majalla al-jadīda, prob. 1932; 198 pp. (*H.*, vol. XLI, Jan. 1, 1933, p. 412; *Mu.*, vol. LXXXII, Jan. 1, 1933, p. 123).
136. Id., *Die Räuber*, transl. by 'Abduh Ḥasan al-Zayyāt as *al-Luṣūṣ*. Cairo, Maṭb. Wādī'l-mulūk, prob. 1929 (*H.*, vol. XXXVII, July 1, 1929, pp. 1139–1140).

136a. Id., *Wilhelm Tell*, transl. by ʻAbbās Abū S̲h̲ūs̲h̲a & Ḥusain Faraj Zain al-Dīn. Cairo; 187 pp. (*Ma.*, XLIII, 1949, p. 295).

137. Id., *Wilhelm Tell*, transl. by Anwar S̲h̲ā'ūl as *Wilyam Till*. Baghdad (?), prob. 1932 (*H.*, vol. XL, July 1, 1932, p. 1341, and *Mu.*, vol. LXXXI, Oct. 1, 1931, p. 371, both of which ascribe the play to Sheridan).

137a. Schmid, J.-C., *Geneviève*, transl. by Nabīl al-Bustānī. Beirut, Mak. Ṣādir, 1933; 81 pp. (*Ma.*, XLII, 1948, p. 454).

138. Shakespeare, W., *Anthony and Cleopatra*, transl. by Muḥammad ʻAwaḍ Ibrāhīm as *Antūnī wa-Kliyūbātra*. Cairo, Maṭb. al-maʻārif, prob. 1945 (*K.*, vol. I, Jan. 1946, p. 397).

139. Id., *As you like it*, transl. by the same as *Kamā tahwāh.* Lit. Ar. prose, following closely the original. Cairo, Mak. al-maʻārif, n.d., prob., 1944; 155 pp.

140. Id., *Coriolanus*, transl. by ʻUmar ʻAbd al-ʻAzīz Amīn as *Kuryūlānūs*, Cairo, Maṭb. al-taqaddum, 1927 (*Fihris*, IV, p. 103).

141. Id., *Coriolanus*, transl. by ʻAlī Imām ʻAṭiyya as *Kuryūlānūs*. Cairo, Maṭb. al-Yūsufiyya, 1927 (ibid.).

142. Id., *Coriolanus*, transl. by Muḥammad al-Sibāʻī as *Riwāyat Kāryūlīnus*, in lit. Ar. prose, following closely the original. Cairo, Mak. al-maʻārif, n.d. (1912); 205 pp.

143. Id., *Hamlet*, transl. by Ṭānyūs ʻAbduh as *Riwāyat Hamlit*. Lit. Ar. prose & verse, with a few omissions (e.g., act I, secne I) or abbreviations in the longer speeches. 1st ed., Alex., prob. 1902. 2nd ed., Cairo, al-Maṭb. al-ʻumūmiyya, n.d.; 110 pp. (*H.*, vol. X, Mar. 1, 1902, p. 356).

144. Id., *Hamlet*, transl. by Kaddūr Fattāl (*BE*, Nov. 1, 1952, p. 3).

145. Id., *Hamlet*, transl. by Amīn al-Ḥaddād as *Hamlit*, in lit. Ar. prose & verse. Cairo, G̲h̲arzūzī, 1907; 70 pp. (*H.*, vol. XVI, May 1, 1908, p. 504; *al-Muqtabas*, vol. III, June, 1908, pp. 355–356; Dāg̲h̲ir, p. 299. *Ma.*, XLIII, 1949, p. 292, names Najīb al-Ḥaddād as the translator).

145a. Id., *Hamlet*, transl. by Muḥammad Luṭfī Jumʻa (*Ma.*, XLIII, 1949, p. 293).

146. Id., *Hamlet*, transl. by Sāmī'l-Juraidīnī as *Hamlit*, in lit. Ar. prose, following the original closely enough. 1st ed., prob. 1921. 2nd ed., Cairo, al-Maṭb. al-Raḥmāniyya, prob. 1932; 128 pp. (*Mu.*, vol. LX, Mar. 1, 1922, pp. 294–295; *H.*, vol. XXX, May 1, 1922, p. 792, and vol. XLI, Jan. 1, 1933, p. 410; Sarkīs, *Jāmiʻ*, I, No. 1168).

147. Id., *Hamlet*, transl. by K̲h̲alīl Muṭrān as *Hamlit*. Cairo, Dār al-maʻārif, 1949; 143 pp. (Dāg̲h̲ir, p. 705).

147a. Id., *Hamlet*, transl. by ʻAbd al-Fattāḥ al-Saranjāwī (*Ma.*, XLIII, 1949, p. 293).

147b. Id., *Hamlet*, transl. by Muḥammad al-Sibāʻī (ibid.).

147c. Id., *Julius Caesar*, transl. by Maḥmūd Aḥmad al-ʻAqqād & Aḥmād ʻUt̲h̲mān al-Qirabī. Cairo, al-Maṭb. al-ʻarabiyya (ibid., p. 296).

148. Id., *Julius Caesar*, transl. by ʻAbd Allāh al-Bustānī, in verse (*GAL*, S. III, p. 416; *Ma.*, vol. XXV, 1927, p. 624. If Dāg̲h̲ir, p. 194, is correct, the transl. was named *Brūtūs ayyām Qaiṣar*).

149. Id., *Julius Caesar*, transl. for school usage by Muḥammad Ḥamdī as *Riwāyat Yūlyūs Qaiṣar*, with an introd. by Muḥammad Kāmil Salīm. Lit. Ar. prose, follows the original closely. 1st ed., prob. 1912. 2nd ed., n.p., Maṭb. Maṭar, 1920; 168 pp. (*Mu.*, vol. XLI, Oct. 1, 1912, pp. 403–404).

150. Id., *Julius Caesar*, transl. by Sāmī' l-Juraidīnī as *Yūlyūs Qaiṣar*. Cairo, Majallat al-zuhūr, prob. 1913 (*H.*, vol. XXI, Mar. 1, 1913, pp. 382–383; ibid., vol. XXXVI, Dec. 1, 1927, p. 203).

151. Id., *Julius Caesar*, transl. by Nāṣhid Lūqā as *Riwāyat Yūlyūs Qaiṣar*. Prob. 1919 (*H.*, vol. XXVIII, Jan. 1, 1920, p. 381; *Mu.*, vol. LVI, Apr. 1, 1920, p. 377).
152. Id., *Julius Caesar*, transl. by Khalīl Muṭran (?) as *Yūlyūs Qaiṣar* (*H.*, vol. XXXVI, Dec. 1, 1927, p. 203).
152a. Id., *Julius Caesar*, transl. by ʻAbd al-Fattāḥ al-Saranjāwī (*Ma.*, XLIII, 1949, p. 296).
153. Id., *Julius Caesar*, transl. by Muḥammad al-Sibāʻī as *Riwāyat Yūlyūs Qaiṣar* Lit. Ar. prose, following the original closely. Cairo, Mak. al-wafd, n.d.; 208 pp.
154. Id., *Julius Caesar*, transl. by Louis Ghannām Thābit. Cairo, 1925 (*GAL*, S. III, p. 197).
155. Id., *King Henry V*, transl. by Sāmī'l-Juraidīnī, as *al-Malik Hanrī'l-khāmis*, in lit. Ar. prose. Cairo, Dār al-hilāl, 1936; 76 pp. (*Mu.*, vol. XC, Jan. 1, 1937, pp. 125–126; *H.*, vol. XLV, Feb. 1, 1937, p. 470).
156. Id., *King Henry V*, transl. by Muḥammad al-Sibāʻī as *Riwāyat Hanrī'l-khāmis*. Lit. Ar. Prob. 1913 (*Mu.*, vol. XLIII, Dec. 1, 1913, p. 592).
157. Id., *King Henry VIII*, transl. for school usage by ʻUmar ʻAbd al-ʻAzīz Amīn as *Hanrī'l-thāmin*, in lit. Ar. prose. Strives to follow the original and has explanatory notes. Cairo, Maṭb. al-taqaddum, n.d. (1925); 311 pp. (*Fihris*, IV, p. 132).
158. Id., *King Henry VIII*, transl. for school usage by Maḥmūd Aḥmad al-ʻAqqād & Aḥmad ʻUthmān al-Qirabī, as *Riwāyat Hanrī'l-thāmin*. Follows the original closely enough, although with some omissions, e.g., the song in Act I, scene I. Cairo, al-Maṭb. al-ʻarabiyya, 1925; 120 pp. (ibid., which wrongly renders translator's name as Aḥmad Muḥammad al-ʻAqqād).
159. Id., *King Henry VIII*, transl. by ʻAbd al-Raḥmān Fahmī as *Qiṣṣat al-malik Hanrī'l-thāmin*, in lit. Ar. prose, attempting to follow the original closely. Introd. by Muḥammad Farīd Abū Ḥadīd. N.p., Maṭb. Jibrā'īl Qārūt, n.d. (introd, signed 1936); 26, 184 pp.
160. Id., *King Henry VIII*, transl. by Muḥammad ʻAwaḍ Ibrāhīm as *Hanrī'l-thāmin*. Cairo, Maṭb. al-maʻārif, 1947. (*K.*, vol. III, Jan., 1948, p. 169).
161. Id., *King Henry VIII*, transl. for school usage by Būlus Iskandar as *Hanrī'l-thāmin* (*H.*, vol. XXXVI, Dec. 1, 1927, p. 203).
162. Id., *King Henry VIII*, transl. for school usage by Yaʻqūb Iskandar as *Hanrī'l-thāmin*, in lit. Ar. 2 vols. 1st ed., Cairo, al-Maṭb. al-Murquṣiyya. 2nd ed., Cairo, Maṭb. ʻAin Shams, 1926 (ibid.; *Fihris*, IV, p. 133).
163. Id., *King Lear*, transl. by Sāmī'l-Juraidīnī as *al-Malik Līr* (acc. to S.J.'s assertion in his translation of *King Henry V*, see above, 155).
164. Id., *King Lear*, transl. by Khalīl Muṭrān as *al-Malik Līr* (*H.*, vol. XXXVI, Dec. 1, 1927, p. 203).
165. Id., *King Lear*, transl. by Ibrāhīm Ramzī as *al-Malik Līr* (Dāghir, p. 403).
166. Id., *King Richard III*, transl. by Khalīl Muṭrān (?) as *Rīshārd al-thālith* (*H.*, vol. XXXVI, Dec. 1, 1927, p. 203).
166a. Id., *Macbeth*, transl. by Maḥmūd Aḥmad al-ʻAqqād & Aḥmad ʻUthmān [al-Qirabī]. Cairo, al-Maṭb. al-ʻarabiyya (*Ma.*, XLIII, 1949, p. 281).
167. Id., *Macbeth*, transl. by ʻAbd al-Malik Ibrāhīm & Iskandar Jirjis ʻAbd al-Malik as *Makbīth*. 1900 (*H.*, vol. IX, Mar. 1, 1901, p. 344).
167a. Id., *Macbeth*, transl. by Ḥāfiẓ Ibrāhīm. Prose. In ms. (*Ma.*, XLIII, 1949, p. 281).
168. Id., *Macbeth*, transl. by Muḥammad ʻIffat as *Riwāyat Mākbīth*. Lit. Ar. verse.

Prob. 1911; 130 pp. (*Mu.*, vol. XL, Feb. 1, 1912, p. 200; cf. *H.*, vol. XXXVI, Dec. 1, 1927, p. 202. *Ma.*, XLIII, 1949, p. 281, reads author's name 'Izzat).

169. Id., *Macbeth*, transl. by Khalīl Muṭrān as *Makbith*. Cairo, Dār al-ma'ārif, 1950; 110 pp. (Dāghir, p. 705).

170. Id., *Macbeth*, transl. for school usage and annotated by 'Abd al-Fattāḥ al-Saranjāwī as *Makbīth*. Cairo, 1924 (*H.*, XXXVI, Dec. 1, 1927, p. 204. *Fihris*, IV, p. 109, reads title *Mākbīth*).

170a. Id., *Macbeth*, transl. by Muḥammad al-Sibā'ī (*Ma.*, XLIII, 1949, p. 281).

171. Id., *Macbeth*, transl. by Aḥmad Muḥammad Ṣāliḥ as *Mākbīth*, in lit. Ar. prose. Some slight changes (an addition at the end of Act I, scene I). Alex., Gharzūzī, 1911; 141 pp. (*Fihris*, IV, 109).

172. Id., *Measure for measure*, transl. by Ḥannā Khabbāz as *Qannāṣat al-mulūk au kaifa taṣīr al-fatāt amīra*. Cairo, Maṭb. al-shams, 1930; 152 pp. (Dāghir, p. 341).

172a. Id., *The merchant of Venice*, transl. by 'Umar 'Abd al-'Azīz Amīn. Cairo, al-Mak. al-mulūkiyya; 28 pp. (*Ma.*, XLII, 1948, p. 450).

173. Id., *The merchant of Venice*, transl. by [Maḥmūd] Aḥmad al-'Aqqād & Raḍwān 'Abd al-Hādī & Aḥmad 'Uthmān al-Qirabī as *Riwāyat tājir al-Bunduqiyya*. Lit. Ar. prose, strives to follow the original closely. School ed., Cairo, Mak. al-Fajjāla, 1926; 120 pp. (*Mu.*, vol. LXIX, Nov. 1, 1926, p. 338; Sarkīs, *Jāmi'*, I, No. 1110).

174. Id., *The merchant of Venice*, transl. by Khalīl Muṭrān as *Tājir al-Bunduqiyya*. Lit. Ar. prose. Cairo, Maṭb. al-hilāl, 1922; 79 pp. (*Mu.*, vol. LX, May 1, 1922, pp. 499–500; *GAL*, S. III, p. 95).

175. Id., *The merchant of Venice*, transl. by Muṣṭafā 'Azīz al-Qurashī as *al-Tājir al-Bunduqī au al-yahūdī'l-murābī*. Cairo, Maṭb. Maṭar, 1922 (*Fihris*, IV, p. 21).

176. Id., *The merchant of Venice*, transl. by Muḥammad al-Sibā'ī as *Tājir al-Bunduqiyya*. 3rd ed., Maṭb. Ra'amsīs; 106 pp. (Sarkīs, *Jāmi'*, II, No. 1111).

176a. Id., *Midsummer night's dream*, transl. by 'Abd al-Laṭīf Muḥammad as *Aḥlām al-'āshiqīn*. Lit. Ar. prose. 1911 (Najm, *al-Masraḥiyya etc.*, pp. 239–241).

177. Id., *Othello*, transl. by Khalīl Muṭrān as *'Uṭail* (or *'Aṭīl*?). 1st ed., Cairo, Maṭb. al-ma'ārif, prob. 1912. 2nd ed., Cairo, Dār al-ma'ārif, 1952; 211 pp. Prod. in Egypt repeatedly since 1912 (*H.*, vol. XX, July 1, 1912, p. 599; *K.*, vol. II, July 1947, p. 1421, and vol. VII, Oct. 1952, p. 994; *GAL*, S. III, p. 95).

178. Id., *Othello*, anonymous adapt. as *Riwāyat Ūtillū au ḥiyal al-rijāl al-ma'rūfa bi'l-qā'id al-Maghribī*. Lit. and coll. Ar. prose. N.p., al-Kutubī, 1907; 60 pp.

179. Id., *Pericles prince of Tyre*, transl. by Maḥmūd Luṭfī Thābit as *Birīklīs amīr Ṣūr*. Prob. 1924. 74 pp. (*H.*, vol. XXXIII, Feb. 1, 1925, p. 562; Sarkīs, *Jāmi'* I, No. 1107).

179a. Id., *Richard II*, transl. by Maḥmūd 'Awaḍ Ibrāhīm. Cairo, Dār al-ma'ārif, 1948; 129 pp. (*Ma.*, XLIII, 1949, p. 120).

180. Id., *Romeo and Juliet*, transl. by 'Alī Aḥmad Bākthīr as *Rūmiyū wa-Juliyyīt*. Prob. 1946 (*K.*, vol. II, Jan., 1947, p. 466).

181. Id., *Romeo and Juliet*, transl. by Najīb al-Ḥaddād as *Shuhadā' al-gharām*. Lit. Ar. prose & verse, with the addition of Ar. songs. Cairo, Maṭb. al-tamaddun, 1901; 48 pp. (*H.*, vol. X, Jan. 1, 1902, p. 227; ibid., XXXVI, Dec. 1, 1927, p. 202; *Fihris*, IV, p. 55. Dāghir, p. 301, mentions another ed., Kafr Shīmā, al-Maṭb. al-Rashīdiyya; 52 pp. Najm, *al-Masraḥiyya etc.*, p. 128, says this transl. was titled *Shaqā' al-muḥibbīn*. Cf. however ibid., pp. 227 *ss.*).

182. Id., *Romeo and Juliet*, transl. by Niqūlā Rizq Allāh as *Rūmyū wa-Julīt*. 1st ed., Cairo (?). prob. 1899. 2nd ed., Cairo (?), prob. 1912 (*H.*, vol. VIII, Dec. 15, 1899, p. 191; ibid., vol. XX, May 1, 1912, p. 511; *Mu.*, vol. XL, Apr. 1, 1912, p. 405. *Ma.*, XLIII, 1949, p. 122, mentions four other translations).

183. Id., *The taming of the shrew*, transl. by Muḥammad Ḥamdī and prod. in Egypt (*BSOS*, vol. VIII, 1937, p. 992, reads translator's name as Maḥmūd Ḥamdī).

184. Id., *The taming of the shrew*, transl. by Ibrāhīm Ramzī as *Tarwīḍ al-namira*. 1932 (?) (ibid. Dāg̲h̲ir, p. 403).

185. Id., *The tempest*, transl. by Aḥmad Zakī Abū S̲h̲ādī as *al-ʿĀṣifa*, in lit. Ar. prose, following the original closely. First publ. in 5 parts of an act each, as suppl. to *Mu.*, vols. LXXV–LXXVI, 1929–1930. Then, in book form, 1930 (*Mu.*, vol. LXXVII, June 1, 1930, p. 109; *H.*, vol. XXXVIII, June 1, 1930, p. 1010; *GAL*, S. III, pp. 117, 1321).

185a.Id., *The tempest*, transl. by Muḥammad ʿAbd al-ʿAzīz Amīn as *al-ʿĀṣifa*. Cairo, 1929 (*Ma.*, XLIII, 1949, p. 133).

186. Id., *The tempest*, transl. by Muḥammad 'Iffat as *Ẕaubaʿat al-baḥr*. Lit. Ar. prose and verse. Cairo, Mak. al-taʾlīf, 1909 (*H.*, vol. XVIII, Dec. 1, 1909, p. 191; *Mu.*, vol. XXXVI, Jan. 1, 1910, p. 75; *Fihris*, IV, p. 45).

186a.Id., *The tempest*, transl. by Yūsuf Iskandar Jirjis as *al-ʿĀṣifa*. Cairo, 1929 (*Ma.*, XLIII, 1949, p. 133).

187. Id., *The tempest*, transl. by K̲h̲alīl Muṭrān (?) as *al-ʿĀṣifa* (*H.*, vol. XXXVI, Dec. 1, 1927, p. 203).

188. Id., *The tempest*, transl. by Nās̲h̲id Sīfīn as *al-ʿĀṣifa*, in lit. Ar. prose. Al-Maṭb. al-Raḥmāniyya, prob. 1929; 158 pp. (*Mu.*, vol. LXXVI, Jan. 1, 1930, pp. 108–109).

189. Id., *Twelfth night*, transl. by Muḥammad ʿAwaḍ Ibrāhīm as *al-Laila al-t̲h̲āniyat ʿas̲h̲ara*. Dār al-maʿārif, prob. 1945 (ibid., vol. CVI, Apr. 1, 1945, p. 413; *K.*, vol. I, Jan., 1946, p. 397).

190. Shaw, G. B., *The apple cart*, transl. by the same as *ʿArabat al-tuffāḥ*. Cairo, Lajnat al-taʾlīf waʾl-tarjama waʾl-nas̲h̲r, 1946; 176 pp. (*K.*, vol. II, Dec. 1946, pp. 307–308; ibid., Jan., 1947, p. 466, the play is ascribed to Shakespeare).

191. Id., *Caesar and Cleopatra*, transl. by Narjis Naṣīf as *Qaiṣar wa-Kliyūbātrā*. Prob. 1946 (ibid., Jan., 1947, p. 466).

191a.Id., *Caesar and Cleopatra*, transl. by Ibrāhīm Ramzī as *Qaiṣar wa-Kliyūbātrā*. Lit. Ar. prose. Cairo, 1914 (Najm, *al-Masraḥiyya etc.*, pp. 256–258).

192. Id., *The devil's disciple*, transl. by Muḥammad Kāmil al-Naḥḥās as *Tābiʿ al-s̲h̲aiṭān*, in lit. Ar. prose. N.p. (Cairo?), Maṭb. al-iʿtimād, n.d. (introd. signed Nov. 1938); 157 pp.

193. Id., *The doctor's dilemma*, transl. by Muṣṭafā Ḥasan Yūsuf as *Ḥairat ṭabīb*. 1947. (*K.*, vol. III, Jan. 1948, p. 169).

194. Id., *Geneva*, transl. by Muṣṭafā Fatḥī & Muṣṭafā Ṭaha Ḥabīb as *Jinīf*, in lit. Ar. prose. Cairo. Mak. al-ādāb, n.d. (preface dated Apr. 1945); 145 pp.

195. Id., *The man of destiny* (?), transl. by Maḥmūd Ibrāhīm al-Dasūqī as *al-Insān al-kāmil*. 1947 (*K.*, vol. III, Jan., 1948, 169. *Ma.*, XLII, 1948, p. 444, mentions another transl. by Muṣṭafā Ḥasan Yūsuf).

196. Id., *St. Joan*, transl. by Aḥmad Zakī as *Jān Dark*, in lit. Ar. prose, following the original closely enough. Cairo, Lajnat al-taʾlīf waʾl-tarjama waʾl-nas̲h̲r, 1938; 8, 355 pp. (incl. illustrations).

197. Sheridan, R. B., *The school for scandal*, transl. by Muḥammad Munīr ʿAbd al-

Ḥamīd, as *Ma'had al-faḍā'iḥ wa'l-wishāyāt*. School ed., prob. 1923 (*H.*, vol. XXXI, May 1, 1923, p. 891).

197a. Id., *Ajax*, transl. by Ṭaha Ḥusain. Cairo, 1939; 90–161 pp. (*Ma.*, XLII, 1948, p. 445).

198. Sophocles, *Antigone*, transl. by Aḥmad Sifta (?) (*BE*, Nov. 1, 1952, p. 3).

198a. Id., *Antigone*, transl. by Ṭaha Ḥusain. Cairo, 1939; 167–230 pp. (*Ma.*, XLII, 1948, p. 444).

199. Id., *Electra*, transl. by Ṭaha Ḥusain as *Iliktrā* in lit. Ar. prose. Cairo, Lajnat al-ta'līf wa'l-tarjama wa'l-nashr, 1939; 6-85 pp.

200. Id., *Oedipos*, transl. by Faraḥ Anṭūn as *Ūdīb al-malik* (Dāghir, p. 150).

200a. Id., *Oedipos*, transl. by Ṭaha Ḥusain. Cairo, 1939; 205–309 pp. (*Ma.*, XLII, 1948, p. 445).

201. Strindberg, A., *The father*, transl. by Wadī' Filasṭīn as *al-Ab* in lit. Ar. prose. Cairo (?), Lajnat al-nashr li'l-jāmi'iyyīn—Mak. Miṣr., n.d., prob. 1945; 85 pp. (*K.*, vol. I, Jan., 1946, p. 397).

202. Tagore, R., *Chitra*, transl. by Fakhrī Shihāb under the same title, publ. in *KM*, fasc. 6, Mar., 1946, pp. 310–322.

Tarbé des Sablons, E. J. L., see: List of Ar. Plays, Transl.—Dennery, A. Ph. & Tarbé des Sablons, E. J. L.

203. Tolstoy, L., *The dominion of darkness*, transl. by Muḥammad al-Mushīr as *Sulṭān al-ḍalāl*. Tunis, prob. 1911 (*H.*, vol. XX, Nov. 1, 1911, p. 128).

204. Id., *The dominion of darkness* (?), transl. from the German by 'Iṣām al-Dīn ibn Ḥafnī Nāṣif as *al-Nūr yuḍī' fī'l-ẓalām*. Lit. Ar. Cairo, Maṭb. al-shabāb, 1926 (*Fihris*, IV, p. 131).

205. Valéry, P., *Amphion*, partly transl. by Khalīl Hindāwī in *Mu.*, vol. XC, Feb. 1, 1937, pp. 185–195.

206. Id., *Sémiramis*, partly transl. by the same ibid., Jan. 1, 1937, pp. 41–51.

206a. Id., *Sémiramis*, transl. by Salīm Sa'da (*Ma.*, XLIII, 1949, p. 126).

206b. Verne, Jules, *Le tour du monde en 80 jours*, adapted into a play by Najīb Kan'ān as *al-Ṭawāf ḥaul al-arḍ*. Prod. in Egypt, Nov. 1905 (Najm, *al-Masraḥiyya etc.*, p. 130).

206c. Voltaire, *Mérope*, transl. by As'ad 'Awwād (*Ma.*, XLIII, 1949, p. 289).

207. Id., *Mérope*, transl. by Muḥammad Khalīl 'Iffat as *Tasliyat al-qulūb Mīrūb*. Lit. Ar. prose & verse. Transl. in A.H. 1306 (approx. 1888). 2nd ed., Cairo, al-Maṭb. al-'umūmiyya, 1909 (*Fihris*, IV, p. 127).

207a. Id., *Mérope*, transl. by Amīn al-Khūrī (*Ma.*, XLIII, 1949, p. 283).

208. Id., *Oedipe*, transl. by Najīb al-Ḥaddād as *Ūdīb*. Lit. Ar. prose & verse. Alex., Maṭb. Gharzūzī, 1905; 20, 95 pp; (Dāghir, p. 301, wrongly thinks this is a transl. of Sophocles' tragedy).

209. Id., *Zaire*, transl. by Najīb Farj Allāh Fayyāḍ as *Zuhaira* (Shaikhū, *Ta'rīkh . . . fī'l-rub' al-awwal etc.*, p. 177).

210. Id., *Zaire*, transl. by Najīb al-Ḥaddād as *Zāyīr* (Dāghir, p. 301).

210a. Id., *Zaire*, transl. by Fāris Kilāb & Elishā' Karam. 77 pp. (*Ma.*, XLIII, 1949, p. 122).

211. Wilder, Thornton, *Our town*, transl. together with Nos. 59, 68 & 103, above. Ed. by Ḥasan Maḥmūd, introd. by Taufīq al-Ḥakīm. Cairo, 1954 (*Muslim World*, vol. XLVI, Apr., 1956, p. 174).

Abbreviations

A=*al-Ahrām* (Daily)
AIEOA=*Annales de l'Institut d'Études Orientales, Alger.*
AJ=*al-Akhbār al-jadīda.*
AL=*Ākhir laḥza.*
AS=*Ākhir sā'a.*
AY=*Akhbār al-yaum.*
B.=*The Bulletin* (of the Egyptian Educational Bureau, London).
BE=*La Bourse Egyptienne* (Daily).
BSOS= *Bulletin of the School of Oriental* (*and African*) *Studies* (London).
Coll. Ar.=Colloquial Arabic.
Dāghir=Yūsuf As'ad Dāghir, *Maṣādir al-dirāsa al-adabiyya*, vol. II, part I.
DLZ=*Deutsche Literaturzeitung.*
ERE=*Encyclopaedia of Religion and Ethics.*
Fihris, IV=Dār al-kutub al-miṣriyya, *Fihris al-kutub al-maujūda fī'l-dār*, vol. IV (1929).
FO=Public Record Office archives (London), Foreign Office series.
GAL=C. Brockelmann, *Geschichte der arabischen Litteratur.*
H=*al-Hilāl.*
HH=*Ha-Mizraḥ He-Ḥadash* (*The New East*, Quarterly, Jerusalem).
JE=*Le Journal d'Egypte* (Daily).
JJS=*Journal of Jewish Studies* (Quarterly, Cambridge, U.K.).
JP= *The Jerusalem Post* (Daily, Jerusalem).
JRAS=*Journal of the Royal Asiatic Society of Great Britain and Ireland.*
JRCAS=*Journal of the Royal Central Asian Society.*
K=*al-Kitāb* (Monthly).
KM=*al-Kātib al-miṣrī* (Monthly).
Lit. Ar.=Literary Arabic.
M.=*al-Miṣrī* (Daily).
Ma.=*al-Mashriq.*
Mak.=Maktaba.
Maṭb.=Maṭba'a.
MEA=*Middle Eastern Affairs* (Monthly, N.Y.).
MSOS=*Mitteilungen des Seminars für Orientalische Sprachen zu Berlin.*
Mu.=*al-Muqtaṭaf* (Monthly).
OA=*Orientalisches Archiv.*
OLZ=*Orientalische Literaturzeitung.*
OM=*Oriente Moderno* (Monthly, Rome).
PE=*Le Progrès Egyptien* (Daily).
RAAD=*Revue de l'Académie Arabe à Damas.*
RC=*Revue du Caire* (Monthly).
RMM=*Revue du Monde Musulman.*
RTP=*Revue des Traditions Populaires.*
RY=*Rūz al-Yūsuf* (Weekly).
ZA=*Zeitschrift für Assyriologie und verwandte Gebiete.*
ZDMG=*Zeitschrift der deutschen morgenländischen Gesellschaft.*

Index